ROCHELLE ALERS

Vows

ARABESQUE®

Recycling programs
for this product may
not exist in your area.

VOWS

An Arabesque novel published by Kimani Press/July 2010

First published by BET Books in 1997.

ISBN-13: 978-0-373-83184-5

© 1997 by Rochelle Alers

www.kimanipress.com

Printed in U.S.A.

Dear Reader,

When *Hideaway* was first published in 1995, I couldn't have anticipated the overwhelming response to the novel, and the characters and stories that followed. Since the very first book, the series has been a reader favorite. In 1997, I published the second book in the HIDEAWAY series, *Hidden Agenda,* which was reissued in November 2009, and the third book in the series, *Vows,* this current reissue. In the past, I've found myself returning to these characters and their lives over and over again. And for me, they continue to be fresh and exciting, and filled with romance.

In May of this year, I released *Breakaway,* the fourteenth book in the HIDEAWAY series, which only adds to the legacy. And for those of you who are fans of the Coles and their extended family and friends, I hope you enjoy this book as much as the others.

Yours in romance,

Rochelle Alers

HIDEAWAY SERIES

Everett Kirkland - Teresa Maldanado * - Samuel Cole - Marguerite Diaz[11]

Martin Cole - Parris Simmons[1]

Oscar Spencer - Regina Cole - Aaron Spencer[5]

Clayborne

Eden

Tyler Cole - Dana Nichols[9]

Martin, II   Astra   Samuel II

Arianna

Josephine Cole - Ivan Wilson

Gisela   Esther   Joseph   Felipe   Ashley

David Cole - Serena Morris[4]

Gabriel Cole - Summer Montgomery[10]   Alexandra Cole - Merrick Grayslake[12]

Immanuel   Anthony   Imani   Victoria   Cordero

Jason/Anna
(twins)

Nancy Cole - Noah Thomas

Timothy Cole-Thomas - Nichola Bennett   Ynez   Grace   Malinda

Celia Cole-Thomas - Gavin Faulkner[14]

Nicholas

Diego Cole-Thomas - Vivienne Neal[13]

Samuel

Matthew Sterling - Eve Blackwell - Alejandro Delgado[2]

Christopher Delgado - Emily Kirkland[7]

Alejandro   Esperanza   Mateo

Joshua Kirkland* - Vanessa Blanchard[3]

Michael Kirkland - Jolene Walker[8]

Teresa   Joshua-Michael   Merrick

Sara Sterling - Salem Lassiter[6]

Isaiah   Eve/Nona (twins)

LEGEND

* - Illegitimate Birth
1 - Hideaway
2 - Hidden Agenda
3 - Vows
4 - Heaven Sent
5 - Harvest Moon
6 - Just Before Dawn
7 - Private Passions
8 - No Compromise
9 - Homecoming
10 - Renegade
11 - Best Kept Secrets
12 - Stranger In My Arms
13 - Secret Agenda
14 - Breakaway

A very special thanks to Minnie—
my late mother, counselor and prophet...

Vivian Stephens—literary visionary...

Mary Oluonye and Marsha Anne Tanksley,
who recognized Joshua as a man for all
seasons long before he appeared in print...

Monica Harris—editor and kindred spirit...

LaVerne—for the gifts from the Spirit...

And for all my readers—this one's for you!

My bitterness will turn into peace,
you save my life from all danger;
you forgive all my sins.

—*Isaiah* 38:17

Prologue

His touch was gossamer, almost magical, his fingers sliding over her breasts and down to her flat belly. Vanessa could not believe the exquisite torture wringing spasms of heat, cold and pleasure from her dormant body. It was as if she had been waiting years, all of her life, for the gratification her husband offered her at that moment.

How could he, this stranger—know her body better than she did? How could he, this man she had only known for eight days—know Vanessa Blanchard-Kirkland better than she knew herself?

His kisses, which had begun as slow and searching, were now strong and urging. "Open your mouth," he ordered softly, coaxing her to respond, and she opened her mouth to his. His tongue slipped inside, awakening a response deep within her.

Her shuttered lids flew up and Vanessa recognized the repressed passion in Joshua's startling, light green eyes. His electric gaze, shocking pale silver hair, and the deep, rich mahogany brown of his tanned skin made him so compelling and magnetic that everything about him was potent and breathtaking.

Closing her eyes she savored the sensation of his flesh melding with hers, making them one. A soft sigh of satisfaction escaped her as she breathed lightly from between parted lips. The rush of heat swept from the soft core of her center and radiated outward like spokes on a wheel.

She rose to meet Joshua in a moment of uncontrolled passion, her eager response matching his. Pinpoints of passion burned brightly as she rose and—suddenly, without warning—fell head-long into darkness and emptiness.

Vanessa couldn't stop her fall as tears leaked from under her closed lids. The recurring dream had attacked again, this time the images more vivid than before. However, this was the first time her missing husband had revealed his face to her in her dream.

Turning her face into her pillow she cried silently, uncon-trollable sobs shaking her body, and it was only later, much later, that she fell asleep again. This time the dream did not come back to remind her that the man she had fallen in love with and married had disappeared without a trace. She didn't know whether she was Vanessa Blanchard or Vanessa Kirkland, married, separated, divorced or widowed.

Bright ribbons of New Mexico summer sunlight slanted across the bedroom floor, and Vanessa knew immediately upon waking that she had overslept. She glanced at the clock on her bedside table and moaned. It was nearly eight-twenty.

Reaching for the telephone, she dialed her boss's private number. The connection was broken after the second ring. "Good morning. Colonel McDonald's office. Miss Grant speaking."

"Jenna, it's Vanessa."

"What's the matter, Vanessa? You sound funny."

She swallowed several times, trying to moisten her dry throat. "I have a sore throat. Please tell Warren I won't be in today."

"Are you taking a personal day?"

"No. Put it down as a sick day."

"I hope you feel better."

"Thank you, Jenna."

Vanessa replaced the receiver and lay back against the pile of pillows cradling her shoulders. Not only was her throat sore and dry, but she knew without looking at a mirror that her eyes were swollen from her crying.

This was the third time within two months that she had called in sick because she had spent the night crying after the disturbing dream woke her. The dream was always the same.

Combing the fingers of both hands through her chemically straightened black hair, she inhaled deeply, closing her eyes. Perhaps if she talked out her dreams with a therapist they would stop haunting her.

She had considered seeking a professional counselor when they first began, but had balked several times because of embarrassment. How could she tell someone that she had met a man while on vacation, married him eight days later, then discovered that he had abandoned her in a foreign country?

There were times when she thought she had imagined him, but then came the times when she knew he was real. Her dreams brought back the memories of the passion she had shared with him; an all-consuming passion she had never shared with any man except the man she had claimed as her husband.

"No," she whispered, shaking her head. No one would believe her.

She lay in bed, willing her mind blank. Soon her breathing deepened and she finally went back to sleep.

It was the telephone and not a dream that pulled Vanessa into awareness. She groped for the receiver several times before locating it.

"Hel-lo."

"Vanessa, are you all right? Do you want me to call Roger and have him stop by and see you after he finishes at the hospital?"

She recognized her sister's voice and smiled. "I'm okay, Connie."

"You don't sound okay."

"I am. Really."

"If you're okay, then why aren't you at work? You never take off from work unless you're sick."

"I have a sore throat."

"Then you're sick. Right after I hang up I'm going to call Roger and—"

"Don't, Connie!" Vanessa shouted as loudly as she could. "I don't need a doctor," she continued in a softer tone. "What I need is someone to talk to," she said quickly, the plea rushing from her lips before she could stop it. Again, her eyes filled with tears.

"Can that someone be your sister?"

Biting down hard on her lower lip, Vanessa nodded. "Yes."

"I'm on my way."

It was done. She was now committed to telling Connie about her dreams. "Thanks."

She hung up the phone, swinging her legs over the side of the bed, and headed for the bathroom. Last night's dream had been too real, but the events leading up to the dreams were also real, and it was time she told someone about the incident that had changed her and her life forever.

She took a leisurely shower, knowing it would take her sister more than half an hour to drive from her sprawling hillside home in *La Tierra,* an area just north of Santa Fe where Connie lived with her cardiologist husband and two school-age sons, to her own modest, three bedroom, Spanish style townhouse.

Patting herself dry, Vanessa took an inordinate amount of time to cream her body with a thick, oil-based, scented lotion. The thin mountain air absorbed all the moisture from her skin, and before the onset of the summer heat she took every step to protect it, at any cost.

She brushed her hair and secured it at the crown of her head with several large pins; peering into the mirror over the bathroom sink, she noted that some of the swelling around her eyes had gone down. Most people would not notice the slight puffiness under her large eyes, but those people did not include Connie. There were very few things she could conceal from Constance Blanchard-Childs.

Returning to her bedroom, she slipped into her underwear, a pair of shorts, and a tank top. She pushed her feet into a pair of well-worn sandals at the same time the doorbell rang.

Vanessa went down the staircase, making her way to the front door and opening it. Connie always parked her racy, red BMW coupe in her driveway instead of the area reserved for visitors.

Connie held out her arms, and she allowed her older sister to comfort her as she pressed a kiss to her scented cheek.

"Come on in out of the sun."

Connie walked into the brick-tiled entryway and took off a pair of oversized sunglasses, fanning her moist face with a mani-cured hand. The resemblance between the sisters was startling. Both were tall and slender, with dramatic, large, dark eyes.

Vanessa closed the solid mahogany door, shutting out the heat. The central cooling and heating systems kept the interior comfortable and virtually dust-free.

"Have you eaten breakfast?" she asked.

"I'll eat after we talk."

The women walked into the living room and sat down opposite each other on a sofa and love seat. Taking a deep breath, Vanessa stared at her sister's attractive face.

"Do you remember when I went to Mexico for vacation?"

Connie nodded. "Of course I do." Her smooth brow furrowed. "Are you in some type of trouble?"

Vanessa pursed her lips. "No, but I'm married to—"

"You're what?" Connie interrupted, the words exploding from her mouth.

"I met a man and married him." She couldn't believe her con-fession sounded so glib.

Connie's eyebrows arched in surprise. "In Mexico?"

"Yes, in Mexico."

Connie moved from the love seat and sat down next to Vanessa. Taking her hand, she shook in her head in amazement. "How could you keep something like this from me? Mercy, Vanessa, I'm your sister."

"If I hadn't had the dreams about him I probably wouldn't have said anything."

"You didn't trust me enough to tell me?" Connie said, anger and disappointment filling her scathing tone.

"It has nothing to do with trust, Connie. It's more like pride and embarrassment."

"The hell with your false pride and being embarrassed. I *have* to know everything."

The anxiety that had filled her waking days subsided with the admission. The fear and the apprehension Vanessa had carried for more than a year eased, and she knew she had made the right decision to tell Connie about the man she had fallen in love with on sight.

"I met Joshua Kirkland on the flight…."

PART ONE

The Seduction

Chapter 1

Vanessa noticed him immediately as he made his way down the aisle of the AeroMexico jet, his darting gaze searching the numbers and letters over each seat.

He was tall and slender, and what riveted her attention was his deeply tanned skin contrasting with his startling, close-cut silver hair. But it wasn't until he came closer to where she sat that she noticed his eyes. They were a cold, pale green.

At first glance she thought he was older, because of his silvered hair, but with his approach she doubted whether he was forty. There were a few lines around his shimmering eyes, and she surmised that he had earned those from squinting in the sun. His impassive expression did not lend itself to a softening of his firm mouth or the crinkling of the lines around his eyes in an open smile.

He was impeccably dressed, unlike her and most of the other casually attired passengers on the Santa Fe flight to Mexico City, via a ninety-minute layover in El Paso, Texas.

His wheat-colored linen jacket, reminiscent of a field of sun-dappled, waving particles of grain, was an exact match for his pale, coarse hair. His pristine white shirt set off the deep, rich color of his face, his silk tie in varying shades of brown and gold, the expertly tailored, double-pleated, dark brown slacks falling from his slim waist to the tops of his imported Italian loafers, and a legal-size leather portfolio with a distinctive world-renowned leather crafter's logo that silently announced *European*.

Vanessa averted her gaze as he stood beside her seat. Out of the corner of her eye she saw him remove his jacket, fold it carefully, then store it in the overhead bin.

She turned her attention to the activity outside the large aircraft, watching as the ground crew transferred luggage from rolling carts to the cargo area of the plane.

"Excuse me, please."

Her head came around quickly and she stared up at the silver-haired man. His voice was deeper than she would have expected it to be, and his accent was definitely *American*. Realization dawned, and she knew he had been assigned the window seat next to her.

He took several steps backward as she stood up and slipped out of her seat. Standing beside him made Vanessa aware of how tall he was. She stood five-nine in her bare feet, and as an adolescent she had towered over most of the boys in her classes until her last year of high school. Her fellow passenger had to be several inches above the six-foot mark.

She registered the warmth of his body and the clean, citrus-based fragrance of his cologne as he moved past her and sat down. Retaking her seat, she secured her seatbelt and picked up the magazine she had bought at a gift shop in the airport.

She soon found herself deeply engrossed in an article on aging and the advantages and disadvantages of cosmetic surgery, shutting out the clamor going on around her as passengers searched for their seats, stored carry-on luggage under seats, or made room in the crowded overhead bins. Flight attendants worked quickly and efficiently to seat everyone before the cockpit crew was cleared for takeoff.

Vanessa had waited more than six months for this long-planned, well-deserved trip to Mexico. As an accountant with a Santa Fe based military defense manufacturing firm, she was responsible for contracts, and Grenville-Edwards had been the winner of a Pentagon bid for the so-called Joint Strike Fighter. The company was expected to build at least 2,800 of the planes, guaranteeing Grenville-Edwards's prosperity well into the next century and the expansion of their work force by thousands of employees.

She had agreed with the *Wall Street Journal* analyst who reported that over the life of the project the fighter could generate sales of more than 750 billion, including spare parts and foreign sales.

Her work at Grenville-Edwards occupied so much of her waking time that a social life had become almost nonexistent for her. She hadn't had a serious relationship in more than four years—not since she had left her native Los Angeles after a broken engagement. At the urging of her sister, she took a leave of absence from the small private college where she taught accounting, and stayed with Connie and her family. The three month leave was extended to six. After securing a position with Grenville-Edwards she relocated to Santa Fe. She lived in her sister's guest house for a year before she purchased her townhouse in a newly constructed private community in a Santa Fe suburb.

She returned to Los Angeles twice a year to visit her parents, and not once did they ever mention the name of the man she had once promised to spend her life with. Kenneth Richmond lived part of the year in L.A. and the remainder in Washington, D.C. He had won a congressional seat from their district, and was now Congressman Richmond.

Thinking of Kenneth wrung a smile from Vanessa. Kenneth Richmond—handsome, brilliant, charming and a consummate womanizer. He would do very well in Washington, where women outnumbered men at least five to one.

The flight attendants walked up and down the aisle, making certain the cabin was secured for takeoff. Vanessa glanced over to her right and noticed a stack of printed sheets resting atop the man's leather portfolio. A company's letterhead indicated a Dusseldorf address, and even though she could not read the language she knew the printed words were German.

Her gaze moved up, studying the clean-cut lines of his profile. His sharp features were perfect and symmetrical, and if it hadn't been for his reserved expression his handsome face would have been almost as delicate as a woman's. High cheekbones blended into a lean jaw and a strong chin. His mouth was firm without being too full or too thin.

Vanessa stared at his long lashes resting on his cheekbones; their soft, charcoal gray color set off the paleness of his penetrating eyes.

Without warning he glanced at her, and she felt heat flare in her face. He had caught her staring. His expression remained impassive as his gaze slowly examined her face, lingering on her mouth, before shifting back to the sheaf of papers on his lap.

The heat in her face increased. She was annoyed at herself for being embarrassed. She was thirty-three years old, and a man she'd found attractive had caught her staring at him.

When, she thought, had she become so involved in her career that she had neglected her own needs? As a normal woman, her physical needs had at one time been strong and passionate.

She couldn't blame Kenneth for her wariness with men. It had been *her* decision not to marry him, and *her* decision to not become involved with some of the men she occasionally dated.

There was one man in particular—her boss. Retired army colonel Warren McDonald, a confirmed bachelor, was pursued by every single woman at Grenville-Edwards regardless of her age. In the six years since he had come to head the company, though, he'd never shown an interest in any woman, except Vanessa.

She did not make promises, because she wasn't certain whether she could maintain them. But she *was* able to keep her promise of not becoming involved with any man she worked with.

Shrugging her shoulders, she pressed her head against the headrest and closed her eyes. She shut out the image of the man sitting beside her and everything else going on in the aircraft as the jet taxied down the runway in preparation for a takeoff.

Gasps of fear echoed throughout the cabin, and Vanessa opened her eyes as her stomach made a flip-flop motion. The Fasten Seat Belt light came on, along with the familiar beeping sound as the aircraft fell several hundred feet before leveling off.

Swallowing back the rush of bile from her empty stomach, she grimaced at the sound of retching from someone seated behind her. Her fingers gripped the arms of her seat in a death-like grip, the veins showing prominently through the flesh on her slender hands. She glanced to her right. She couldn't see out the window. It was apparent that the man sitting beside her had lowered the shade. He had put away the report he'd been reading and sat with his eyes closed, while his hands rested atop the leather case. How could he sleep, when they had flown into something which threatened to break the jet into tiny pieces?

The pilot's voice came through the speakers. "We'll be experiencing some turbulence until we fly over Alamogordo. After that we'll have smooth flying and clear skies, and we expect to touch down in El Paso on time." Vanessa did not care if they landed in El Paso "on time." All she wanted was to step foot on a solid surface, and in one piece.

Fifteen minutes later, the storm left behind, a collective sigh of relief went through the jetliner.

The AeroMexico plane touched down in El Paso and Vanessa

unsnapped her seatbelt and readied herself to deplane. She would use every second of the ninety-minute layover to calm her frayed nerves. Gathering her handbag, she made her way down the aisle and out to the terminal.

She noticed that most of the passengers were subdued as they filed out into the terminal. Most were probably remembering the frightening moment of free fall when they flew into the thunderstorm.

She detected the heat of a body pressed close to hers, and the familiar scent of clean, citrusy cologne. Turning slightly, she glanced over her shoulder and encountered the pale gaze of the tall man. He had retrieved his jacket and it hung elegantly from his broad shoulders.

"I think you could use a cup of coffee," he stated without preamble. "You didn't look very well while we rode out the storm," he added when she arched a questioning eyebrow.

How would he know how she looked? Vanessa thought. He'd sat, eyes closed, totally relaxed. And it wasn't as if she'd cried out or retched, like the man behind her.

"There's a restaurant at the far end of the terminal that serves excellent coffee," he continued. "Perhaps you'd like to join me?" He said the words tentatively, as if testing her reaction and his own for extending the offer. His gaze burned into hers while a muscle barely tensed in his lean jaw.

She was piqued by his cool, detached manner. He hadn't exchanged a word with her during the flight, preferring instead to read or feign sleep, yet he now wanted to engage her in conversation and share a cup of coffee.

"Mr—"

"Kirkland," he supplied quickly. "Joshua Kirkland."

Tilting her chin, Vanessa flashed an artificial smile. "I don't think so, Mr. Kirkland."

Joshua merely inclined his head at her refusal. "Then I'll see you back on the plane, Miss—"

"Vanessa Blanchard." The two words were layered with ice.

"Miss Blanchard," he repeated, watching as she turned and walked away. He stared at the curling mass of heavy black hair falling around the nape of her slender, swanlike neck. Her long, flared, cotton jersey tailored dress moved softly on her tall frame, its soft coral color flattering the intense vibrancy of her deep brown skin. Joshua stared at her departing figure until she disappeared from his field of vision, then walked over to a wall with a bank of telephones; he picked up the receiver of one designated for calling cards calls only.

Dialing a series of numbers, he waited for a break in the connection. The caller on the other end of the wire identified himself.

"I've made contact," Joshua said tersely.

"How is she?"

"She'll do."

A low chuckle came through the receiver. "I knew you'd say that."

His solemn expression did not change. "Is there anything else?"

"Yes, there is. I thought I'd tell you before you hear it in the field."

"What is it?"

"The odds are fifteen-to-one—in her favor."

"All of you are sick," Joshua said softly before hanging up.

He had expected more from the people he worked with, but then, why would he? Most of them were serious-minded people who were entrusted with extremely dangerous assignments, and a bit of joviality was a welcome respite in the shadowy world of military intelligence.

It had become an inside joke that one day a woman was going to get him to commit, though at thirty-eight it hadn't happened. He had come close with Sable St. Clair, *and* he was certain it would not be Vanessa Blanchard. She was his target, and in no way would he become *that involved* with a woman he'd been assigned to investigate.

He would use every available means necessary to get the information he needed from Vanessa Blanchard. Then, as quietly as he would walk into her life, he would walk out.

Chapter 2

Vanessa sat in a small booth in the airport coffee shop sipping a cup of excellently brewed coffee while flipping through the pages of her magazine. The coffee's warmth eased down the back of her throat and settled in her chest. Within seconds her anxiousness eased, and she temporarily forgot the fearful moments of the flight from Santa Fe to El Paso.

She felt a slight tug on her hair. She turned on the leather seat and stared at a small child who stood on the seat of the adjoining booth. Her large dark eyes sparkled as she smiled at the little boy.

"Hello," she crooned softly. His brilliant hazel eyes, framed by long dark lashes, widened with her greeting.

"Billy, sit down and leave that lady alone," admonished the boy's mother.

Billy quickly reached out and pulled at another curl falling over her forehead. Vanessa reached up, trying to extract his tiny **hand, but he tightened his grip and pulled harder.**

She could not believe she was being assaulted by a child who could not be more than three years old.

"Billy! Billy!" The child's mother screamed hysterically while he laughed and pulled harder.

One by one, Vanessa eased each of his fingers from her hair, her scalp tingling where she was certain she had lost more than a few strands.

Her face flushed a deep red from anger and embarrassment, apologizing profusely, Billy's mother scooped up her child and fled the coffee shop.

Vanessa stood up and massaged her scalp, watching the two as they disappeared into the throng passing through the terminal. Her gaze shifted and she saw Joshua Kirkland standing near the entrance. A slight smile ruffled his mobile mouth. It was apparent that he had witnessed the entire scene.

Reaching into her handbag, she pulled out several bills and left them on the table. She managed a tight smile for the waitress who had served her. Then, tilting her chin, she walked toward the entrance.

Joshua did not move as she neared him and her bare arm brushed the sleeve of his jacket. Lowering his head slightly, he whispered softly, "You don't look the type to beat up on little kids."

She took a quick, sharp breath. "In case you didn't notice, it was Pee Wee Hulk Hogan who was trying to make me a candidate for Rogaine!"

He stared down at the wealth of black curls falling over her forehead, trying not to laugh at her scowling expression. He had just walked into the coffee shop when he heard the woman screaming her son's name. He hadn't seen Vanessa's face because the child's body blocked his view, but he knew her because of the color of her dress. And it had taken all of his control not to rush over and rescue her from the willful little boy.

"Did he hurt you?" he questioned, his voice filled with concern.

Vanessa massaged her scalp, shaking her head. "Only my pride."

"Do you think it's safe to enter?"

She gave Joshua a warm, open smile for the first time. The expression transformed her face, startling him with her soft, natural beauty. Her hair—her crowning glory—was a luxurious, raven black. It curled over her forehead and brushed the high, exotic cheekbones in her delicate face. Her large eyes, framed by long, thick lashes, were the same blue-black shade as her hair. He could only describe her coloring as rich—a rich orange-yellow layered with shades of browns, from maple to umber.

"I don't know, but if you decide to go in, it's at your own risk," she teased.

He arched a pale eyebrow. "I feel lucky today. I'll try it."

"Good luck," Vanessa returned, smiling and walking away from him.

For the second time that morning, Joshua waited and watched Vanessa Blanchard walk. He had only nine days to get what he wanted from Vanessa. He had engaged her in conversation *and* coaxed a smile from her, but the conversation did not yield the information he sought.

What Joshua Kirkland would not readily acknowledge was that she also had elicited a smile from him, and for the first time since he returned to the shadowy world of military intelligence, he looked forward to gleaning information from a woman—especially if that woman was Vanessa Blanchard.

Vanessa waited until the final announcement to board her flight to Mexico City blared from the terminal speakers before returning to the gate. Flashing her boarding pass, she entered the aircraft. Time had passed quickly. She had spent the ninety minutes browsing throughout the many souvenir shops. She had entered and exited each shop empty-handed. Her trip to Mexico had a twofold purpose: shopping and relaxation.

In keeping with the culture of the inhabitants of the Southwest region, she had begun decorating her home with a blend of Native,

African and Mexican-American furnishings. It had taken more than two years to find the bed she wanted for the master bedroom, the sofa, love seat and tables for the living room, dining-room table, chairs, credenza, and buffet server, and guest bedroom furniture. Her long awaited trip to Mexico was for the express purpose of buying accessories: rugs, pottery and native artifacts.

She made her way to her seat and sat down. Joshua Kirkland, already seated and belted in, did not avert his gaze from the window and the activity on the ground below.

No hint of emotion showed on Joshua's face as he registered the now familiar warmth and fragrance that belonged exclusively to Vanessa Blanchard. Even without glancing at her, he knew exactly what she looked like. In fact, he probably knew more about Vanessa than she knew or remembered about herself.

Her file at a Pentagon office, labeled Top Secret and Priority, had been handed to him during a meeting with the members of the Joint Strike Fighter committee. A prior year's financial audit of Grenville-Edwards had uncovered several improprieties; an official inside source at the aerospace plant had leaked information linking someone at the plant with sub-contracting to a subsidiary manufacturer who was selling classified components for laser guided bombs to a guerilla group in Central America. The audit uncovered that more than two million dollars had been diverted into nonexistent escrow accounts since Vanessa had headed the contracts department. What the Joint Strike Fighter committee wanted to prevent was a similar compromise of national security if any of the specifications for the new fighter aircraft were sold to a foreign nation without authorization.

A Justice Department investigation had examined every phase of her life—personal and financial—and had come up with nothing which would link her to the receipt of monies from the sale of the classified military components. However, a subsequent pending file was also set up: U.S. v Vanessa Blanchard. Charge—Industrial Espionage.

The government wanted to indict her for industrial espionage, while Joshua thought the charge should be treason. For a few dollars she had sold out her country; a few dollars no one, not even the most accomplished accountants, had been able to locate.

His mission was to identify her contact, and it was his intent to get the information he needed from her with or without her consent.

Pressing his head back to the headrest, he closed his eyes and feigned sleep during the flight from El Paso to Mexico City. He listened as Vanessa thanked the flight attendant for her green salad lunch. He recalled an entry under her medical history on the dossier the investigators had collected on her—she had experienced food poisoning on a flight to New York during her senior year in college. It was apparent that she still did not trust the ubiquitous airline cuisine.

He listened intently to the soft whisper of her breathing, counting the measured beats. She was calm and relaxed. Stealing a glance at her profile, he felt his own breathing falter before starting up again.

Vanessa Blanchard was an exotically beautiful woman. The delicate black curls falling over her forehead made her look soft and vulnerable, and Joshua did not want to believe that she had betrayed her country for financial gain.

But, *had* she done it for financial gain? The investigators were unable to trace the two million dollars, and Vanessa Blanchard's lifestyle had not changed dramatically since she had come to work for Grenville-Edwards. She had placed a standard ten percent down payment on her house and paid her mortgage at the same time every month for the past two years. There were no large purchases of luxury cars, expensive jewelry or extravagant trips. They knew she flew to Los Angeles every Thanksgiving and Christmas to visit her parents. Other than her sister, brother-in-law, and two nephews, she did not have a wide circle of friends. She was well liked at Grenville-Edwards and participated in most job-related social activities.

It was the men, or the lack of men, in her life that intrigued Joshua. Except for an occasional date for dinner or a movie, Vanessa did not have a significant other in her life. It appeared that she did not have a lover. That would make his mission much easier.

A rare smile ruffled his firm mouth. He would seduce her!

The notion of seducing Vanessa Blanchard shocked him. It was something he had never done before—professionally or personally. It simply wasn't his style. What he could not explain or understand was that there was something about this woman that made him want to know her—in the most intimate way possible.

Vanessa turned to her right, capturing Joshua's gaze. This time his eyes were brilliant emerald instead of pale, transparent peridot. She returned his smile. "You slept through lunch." Her voice was warm as heated honey.

His smile widened. "I'd asked the attendant not to wake me. An hour after we land I'm scheduled to have a business lunch. I've found that too much food in a warm climate usually dulls the mind."

Vanessa shifted a beautifully arched eyebrow. "So, you're going to Mexico on business?"

He shook his head. "Business *and* pleasure." He'd told her the truth, because *she* would be his pleasure. "And yourself?"

"Pleasure."

Joshua made certain to keep his smile in place as he contemplated her response. He knew she had planned a trip to Mexico six months before, and wondered if perhaps she was to have met her contact at that time. Was this trip to make up for the prior, aborted one?

"Are the people you're meeting with German? I noticed the report you were reading was in German," she explained quickly when his smile faded and a glaze of frost swept all of the color and warmth from his gaze.

"No. They're Mexican," he explained quietly. "I oversee North American operations for a German investment company."

He had used this cover so often that the words flowed smoothly and without hesitation. The report Vanessa had seen him reading was not an update on a Mexican investment firm, but a cryptograph. His mission in Mexico was twofold: uncover Vanessa Blanchard's contact, and mobilize a drug sweep which he had given the code name Operation MESA.

The Drug Enforcement Administration was certain that one of their agents had alerted Mexican drug smugglers of impending raids by a concert of Mexican and U.S. DEA personnel. Classified maneuvers were leaked soon after they were formulated.

As an expert cryptographer, Joshua had been recruited because a cache of weapons stolen from a Texas fort were smuggled into Mexico, then sold to a Costa Rican military official who was quietly amassing his own private army to overthrow his democratic government.

The pages Vanessa saw him reading were filled with dates, times, and places where U.S. and Mexican drug enforcement personnel would strike with the speed of lightning, filling their nets with high-level traffickers.

The man Vanessa found so attractive intrigued her. "Are you also fluent in Spanish?" she questioned. Again a smile played about his handsome mouth as he nodded. "And what else?"

"Italian, Russian, and French."

Her eyes widened with this disclosure. "I barely get by with English, and you speak six languages."

"Five."

"Six," she insisted. "Or don't you count English?"

Joshua arched a pale eyebrow. Vanessa Blanchard had a quick mind—quick, sharp, and devious. And she was smart enough to hide two million dollars where men who were labeled accounting experts could not find it.

"You're right. I didn't count English." His piercing gaze was fixed on her lush mouth. "I've told you everything about myself, Vanessa Blanchard, so it's now your turn."

"I hardly think so," she teased lightly. "All I know is your name, you're flying to Mexico City on business, and that you speak—"

"And pleasure," Joshua interrupted, his voice lowering seductively.

"And pleasure," Vanessa conceded. "I also know that you say you speak six languages."

As he leaned to his left, Joshua's warm, moist breath caressed her cheek. "What else do you need to know? Vital statistics? I'm thirty-eight," he continued, not giving her a chance to answer. "I was born and raised in Miami, Florida. My parents are African-American and Cuban-American. I learned Spanish from my mother, and picked up the other languages from traveling. I'm six foot three inches and I weight one hundred and eighty pounds. I'm also single and have no children," he concluded with an irresistibly devastating grin. He noticed Vanessa's downcast gaze, thinking perhaps he'd embarrassed her. What he had revealed to her was valid, because he wanted her to know enough about him not to be wary.

It wasn't embarrassment that made Vanessa cautious, but Joshua's sudden attempt to engage her in conversation, *and* the fact that he was so willing to talk about himself. They were less than half an hour from Mexico City and he was coming on to her.

Glancing up at him, her smooth forehead furrowed in a frown. "Why are you telling me about yourself? You barely looked at me or said more than three words to me during the flight from Santa Fe to El Paso."

Joshua was not rebuffed by her sudden withdrawal. If she *was* a part of an espionage ring she would always be alert to anyone who tried to get too close to her. A wry smile softened his features. She would be a worthy target.

"You're right about my only saying three words to you, but you're very wrong about my not looking at you. I noticed you the moment I stepped foot onto this aircraft, and I couldn't believe my good fortune once I realized we were sitting together." What he did not tell her was that their seating was pre-arranged.

She met his level stare, noticing the darkening of his penetrating eyes as the blood heated up in her face and spread slowly over her neck and chest. His gaze inched down to her chest, where the tightening of her nipples was discernible through the cotton dress; she was angry with herself for responding to him, and that he knew she wasn't unaffected by his blatant masculinity.

"Why are you coming on to me?" she whispered.

Joshua's familiar impassive mask was back in place. "Because I was hoping that maybe we could share dinner one of these nights. After all, we're fellow Americans and we're both traveling alone. I'm more than familiar with being in a foreign country, where I need to hear the bastardized English which we seem to change every two or three years."

"But you speak Spanish, so you shouldn't feel like a foreigner. I'm the one who only has a rudimentary knowledge of the language. I know enough Spanish to ask directions," Vanessa argued.

"How about ordering food?" he challenged.

"Chicken is *pollo,* and meat is *carne.*"

He shifted an eyebrow. "If that's the case, then please forgive me for being forward, Miss Blanchard. I meant no disrespect."

He moved away from her and stared out the window, his jaw tightening. She wasn't going to cooperate. Dammit! He only had nine days to get what he wanted from her. That wasn't going to happen if she refused to see him.

Vanessa placed a slender hand on the sleeve of his crisp, white shirt and Joshua jumped as if she had burned him. "I'm sorry," she apologized. "I didn't mean to sound like a shrew."

His head came around and he stared at her with a deadly calm which chilled her. It was a look that those who were familiar with Joshua Kirkland recognized immediately. It was cold and lethal.

"I don't need your pity."

"And you don't have to be so rude!" she snapped in anger.

He exhaled audibly and covered her hand with one of his. "I

meant no harm, Vanessa," he countered in a softer tone. "All I asked is that we have dinner together. You acted as if I'd asked you to go to bed with me."

Vanessa felt properly chastised. She'd planned to spend ten days in a foreign country, traveling alone, and what harm would it do if she accepted his invitation to have dinner? And it wasn't as if she hadn't been attracted to him. She would accept, but it would be on her terms.

"Tomorrow night. At my hotel." A part of her hoped he wouldn't be available.

Only his iron-willed control prevented Joshua from revealing any hint of satisfaction. "It happens I'm free tomorrow evening. Where are you staying?"

"La Mérida."

He studied her thoughtfully for a moment, something lazily seductive in his look. "I'll meet you in the lobby at eight."

Extracting her hand, Vanessa nodded. "You've got yourself a date."

The flight attendants walked up and down the aisle, checking whether seat trays were put away, seats were in the upright position, and carry-on bags were secured as they prepared for their final descent.

Vanessa closed her eyes and inhaled deeply as the plane lost altitude, her fingers gripping the armrests; she felt the warmth and strong grip of a hand on her right one. Joshua's thumb grazed her knuckles, massaging them until her grip loosened.

The jetliner touched down with a squeal of rubber hitting the tarmac, and she opened her eyes and rewarded him with a dazzling smile.

For the second time since he had met Vanessa Blanchard face-to-face, Joshua was stunned by her sensual beauty. He looked forward to spending time with her—alone.

He followed Vanessa off the plane, waited with her while she filled out a baggage declaration form, then made certain she secured ground transportation to her hotel.

Leaning in through the cab window, he winked at her. "Tomorrow night at eight," he reminded her.

"Tomorrow night at eight," she repeated.

He watched as the car sped away from the curb. Shifting a garment bag over his shoulder, he picked up his single piece of luggage and walked over to an awaiting taxi.

Day One—he had met Vanessa Blanchard, engaged her in conversation, and secured a promise of a dinner.

Chapter 3

Vanessa settled into her hotel suite, pleased with her opulent surroundings. The hotel staff were professional and bilingual, reminding her that if she needed anything all she had to do was to pick up the telephone.

Closing the door behind the departing concierge, she headed for the bathroom. Stripping off her dress and underwear, she covered her hair with the ubiquitous hotel shower cap from a small wicker basket on the vanity filled with a typical hotel supply of soap, shampoo, lotion and other grooming aids.

Minutes later, she stood under the warm spray of water, reveling in its rejuvenating power. She showered twice each day and allowed herself a leisurely bath once a week. Filling her bathtub with a rich, scented, bubbling bath oil on Sunday nights had become a ritual once she moved from Los Angeles to Santa Fe.

Her life changed dramatically once she had come to work for Grenville-Edwards. Unlike with teaching, she worked year-round, and a normal, scheduled, nine-to-five workday was the exception rather than the norm. She was very good at what she had been hired to do and paid very well for her expertise. She had attended meetings which lasted twelve hours. Grenville-Edwards had become the largest corporation in the Southwest in the manufacture of aerospace components, and the corporate giant had no intention of losing that distinction.

But right now she forgot about contracts, budgets, and anything and everyone at Grenville-Edwards as she prepared to enjoy her Mexican vacation.

She emerged from the bathroom and walked into the adjoining bedroom, a bathsheet wrapped around her moist body. She went through her normal ritual of moisturizing her body from head to foot, then slipped into the underwear she had laid out on the king-size bed.

Making her way to the closet where she had hung her clothes, Vanessa surveyed the dresses, blouses, and slacks, knowing she would have to take advantage of one of the hotel's amenities—most of the garments needed to be ironed.

She selected a pale blue chambray shirt with a long, slim matching skirt. At five-foot-nine inches she favored mid-calf garments that flattered her slender body. It was only on rare occasions that she wore anything above her knees.

Right now it wasn't her wardrobe that filled her thoughts. She had planned her itinerary carefully, using Mexico City as her home base. Her list included wooden masks from the capital city, ceramics from Puebla, silver, woven shawls, or blankets from Taxco or Oaxaca. Her excursions to these other cities would be by bus or train.

After slipping into a pair of comfortable leather low-heeled shoes and securing most of her precious and sought after American dollars in the hotel safe, she headed toward Mexico City's business district with a small shoulder purse slung across her chest.

Vanessa was assailed by sounds and sights which threatened to overwhelm her. Traffic jams at every intersection made vehicular transit horrendous and the air quality unpleasant and unhealthy. The streets were clogged with well dressed locals, designer-clad tourists, and many shabbily dressed natives, each jostling for his own personal space. The sounds of rude car horns and radios blasting *salsa* filled the air.

She passed a group of young Mexican men who stared and called out to her, and even though she did not understand what they were saying, she knew enough not to make eye contact or appear insulted. There was much to be said for a woman in a foreign country without a male escort.

Male escort! Since she left the airport she had temporarily dismissed Joshua Kirkland, even though she had promised to have dinner with him in the hotel's supper club. Most of the clothes she packed were casual and practical, because she intended to use room service for most of her meals. That meant she had to buy something suitable for tomorrow evening.

Damn you! she thought angrily. Mentally assessing how much money she had in her purse, she headed toward the *Zona Rosa,* a shopping district that boasted shops similar to those found along New York City's Fifth Avenue.

She strolled along *La Rosa,* peering into the windows of the many prestigious shops and boutiques. Glancing at her watch, she realized it was near time for *siesta.* She had to buy what she wanted in forty minutes or wait another two hours for the shops to reopen for the late-afternoon crowds.

Walking into a shop which featured upscale dresses in the showcase window, Vanessa smiled as a beautiful, young sales-clerk came forward to greet her.

"¡Buenas tardes!" she said, trying out her limited high school Spanish. *"Quisiera comprar un vestido."*

The salesclerk lapsed into a stream of rapid Spanish, and Vanessa stared blankly at her. Her expression of confusion was obvious when an older woman came to the front of the shop and spoke softly to the clerk, telling her to draw the awning in prep-aration for their *siesta.*

The shop's owner, her face and body giving no indication of

her six decades of life, was exquisitely attired in a white silk sheath which clung to every line of her professionally nipped and tucked frame. She smiled at Vanessa. "May I help you?" she questioned in flawless English.

Vanessa returned the warm smile with one of her own, relieved that she did not have to continue groping in her halting Spanish. "I need a dress," she stated, repeating what she had told the salesclerk.

"A dress to make a statement, or one to get attention?"

Arching an eyebrow, Vanessa stared, speechless for several seconds. "That's a very interesting question."

"I ask that of all of my customers." The proprietor extended a delicate, pale hand. "I'm Elise Wilcox-Santana."

She took the proffered hand, replying, "Vanessa Blanchard."

"Well, Miss Blanchard, you didn't answer my question."

She didn't answer because at that moment she couldn't. If Joshua had been present, she would have replied, 'To make a statement.' Because he wasn't, Vanessa was uncertain how he would react to her if she decided to purchase a suggestive or provocative garment.

The silent, sensual energy he had projected made her want to know him, be with him. However, without his strong, masculine aura to cast a spell over her she vacillated.

But did she really want to be pragmatic? How long had it been since a man, any man, had intrigued her? *Four years,* a voice whispered to her—not since Kenneth.

A voluptuous smile softened her full lips, assuaging her momentary uncertainty. "I want one that will get attention."

Elise Santana pressed her manicured hands together, obviously pleased with Vanessa's decision. "What size are you?"

"Six."

The two women spent part of the *siesta* selecting and trying on dresses that would get Joshua Kirkland's attention. Vanessa wondered how her mysterious traveling companion would react when he saw her in the dress she had finally decided to purchase.

Elise was smugly pleased with Vanessa's selection as she led her to the section of the upscale boutique where she displayed elegant accessories. Vanessa chose undergarments, a pair of three-inch, black satin, sling-strap pumps and a small, black satin evening purse.

A shiver of anticipation and excitement quickened her pulse as she handed Elise a credit card, and it was only when she had bought and paid for her purchases that she realized that the past four years had been spent in waiting.

She wanted Joshua Kirkland, if only to make her see herself as a woman who needed more than a career. Her chest swelled with an emotion she had thought long dead—she wanted the man!

Joshua arrived at La Mérida fifteen minutes before his appointed meeting with Vanessa, confirmed his reservation of a table for two in the hotel's supper club, then returned to the lobby to wait.

The hotel she had elected to stay in was one of the older establishments in Mexico City, and filled with Old World charm. The interiors complemented the hotel's seventeenth-century appearance. Its architecture and furnishings were reminiscent of the spacious haciendas erected by the Spanish grandees in Old California.

Sitting in a corner, his presence partially obscured by the fronds of a large palm plant, he surveyed the bank of elevators, and without looking at his watch he knew he had been waiting for more than a quarter of an hour.

She's late. The two words attacked him savagely. He detested tardiness, and he also knew that Vanessa Blanchard had never come in late in the three and a half years she had worked for Grenville-Edwards.

So why was she late? Did she intend to stand him up?

These questions hadn't quite fled his mind when the doors of one elevator opened and Vanessa stepped out into the lobby.

For a reason he could not explain or understand, Joshua was

not able to stand and go to her. Not now. He wanted to give himself the opportunity to quell the silent storm raging throughout his body.

He stared numbly, watching as she made her way across the carpeted floor. His gaze fixed on her feet and traveled slowly upward. Her long legs, which seemed to never end, were encased in sheer black hose, and he was momentarily stunned at the undulating movement of firm muscle in her calves and thighs as she glided over to him.

Her black dress, what there was of it, was off the shoulder and clung to every curve of her incredibly tight, slender body. It showed off the perfection of her long neck, the concave hollows above her collarbones, and at least four inches of flesh above her knees. The long sleeves concealed her arms and offered the only hint of modesty. But there was no way the dress could be modest on Vanessa Blanchard. On another woman, perhaps, but not her.

He rose to his feet and the fire burning within him was reflected in the deepening green of his electric gaze. Vanessa had styled her hair in a mass of black curls and swept them up in seductive disarray, adding, with her heels, another four to five inches to her already statuesque figure.

Joshua moved forward to meet her, and he detected the haunting scent of her perfume as her warmth overpowered him. Her lightly made up face hypnotized him as his gaze bore into hers. What stood before him was a woman who had not adorned herself with any jewelry, yet had become the most exquisite jewel he had ever encountered.

He had planned to seduce her, but somehow Vanessa had reversed their roles. She was seducing him!

Vanessa saw the stunned look on Joshua's face and successfully concealed a smile as she extended her manicured fingers. She had gotten his attention.

"¡Buenas noches!" she said, smiling.

Joshua took her hand, cradling it in his larger one before

turning it over and pressing a gentle kiss on her inner wrist. She stiffened and he tightened his grip.

Exerting the slightest pressure, he pulled her closer until her full breasts grazed the crisp front of his white shirt. Lowering his head, he brushed his lips over hers.

"*¡Buenas noches!*" he returned, the Spanish greeting flowing fluidly off his tongue. Pulling back slightly, he stared down at her. Biting down on his lower lip, he tasted the sweetness of her mouth a second time. "You look exquisite."

Vanessa's lipstick, the deep shade of a ripe burgundy cherry, shimmered on her temptingly curved mouth, bringing his gaze to linger on the spot. There was something about her smile that nearly crushed the iron-willed control he had managed to maintain all of his life. He didn't know whether it was her lips, the perfection of her straight, white teeth, or the way that skin around her large eyes crinkled at the corners that sent ripples of desire shooting through his groin.

Vanessa lowered her lashes in a demure gesture. "Thank you."

His breath caught in his chest, then started up again. How could she dress so provocatively yet react to his compliment with such affected innocence?

Who was the real Vanessa Blanchard—the sexy nymph standing before him, or the career-minded woman who had dated only three men during the time she had been under surveillance? And of those three, she had seen one only twice!

"Are you ready?"

Vanessa inhaled sharply as his right hand went to the small of her back. How was she going to make it through the evening with a man whose stunning virility seemed to suffocate her?

His expertly tailored, dark suit caressed the slim lines of his tall frame, and the stark whiteness of his shirt offset the deep color in his lean, brown jaw. A Windsor-knotted silk tie in rich tones of navy and silver under a curved spread collar caught her attention as she stared at his bronzed throat. Her heels had put her within three inches of his impressive height.

Raising her gaze, she met his, and what she saw rocked her to her core. Joshua Kirkland had lied to her. He wanted more than dinner. He wanted her in his bed!

Tilting her chin, she managed a nervous grin. "I've been ready for hours." And she had; she had been ready for years.

The heat from Joshua's hand swept through the fabric of her dress, searching, scorching, and searing her naked flesh beneath the black jersey material with a sensual fire. How could the mere contact of his fingertips remind her of how much she had missed a man's touch?

She was pleased Joshua had asked her out to dinner and pleased that she had accepted. She would share dinner with him, enjoy his company, then bid him good night.

Chapter 4

Joshua felt a rush of masculine pride the moment he and Vanessa stepped into the dimly lit supper club. Most male gazes were directed at her: the maître d', waiters, busboys, and diners. Their reaction to Vanessa was similar to his. She was breathtakingly stunning. And she was *his* dining partner for the evening.

He spoke quietly to the maître d', and within seconds they were shown to their table. The location of the table was perfect. It was close enough to the raised stage, where a band played melodiously behind a man and woman singing a passionate love song to each other.

After he made certain Vanessa was comfortably seated, he took his own seat. Enthralled by her perfect profile, Joshua watched as she listened to the vocalists singing a popular Spanish song.

Vanessa turned back to him, a questioning look in her expressive eyes. "What are they singing about?"

He leaned forward over the small, round table, the flickering candle in a votive glass creating light and dark shadows across his lean face. "He's asking her for forgiveness and under-standing."

"Forgiveness for what?"

"A single indiscretion."

She arched a delicate eyebrow. "In other words, he was un-faithful?"

Joshua nodded. Vanessa's expression made it seem as if she had been the wronged party. "Quite unfaithful," he confirmed.

"Is she going to forgive him?"

He listened for a few moments, nodding. "Yes. But only if he agrees to marry her. Otherwise it's over between them."

Vanessa thought of Kenneth and his many indiscretions. "Why would she want to marry a man knowing he's going to be unfaithful to her?"

The moment the question left her lips she knew she had revealed too much about herself. Kenneth Richmond's infidelity had made her overly cautious with the opposite sex. Focusing her attention on the menu on the table, she picked it up and pre-tended interest in the many selections listed in Spanish.

Staring across the table at her bowed head, Joshua said quietly, "Love. Because she loves him she's willing to forgive him."

Vanessa glanced up as her lips twisted in a cynical smile. "There isn't that much love in the world."

He recalled the entry in her file about her liaison with Kenneth Richmond. They had been engaged, but it ended within six months. The investigator never discovered the reason for their breakup. But now he knew—infidelity.

Joshua displayed a knowing smile. "I agree with you."

Her mouth formed a perfect little *O* before she pursed her lips tightly. She hadn't expected him to agree. "Are you saying that you would never be unfaithful to your wife?"

He relaxed against the back of the chair, staring intently at her. It was as if he could hear her silent plea for him to help her overcome the mistrust, show that all men weren't selfish, las-civious monsters who thought only of their own needs or desires.

"I would not only not be unfaithful to my wife, but to *any* woman I found myself involved with."

Vanessa searched his features for a hint of guile, but found none as she tried to assess his impassive countenance. His statement that he would be faithful sounded like a challenge. But was it one she could afford to accept?

"You sound so noble, Mr. Kirkland," she drawled sarcastically.

Successfully concealing his frustration, Joshua inclined his head. "Thank you, Miss Blanchard."

Inwardly he cursed and thanked Kenneth Richmond. He cursed him for making Vanessa reticent with men. He thanked him because she hadn't been involved with any man for more than four years, and that would make his assignment much easier than he had originally thought.

He knew instinctively that Vanessa was a passionate as well as a sensual woman, and he also knew that she was comfortable with her femininity. Her revealing attire confirmed that.

For the second time since he had met Vanessa Blanchard Joshua displayed a warm, easy smile. The gesture deepened the attractive lines at the corners of his luminous eyes, darkened their color from a light peridot to a rich emerald green, and displayed his straight, white teeth.

"I've invited you to dinner so that both of us can enjoy an evening filled with an excellent wine, good food, and enjoyable entertainment. Would you mind if I ordered a bottle of champagne to begin?"

Vanessa returned his smile, replying, "Not at all."

She again surprised him with the transformation of her features. Whether she was aware of it or not, she was born to smile, he thought; at that moment he pledged that over the next eight days he would make certain to brighten her eyes, soften her mouth with laughter, *and* identify her contact.

Gesturing to a waiting sommelier with a barely perceptible motion of his left forefinger, he ordered a bottle of vintage French champagne in fluid Spanish.

A waiter replaced the departing sommelier, asking if they were ready to order. He had directed his question to Joshua, though his dark gaze lingered leisurely on Vanessa.

"The lady and I will let you *know* when we are ready to order dinner." Though he spoke politely, there was no mistaking the slight reprimand in Joshua's tone.

"Sí, señor." The white jacket-clad waiter quickly backed away from the table. The maître d' had given him explicit instructions to take good care of the pale-haired Señor Kirkland, and that was what he wanted to do. But the man the maître d' then referred to as *El Rubio* frightened him. One glance at *El Rubio*'s cold gaze made him feel as if he had glimpsed the eyes of death.

The sommelier returned, showed Joshua the label on the bottle of champagne, then expertly extracted the cork. Their waiter reappeared with two fluted glasses and a crystal ice bucket filled with cracked ice. After settling the bottle into the ice, the sommelier and waiter retreated silently.

Vanessa was puzzled that Joshua hadn't requested a wine list when ordering a champagne rare as a 1938 Châteauneuf-du-Pape.

"How did you know La Mérida stocked that particular brand of champagne?" she questioned.

"I called them last night and asked. Why?"

"Do they stock it?"

"No. But they offered to pick up a few bottles from another hotel that does. Is there something wrong with this brand?"

She stared wordlessly across at him, her heart pounding. Did he actually know, or was it just a coincidence? "That brand of champagne is the only one that I can drink." To her surprise, Joshua showed no reaction to her disclosure, and as their gazes met she felt a shiver of uneasiness.

"How propitious. We have something in common, because it happens to be a favorite of mine." He dropped his gaze and a sweep of charcoal gray lashes brushed his cheekbones. He hadn't lied to her, because it *was* one of only two brands he would drink. "I think of it as a good omen. Don't you?" Tilting his chin, he winked at her.

"I'll let you know," she replied, not committing herself.

The tenderness in his expression made his face appear boyish. But Vanessa knew there was nothing boyish in a thirty-eight-year-old man who was proficient in six languages; a man who traveled throughout the world to earn his living.

She touched her left earlobe where she normally wore a small gold hoop. She had acquired the habit of touching her ear whenever she was deep in thought, and now she wondered what she was doing sharing dinner with a man who was a complete stranger—an attractive one, but still a stranger. Had she acted too hastily? Perhaps she shouldn't have accepted his invitation. Why had she waited to leave the United States to accept a date from a man, when she had declined numerous offers from men she knew?

Pushing back his chair, Joshua crossed one leg over the opposite knee. "When will you let me know?"

She managed a small smile. "Tonight."

"Tonight?" he questioned, arching an eyebrow.

"Just before I close the door to my hotel room and bid you *buenas noches*."

He pressed the knuckles of his right hand to his mouth, shaking his head. As he glanced up, his eyes sparkled with laughter. "You really know how to hurt a guy."

Vanessa also laughed, the sound light and tinkling. "What do you expect, Joshua?" His hand dropped and he stared at her, a strange expression on his face. Her own body stiffened. "What's wrong?"

His gaze traveled slowly over her face, lingering on her mouth. "That was the first time you called me by my name."

"Joshua," she repeated in a soft whisper.

His mouth curved with tenderness as a sensuous flame fired his electric gaze. "Do you really want to know what I expect?"

Resting her elbows on the table, Vanessa laced her manicured fingers together. "And do *you* expect me to answer that?"

"I expect you to tell me *something* about Vanessa Blanchard."

"There's not much to tell."

Pushing his chair farther away from the table, he rose to his feet. "Let me be the judge of that. You can tell me about yourself while we dance." The two singers had left the stage, leaving the band playing a slow, rhythmic composition. He took four steps, circled the small table, and extended his hand.

She stared at his proffered hand. "I don't dance."

A corner of his mouth lifted. "It's slow, and all you'll have to do is follow me."

"Don't blame me if I step all over your shoes and ruin the leather," she warned with a smile, rising to her feet.

He curved an arm around her narrow waist and led her out onto the floor, where a half dozen couples swayed in time to music with a distinctive Latin beat.

"I'll buy another pair," he whispered against her ear, while swinging her into a close embrace, his right arm tightening comfortably around her waist.

Vanessa felt the press of Joshua Kirkland's body against hers, and she registered the silent, sensual aura that drew her to him although she fought the pull. Her left hand rested on his shoulder, then moved up, grazing the collar of his suit jacket.

"Tell me about Vanessa," he urged, whispering into her hair and eliciting a slight shiver from her.

She reveled in the slim hardness of his body and the hauntingly erotic scent of his cologne, sighing. "Vanessa Blanchard is a thirty-three-year-old accountant who lives in Santa Fe. End of story."

"Married?"

"No."

"Children?"

"No."

"Is there a significant other in your life at this time?"

"End of story," she enunciated with a tone of finality.

Joshua chuckled and pulled her closer, but didn't press her
for more than she was willing to disclose. He still had time.
Closing his eyes, he committed everything about Vanessa to
memory: her breasts burning his chest, the narrow curve of her
waist and womanly flare of her hips, the solid tightness of her
slender thighs pressed against his, the silky feel of her flawless
face, and her hypnotic, feminine scent.

He lowered his head and nuzzled her ear, his warm breath
feathering over her neck. She stiffened and he tightened his hold
until she relaxed, her curves melding to his.

"For someone who doesn't dance you are very good, Miss
Blanchard."

"That's because you're an excellent lead."

She closed her eyes, following his intricate steps and losing
herself in the music, the moment, and the man.

Dancing with him reminded her of what she had been
missing. She was a normal woman—with needs and desires; she
wanted to be in love, marry, and eventually have children; she
wanted a man to love and protect her.

She had been alone for so long that she'd grown used to it.
Her work at Grenville-Edwards and her hobbies kept her so
busy she did not think of herself as lonely. She lived alone, but
she was never lonely.

The music ended and Joshua and Vanessa stood in the middle
of the dance floor, smiling at each other. Then, without looking
away, she backed out of his grasp. He stepped forward, closing the
distance, and placed an outstretched hand at the small of her back.

"Thank you for the dance," he said in a hushed tone.

Vanessa nodded, permitting him to lead her back to their table.
She watched Joshua pour the pale, bubbling champagne into the
two glasses, admiring the perfection of his slender hands. They
were beautifully formed, the fingers long, tapered and well-
groomed.

He handed her a half-filled glass, then lifted his own. "To
Mexico and…"

His gaze lowered, as had his voice, and he did not say what he wanted to say. If necessary, he planned to seduce Vanessa, but what bothered him was that he *wanted* to seduce her.

"And an evening filled with excellent wine, good food, and enjoyable entertainment," she said, completing his toast and repeating his statement.

"*¡Salud!*" he returned, touching glasses before he took a deep swallow of the cooling wine. It was what he needed to ease the warmth which built up in his chest when he realized where he wanted Vanessa, and what he wanted to do to her.

"*¡Salud!*" She put her glass to her lips and sipped the premium champagne, savoring the bubbles settling on her tongue.

Joshua stared at Vanessa over the rim of his glass, wondering what it was about her that made him think only of her and not the mission he was committed to completing.

When he had taken Vanessa into his arms and danced with her, he had consciously pushed the reason he had followed her to Mexico out of his mind, and in forgetting about his mission he had realized how much he wanted to live a normal life. A life free of the risks of surveillance.

He had grown tired of sleeping in strange hotel beds and living out of his suitcase years before, and left the shadowy world of military intelligence for four years. But he had come back, back to snare a woman whose above-average intelligence had baffled the government's team of accounting experts.

The accountants were frustrated because they could not find the Defense Department's two million dollars. Joshua considered the money inconsequential when he thought of how the country's national security had been compromised with the sale of the classified components for the laser-guided bombs. That meant no U.S. citizen was safe—on the ground or in the air.

As he concentrated on the reason why he was sitting across the table from Vanessa Blanchard, his familiar detached expression was back in place.

"Are you ready to order?" he queried.

Vanessa missed the cold and impersonal tone in his voice as she spread her menu out in front of her. She studied the section labeled *pollo*.

Touching her left earlobe with her forefinger, she said quietly, "I'll have the grilled peppers with chicken."

"Good choice. I'm going to order the fish in a garlic sauce."

Joshua gave the waiter their orders. Then he and Vanessa sat silently, drinking champagne.

If Vanessa was perplexed by the sudden shift in Joshua's mood, she did not reveal it as she sat opposite him eating her spicy chicken entrée and drinking champagne.

She noticed that he preferred the European style of eating, with his fork in his left hand rather than the right that Americans favored. Everything about him was exacting—from his dining etiquette to the way he interacted with her. There was something in his manner that conveyed that Joshua Kirkland was perfect—a little too perfect.

He appeared to have it all: looks, intelligence and, judging from the cut of his expertly tailored, dark blue suit, money. The longer she remained in his presence the more she wondered why some woman hadn't claimed him for a husband.

"You're not originally from Santa Fe, are you?" Joshua asked, breaking the comfortable silence.

Lowering her fork, Vanessa gave him a direct stare. "How did you know?"

"You don't sound like someone from the Southwest. You must remember that I do a great deal of traveling, and I've learned to listen to accents, dialects, and regional inflections."

"Well, Mister World Traveler," she teased, "where do you think I'm from?"

Joshua's rare smile was back in place. "Somewhere along the West Coast. California, Oregon, or Washington state."

"California," she confirmed. "Which city?"

Closing his eyes, he toyed with the stem of his wineglass.

"You don't sound like San Francisco or Sacramento, so it would have to be southern California."

"Which city?" Vanessa repeated.

"San Diego or Los Angeles."

He opened his eyes, confidence shining from their depths. Even if he hadn't read the information the Justice Department gathered on Vanessa Blanchard, he still would have been able to uncover a lot of information about her by mere observation.

"San Diego." He had deliberately given her a wrong answer.

"Los Angeles," she confirmed, this time with a warm smile. "You're very good, Joshua."

He inclined his head. "Thank you, Vanessa."

"You say you travel a lot. Do you like it?"

A furrow creased his smooth forehead. "I used to."

"Why not now?"

"I'm at the age where I want a place to call home. A place I'm guaranteed to come home to every night."

She registered the longing in his voice. "Where is home now?"

"Florida and Jamaica."

"Jamaica in the Caribbean?"

"Yes."

Now her curiosity was piqued. "How much time do you spend there?"

"Not enough." A muscle flicked uneasily in his lean jaw. "The house is more than a hundred and eighty years old, and is one of the most intact structures in Ocho Rios. I was able to buy it for a fraction of its worth because the locals say it's haunted."

Vanessa went still, her eyes widening with this disclosure. "Haunted how?"

"The house was built in eighteen thirty-six as a honeymoon retreat for the members of a well-to-do British family. Every woman who married into the family and spent her honeymoon at the house died within the first year of her wedding."

"How did they die?"

Shrugging his broad shoulders and arching a pale eyebrow,

Joshua said, "Rumors say they were poisoned. By whom, no one knows."

"Do you believe in the superstition?"

A mysterious smile touched his mouth. "It wouldn't make a difference if I did, because I claim no blood ties to the family who owned the house."

"What did they do with the place?"

"It was abandoned when Jamaica claimed its independence and went into receivership for taxes. I found it unusual to purchase a house with all of its original furnishings still in it. Most former owners sold off heirloom pieces to pay for taxes or other debts."

Vanessa studied his face, unable to assuage her attraction for the enigmatic stranger she had consented to share dinner with. He was nothing like men she had dated in the past. Most of them had dominated the conversation, bragging about their attributes and successes, hoping to impress her, while Joshua only revealed what she had asked of him. He seemed more interested in her than she in him.

"The house must be quite elegant," she said, trying to envision the contents of a nineteenth-century West Indian home.

A faraway expression crossed Joshua's face and his eyes searched Vanessa's, reaching into her thoughts. "It's not as elegant as it is peaceful. It's a refuge if you're hurting and need a place to heal."

She laughed. "Do I look as if I'm hurting?"

"No one is exempt from pain—physical or emotional." This time there was no hint of a smile or amusement in his eyes.

A flicker of apprehension coursed through Vanessa as she remembered the pain of Kenneth's infidelity—pain which caused her to flee Los Angeles for New Mexico. She had told herself that she wasn't running away, but no one was fooled by her assertion that she needed a change. Her family never questioned her motives, knowing she had to leave California because the media had begun to follow her. Reporters wanted to know why she had decided not to marry the most talked about, dynamic, young politico in modern California's history. Photographers camped out in front of her house, or followed her to the college where she taught accounting courses. It was a time when she probably could've used Joshua's Jamaican retreat.

Picking up her cloth napkin, she dabbed at her mouth, drawing his gaze to the spot. A quick glance at the gold watch on Joshua's wrist indicated it was nearly ten-thirty. She had to be up early the following morning to catch a bus to Puebla.

"I'm sorry to have to end a most enjoyable evening, Joshua." Putting aside her napkin, she rose to her feet at the same time he circled the table and pulled out her chair.

"Can we have a repeat of tonight?" he questioned close to her ear.

Vanessa glanced up at him, her heart hammering wildly in her chest. He was close, too close to permit her to breathe normally. His pale eyes in his mahogany brown face reflected an eerie magnetic glow that sucked her in and refused to let her go. His gaze was hypnotic, mesmerizing. What spell had he cast over her?

"When?" she asked, her voice a breathless whisper.

"Tomorrow night."

She hesitated, torn by conflicting emotions. She enjoyed his company, but she had not come to Mexico to initiate a friendship with a man, especially a man like Joshua Kirkland, who fascinated and frightened her at the same time.

As he lowered his head, his lips brushed her ear. "Please, Vanessa. I usually don't have to beg a woman to share a meal with me," he whispered arrogantly.

Her head came up, her mouth only inches from his. Giving him a saucy smile, she replied, "I take it they usually beg you?"

Joshua's lids lowered, concealing his enthralled gaze as laughter filled his chest. "Sometimes. But *never* for food."

It took several seconds before she understood his double meaning. Placing a slender hand against his chest, Vanessa pushed him gently. "I won't beg you for either."

He took her hand and held it firmly as his warm champagne-scented breath swept over her moist face. "I'm not asking you to beg me for anything."

"Why me, and not some other woman, Joshua?"

A frown settled into his features. *Why you,* he thought. *Because you are a traitor, Vanessa Blanchard. And it's my job to snare traitors who jeopardize our country's national security.*

"Because I like you," he stated simply. She was the first woman he'd met who was as stunningly beautiful as she was intelligent, and because she was it made his job easy.

Vanessa had to admit to herself that she liked him. Liked him enough to want to see him again.

"I can't see you." Joshua stared at her, disappointment shadowing his features. "Not tomorrow evening," she added. "I'm free the following evening, if you are."

A slight smile touched his sculpted mouth. "I'll make certain I am."

Their waiter approached the table and handed Joshua a small, leather-bound case containing the bill for their dinner. He glanced at the total and reached into the breast of his jacket and withdrew a billfold. He extracted enough Mexican pesos to pay their meal and beverage—twice.

"Mil gracias," he said quietly to the waiter, leaving the man staring at the money. Smiling openly at Vanessa, he escorted her out of the supper club and into the lobby of the hotel.

Reaching for her hand, he led her to the elevators. "I'll see you to your room."

She tried pulling her fingers from his loose grip and failed. Joshua was much stronger than he appeared. "I can assure you that I won't get lost between the lobby and the third floor."

He gave her a sidelong glance. "Have I not been the perfect gentleman tonight, Miss Blanchard?"

"Well…yes."

"A gentleman always sees a lady to her door."

The ornate brass doors of the elevator opened and they waited until a formally dressed couple exited. Vanessa did not miss the surreptitious glance the woman threw Joshua as she walked past with an exaggerated wiggle of her hips.

She stepped into the elevator, Joshua following and pushing the button for the third floor. The car rose quickly and smoothly, stopping at her floor; she opened her small evening bag and withdrew a plastic, magnetic coded key.

"Which room?" he asked, taking the key from her hand.

"Three fourteen."

Their footsteps were muffled by the thick carpeting as they made their way down the hall. Vanessa stopped in front of the door to her room. Joshua inserted the key in the slot and a small light gleamed a green signal. He pushed the door open and stepped into the entry.

Vanessa walked in and took the key from his outstretched hand. Tilting her chin, she smiled up at him. The light she had left on in the entry gleamed down on his hair, which appeared nearly white in the muted glow. "Thank you for dinner, Joshua."

Shaking his head, he flashed a warm smile. "I should be the one thanking you." Leaning over, he kissed her cheek. *"Buenas noches."* Winking at her, he closed the door behind him.

She stared at the space where he'd been, blinking. A slight smile softened her mouth. He was right: he was a gentleman; they had shared a date; there were no strings attached.

Shrugging her slender shoulders, she flicked off the light in the entryway. What did she have to lose by seeing him again?

"Nothing," she whispered as she slipped off her heels and headed for the bedroom. Nothing at all.

Joshua walked across the lobby of his hotel, heading for the front desk. He asked the desk clerk for his key, and if there were any messages for him. The clerk handed him the key and a white, business-size envelope with the hotel's logo in the upper left corner and his room number written across the front. He knew without opening the envelope what it contained. Heading for the bank of elevators, he walked into an empty car and pressed the button for his floor.

Three minutes later he opened the door of his hotel suite on the twenty-second floor. There had been a time when he would've torn open the envelope to read its contents as soon as he took possession of it, but after years of experience, coupled with an iron will and self-control, he could wait until he entered the bedroom and changed out of his suit, shirt, and tie and into a pair of black sweatpants.

Making his way back to the suite's expansive living room, he filled a snifter with ice and a lemon-lime flavored seltzer from the wet bar. He took several deep swallows of the cooling liquid before picking up the envelope, which he'd left on a side table. The snifter replaced the envelope. Turning on the table lamp and slipping a finger under the flap, he withdrew a single sheet of paper. Pale green eyes swept over the neatly handwritten notations.

29 April: left La Mérida at 0850—toured Plaza del Angel. 1125—taxi to Bazar Sábado—purchased silver jewelry for female. 1318—dined alone. 1501—returned to La Mérida.

Frustration tightened Joshua's jaw as he crumpled the sheet of paper in his left hand and dropped it to the floor. The person he had assigned to follow Vanessa did not see her meet with anyone. She toured, shopped, dined, then returned to her hotel for her dinner date with him; how long, he wondered, was she going to play the tourist before she met her contact? And how long did he have before his contemplated seduction failed, and he would have to exercise an extremely conclusive method of extracting information from her?

He walked silently on bare feet on the deep pile of the pale gray carpeting, over to the wall-to-wall windows. Not bothering to close the dark gray, silk-lined drapes, he stared out at the sparkling lights of nighttime Mexico City. Images of Vanessa whirled around in his mind, and he recalled everything about her. He could still smell the natural scent of her flesh beneath her seductive perfume, recollect the velvety feel of her cheek against his as they danced, her willowy, seductive feminine curves pressed against his body, and the sweet, ripe taste of her lips when he kissed her. The kiss had been just a brushing of the lips, and it had taken all of his restraint not to deepen it.

He had spent most of their time together over dinner watching her mouth. The deep burgundy color on her lower lip reminded him of an overripe cherry bursting with sweet, thick juice. Vanessa Blanchard was beautiful and sexy—the sexiest woman he had ever encountered during his travels throughout the world—and he looked forward to seducing her with an emotion so foreign to him that at that moment he was unable to fathom it.

The only other woman he had permitted himself to become involved with had been beautiful as well as innocent. Sable St. Clair possessed an innocence that initially made him want to protect her. Sable did not want his protection; she wanted marriage and children, and at that time in his life he was unable to offer either. She cried quietly, then told him she was leaving, and he did not try to stop her. He had permitted Sable to walk out of his life without a word of protest.

He knew instinctively that Vanessa was no Sable. She did not need him or any man. And that made his assignment even more frustrating and challenging.

Joshua also knew that he could not afford to waste a day not seeing her. Turning away from the window, he clasped his hands behind his back and stared at the crumpled ball of paper. He had to find a way to meet with her within the next twenty-four hours; he had to find a way to make Vanessa *need* him.

A satisfied look softened his jaw as he contemplated what he intended to do, and mentally catalogued the day's events.

Day Two—he shared a kiss, dinner, and dancing with Vanessa Blanchard and secured a promise for another liaison for dinner.

Chapter 5

It was the sound of thunder and lightning that woke Vanessa from a deep sleep, not the hotel's front desk wake-up call.

Turning over onto her back, she peered at the drawn draperies, unable to discern a hint of light even though it was nearly seven o'clock. She smothered a groan as she threw an arm over her forehead. How was she going to shop and sightsee in a torrential downpour?

Sighing heavily and pushing herself into a sitting position, she massaged her temples with her fingertips. She didn't need a medical expert to tell her that the dull throbbing in her forehead and acrid taste on her tongue were from the prior evening's champagne. How many glasses had she consumed? Two? Or was it three?

If it had been three, then she'd exceeded her limit. Champagne usually made her feel giddy while she drank it, but lethargic the day after. And she wondered about Joshua. How was he feeling this morning? She was certain he had drunk more than she did.

The thought of Joshua brought a smile to her face. What was

there about him, other than his overall appearance, that drew her to him? It wasn't just that he was charming when he chose to be; it was something else she couldn't quite identify.

She knew instinctively that he was *all male.* Just the way his eyes lit up and swept over her body when she walked across the lobby last night reinforced that. He'd liked what he saw as much as she'd liked what *she* saw when he came forward to meet her. He'd kissed her, lightly, and later she'd realized that he was as stunned by the gesture as she was.

The telephone chimed twice with two consecutive rings, momentarily shattering her musings about Joshua Kirkland. She leaned over to the bedside table, picked up the receiver, then replaced it on its cradle.

Despite the rain, she decided to continue with her plans.

She had exactly two hours to get herself ready for the bus tour that would take her to the state of Puebla. The travel brochure stated that the trip would take about three hours via the scenic route. The three-hour journey would also include a detour to view two volcanoes, Popocatépetl and Ixtaccíhutal, up close.

Picking up the telephone, Vanessa dialed the extension for room service and ordered breakfast, requesting that it be delivered to her at eight.

Throwing back the sheet covering her nude body, she swung her legs over the side of the bed and headed for the bathroom.

At exactly eight o'clock Vanessa answered the door. Her breakfast had arrived. A smiling young woman pushed a serving cart into the room, followed by an older man carrying a large bouquet of pale pink flowers in a towering rectangular vase.

She noticed her name and room number written on the envelope attached to the clear cellophane covering the exquisite bouquet, and her pulse quickened. Only her sister and her boss, Warren McDonald, knew her hotel, and she doubted whether Connie would send her flowers. They had to be from Warren.

"Put them over there, please," she said to the man laboring

under the enormous weight of the vase. She watched as he gently placed the vase in the center of an oval table near the windows. Reaching for the stack of Mexican coins she kept on the top of the double dresser, she handed several to him.

"No, *gracias, Señorita,*" he protested. "I cannot take your money."

She gave him a puzzled look. She was not aware that the hotel staff could not accept gratuities.

"*El Señor* made certain to pay me."

"*Muchas gracias,*" she said with a smile.

"*De nada,*" he returned, nodding and walking out of the room behind the departing maid.

Vanessa plucked the small envelope from the cellophane wrapping. *El Señor made certain to pay me.* That meant it *was* from a man, and that man had to be Warren.

But why have flowers delivered to her when she was on vacation? Why had he continued to pursue her after she told him candidly that she would not become involved with him because they worked together and he was her *boss?*

She removed the cellophane, finding roses, tulips, lilies, and orchids, all in the same pale pink shade, then withdrew a card from the envelope. She stiffened. The flowers weren't from Warren. They were from Joshua Kirkland!

Her gaze raced over the neat, precise handwriting, not once, but twice. Closing her eyes, she could still see the words inscribed on the square of vellum: *Vanessa—Please accept my humble thanks for the most memorable night I've ever experienced in Mexico City. I hope more will follow. Sincerely—Joshua K.—Clarion Reforma Suites—Room 2204.*

Opening her eyes, she smiled. There was nothing humble about Joshua Kirkland. If anything, he was arrogant, too arrogant, and very, very confident. He was arrogant, confident, *and* charming, and the fact remained that she *would* see him again. At least one more time. First she would eat her breakfast, then call and thank him for the flowers.

She picked over her breakfast, barely eating her eggs and tacos, preferring instead to drink the strong, flavorful Mexican coffee. She swallowed two aspirins, hoping her dull headache would subside. She'd looked forward to the leisurely bus ride to Puebla.

Her gaze lingered on the flowers and she put down her coffee cup and made her way over to the telephone. Picking up the receiver, she asked the hotel operator to ring the Clarion Reforma Suites. The front desk at Joshua's hotel answered and she asked for his room. The phone rang six times before it bounced back to the desk.

"There is no answer in Room two two oh four. Perhaps you would like to leave a message," said a man in slightly accented English. She hesitated, then left her name and number.

The pain in her temples had begun to ease by the time she slipped her sock-covered feet into a pair of running shoes. She pushed a lightweight windbreaker with a hood into her leather backpack, along with her wallet, sunglasses, khaki-colored baseball cap and the bottle of aspirin.

Checking her face in the mirror over the sink in the bathroom, Vanessa winced. There was still a slight puffiness under her eyes. She tucked in several strands of hair with her fingers, securing them in a chignon pinned loosely at the nape of her neck. With her face washed clean of makeup and dressed in a T-shirt, well-worn comfortable jeans, and a pair of running shoes, she was the epitome of a laid-back tourist.

She returned to the bedroom and gathered up her backpack and key. Her gaze swept around the room, lingering on the vase with the flowers before she opened and closed the door behind her. She took the elevator to the lobby, realizing as she left her key at the desk that her headache had vanished. The rain had also stopped, and the sun tried vainly to pierce the veil of smog that lingered over Mexico City.

In front of the hotel, Vanessa walked over to the waiting bus which would take her to Puebla for a day of shopping and sightseeing. Smiling at the driver seated behind the wheel, she knew she was going to have an enjoyable day.

Joshua opened the door to his hotel suite, watching a youthful-looking Cordero Birmingham give him a look which spoke volumes. The natural color had drained from his face, leaving it a sickly yellow shade.

"Where—where's Nathanial Webb?" Cordero sputtered, recovering quickly and finding his voice. He had been told he would meet the Director of the Drug Enforcement Administration, not U.S. Army Colonel Joshua Kirkland.

Joshua's impassive expression did not alter as he noted subtle changes in the man he had been ordered to contact. Cordero Birmingham was thirty-five but appeared ten years younger. He was an even six-foot, slim, and claimed smooth golden skin over high cheekbones. His hair was a thick, wavy, burnished copper, and his eyes a startling, topaz blue under dark eyebrows. There was a slight hardness around his mouth until he smiled. He claimed a perfect set of shimmering, white teeth.

"Nate's been relieved of duty for this maneuver."

Cordero followed Joshua into the living room and sank down into a plush armchair. "Why? Who's replacing him?"

Clasping his hands behind his back, Joshua stared, coldly drilling Cordero to his seat. "I'm replacing Nate, because they suspect a mole in his operation."

Inhaling audibly, Cordero let out his breath slowly. "Who?"

"That's what Matthew Sterling is going to uncover. Tell him to take out the mole and leave Delgado in place."

The United States government had many private citizens on their payroll for undocumented covert activities, and Joshua knew that Matthew Sterling was one of the best. They had collaborated on a maneuver in the Salvadoran jungle, and had barely gotten out of the Central American country alive. A guerilla's bullet had found its target inches above Matt's heart, and his movements had given away their position. Joshua had been responsible for injecting Matt with a narcotic powerful enough to render a man immediately unconscious and kill with a single dose—any man except Matthew Sterling. Matt survived, and their mission was successful.

Cordero shook his head, frowning. "I don't know if Mateo's going to like this change of plan. He's to be married at eleven o'clock today."

Joshua stared at the younger man without blinking. "I'll meet you in the airport tomorrow night at twenty-three hundred hours," he ordered in an emotionless tone.

"Where?"

"AeroMexico's departure terminal. I'll let you know who to contact for the pickup of marijuana, and I'll also arrange for the transfer." U.S. DEA agents had infiltrated several drug cartels, identifying them for his Operation MESA. The telephone rang, but he made no move to answer it. He counted off six rings before it stopped.

Joshua turned his back, and it was a full minute before Cordero realized he had been dismissed. Rising to his feet, he bowed slightly at the man who had personally come to Mexico to deliver his orders. A sardonic smile revealed his sparkling teeth as he made his way across the luxurious hotel suite. He opened and closed the door quietly. It was only then that Joshua turned around, to make certain he was alone.

He picked up the telephone and retrieved the call from the hotel's operator, his eyebrows arching slightly. Vanessa had called. Now she knew where to find him when she needed him.

Vanessa returned to Mexico City and La Mérida exhausted and satisfied. She'd found the ideal planters for her enclosed patio. The large terra cotta vessels were hand-painted reproductions with ancient Mexican hieroglyphics. The urns were perfect for the saguaro cacti she intended to order from a popular Santa Fe nursery. The Puebla shopkeeper assured her that the specially ordered ceramic planters would be shipped to her home within a month of her return to the States. She'd left the shop, knowing the one month he'd promised would more than likely be two.

Retrieving her key from the desk, she made her way to the elevators. Riding the bus for six hours and walking endlessly around a city which boasted architecture from the sixteenth through the late seventeenth centuries to modern office buildings and a few hotels had taken their toll. All she wanted was a bath and her bed.

As she inserted the key in the lock to her room she heard the shrill ringing of her telephone. Pushing open the door, Vanessa stood still, her heart pumping wildly in her chest. She took two steps into the entry and felt personally violated. Someone had ransacked the place! Fear and rage warred inside her as the phone continued its incessant ringing.

She rushed into the bedroom, snatching up the receiver and holding it with both hands to keep it from slipping from her trembling fingers. "Hello." Her voice was a hoarse whisper.

"Vanessa?"

She recognized the other voice immediately. "Josh-u-a."

"Vanessa? Are you all right?"

Sinking down to the floor beside the bed, she closed her eyes and bit down hard on her lower lip until it throbbed like a pulse. "Someone's been in my room," she gasped, struggling for a normal breath.

"Who, Vanessa?"

She registered the impatience in Joshua's voice, and it angered her. Why was he asking a question she couldn't answer?

"I don't know," she snapped. "I just walked in and found everything turned upside down. Whoever it was stripped my bed, and they've gone through the closet and dresser drawers."

"Don't touch anything," he ordered. "When you hang up, call hotel security. I'll be there as soon as I can get a car."

"Joshua—" She heard the steady drone of the dial tone. He had hung up. Pressing her head back against the edge of the mattress, she depressed the hook, then dialed the hotel's operator. The operator said she would have security personnel at her room within minutes.

Why would anyone want to steal from her? She hadn't brought any jewelry with her. Most of her money was locked in the hotel's safe, and when she ventured out she carried only a small amount of Mexican currency and her credit cards.

The *whys* attacked her until she did what she rarely did—cried.

Two men carrying walkie talkies swept into the room, not bothering to close the door and barking questions at Vanessa.

She shook her head like someone drugged. "I don't know," she said over and over until she felt like screaming.

"Did you notice anyone following you, Señorita Blanchard?" asked the shorter of the two men.

"Why would anyone want to follow me? For what?"

His dark gaze lingered on her face before slipping down to her chest and the jeans hugging her slim hips. "That's what I'm trying to uncover."

"Is anything missing?" asked a familiar male voice in Spanish.

Vanessa spun around as she rose from the chair where she'd sat during the questioning. "Joshua," she sighed breathlessly. It had taken him less than fifteen minutes to come to her.

He crossed the room quickly, stepping over bedclothes and articles of clothing that Vanessa had stored in the chest of drawers and closet. She did not disappoint him as she flung herself into his outstretched arms.

A shudder went through his body as he cradled her gently, offering comfort and safety. The need to protect her surfaced, along with a craving to possess Vanessa Blanchard totally. He wanted her body, and more.

One hand made circular motions on her back, while the other cradled the back of her head to his shoulder. "I'll take care of everything, Angel."

She nodded, fighting back tears. She didn't want to show weakness, especially in front of Joshua. She'd managed to stem her flow of tears before the other two men arrived, but now they threatened to flow again.

Reluctantly he released her, and she covered her mouth with one hand and sank back down to the chair. His penetrating green eyes burned into hers, and there was something in his gaze that said he would take care of everything—and her.

Joshua took charge, demanding that the two men tell him what they had asked Vanessa. They reported that she hadn't kept any jewelry or money in the room, therefore there was none to report stolen. Neither of them could understand why Señorita Blanchard's room was ransacked.

Joshua did not tell them, of course, that he'd ordered The Shadow to break into her room and make it look like a burglary because he knew instinctively that Vanessa would be frightened enough to come to him—come to him because he'd offer to protect her.

"Before you make the determination that only her room was *ransacked,* I suggest you check with the other guests in your hotel," he countered.

The shorter man took charge. "We will check, Señor—"

"Kirkland," he supplied. "I will help Señorita Blanchard pack her—"

"There's no need for her to leave La Mérida, Señor Kirkland."

Joshua shot him a lethal glare. "There is every need if her safety is at risk. She could've been here when whoever it was broke in. And if it were to happen again, can you guarantee that she would not be harmed?"

"No, Señor Kirkland," said the other man. "Do you want us to notify the police?"

"I'll let you know after we've gone through everything."

"*Gracias,*" the men said in unison. They didn't want a police presence. The other guests would become aware of what had happened in 314. La Mérida had spent many years acquiring the reputation befitting a four star hotel. An incident like this one would tarnish their reputation and limit future business.

"We will make certain the management compensates Señorita Blanchard for her trouble," the taller of the two stated with a wide grin. "And we'll send someone from housekeeping to help her pack."

Pleased that they had managed to defuse what could've become a volatile situation, they left the room.

Joshua did not acknowledge their offer as he turned back to Vanessa. She sat on the chair, legs drawn up under her body, head thrown back, and her eyes closed. She looked nothing like a traitor, but did anyone who sold classified secrets ever look like one?

Walking over to her, he hunkered down next to the chair. "Vanessa," he crooned softly, rubbing the back of his hand over her cheekbone. Her large eyes opened and she blinked, then focused her gaze. "You're going to check out of this place and stay with me."

"I can't." She stared over his head at a pattern on the wallpaper behind the bed.

"You can, and you will." His face was a mask of stone. "I have enough room in my hotel suite for three people without anyone bumping into another."

Vanessa shook her head, refusing to relent. "I want to stay here. I'll move into another room on a different floor."

"What if it happens again?"

She sat up, unfolding her legs. "Why would it?"

"I'm not saying it would. But I would feel better if I didn't have to race across town to check on you." He pointed to the overturned vase and the flowers resting in a widening pool of water on the carpet. "And it pains me that you treat my carefully chosen gift of appreciation in such a deplorable manner."

She smiled for the first time since walking into the room that evening. A feeling of relief surged through her, and she rested her head against his shoulder. How she wanted to take him up on his offer! She needed him to make her feel safe.

"I'm usually not so ungrateful. I did try to call you."

Shifting his head slightly, he pressed his lips to her hair. "To tell me what?"

"To thank you for the flowers."

"Thank me by staying with me."

Vanessa sat up straighter. "I want to," she admitted, "but I can't. I won't allow something like this to turn me into a coward. And if I hide now, then I'll never stop hiding. Thank you for the offer, but I'll just move into another room," she insisted stubbornly.

Joshua stood up, pulling her to her feet. He cupped her face between his palms, making her his willing prisoner. "What happened here has nothing to do with cowardice. It's about not challenging a lunatic who gets his or her kicks by breaking into hotel rooms and destroying everything in sight."

A distinctive tapping on the door, followed by a woman's voice, preempted whatever Vanessa was going to say.

"Come in," Joshua called out.

A petite woman wearing the uniform of the hotel's house-keeping staff stepped into the room. Joshua told her in rapid Spanish what he wanted her to do while Vanessa excused herself and walked into the bathroom.

She could not stop the gasp of horror escaping her gaping mouth when she saw remnants of several items of intimate apparel hanging on the shower rod. Her panties and bras were splattered with what seemed like red paint, mimicking blood. The ransacking of her room had not been just a moronic prank. It was now apparent that whoever had broken into her room was deranged *and* probably a sexual deviant, as well. Backing slowly out of the bathroom, she retreated to where Joshua stood supervising the cleanup. She tugged at the sleeve of his black linen jacket.

He looked down at her, recognizing the fear—stark, wild and vivid—in her tortured gaze. Her fingers tightened on his arm.

"What is it, Vanessa?"

Fearful images crowded her mind and she breathed in quick,

shallow gasps to slow down her runaway heart. "I want out of here. I can't stay in this place."

Joshua did not understand what could've made her change her mind so quickly. His gaze narrowed. "What's the matter?"

Closing her eyes, she tried forcing air into her constricted lungs. "Look in the bathroom."

He made his way to the bathroom and his reaction to seeing Vanessa's underwear spattered with a red substance was a burning rage that swept over him like a volcanic eruption.

The man who had been dubbed The Shadow—because of his ability to follow a person without being detected—had traumatized Vanessa instead of just frightening her.

Joshua's eyes paled to a translucent green while his jaw tightened. The Shadow would soon learn that following a directive meant just that. He would not tolerate superfluous theatrics.

Returning to the bedroom, he stared at Vanessa as she stood at the window, looking out with unseeing eyes. His gaze moved leisurely over her slim hips in revealing jeans. Seeing her rounded bottom attractively outlined in the denim failed to arouse him. What he did feel was a munificent need to take care of her.

The woman was a traitor, and he still was drawn to her!

Closing the distance between them, he pulled her gently against his chest in a close, comforting embrace. Lowering his head, he pressed his lips to her sweet, fragrant hair.

"Don't be afraid, Angel," he whispered quietly. "I'm going to take care of you. You'll be safe with me."

Vanessa sagged weakly against his stronger body and nodded. She couldn't fathom the emotion, but suddenly without warning she felt safe with Joshua, safer than she had ever been in her life.

Chapter 6

Vanessa sat on a large plush chair in a living room at the Clarion Reforma Suites. Joshua hadn't lied to her. His accommodations were spacious enough for two or three people. The suite contained two bedrooms, the larger with an adjoining bath and dressing room, a living room, dining area and an efficiency kitchen.

She returned Joshua's unwavering gaze as he stood in front of the expansive windows with his hands clasped behind his back, while the hotel maid put away her clothes in the smaller bedroom.

He watched her the way a predator studies its prey before attacking, and she wondered what was going on behind his solemn expression. Had he regretted suggesting that she share his suite? Did he think she'd met someone, spurned him, and the person now stalked her?

She suddenly realized that Joshua was dressed entirely in black: his jacket, slacks, shirt, and shoes. For the first time since she'd met him he didn't appear to be what he said he was—an international businessman. There was something about his eyes, his stance, penetrating gaze, and uncanny stillness that projected an aura of danger. The man standing before her was dark except for his hair and eyes; lean and dangerous.

"I'm leaving here tomorrow morning," she stated quietly, deciding that she had to get away from him as smoothly and quickly as she possibly could.

A pale eyebrow shifted at her disclosure. "You're going back to the States?"

Vanessa rose gracefully from her chair, transfixing Joshua with the slender, supple lines of her feminine form. "No. I'm going to check into another hotel."

He moved toward her, seemingly floating and narrowing the space between them in seconds. She moved back and sat down on the chair she'd just vacated, and the backs of her knees hit the seat.

"I can't permit that," he said in a low, ominous tone.

She felt a wave of momentary panic. His voice was absolutely emotionless, chilling her. She tilted her chin, and her eyes widened when he stood over her.

"You can't stop me."

He nodded. "You're right about that. But I also can't protect you if you leave."

She felt a resurgence of confidence. "I don't need protecting."

"What if what occurred in your room happens again?"

"Why should it?" Vanessa countered.

Joshua's eyes paled. "Because you're a woman traveling alone in a foreign country. You don't know if some psychopath is following you because he likes what he sees. You *are* aware of what you look like?"

"What's that supposed to mean?"

A slight smile softened his sensuous mouth. "You have eyes, Vanessa. Surely you're aware of your beauty."

"Whether I believe I'm beautiful or not is not a topic for debate. I admit that I was a little shaken by the simulated blood on my underwear, but I've gotten over that. I'm grateful to you that—"

"I don't need your gratitude," he interrupted.

"Well, that's all I can offer you at this time," she countered. "I'll accept your invitation to spend the night here, but I intend to check out in the morning."

Joshua decided not to argue with her. The fact that she was willing to share his suite for the night was enough—for the moment.

"Is there anything I can get for you?"

She managed the beginnings of a smile. "Only what I've wanted since I got off that bus almost two hours ago. A hot bath and a clean bed."

Hunkering down in front of Vanessa, Joshua grasped both of her hands in a firm grip. He registered the shiver of uneasiness shaking her body, and he knew she wasn't as unaffected by the break-in as she appeared.

He studied her, seeing her fragile vulnerability. The need to protect her was overwhelming; the emotion nearly suffocated him with its ferocity.

But she's a traitor, a voice in his head shrilled, *a beautiful, sexy, gutsy, brilliant traitor.* He wondered whether he was attracted to her because of her beauty or in awe of her tenacity.

"Do you want anything to eat or drink?"

She shook her head. "No, thank you. Just the bath and a bed will do."

He rose to his feet, pulling her up with him. "A bath and bed coming up."

Vanessa gave him a warm smile. His breathing stopped, then started up again at her inviting, sensual expression. His reaction to seeing the transformation of her features when she smiled was something he knew he would never get used to.

Releasing her hands, he made his way to the bedroom to instruct the maid to draw a bath for her.

Vanessa sank down into a bathtub filled with warm, scented bubbles. She felt the tension and rigidity leaving her body almost immediately. She had not wanted to let Joshua know just how unnerved she had been by the break-in at La Mérida.

The fact that nothing had been taken was more unsettling than an actual theft would have been. And she refused to think about what he had identified as red nail polish on her under-wear, because she did not want to think the person intent on breaking into her room was not only a thief but a depraved sexual deviant.

Joshua conferred with the two men from La Mérida's security team before she'd checked out, and they had reassured him that no other room had been burglarized; that meant she had been a specific target. She wondered of whom, and for what purpose.

The soft music filtering through the concealed speakers in the spacious pale blue and raspberry bathroom lulled her into a state of somnolence as she rested the back of her head on a sponge pillow and closed her eyes. Tiny droplets of water dotted her face and curled her relaxed hair around her hairline.

She had no idea how much time had elapsed when she heard the tapping on the door. Sitting up, she realized the bubbles had disappeared and the water had cooled.

"Yes," she called out.

"Are you all right?" Joshua asked.

Vanessa smiled, picking up a bath puff and trickling water over her breasts. "I'm fine. I'll be out in a little while."

It was another twenty minutes before she stepped out of the bathroom, wearing a light gray, oversized T-shirt with a pair of matching leggings. Her hair being swept on the top of her head allowed for an unobscured view of her face and neck.

She stopped suddenly, and a small gasp of surprise escaped her. Joshua leaned against a wall, waiting for her. He'd changed from his slacks and silk shirt into a pair of black, drawstring, cotton sweatpants and tank top.

He appeared taller in the revealing black attire as the muted overhead light shone down on his bare arms and shoulders. Lean, compact muscles flexed fluidly under his brown flesh when he crossed his arms over his chest.

His languid gaze moved slowly over her features, lingering on her mouth before moving up to her eyes. "I didn't mean to startle you. I made some tea and I wanted to know whether you'd want a cup."

Vanessa felt a shiver race through her body at his penetrating stare. Whenever he stared at her she felt as if he was looking for something from her. What it was, she didn't know.

Clutching the clothing she had worn earlier that day to her chest, she hoped it would serve as a barrier between them. Joshua stood more than three feet from her, yet his presence overwhelmed her with the raw power he emanated so effortlessly.

"I would like a cup, thank you." Her voice was breathless, as if she had run a long, grueling race. "Let me put these away, then I'll join you." She walked toward her bedroom, while Joshua turned and made his way to the kitchen.

The bedroom was luxurious, and no expense had been spared with the furnishings. Massive mahogany furniture dominated the space. Its deep, rich color was offset by stark white carpeting and window and bed dressing. It was the smaller of the two bedrooms in the suite, yet it was still larger than the space she had occupied at La Mérida. She placed her jeans and T-shirt on a chair before she left the bedroom.

Joshua had set the table in the dining area with a fragile bone-china teapot and matching cups and saucers. A serving plate in the center of the table was filled with a variety of golden butter cookies. He stood behind a chair, waiting to seat her.

"Did you bake the cookies?" she teased, taking the seat. He leaned over her head and she felt the warmth of his body and his breath.

"They're from the hotel's kitchen," he whispered close to her ear.

Glancing back over her shoulder, Vanessa stared up at him. "Can you cook?"

He flashed a mysterious smile. "Yes, I can." Straightening, he walked around the table and sat down opposite her.

"What's your specialty?" she questioned as he reached for her cup and filled it with a fragrant, steaming, pale green liquid.

"Southern and Caribbean cuisine."

She stared at him as he filled his own cup. "Who taught you?"

A muscle tensed and throbbed noticeably along the left side of his face before easing. All warmth in his eyes fled, leaving them cold and forbidding, and she chided herself for probing.

"My mother," he answered after a lengthy silence, watching as she picked up her cup and took a sip of the imported tea. "How about yourself? Do you cook?"

"I'm learning," she admitted softly.

"Learning?"

Replacing her cup gently on its saucer, Vanessa folded both hands on her hips and glared at him across the table. "If I knew how to say the word in another language for you I'd do it." She noticed the smile curving his mouth. "You think because I'm a woman I'm supposed to know how to cook, don't you?"

Shrugging his bare shoulders and holding up his hands, Joshua shook his head. "That's where you're wrong. I'd never assume that." His expression mirrored innocence.

Sure, Vanessa thought. There was something in Joshua Kirkland's bearing that silently screamed that he could be extremely sexist when he chose to be.

"You don't believe me, do you?" he questioned. She refused to answer him. "We're supposed to have shared dinner out tomorrow evening, but instead I'll cook for you."

She was mildly surprised by his offer. "You'd do that?"

"I'd do *anything* for you, Vanessa," he countered in a deep voice simmering with barely checked passion. "All you have to do is ask."

His declaration alternately frightened and thrilled her as a pulse throbbed erratically in her throat. Her mouth felt dry, and she took another deep swallow of tea.

"You're coming on to me again, Joshua."

Placing an elbow on the table, he rested his chin on a fisted hand. "You accused me of that before and I denied it," he said, reminding her of her accusation during the flight to Mexico City. "But this time I'm guilty as sin. Can you handle that, Vanessa Blanchard?"

She couldn't handle it, and she was ready to bolt from the table. She was thirty-three years old, experienced with men, and here she was trembling like a frightened virgin before her first sexual encounter.

Tilting her chin, she gave him a challenging look. "And if I couldn't handle it, Joshua Kirkland, what would you do about it?"

Leaning back on his chair, while crossing his arms over his chest, he smiled and nodded in approval. Though not one to engage in mind games, he enjoyed the sexual sparring with Vanessa.

"I'd wait," he replied quietly. "I'd wait for you to come to me."

She stood up, and he rose with her. "Wait on, Mister!" she spat out. There was no way she was going to fall into bed with a stranger. "Good night." Pushing back her chair, she turned in the direction of her bedroom.

Joshua stared at her departing figure, smiling. "There's a lock on the door separating our bedrooms. If you change your mind just leave it unlocked," he called out.

Vanessa made it to her bedroom and closed the door softly. What she wanted to do was slam it and rid herself of some of the frustration building up in her celibate body. Joshua had become a blatant reminder of what she had once shared with a few men; what she consciously wanted to share with him.

Stripping off her clothes, she slipped under the sheet and turned off the lamp on the bedside table. All she wanted to do was sleep, sleep so she would forget about the person or persons who had ransacked her room at La Mérida, and the man who had assumed the responsibility of becoming her protector.

Joshua Kirkland was too attractive, confident, too sensual and virile, and much too arrogant.

Vanessa sat up quickly and flicked on the lamp. She had forgotten to check the door separating their bedrooms. Crossing the room, she turned the lock, listening to the soft click.

Seconds later, she returned to the bed and plunged the room into darkness. Soon the space was filled with the soft whisper of her breathing as she sank into the comforting arms of a dreamless sleep.

Chapter 7

Joshua sat at the table, staring at the space where Vanessa had been. Within the span of three days she read him better than anyone ever had. Not even his family knew him that well.

He had come on to her because he wanted her with a raw, unbridled passion he had never felt for any woman, and the wanting had nothing to do with his mission. Without her saying, *"take me," "love me,"* or *"protect me,"* it was something he wanted to do.

He had retired once, and perhaps he shouldn't have come back. Had he lost his edge? Had he allowed his emotions to dictate to him, so that he'd nullify his orders?

His desire for her went beyond a simple slaking of sexual tension. And he knew enough about himself to know that if he made love to her he would not be able to walk away from her.

Looking down into the china cup filled with tea, he recalled poignant episodes in his life as if they were frames of film. He summoned his mother's face, a face so much like his own, a face that rarely displayed a smile. He thought about the man whose last name he claimed, who would not claim him as "son."

He also thought about another man who was his father, a man who had denied him even before he was born, whom he would never call "father."

The realization rushed through him with the force of an erupting volcano. He wanted a family! Not brothers or sisters— those he had—but a wife and his own children. A woman he could acknowledge before man and God, and children he would love, cherish, and protect with his last breath.

And there was something about Vanessa Blanchard that elicited the strong, driving desire to marry and procreate.

Inhaling deeply and letting out his breath in an audible sigh, Joshua Kirkland knew what he wanted to do. He did not love Vanessa, yet he wanted her. He would get the information he sought from her, then he would protect her from any legal prosecution.

He poured out the lukewarm tea, refilled the cup from the pot, then sat staring out the window. He drank two cups before he cleared the table.

Walking into his bedroom, he glanced at the door separating his room from Vanessa's. He made his way over to it and turned the knob gently. A smile deepened the minute lines around his eyes. She had locked it!

There will be another time, he told himself.

Day Three—Vanessa would spend the night with him, but not in his bed.

Vanessa woke to the sounds of a driving rain battering the windows and the rumble of hunger gripping her stomach. Flicking on the lamp and peering at her watch on the bedside table, she groaned. It was only four o'clock. It was another two hours before the sun came up.

She glanced over at the door connecting the bedrooms, then fell back against the mound of pillows cradling her shoulders. She had to get up and prepare to check into another hotel.

The thought of trying to secure lodging weighed on her like a heavy blanket. Instead of touring and shopping she would have to call hotels. Slipping out of the bed, she moved quietly across the room and opened a drawer of a chest-on-chest. She withdrew a caftan and pulled it over her naked body before selecting underwear, a pair of jeans, and a T-shirt. She would get dressed, eat breakfast, and then check out of Joshua's suite.

Opening the door to her bedroom, she peered out. Joshua had left a lamp on a side table in the living room on, and the glow radiating through the crystal base provided enough light for her to make her way across the living room and into the bathroom, where she managed to shower, dress, and secure her hair into a sleek French twist in twenty minutes.

The now familiar scent of a citrus-based aftershave met her as she left the bathroom, and she knew Joshua was also up. Walking into the living room, she saw him seated at a desk in an alcove reading, and even though her bare feet made no noise on the carpeted floor his head came up alertly, as if she had made a sudden noise or motion.

"Buenos días," he said, rising and coming toward her. "I hope you slept well."

Vanessa gave him a warm smile. "Good morning. I slept quite well, thank you."

She took in everything about him in one glance. The smooth, brown flesh over his jaw glowed from a recent shave, and his hair, still damp from his shower, appeared burnished instead of white-gold. This morning he had selected a pair of startling white jeans, running shoes, and T-shirt. His spotless attire highlighted the deep, rich color of his skin, and the jeans riding low on his hips accentuated their slimness. The casual garments had transformed him from an erudite businessman to a laid-back tourist.

He's a chameleon, she thought. Just when she thought she'd categorized Joshua Kirkland, he changed before her eyes, and she wondered just who he was.

"Do you normally get up this early?" he asked.

Vanessa shook her head. "No, I don't. But I must confess that hunger is one of the motivating factors this morning."

Crossing his arms over his chest, Joshua gave her a knowing smile. "Then I'd better order breakfast for us."

She folded her hands on her hips and cocked her head at an angle. "At four-thirty in the morning?"

Reaching out, he ran a forefinger over the outline of her delicate jaw, lingering under her chin. "The hotel offers twenty-four-hour room service."

Vanessa felt the heat flame in her face under his touch when his smile broadened with a trace of eroticism. She wanted to pull away, but didn't, because each time he touched her she was reminded of his sensual attractiveness.

"What is the other motivating factor?" he whispered, leaning in closer.

Her eyes widened as she studied the darkening of his probing gaze. "I have to find another hotel."

His hand dropped abruptly, though his expression did not change. "I'll call the front desk and have them locate one suitable for you."

It was obvious that he wasn't pleased with her insistence that she leave his suite, but Vanessa knew that there was no way she could live with Joshua and not respond to his overt seduction. He'd made it quite clear over tea the night before that he wanted to sleep with her.

"Thank you, Joshua."

Trapping her with his penetrating stare, Joshua saw what Vanessa tried vainly to conceal from him. She was uncomfortable with him and anxious to leave. If she was to meet her contact she wouldn't be able to do it with him clinging to her, and he had to keep reminding himself that one of the reasons he was in Mexico was to uncover Vanessa Blanchard's contact.

"There's no need to thank me, Vanessa. I told you before

that there isn't anything I wouldn't do for you. All you have to do is ask."

She nodded, then watched as he made his way to one of the many telephones placed throughout the expansive suite. He picked up the receiver and dialed a number. She did not understand any of what he'd said in Spanish before he depressed the hook and dialed another number. She caught several words from this conversation—like *"señorita"* and *"Americana"* before he ended the call.

Watching her watching him, Joshua noted the expectant expression on Vanessa's face. He did not think she would be too pleased with the news he had to tell her.

"I've just been informed that there's a weather emergency."

She took several steps toward him, then stopped. "What do you mean?"

"The desk clerk just informed me that nearly two inches of rain have fallen in the past three hours, and that most of the roads leading into or out of the city are flooded. The judicial police have issued a stern weather emergency warning that anyone caught driving will be fined or jailed for ignoring the ban."

Gritting her teeth in frustration, Vanessa swallowed the words forming on her tongue. How had the weather conspired against her so that she couldn't get away from this man? What was it about Joshua that forced her to be inexorably linked to him?

"What am I going to do?"

"You'll stay here until the weather clears."

"I don't want to stay here."

"You don't have much of a choice," he countered.

Vanessa noticed the beginnings of a smile inching his sensuous mouth upward. She was irked by his obvious amusement at her not being able to escape him.

"You like this, don't you?" she accused.

He arched a pale eyebrow. "You want me to lie and say I don't?"

She gave him a hostile glare before turning and making her way to the expansive windows lining the living room wall. She opened the dark gray drapes and tried to see beyond the wall of torrential rain which fell in a slanting pattern and obliterated everything in sight. It was the beginning of May and the beginning of the rainy season.

Crossing the room and standing behind Vanessa, Joshua placed both hands on her shoulders. His touch was impersonal, comforting.

"There's not much we can do until the rain stops," he said softly, his breath sweeping sensuously over the back of her neck. "I'm going to have to postpone a business meeting until the travel ban is lifted."

Vanessa felt properly chastised. Here she was worrying about going on a shopping spree when Joshua was probably responsible for millions of dollars for his German-based investment company.

Her shoulders rose and fell as she sighed. "I suppose we're going to have to wait it out."

He turned her around to face him. The top of her head was level with his nose. His gaze moved with agonizing slowness over her face, and lingered on her mouth.

"What do you want to do to pass the time?"

Her eyes widened. "What *can* we do?"

"We can swim—"

"Not," she interrupted, putting up a hand. "It's because of water that we're having this discussion."

He nodded, giving her an easy smile. "You're right about that. Well, there's racquetball or billiards."

Vanessa's eyes glowed with anticipation. It had been a long time since she'd enjoyed a game of billiards. But she didn't want Joshua to know that she played the game—very, very well.

"I've always wanted to learn how to shoot pool." There was just enough longing in her voice to appeal to his machismo.

"I'll teach you if you'll join me in a game of racquetball."

She extended her right hand. "You've got yourself a deal."

Ignoring her proffered hand, he lowered his head and pressed his lips to hers, caressing her mouth more than kissing it. "Deal," he whispered, staring down into her surprised gaze.

It was the second time Joshua had kissed her, and both times it had been a brushings of the lips rather than a joining of mouths. The feathery touch of his firm mouth tantalized and frustrated her. What she wanted was a forceful domination of his mouth, so that she would lose herself in his kiss. She wanted, as well as needed, him to assuage the dormant feelings racing along her nerve endings.

Her fingers curled into tight fists as she backed away from him. His expression was closed but the deepening green of his eyes reflected the passions he was unable to conceal, and she knew Joshua wasn't as unaffected by the kiss as he appeared.

He hooked his thumbs in the waistband of his jeans, and his expression softened as he watched Vanessa compose herself. She squared her shoulders, tilted her chin, and crossed her arms under her breasts. She gave him a slow smile, and he was lost—spellbound.

"*Every* time you do that you take my breath away," he confessed, his voice dropping to a velvety whisper.

Her smiled faded. "Do what?" She couldn't stop the tremor in her own voice.

Joshua moved closer. "Smile."

Her mouth dropped slightly, giving him the advantage he sought as he swept her into the circle of his embrace. His hands, locked around her waist, brought her close until her middle was fused to his.

His head dipped, and when he settled his mouth over hers it was no gentle brushing of lips but a total possession that robbed Vanessa of her breath. Her knees buckled, and he tightened his hold on her until the lean, hard lines of his body burned her through her clothing.

He kissed her slowly, his lips moving and tasting every inch of her mouth, and Vanessa rose on tiptoe, returning the kiss as dormant fires blazed to life. Her hands cradled his lean cheeks and Joshua lifted her effortlessly from the floor until her head was level with his.

His tongue eased into her mouth, caressing, tasting, and coaxing, until she moaned with passion summoned from somewhere she didn't know existed. Her moans became whimpers as his breathing deepened.

She pressed her body closer, wanting Joshua to absorb her into himself. Memories of every man she'd ever known faded when a warming shiver of desire coiled at her center, threatening to explode. The strength of his arms was so male, so protective; she wound her own arms around his neck, clinging to him and marveling at how safe he made her feel.

Joshua kissed Vanessa with a hunger that belied his outward self-control, and it was only now that he had tasted her mouth that he realized that he wanted more—much more.

The heated blood rushing through his body pooled in his groin, and he knew with the hardening of his flesh that he had lost control. What was it about Vanessa Blanchard that caused him to lose himself in her sexy smile and scented body? How could she turn him on so easily?

"Joshua," Vanessa murmured. She repeated his name once more before he reacted.

"What is it?" he breathed into her open mouth.

"Someone's at the door."

He eased his hold on her body and lowered her on bare feet to the carpeted floor without freeing her from his embrace. His mouth hovered above hers as he struggled to regulate his rapid, labored breathing.

Closing his eyes against her stunned expression, he buried his face against her warm throat. "It's probably our breakfast. But what I want to eat is definitely not on that serving cart."

Not trusting herself to remain in his arms, Vanessa pushed against his chest. "I need to eat what's on that cart, so you'd better answer the door."

"Don't go away." Reluctantly he released her, making his way to the door while she groped for a chair in the dining area. Her nerves were screaming as if thousands of tiny insects had descended on her bare flesh. Closing her eyes, she bit down on her trembling lower lip. He'd done what she wanted him to do. He'd kissed her. But now she wanted more than his kisses.

Don't go away. Where would she go, even if she could escape him?

She suddenly realized that she wasn't as frightened of Joshua as she was of herself. She knew what he wanted, and she also wanted it. But could she sleep with him, a stranger, then walk away unaffected? Could she take off her clothes and lie with a man who reminded her of what she should feel as a woman, as a female?

Yes! screamed a voice within her, while another voice calmly said *no*.

How had she gotten herself into this dilemma? More importantly, how was she going to extricate herself?

Chapter 8

Vanessa stared at the waiter as he set the table with china, cutlery, and serving dishes, while Joshua watched her. She felt the heat of his gaze, and she refused to look at him. She didn't want him to see that her feelings for him were intensifying, and that she was caught up in her own conflicting emotions. A delicate, slender thread had formed between them when they exchanged the passionate kiss, and she was swathed in an invisible warmth of desire that she wanted to hold on to.

Even in the silence she could still hear his soft voice that seemed to come from deep within his chest. The sound was a rich, honeyed, controlled baritone that mesmerized her. She found that listening to Joshua speak was almost as sensuous as his touch. If she took his breath away when she smiled, then he made her heart stop when he touched her.

Joshua signed the receipt the waiter handed him and thanked him for the quick service. He waited until the man left the suite before he sat down opposite Vanessa.

He smiled, noticing her mouth was swollen from his kiss. Vanessa Blanchard hadn't held back, eliciting from him a rush of heated desire that made him want to strip the clothes from her body and take her on the carpeted floor; his desire for her had forced him to forsake his self-control, though he hadn't wanted to make love to her, but mate.

No, he would not take her on the floor like a rutting beast after a female in heat, but in a bed, and with all the tenderness and passion she would expect from a lover.

"Shall I serve you?" he asked quietly.

Vanessa's head came up and she met his gaze for the first time since they'd shared the kiss. His mesmerizing eyes were now a deep, verdant green. "Please."

She watched as he uncovered a large dish, her gaze fixed on his hands. Faint blue veins showed through brown flesh dusted with a sprinkling of short, gold hair. His long fingers were beautifully tapered and well-groomed, and were capable of uncanny strength. She'd felt the strength in those hands when they'd tightened around her waist and lifted her effortlessly off her feet.

Her gaze moved up, searching Joshua's composed features for remnants of passion. Nothing in his expression revealed that only minutes before his mouth had demanded she respond to his kiss, his body had hardened with lust, and his breathing had deepened with a shuddering desire.

Vanessa had known of the strong passion within herself, but it was only now, for the first time in a very long time, that she recognize her own needs; it was her own driving need for Joshua Kirkland that shocked her, because she knew there had been something special about him from the very first time she saw him; a special quality that would not permit her to resist the expert seduction he had openly admitted.

Since she'd moved to Santa Fe there had never seemed enough time for romance in her busy schedule. There hadn't even been enough time for a vacation—until now—and the realization swept over her that if she didn't flee room 2204 as soon as the rains stopped she would wind up in Joshua's arms again, and in his bed.

He flashed a slow, mysterious smile, handing her a plate filled with fluffy scrambled eggs, slices of crisp bacon, baked ham, and potatoes with onion and peppers. She took the plate, murmuring her thanks.

She had momentarily forgotten about the person or persons who had ransacked her room at La Mérida, because sitting across the table from Joshua and eating in silence while the rains slashed the earth with fury had made her feel secure and very safe. She didn't know what it was about her dining partner, but something within him transmitted wordlessly that she would have nothing to fear as long as he offered his protection.

Joshua was not put off by Vanessa's silence. He hadn't expected her to be talkative or animated. He'd kissed her, something she hadn't expected him to do, and he knew she'd surprised herself when she kissed him back. Her knees had given way, and if he hadn't tightened his grip on her body she would've fallen to the floor. That position would've been disastrous for both of them, because he *would have* been tempted to take her on the floor even if she protested.

He was stronger than she was, and he could overpower her at any time, but what he wanted to do was court her, seduce her, then have her come to him without guilt or remorse. He wanted her to want him as much as he wanted her.

He did not fool himself into believing his wanting Vanessa had anything to do with getting information from her. *That* he could do without sleeping with her. With a syringe filled with sodium amytal he could prove conclusively whether she was involved with the sale of classified military components.

He could get what he wanted from Vanessa Blanchard without drugging her, though, and having her offer up her body to him would be an added bonus.

Vanessa held out her cup for Joshua to refill it from a pot of excellently brewed coffee. After being in Mexico for three days she had come to look forward to and savor the rich, strong, Mexican blends. She was on her second cup, while Joshua hadn't drunk his first. She remembered he'd declined the waiter's offer of coffee after their dinner at La Mérida.

"Don't you like the coffee?" she asked, her midnight gaze fixed on his attractive mouth.

He looked at her as if photographing her with his eyes. "I grew up drinking coffee with milk and sugar added to it after it was brewed. Then it was reheated and served hot." Studying her bemused expression, Joshua continued, "I began drinking coffee as a child. I loved the smell of it brewing, and the taste even more. My mother used to dilute a portion with a lot of milk and sweeten it with sugar."

She smiled at him. "How old were you when you began drinking coffee?"

He shrugged a broad shoulder under his T-shirt. "Six, maybe seven."

Vanessa shook her head. "You were young. I didn't start drinking it until I was in college."

She met Joshua's direct stare with one of her own, enthralled with the tenderness of his expression. It was the first time since she'd met him that he appeared truly passionate, with all of his emotions on the surface. "What other addictions do you have?" she questioned softly.

Joshua hesitated, measuring her for a moment; *she* was becoming an addiction. He wanted to see her, touch her. There was something about Vanessa Blanchard that reached out and called out to him that she was to become a part of him and a part of his life.

"You," he replied in a deep, soothing, hypnotic whisper.

Vanessa felt her pulse race, and it throbbed noticeably in her throat. A flicker of apprehension coursed through her before she managed a relaxed smile. "You're kidding, aren't you?"

"No, I'm not," Joshua answered. "When you smile, something inside of me..." He paused, unable to come up with an apt description of his emotions. "Your smile is very erotic," he said instead.

She arched an eyebrow. "Erotic?"

He cocked his head at an angle, studying her intently. "If not erotic, then sensual. It reminds me of a sunrise."

Vanessa laughed, the soft, haunting sound floating up from her chest. "What a strange metaphor."

"A very fitting metaphor," he countered. "Your smile lights up and transforms your entire face."

She sobered, staring at Joshua and becoming increasingly uneasy under his scrutiny. His seduction had become so subtle, almost invisible, that she found herself snared in his web, though she was fully aware of his intent.

What hidden, invisible powers did he possess that made her want to take off her clothes and lie with him? *It's been too long,* she told herself. The last man she'd found herself attracted to was Kenneth, but even he hadn't affected her the way Joshua Kirkland did.

Joshua was quiet, subtle, yet something told her that he was also dangerous. He wasn't dangerous in the menacing sense, because she felt very safe with him, but no-nonsense dangerous. She knew instinctively that a relationship with him would be intense, satisfying, and above all else honest.

"I think of you as a throwback to another time, when knights rescued damsels in distress."

Joshua merely nodded at her assessment of him. What Vanessa didn't know was that she would need rescuing once she was charged with espionage, or conspiracy to commit espionage.

Placing an elbow on the table, he leaned forward, a slight smile touching his mouth. "Are you a damsel in distress?" he questioned, knowing she would never openly admit to the dangerous game she had elected to play. Spies were usually greedy, guarded and deceitful, not candid.

Vanessa smiled again, the gesture lighting up her eyes. "I'm certain I'll be, after you trounce me in billiards and racquetball."

"How competitive are you?"

Her eyes narrowed as she wrinkled her nose. "*Very*. Why?"

"So am I," he admitted. "And because we both are, then I'm *also* at risk of having to be rescued."

Raising her cup to her mouth, Vanessa took another sip of coffee. "We'll see," she said in a quiet voice. "We'll see."

Vanessa leaned against the pool table in the hotel's gaming room watching Joshua chalk the tip of a cue stick, a slight smile softening her mouth. He had patiently explained the rules of the game while she waited just as patiently to begin play.

What she didn't disclose was that her father, who had become a skilled amateur pool player, taught her the game before she was tall enough to see over the table. She'd stood on a stool and watched Mason Blanchard as he drove ball after ball into the pockets.

When she and Joshua entered the gaming room she had been surprised that they weren't the only ones taking advantage of a half dozen or more billiard tables set up in the expansive space. Seeing her questioning expression, Joshua had explained that the hotel catered exclusively to the business traveler. All of the rooms were suites, with efficiency kitchens, and twenty-four-hour services that included room service, concierge, valet parking, a heliport, limousine service, and free car wash. Each executive suite featured a sauna or Jacuzzi, while his in the Clarion Suites had both. He then hinted that she would probably utilize both after their strenuous game of racquetball. She'd thanked him with a facetious smile, while pondering the intimacy of using the bathroom adjoining his bedroom again.

The sound of a Ping-Pong ball pouncing off paddles and the distinctive clacking of pool balls being hit resounded through-out the room. Vanessa glanced around, realizing she was the only woman present. Either the businessmen who had checked into the Clarion Reforma elected not to travel with their significant others, or the women did not see the value in getting up before dawn to engage in table games.

Putting aside the chalk, Joshua beckoned to Vanessa. "Come here," he ordered softly. She straightened from her leaning position and moved over to him. "Stand in front of me and I'll show you how to hold the cue stick."

She manuevered in front of him and the whisper of his breath on the nape of her neck caused a shiver to shake her body; she was certain Joshua had registered it as he moved closer until his chest was pressed flush against her back. The heat from his body seeped into hers, bringing with it a wave of moisture between her breasts.

"Because you're right-handed," he said quietly near her ear, "you'll grip the handle of the cue stick loosely in that hand." He slipped the smooth length of wood in her right hand. "Lean forward slightly," he continued, "and rest your left hand on the edge of the table."

Vanessa couldn't concentrate on what he was saying. She felt every bone, muscle, and curve of his body molded intimately against her back and buttocks, and she knew she had made a mistake not telling him that she knew how to play pool, because every nerve in her body tingled with rising desire.

Savoring the clean masculine smell of him as he pressed closer, she knew she couldn't deny the pulsing knot that formed in her stomach and moved lower with a slow, hot ache between her thighs.

"Joshua." His name was a shivering whisper. She was unable to disguise her desperation *and* her vulnerability.

He leaned even closer. "What's the matter, Angel?"

"Please."

His mouth brushed over her left ear. "Please what?"

She was trapped, between his body, the table, and the potency of the force field he exuded so effortlessly. Closing her eyes, she wondered what was she doing with this man who had seemingly cast a spell over her so that she couldn't escape him.

"How do you expect me to trounce you if you won't teach me the game?"

His warm breath singed the back of her neck. "I am teaching you."

She opened her eyes, smiling. "I don't see anyone else in the room using your method, *Professor Kirkland.*"

"That's because none of their students look the way you do."

"Let me go, Professor. The bell just rang signaling the end of class." Her words were playful, but the meaning wasn't. He stepped back and Vanessa was able to breathe normally for the first time in more than two minutes. Turning, she glanced up, and her smile widened when she saw the broad grin Joshua gave her.

"I thought you needed a little remediation," he offered as an apology.

"Let me try it on my own. Then you'll be able to assess whether I need remediation."

Picking up his own cue, he chalked it, saying, "I'll break, and then you're on your own."

Vanessa watched the lean body swathed in pristine white as he drove his cue stick into the white ball, scattering others over the green felt, and three of them rolled into two leather-laced pockets at the corners of the table.

"Very nice, Joshua." He smiled at her, nodded, and stepped away from the table.

Inhaling, she gripped the handle of her cue loosely in her right hand while anchoring the tip between the first and second fingers of her left hand. It was over before it began as she drove all of the balls into the pockets in three moves.

She didn't have to look at Joshua to see his stunned expression. "Rack them," she ordered, chalking her cue.

Silently, he complied, folded his arms over his chest, and stood back watching as she slowly and methodically drove all of the balls into the pockets. Vanessa was unaware that all play at the other tables had stopped, the men moving closer and staring at her in disbelief.

I've been had, Joshua thought, his mouth tightening in annoyance. But the emotion faded quickly, admiration taking its place. Unfolding his arms, he applauded slowly, the sound shattering the stunned silence in the large room. Soon the other occupants applauded, and Vanessa lowered her head in a modest gesture.

Amusement shimmering in her eyes, she flashed a hypnotic smile, her gaze sweeping over the men standing around the table. "Would anyone like a turn with me?"

Before any of the men could accept her offer, Joshua moved to her side, the fingers of his left hand curving firmly around her upper arm. "You'll only go *one-on-one* with me," he warned softly.

Her eyebrows shifted upward in an expression of innocence. "I won't take their money, if that's what you're worried about."

He glanced over his shoulder, his cold glare drilling the men standing around and watching the interchange between himself and Vanessa. Turning, they went back to what they were doing before she began her awesome exhibition.

His cold gaze shifted back to her. "I'm not worried about you taking anyone's money."

"Then, what is it?" she asked, meeting his steady gaze with her own.

"I didn't bring you here to share you with other men."

She didn't have to search for the meaning behind his words, because after three days Vanessa knew Joshua to say exactly what he meant. Despite this, a flicker of anxiety still coursed through her.

The smoldering flame she saw in his gaze warmed her, and her body overrode her common sense when it ached for his touch. His attraction appealed to her vanity, and the depth of her femininity that no man had been able to penetrate. Without touching her he was able to elicit a profound sexual longing. A longing that intensified with every second she remained in his presence.

"There's no need for jealousy, Joshua," she said glibly. "I'm sharing a suite with you, not these other men."

But what I want is for you to share my bed, he thought. His need to extract information from her was no longer paramount. Having Vanessa and making her his own had taken precedence.

His grip on her arm loosened, the fingers caressing the silken skin below the sleeve of her T-shirt. "That you are."

The three words swept over Vanessa like a shimmering wave of sunlight, and she realized it was only a matter of time before she would share her body with Joshua Kirkland. Where? When? Those questions she couldn't answer, but she did know that it would happen.

Raising her chin, she gave him a saucy look. "Do you want to play another game?"

"You're giving me the chance to salvage what's left of my masculine pride?"

"Of course." Rising on her toes, she kissed his cheek.

Smiling down at her, he asked, "Where did you learn to play like that?"

"My father taught me."

"He's a pool shark?"

Vanessa laughed. "No. He's a physician. *His* father was a pool shark. I was told he supplemented his meager income very well with a game or two with so-called experts who tried to beat him."

"So, it's in the genes."

"Guilty as charged," she stated with a wide grin.

Joshua went completely still. Were those three words prophetic of what a jury would conclude after her trial?

The fear of Vanessa jailed, then going to trial, summoned a panic he had never acknowledged in his life. He'd agreed to do a job for the United States government, but for the first time since he'd been recruited into the world of military intelligence he considered not following orders—because he'd never used his body to get information from a subject.

But, he wondered, how could he give his superiors what they wanted while protecting Vanessa from prosecution?

The *hows* and *whys* attacked as he watched Vanessa retrieve the balls. He examined the lush curves of her slender body, her delicate profile, the shape of her intoxicating mouth, and knew there was only one way he could protect her.

He smiled, his eyes darkening to a rich avocado green. Before Vanessa left Mexico she would become Mrs. Joshua Kirkland.

"I have no doubt that you're going to beat me again," he stated quietly, leaning in toward her, "but I must also warn you that I'm not a very good loser."

Arching an eyebrow, Vanessa glanced up at him over her shoulder. "Are you serious?"

"Quite."

Turning and facing him squarely, she tilted her chin. "And what do you *intend* to do *if* I beat you again?"

His electric gaze bore into hers, burning her face, her mouth, as a mysterious smile softened his mouth. "Trounce me again, and you'll see."

This time her eyes narrowed. "Are you threatening me, Joshua Kirkland?"

"No, Angel, I'm just warning you."

"Then, I'll consider myself warned."

Chapter 9

Vanessa and Joshua stood at opposite sides of the elevator, staring at each other. After two games of pool, which she handily won, they played racquetball, and because she hadn't permitted him the advantage when they played pool, he hadn't given her any quarter during two very strenuous games. It was obvious their competitive tendencies were in full force.

"I beat you and you beat me," she said, staring up at the lighted numbers on a panel over the door.

Not replying, Joshua continued his visual examination of her profile. He had warned her to test her. He had to see whether she would waver under his warning, and she hadn't. There was no doubt that Vanessa Blanchard did not frighten easily, nor would she divert her focus from a task. It appeared she played hard, *and* she played to win.

Who, he wondered, had approached her to pass along the classified information on the laser-guided bombs? Why had she sold the classified documents? Where had she hidden the two million dollars? If she did it for the money, what had she needed it for? And who was she to meet in Mexico?

She had thought his warning a threat, not knowing that he would never do anything that would harm her or put her in more danger than she was already in. His realization that he would offer marriage to protect her indicated that his need to protect her from prosecution merely obscured deeper feelings he refused to acknowledge. There was no doubt he desired her, but he was unable to concede that he was falling in love with Vanessa Blanchard.

"You didn't beat me, Vanessa," he drawled, forcing a thread of anguish into his voice. "But what you did do was humiliate me in front of at least a dozen *men.*"

The elevator arrived at the twenty-second floor, and they stepped out to the carpeted hallway. She waited until Joshua opened the door to their suite before saying, "And you didn't humiliate me when you beat me at racquetball?"

He placed the key on a side table, then walked back to where she stood by the door. Cupping her face in his hands, he brushed his mouth over hers. "No, I didn't."

"Yes—you—did," she countered firmly between his soft, nibbling kisses.

"No, no, no, I didn't." Each of his denials was punctuated with a kiss over an eye and on the tip of her nose.

Vanessa pressed her face to his shoulder, inhaling the erotic fragrance of his cologne as it mingled with the clean scent of sweat drying on his T-shirt. "Why are we arguing about this?" Her voice was soft and muffled against his solid shoulder.

Joshua kissed the top of her head. "I'm not arguing, Angel." His hands searched under the hem of her T-shirt, massaging the tight flesh over her ribs.

Her breath came in quick gasps from the radiating pleasure, and she moaned softly. "What are you doing?"

Pulling back, he captured her tortured gaze, trapping her within the aura of his sensual masculinity. "I'm seducing you, Vanessa Blanchard. Do you have a problem with that?"

Ensnared by her own burning desires, with his hands moving up and down her back in a titillating rhythmic motion, she was unable to respond to his query.

"All you have to do is tell me no, and I'll stop," he continued. Vanessa leaned into him, and it was Joshua's turn to try to catch his breath. The full crush of her breasts burned him through his own shirt.

How could she deny what she felt, had been feeling, since she first saw Joshua Kirkland? Shaking her head, she closed her eyes. His compelling personality, the warmth of his protection, and the repressed desires fusing them together wouldn't permit her to reject him.

"I can't say no." The admission came deep from a place so unknown, so foreign, that a shudder of fear ripped through her.

He registered the shudder and tightened his claim on her body. His hands moved around to her flat belly, feathering up to her chest. Her breasts swelled against the lace of her bra, growing heavy in his hands.

His hot breath seared her face seconds before he took her mouth with the almost savage intensity and speed of a hawk swooping down on its prey.

"And I don't think I can stop," he confessed against her moist, parted lips. His kiss burned her mouth, and the fire he ignited spread to other parts of her body.

And he hadn't lied. With any other woman he'd be able to stop and walk away, but not Vanessa. He'd told himself that he wanted her because he wanted to protect her. Was it because she flashed a pretty smile, or was it because he'd found her sexy, sexier than any woman he had ever met?

Or was it because his attraction to Vanessa reminded him of how sterile his life was? It was always his mission, and only his mission. The people who worked out of the office at the Pentagon had become his extended family, and the women he "saw" occasionally offered only temporary diversions, while most of the time they bored the hell out of him.

Vanessa was one of a few women he'd spent more than an hour with who hadn't bored him. She challenged as well as seduced him, and instinctively he knew he could grow old with her.

Explosive currents of desire throbbed through his groin, and he realized that he had reached the point of no return, the fragile thread of control threatening to break with each second Vanessa remained in his arms. "Do you want me to stop, Angel?"

"No! Don't...please don't stop," she pleaded shamelessly.

Needing no further prompting, he swung her up in his arms and headed for his bedroom. Lust and desire merged, surging uncontrollably through him. His whole being was filled with a waiting, a waiting to bury his flesh deep in hers, making them one.

Vanessa closed her eyes and tightened her grip around his neck. "You'll have to protect me," she whispered, her words muffled against his warm throat.

"I'll protect you," he promised, "from everything."

Joshua felt the stirring of his own sexual arousal as he placed Vanessa in the middle of his king-sized bed. His heart rate quickened, his labored breathing deepened, and he felt the familiar closing of the outflow of blood in his manhood as it filled with a rush of dizzying desire. He hadn't yet joined his body with Vanessa's, yet his passion for her was fever-pitched. He resisted the urge to turn on the lamp in the darkened room, because he needed her relaxed so he could bring her maximum pleasure.

Vanessa's legs trembled as she tried to stop her voracious craving for Joshua from taking over her mind and body. His hands slipped up her rib cage, ever so slowly, and inched the T-shirt up her chest and over her shoulders.

It was only seconds, but it seemed like hours before he divested her of the shirt, and instead of releasing the clasp on her bra he slid his fingers under the demi-cups and cradled her breasts gently. His thumbs grazed the nipples until they hardened and tingled for escape from the delicate scraps of lace.

Joshua felt the areolae pebbles under his fingertips, and he reached around to unhook her bra, freeing her breasts. Lowering his head, he drew one breast into his mouth, then switched to the other, sucking and nibbling gently around each nipple. He teased them mercilessly between his teeth until she gasped loudly and arched up off the mattress.

He moved up, his mouth searching for hers, and she returned his kiss with a savage intensity that sucked the very breath from his lungs. Her tongue plunged into his open mouth at the same time her fingers bit into his scalp.

Liquid fire rippled through Vanessa's veins as a rush of sexual awareness she had never experienced before threatened to consume her. She was fully aware of the hardness between Joshua's thighs probing strongly against hers. Why was he waiting? Why wouldn't he take her and end her torture?

Unsnapping the waistband on her jeans, he eased them down her hips and legs before his hand searched under the triangle of silk concealing her femininity. Her warmth scorched his palm, then cooled as a gush of moisture bathed his fingers. He had wanted their first time together to be slow, leisurely, so they both would experience maximum pleasure, but now he knew it wasn't possible. The magnitude with which Vanessa responded to him was stunning, and as he aroused her his own passion grew hotter, stronger.

Her silken panties followed her jeans, falling to the carpeted floor. Seconds later his T-shirt, jeans, and briefs followed. Vanessa had asked him to protect her, and he would. There would be time for a child—their children—later.

Placing his hands on her thighs, he eased her knees apart and settled his body within the cradle of her femininity. She gasped loudly again, this time at the probing assault on her celibate flesh.

Joshua withdrew immediately, cupping her face in his hands. "I'll go slow," he crooned against her parted lips. "I'll try not to hurt you."

Feeling the tension leaving her limbs, he tasted her mouth, then the tip of her nose, chin, and throat, lingering at the runaway pulse.

His mouth continued its downward course, branding Vanessa his possession as she moaned and writhed in an ancient rhythm that needed no prompting or tutoring.

She felt the scorching heat from his mouth at the apex of her thighs, his tongue worshipping the delicate folds hiding her femininity.

"Josh—" His name died on her lips when a spasm of pleasure coiled at the base of her spine, then exploded.

He moved fluidly up from between her thighs, raising and supporting her hips with both hands as he thrust into her pulsing flesh with the force of a tornado racing across a swath of land, sweeping up everything in its path.

The impact of their lovemaking matched and surpassed the storm lashing the city with its fury as they climbed to heights of ecstasy in an act that had become not lovemaking, but raw, unadulterated possession.

Vanessa's sighs of repletion hadn't faded completely when Joshua reversed their positions and held her tightly to his damp chest. She felt his thundering heartbeat under her breasts as he reached over and turned on the lamp on the bedside table.

Burying her face against his warm neck, she pressed a kiss under his ear. He growled deep in his chest and caught the tender flesh at the base of her throat between his teeth, leaving a visible imprint of his claim.

She moaned sensuously under his tender assault and he raised his head and stared up at her. The soft, golden light slanted across her face, highlighting the expression of satisfaction curving her temptingly lush mouth.

He methodically removed the pins holding her hair in place, permitting the thick strands to fall around her neck in sensual disarray. A gentle smile softened his features, allowing him to appear noticeably younger than his thirty-eight years. "I like you with your hair loose."

Vanessa lowered her head, resting her forehead on his shoulder. She didn't want to talk, because she wanted to remember and savor the moment when they had become one. Inhaling deeply, she committed the smell of his flesh to memory, because something unknown told her that once she left Mexico she would also leave Joshua Kirkland—forever. Waiting until his hold on her waist eased, she slipped smoothly out of his embrace and lay on her side.

Turning over to his left, Joshua cradled Vanessa until her hips were molded to his groin. He pressed his lips to her hair, breathing in the delicate fragrance clinging to the strands.

"Are you all right?" His voice was filled with concern.

Closing her eyes, she smiled. "Yes."

"I didn't hurt you, did I?"

Turning in his embrace, she stared at him staring back at her. She placed a finger over his lips, then her mouth replaced it. "No, you didn't hurt me."

He caught her hand and kissed each finger as she examined the thick, coarse, pale hair covering his scalp. "You're a lot smaller than I expected you would be. I—"

Her mouth covered his, stopping his words. "Don't, please. Let's enjoy what we have until it's over."

He went completely still. "Is that what you want, Vanessa? You want it to be over?"

"It'll be over for me when I leave Mexico."

"What about me?"

"What about you, Joshua?" She pulled away from him, drawing a sheet over her naked breasts. "You'll probably leave Mexico and fly to some other country, where you'll meet another woman to seduce."

She really did not want to think about him sleeping with another woman, but one thing she knew she was, and that was realistic. She probably wasn't the first woman he had slept with while on a business trip, and she wouldn't be the last.

His eyes paled as he stared at her as Vanessa registered something menacing about him.

"Is that how you see me? Do you actually think that I

make it a habit of picking up women to sleep with when I travel on business?"

Flinging off the sheet, she swung her legs over the side of the bed and strode naked across the room. "I don't know what to think. I don't even know you," she flung over her shoulder.

Moving quickly, Joshua left the bed and caught up with Vanessa before she reached the door connecting their bedrooms. Standing with his back to the door, he braced his arms over it, preventing her from escaping him.

Leaning down from his impressive height, he thrust his face close to hers. "You're right about that. You don't know me. In fact, you know nothing about me. If you did, then you'd know that I don't want to lose you."

There was no emotion in his voice, and that unnerved Vanessa more than his unexpected admission. She felt as if a hand had closed around her throat, not permitting her to come back at him.

Silence descended upon them like a weighted fog, cloaking and smothering in its intensity. The sound of labored breathing shattered the stillness as Vanessa and Joshua engaged in a virulent debate without words.

Her gaze shifted from his impassive expression to his smooth, bared chest, then returned to his face. She studied him, feature by feature, trying vainly to see another side of the stranger she'd just slept with.

"What's that supposed to mean?" she questioned, recovering her voice.

His eyes widened. "Exactly what I said. I don't want you to move out, and when I return to the States I want you to come back with me."

Vanessa couldn't help herself. She burst out laughing. "I go back with you and do what? Give up all I've worked for to sit around and wait while you jet around the world?"

Joshua struggled to control his temper. She wasn't going to make it easy for him. There would be no way he could protect her from prosecution unless she cooperated with him.

"I'd never expect you to sit around and wait for me."

"So I'd lie in bed and wait for you, instead of sitting."

"That's enough," he warned, his voice rising slightly.

Her temper rose to match his. "How do you see me, Joshua? Did you think I was so desperate for male company that I slept with you because you were the only one offering?"

"Why *did* you let me make love to you?" he shouted at her.

There was a long, rigid silence, her chest rising and falling heavily with every breath she took. Joshua Kirkland had stripped her bare—figuratively and literally. He wanted the truth and she would give him the truth.

"I slept with you because I'm attracted to you. You have to know that you're a very sensual as well as a very intriguing man."

He took a step, closing the distance between until they were less than a foot apart. "What about emotions, Vanessa? Do you at least feel *something* for me?"

Tilting her chin in a gesture of defiance, she gave him a steady stare. "I like you. Is that what you want to hear?"

His lips twisted into a cynical smile. "It's better than if you despised me."

"Don't put words in my mouth. I never said that I despised you."

His hands slipped up her arms, bringing her closer, and she was conscious of where his naked flesh touched hers. His splayed fingers moved to her hips as he lowered his head and drank deeply from her sweet mouth. He wasn't disappointed when Vanessa returned his kiss with all of the passion she was capable of offering him. Both were breathing heavily when the kiss ended.

Shimmering green eyes burned her face as she glanced up. "When are you going to stop seducing me?" she whispered.

"Never," he crooned moments before he claimed her mouth again.

Chapter 10

Vanessa lay sprawled between Joshua's outstretched legs in the oversized Jacuzzi, her head resting against his chest. The warm, swirling waters in the tub helped ease the slight tenderness between her thighs, while she luxuriated in the feel of his strong fingertips as he shampooed her hair.

"Angel?" he whispered close to her ear.

"Hmm."

"Don't fall asleep on me. I still have to rinse your hair."

Smiling, she didn't open her eyes. "If I fall asleep, it's your fault. I ask for lunch and you fill me up with wine and pâté."

He chuckled. "It was too late for lunch, so think of them as pre-dinner appetizers."

She and Joshua had made love a second time, then fallen asleep in each other's arms, waking hours later to lengthening afternoon shadows and a softly falling rain.

Joshua had suggested she relax in the Jacuzzi while he prepared something to eat. His *something* had turned out to be an excellently prepared *pâté de foie gras* on delicate, stone ground wheat crackers and a chilled bottle of white wine. When she'd raised a questioning eyebrow he'd explained that he needed to replenish the contents of the wet bar.

He had placed a tray with the wine, crackers, and pâté on a table near the Jacuzzi. He then surprised her when he positioned several lighted candles on shelves in the bathroom, turned off the lights, stripped off his clothes, and joined her in the Jacuzzi, where they spent the better part of an hour eating, drinking and lounging in the warm, swirling water.

"What's for dinner?"

His fingers stilled their massaging, rhythmic motions on her scalp. "It's a surprise."

"You're just full of surprises, aren't you?" she teased.

If only you knew how many, he mused, wondering how she would react to his marriage proposal and his eventual disclosure of who he was working for.

"Is there something you don't like, or are allergic to?"

"I'm allergic to anchovies, and I don't like rhubarb and brussels sprouts."

"I don't think any of them are on tonight's menu."

Opening her eyes and raising her chin, she smiled up at Joshua. A sheen of moisture dotted his face and spiked his lashes. "Aren't you going to give me a hint?"

He shook his head slowly while studying her face with his enigmatic gaze. Retrieving a loofah sponge from the water, he squeezed it over her head, gently rinsing the shampoo from her hair. The water trickled over her head and shoulders and down the curves of her small, firm breasts. His gaze drank in her beauty, stunned by the perfection of her face and body.

She is as beautiful as she is devious, the silent voice whispered to him, and his expression hardened. Despite what he felt and was beginning to feel for Vanessa, he had to remember what she was: *traitor, spy, witch.* A beautiful witch who'd cast her spell over him so that he couldn't escape her if he tried.

He placed the sponge on the tray with the half-empty bottle of wine. "I'm finished."

She squeezed the excess water from her hair. "Thank you." She would finish rinsing it in the shower.

Her eyes widened in awe as she watched Joshua rise from the water, step out of the sunken bathtub, and walk over to the rack cradling thick, thirsty towels. His wet body gleamed in the glow of the flickering candles, the muted light turning him into a towering statue of polished bronze.

Vanessa noted for the first time that there wasn't an ounce of fat on his tall, spare frame, and she couldn't pull her gaze away as he went through the motions of drying his body. Every move was fluid and measured, as if in a choreographed dance. He was so quintessentially male that she found it hard to draw a normal breath without heat suffusing her face and body.

Who are you, Joshua Kirkland? She hadn't realized that the silent question had nagged at her from the first time she saw him on the plane. He appeared perfect, so perfect that she had taken off her clothes and lain with him only four days after their meeting.

What, she wondered, was there about him that had made her so shameless? He'd been forthright with her when he told her he wanted to seduce her, and yet she had begged him to make love to her.

Why, at thirty-three, had she become so bold, so brazen, when she never had been before? Why had it taken Kenneth Richmond four months to get her into his bed, while it had taken Joshua Kirkland only four days?

All of the *whys* tumbled over each other in her head until Joshua walked over to the Jacuzzi, hunkered down, and kissed her mouth.

"Take your time getting dressed. I'm going to order dinner."

Her dark eyes searched his face. "I thought you were going to do the cooking."

"I am." He smoothed back her eyebrows with a forefinger. "I have to call the kitchen and see what they have."

She nodded, watching him as he straightened and walked out of the bathroom and into his dressing room. She lounged in the healing waters for another ten minutes, then stepped out and made her way over to the shower stall to rinse her hair and body.

When Vanessa walked out of her bedroom and into the living room she was met with several tantalizing cooking aromas. A blending of exotic spices wafted through the suite, reminding her of how much she needed to put something in her stomach.

The table in the dining alcove was set with china, fragile stemware and gleaming silver. She noted wineglasses, water goblets and tiny cordials, and each setting also claimed several forks. It was apparent that Joshua intended to prepare a dinner with several courses.

When he'd asked whether she cooked, she had replied that she was learning, and that she was. Her older sister Connie had been the one who loved tinkering in the kitchen and experimenting with exotic dishes, while *she* had preferred solitary pursuits like reading, listening to music and writing lengthy letters to her many pen pals.

After securing a teaching position, she set up her own apartment and bought all of the top of the line cooking gadgets, but continued to eat at local restaurants. It was only after relocating to Santa Fe that she realized she didn't want to spend the remainder of her life eating out, and enrolled in a mail order cooking course.

Some of the meals she prepared were too elaborate for one person, but it gave her a sense of accomplishment when the presentations mirrored the photographs in the large, loose-leaf binders. The ultimate taste test was usually satisfying, although some of the dishes requiring piquant spices were a little too stimulating for her delicate taste buds.

She moved away from the dining area and into the kitchen, where Joshua stood at a counter stirring something in a small mixing bowl. A slow smile crinkled the skin around her eyes as she watched him. There was something attractive about a man in a kitchen—whether he was cooking or washing dishes.

Her gaze moved appreciatively over his celery green, short-sleeved silk shirt and black tailored slacks. The color of the shirt was an exact match for his luminous eyes.

"You look and smell wonderful," he remarked, not glancing her way.

Vanessa folded her hands on her hips. "How would you know? You haven't looked at me."

"Peripheral vision, Angel. And I don't have to look at you to smell you."

She walked over to him and pressed a kiss to his smooth cheek. "Thank you." The warmth and the seductive fragrance of his aftershave enveloped her in a sensual cocoon of longing.

Before she could pull away she found her body molded against the length of his, and her mouth ravished in a tender assault that robbed her of her breath.

Joshua pulled back, staring at the shocked expression on her face. "You're quite welcome," he whispered.

His gaze feathered over her bared shoulders under a lemon-yellow silk dress that skimmed her body and ended mid-calf, before reversing direction and lingering on her hair. She'd blown it out and, utilizing a curling iron, had curled it in a mass of tiny curls that caressed her face and danced along the nape of her long neck.

"I don't think I'll ever get used to your beauty."

His voice was filled with awe and passion as he cradled her face between his hands. His thumbs toyed with the tiny gold hoops in her pierced lobes. He tried seeing into the depths of her dark eyes, hoping beyond hope that she was innocent of spying against her country. At that moment he wanted to pretend that she wasn't who she was, and he wasn't who he was.

When, he thought, had the seduction changed so that his actions were no longer calculated, but real? Too real for him to ignore that his feelings for the woman in his arms ran deep, deep and passionate.

I want her for myself! He wanted her in bed and out of bed. The realization of why he'd lured Vanessa to his hotel suite ripped through him like a knife. The woman he'd been directed to follow and investigate was the woman he knew he wanted to spend the rest of his life with.

Lowering his head, he buried his face in the curls framing her face, struggling to keep from blurting out that he was falling in love with her. He was thirty-eight, and all of his life he had practiced hiding his emotions, and he'd become an expert—except now.

What was there about her that stripped him of his self-control, leaving him vulnerable to pain and anguish? He had grown up seeing enough pain to last him two lifetimes, but he was helpless against Vanessa and the spell she wove over him.

"What's for dinner?" she breathed against his throat.

"You," he growled, swinging up her in his arms and striding purposefully toward his bedroom.

Vanessa, holding tightly to his neck, closed her eyes. There was something so primitive, so savage, in the single word that it left her trembling with a need that went beyond logic or reason.

He placed her on the bed, his body following, while his hands searched for the opening of her dress. He moaned in frustration when he couldn't find the hidden zipper under her left arm. Her fingers were busy trying to undo the buttons on his shirt, and in her haste several were ripped from the silken garment.

Thwarted by trying to remove her dress, Joshua raised his body and unbuckled the belt around his waist and pushed his slacks down around his hips.

Heavy, labored breathing punctuated the silent space, followed by the whisper of fabric being pushed aside and the satisfying moans of flesh meeting flesh.

Surely I'm going to die from the pleasure, he thought as he pushed into the hot, tight, wet flesh sheathing his own hard, blood-engorged sex.

Everything was magnified in the blackness of the bedroom:

the scent of their lovemaking mingling with their perfumed bodies, the soft sounds of sexual pleasure, and the silken feel of her legs clasped tightly around his waist.

Heat, chills, and waves of ecstasy swept over Vanessa as she tried, and failed, to keep the moans from escaping her. She forgot about everything as she gave herself up to the burning desire shaking her from head to toe.

She gasped, her body arching as the first ripple of release gripped her, subsided, then gripped her again—this time longer and stronger than the first. Waves of ecstasy throbbed through her until she threw back her head and cried an awesome moan of erotic pleasure as Joshua's own groans overlapped hers, his breath coming in long, surrendering gasps.

Joshua lay heavily on Vanessa, the remnants of passion ebbing. The enormity of what they'd shared washed over him as if he'd plunged head first into an ice-covered stream.

"Joshua?" Her voice was soft and quivering in the silence.

He nodded rather than speaking, because he knew what she was going to say before she spoke.

"What did we do?"

Cradling her tightly, he reversed their positions. "We just made love, darling."

Vanessa tried pulling out of his embrace and failed. "That's not what I'm talking about, and you know it. Sleeping with you is one thing, but becoming pregnant is out of the question."

His hold on her waist tightened. "Is the possibility of having my child that repugnant to you?"

She swallowed several times, trying to moisten her dry throat. "It's not repugnant, it's just out of the question."

"Why?"

"Need you ask why?"

"Yes," he shot back, not bothering to hide his annoyance.

"I don't know you, Joshua. You're a stranger and—"

"A stranger who has made love to you three times. I think we've progressed beyond the stranger stage, Vanessa."

"I'm not ready to have a child," she argued. "I usually plan what I want to do with my life, and having a child before I'm married is not something I've planned."

He almost laughed aloud. Now she was beginning to cooperate.

"Marry me."

She went completely still as if she'd been shot. "No!" she whispered.

"Why not?"

"Because I don't know you."

He chuckled. "Is that all that's stopping you?"

"Of course not. People who marry usually love each other."

"Do you think you could love me?"

Vanessa hesitated, unable to think clearly. She had slept with a man she'd known for four days, and there was the possibility that a new life was growing in her womb at that very moment.

"Do you?" Joshua repeated.

"Given time, I suppose I could."

Raising his head, he searched for her mouth and found it. His lips coaxed hers until they parted. "I'm an impatient man," he breathed into her mouth, "and I don't want to spend years chasing you. Marry me and I swear that I'll love, honor, and protect you for the rest of my life."

"No," she whispered tearfully. "I can't."

"What if you're pregnant?"

"I'll deal with it," she said stubbornly.

"By yourself?"

"Yes, by myself."

He released her and reached over and turned on the lamp, flooding the room with light. Turning back to Vanessa, he caught her shoulders firmly and pulled her up to his chest.

"That's where you're wrong," he said quietly. "Whatever you decide to do I'll be there with you."

Nodding, she adjusted her dress, pulling it down over her hips and smoothing out the wrinkles. She realized he hadn't said I'll be there *for* you, but I'll be there *with* you. It was apparent that he was not going to let her escape him.

She didn't tell him that if she were pregnant she would have the child, because even though she couldn't admit it openly she knew that she was falling in love with Joshua Kirkland.

She pulled away from him. "Excuse me, but I have to change my clothes."

Joshua watched her intently as she slipped off the bed, her gaze downcast. Her back was ramrod straight when she made her way across the bedroom.

"Vanessa." He'd spoken her name so softly that he doubted whether she'd heard it, but she stopped, not bothering to turn around. "I love you."

The moment the three words were uttered he knew they had come from the depths of his soul, and he was momentarily speechless with the revelation. Never had he ever openly declared that he loved any living mortal. The word *love* was as foreign to him as the emotion.

Why Vanessa? Why her, and not some woman from his past?

The questions nagged him as emotions he didn't know he had attacked relentlessly. Why a spy?

He wanted to protect her, and he was willing to marry her to do that, but what he didn't want to do was love her; he had grown up seeing how the pain of loving could destroy a life.

But what if she's pregnant? What about your child? The thought that perhaps Vanessa could be pregnant quieted the riot of uneasiness assailing him. How different his child's life would be from his own, and if he had to surrender to loving, it would be to his child.

The seconds stretched into a long, suffering minute before she turned and faced him, her large dark eyes shimmering with moisture.

"Don't," she whispered. She didn't want him to love her, because she knew that she was falling in love with him. If he didn't love her, it would be easier for her to walk away from him.

When she left Mexico for the States all she wanted to take home was the memory of Joshua Kirkland and nothing else.

"Don't tell me what to feel," he countered. "I love you, and I'll say it over and over until you marry me."

She couldn't believe what she was hearing, or believe what she was feeling. Joshua's statement echoed the deep emotions she wasn't able to deny. How had it happened? How could she have fallen in love with him so quickly? What was it about him that frightened and fascinated her at the same time?

Only one other man had proposed to her, and he had loved her and any other woman who was available to him. Would Joshua also be unfaithful to her?

The statement he'd uttered over dinner at La Mérida came rushing back. *Not only would I not be unfaithful to my wife, but to any woman I found myself involved with.* She didn't know why, but she believed him.

Retracing her steps, she returned to the bed and fell into his arms. She kissed him, communicating wordlessly that she had conceded. She would stay with him, and she would become his wife.

Chapter 11

A slow, warming sense of peace filled Joshua as he cherished the softness of Vanessa in his embrace. Everything that surrounded them was so right, so perfect. It was as if all of the bitterness he'd carried for years had vanished, a gentle, comforting peace taking its place.

"Tell me what you want. What you need from me," he whispered in her hair.

Rubbing her nose against his smooth jaw, Vanessa smiled. "I want you to love me as unselfishly as I'm certain I'll come to love you. And when I marry you I want it to be forever."

"Where do you want us to live?" he asked.

"I want to stay in Santa Fe." Pulling back slightly, she stared up at him. "That means you'll have to relocate."

Joshua shook his head, smiling. "That's not a problem. I think you ought to know that aside from the house on Ocho Rios, I also have a condo in Palm Beach, Florida."

"You're not thinking of selling them, are you?"

"No. We'll use the house in Jamaica as a vacation retreat, and we'll stay at the apartment in Florida whenever we visit my relatives."

Placing her cheek against his breast, she listened to the strong, steady beating of his heart, curving an arm around his neck. "Do you think they'll like me?"

A chuckle rumbled in his chest. "They won't have a choice. The men in my family have a penchant for beautiful women."

"That means your mother must be beautiful."

His muscles tensed suddenly under her fingertips. "My mother *was* very beautiful." He paused. "She died five years ago."

Closing her eyes, Vanessa tightened her hold on his neck. "I'm sorry, Joshua," she whispered. If he was thirty-three when his mother died, then, she wondered, how old could she have been?

Closing his own eyes, he sighed heavily. "She's at peace."

There was a strained silence before Vanessa spoke again. "What is it you want from me?"

"I want to spend the rest of my life with you in a marriage based on love, honesty, and fidelity," he replied without hesitating. "And I also want children."

"How many?"

"As many as you'll give me."

"How many can we afford?"

"At least a dozen."

"A dozen!" she exclaimed. "I don't think so, Joshua Kirkland."

"Then we'll begin with one."

Sobering quickly, she kissed his earlobe. "What do you need from me?"

"I need you to trust me to take care of you *and* protect you."

A frown furrowed her forehead, and she pulled out of his embrace. "Is there a reason why I shouldn't trust you?"

He stared back at her, his gaze unwavering. "No."

"I—"

The chiming of the telephone preempted further conversation, and Joshua reached over to the bedside table and picked up the receiver.

"Sí." His greeting was soft and controlled.

"Birmingham," came a masculine voice on the other end. "We're going to have to reschedule," he said in Spanish.

"Meet me in San Miguel in five days. I'll be seated in the last pew of *La Iglesia de los Santos* at oh nine hundred," Joshua said in the same language. "And I want you to give your boss a message from me."

"What?"

"Pull The Shadow."

"I thought The Shadow was to stay in place until Operation MESA goes down."

His jaw hardened, and he turned his back to Vanessa. "Tell Blackwell to pull him or I'll make him disappear permanently," he ordered in a soft, lethal tone.

"I read you," Cordero Birmingham replied before the connection was broken.

Replacing the receiver in its cradle, Joshua turned back to Vanessa, a warm smile replacing the hardness that had settled into his features. He had five days to marry Vanessa, uncover her contact, and set the wheels in motion for Operation MESA.

He reached for her and pulled her to his chest. "What had you planned to do tomorrow?"

"What I'd planned to do today."

"Shop?"

She smiled down at him. "Shop until I drop."

"Where?"

Oaxaca."

"That's not a day trip," he reminded her.

"I know. I'd planned to take the 7:00 p.m. train down, stay overnight, and return the following day."

"I have a proposition to make to you."

Vanessa's mouth hovered over his. "What?"

"We check out, rent a car, and travel. I'll take you wherever you want to go. I'll even act as interpreter so that the local merchants don't cheat you."

"What about your business clients?"

"I don't have another meeting until the sixth."

She calculated quickly. That gave her and Joshua another five days together. "Will we have to come back to Mexico City for your meeting?"

Joshua wondered just how much of his telephone conversation Vanessa understood. Was she fluent in Spanish? She'd admitted to having only a rudimentary knowledge of the language.

"No," he admitted.

"I'm scheduled to return to the States on the seventh," she reminded him.

"What time is your flight?"

"8:50."

"Morning or evening?"

"Evening."

He kissed the end of her nose. "I'll call the airline and change my ticket, then we'll fly back together." Sitting up, he pulled at a curl over her forehead. "I promised to feed you, didn't I?"

"You started to, but somehow you got distracted," she said with a teasing grin.

"That's because you're quite a distraction, Miss Blanchard."

Vanessa moved off the bed, blew him a kiss, and strolled across the room with an exaggerated wiggle of her hips. "You must work on your self-control, Mr. Kirkland," she warned over her shoulder, walking out of his bedroom and into her own.

Joshua stared at the space where she had been, still seeing her enchanting face and alluring body. The scent of her was stamped on his skin, like a signature. All that was needed was a smile, a caress, or a kiss from her, and he was lost, trapped in the seductive web she had woven.

The script was written, but their roles were reversed. Vanessa had become the seducer.

* * *

Joshua sat across the table, watching Vanessa pick absent-mindedly at the food on her plate. He'd prepared shrimp and plantains on skewers with a mango mayonnaise, avocado halves filled with a succulent lobster dip, a tropical green salad and grilled rib lamb chops with savory white rice. He noticed she hadn't touched her wine, but had elected to drink water.

Placing his fork aside, he stared at her bowed head. "Is it too spicy?"

Her head came up quickly. "No, not at all."

"I thought you were hungry."

She stared back at him, her gaze direct and steady. Exhaling audibly, she apologized. "I'm sorry. You went through a lot of work to prepare dinner."

"I had to eat, too." He studied her thoughtfully. "What's the matter, Vanessa?"

"I've been thinking—" Her words trailed off.

"Do your thoughts have anything to do with me?" he asked perceptively.

Vanessa nodded. The day had been filled with surprises and revelations she never could've imagined. "I keep asking myself if I'm losing my mind, if I know who I am. My being here with you, sleeping with you, feeling what I do for you, and even going so far as to contemplate marrying you. I've tried convincing myself that it's a dream, and when I wake up you won't be here, that my sleeping with you was just a sexual fantasy because I've been celibate for so long."

A slow smile parted Joshua's lips. "I'm not an apparition, darling, and what we've shared is real, very real." His expression grew serious. "Perhaps what you're feeling is guilt."

"What about?"

"Sleeping with a stranger." She glanced away, and he knew he'd identified her apprehension. "How do you propose we resolve your uneasiness?"

Again Vanessa realized he'd said *we,* not *you* or *I,* and despite his closed expression she sensed his vulnerability. She did not want to reject him, could not without causing pain for both of them, but she couldn't continue the headlong flight into a morass of passion where she lost herself each time she joined her body with his.

"I don't want us to make love again until after we're married," she stated, her voice coming out in a breathless whisper. "I hope that will help me to assess my true feelings for you, without confusing them with sex."

His eyes paled, raw hurt glittering in their depths like bits of stone. The victory that Joshua had savored earlier dissipated, leaving in its wake anger and disappointment. *One step forward and two steps back,* he raged silently.

"What I feel for you has nothing to do with *sex!*"

"I'm not talking about you, Joshua," she countered, her voice rising slightly. "All I'm asking for is time," she continued, this time with an unexpected, gentle pleading creeping into her tone.

He stared at the hopeful expression on her face, unmoving, seeing the emotional struggle going on within her as a shadow of pain filled her large, dark eyes.

I love you, a part of him crooned silently, a part he had never revealed to anyone, not to any woman. His heart turned over in compassion at Vanessa's pleading that he understand her turbulent emotions.

He managed a half-smile. "Take all the time you need."

Her eyes filling with tears of relief, Vanessa stood up and circled the table. Joshua pushed back his chair, gathered her into his arms, and held her gently. She felt his even breathing against her cheek as she pressed her lips to his.

"You make it so easy to love you, Joshua," she whispered, then buried her face against his throat.

It was past midnight and Joshua lay in the darkened bedroom, listening to the sound of soft, gentle breathing and savoring the perfumed, scented softness of the slender body next to his own. He'd honored his promise that they would not make love again until they were married, though his body ached for her. She aroused a desire in him that he hadn't experienced since adolescence, while she made him smile and look forward to marrying and fathering children.

An indefinable feeling of peace swept over him as he tightened his hold on her waist.

Day Four—he had gotten Vanessa Blanchard to share his bed, and a promise that she would also share his future.

Chapter 12

Vanessa shook Joshua gently, rousing him from sleep. His eyes opened and he stared up at her, smiling. She'd opened the drapes, and the early morning sunlight pouring in through the windows highlighted the shimmering excitement in her large, dark eyes.

She sat down on the edge of the bed. "I've showered and dressed, while you're still lounging," she teased.

"I've been awake for hours," he countered. And he had, his mind filled with the details for Operation MESA. "You left the bed at exactly 5:53."

A shock flew through her. How did he know what time she'd gotten up, when he'd been asleep? She had been certain he had been asleep, because his breathing was even and deep and he hadn't even stirred when she pulled out of his embrace.

"How did you know that?" There was no disguising the tension in her voice.

Pushing himself into a sitting position, Joshua gestured to the travel clock on the bedside table. "I looked at the clock."

Vanessa glanced over at the clock as if seeing it for the first time, the slight frown that had furrowed her forehead disappearing. She didn't know what it was, but she couldn't rid herself of the belief that Joshua wasn't truly what he presented to her. There was something curious, odd, about him. His quixotic behavior was totally incongruent with his impassive expression, because the times she had noted his expressionless face she hadn't been able to suppress her fear of him. However, the fear fled with the sound of his sensual voice and the touch of his seductive hands. He was a stranger, and she knew even if she married him and spent the remainder of her life with him he would always be a stranger.

"Get up, sweetheart," she crooned, pulling on his arm. "I'm already a day behind schedule."

Joshua wanted to ask who she was to meet that made her so impatient to leave Mexico City, but didn't. His admiring gaze swept over her melon-colored, sleeveless cotton shift, then moved up to her hair pinned at the nape of her neck in a simple chignon. She looked chic and innocent at the same time. Her perfect face with the large, trusting eyes made her appear virginal, untouched. He hadn't been the man to claim her virgin body, but he would make certain no other man would ever touch her again. She was *his*.

"How far is it to Oaxaca?" he asked before he kissed her bared, scented shoulder.

"Almost three hundred and fifty miles."

"If that's the case, then we'll fly down and pick up a car at the Oaxaca airport."

Vanessa pulled back and stared up at him. "Fly?"

He ran a forefinger down the length of her nose. "Yes, fly. How alert will you expect me to be after driving more than five hundred kilometers?"

"Something tells me that you'd still be alert even if you were deprived of sleep for more than twenty-four hours." She patted his bare chest. "Get out of bed, Joshua, or I'm going to leave you right here."

"I see that you're not going to be an easy wife."

"I'm going to be a wonderful wife, and you know it," she countered, hugging him tightly.

"I'm sure you will." He swept the sheet back from his body and swung his legs over the side of the bed. "Will I have to salute you, or answer with 'yes, Ma'am and no, Ma'am'?"

"If you keep testing me, Joshua, you'll find out."

Reaching for her with blinding speed, he kissed her hard, then released her before she could react. "That should hold you until I get ready."

Vanessa sat, momentarily stunned. A smile curved her mouth as she looked forward to what she knew would be a passionate future with the man who, in five days, had become as essential to her as eating and sleeping.

Vanessa watched as her luggage, along with Joshua's, was wheeled out to the rental car at the Oaxaca airport and stored in the trunk by an airport baggage handler. A shimmering sun in a bright, cloudless sky indicated no rain for Mexico's southern region as well as rising temperatures predicted to peak in the low nineties. She smiled. After four days of smog and rain in Mexico City it was startling to see the undefiled blue of the sky.

Joshua tipped the handler and helped her into the car, then settled in beside her. He adjusted a lever under the front of his seat until his long legs were comfortably stretched out under the steering wheel.

Turning to his right, he examined her enchanting profile, his gaze lingering on the hollows under her cheekbones and the length of her long, smooth neck. *She's a swan who was never an Ugly Duckling.*

Vanessa turned, her gaze meeting his. He seemed to be waiting, for what she didn't know. Was he waiting for a command from her that he pull out of the parking lot?

"Yes?" Her voice held a breathless quality that she didn't recognize as her own. "Yes?" she repeated when he did not answer or move. She was as still as he was, despite the erotic shock racing through her. All that Joshua was, all that he felt at that moment, she was and felt. Without a word, without a gesture, she knew that he truly did love her.

"I love you so much," he whispered quietly and reverently.

His confession filled her entire being, and she didn't know why but she wanted to sob. Resting her forehead on his shoulder, she closed her eyes and inhaled his now familiar scent.

"And I love you, too, Joshua Kirkland," she confessed for the first time. "I will marry you, and when I return to the States it will be as your wife."

Only her belt prevented him from pulling her from her seat and onto his lap as his mouth covered hers in a gentle, possessive joining. The kiss they shared was tender and confident, and promised more, much, much more.

Joshua pulled back, breathing heavily. His lowered lids concealed his innermost feelings from her. "I can't form the words to tell how I feel at this moment. All I can say is thank you."

He released her and started up the car. The seduction had worked. But he wondered who was the winner—he, or Vanessa.

Vanessa was totally enchanted by Oaxaca. The city claimed no high-rise hotels or resorts, but beautifully restored properties that overlooked the deep, arid valleys of the Sierra Madre mountains.

They checked into the Victoria, a two story, salmon-colored complex built on a hill overlooking the city. Joshua had decided on absolute privacy when he selected a bungalow rather than a suite within the main building. The Victoria also claimed picture-perfect bougainvillea vines strewn throughout the property, an excellent restaurant, tennis courts, heated pool and a disco.

Joshua closed the door behind the departing bellhop and extended his arms. Vanessa did not disappoint him when she walked into his embrace.

Resting his chin on the top of her head, he closed his eyes, luxuriating in the feel of her body molded to his. The frantic craving to make love to her had subsided with her promise of marriage. Within the next three or four days he would claim her as his wife.

What he had to do was buy her a ring and a wedding gift, and find a priest who would marry them without a posting of banns or the formalities which usually preceded a Roman Catholic ceremony. He and Vanessa would marry before he met Cordero Birmingham in San Miguel. The meeting with Birmingham would conclude his involvement with Operation MESA. Then he would be able to concentrate fully on uncovering what he could about Vanessa and the sale of the classified components.

"What do you want to do now?" he asked her.

"I want to tour the *Mercado Juárez* and the *Mercado Veinte de Noviembre* today, and the *Mercado de Artesanías,* if there's enough time."

Joshua concealed a smile as he pulled back and stared at her. There was no doubt that she had done her homework. She knew exactly where she wanted to go. "How about tomorrow?"

"Tomorrow I go to the galleries. Someone at work gave me the name of a proprietor at one of the galleries in the *Galería de Arte de Oaxaca* who sells exquisite pieces of gold and silver designed in the style of the jewels found at the *Monte Albán* archeological ruins."

He felt a rush of excitement with this disclosure. The person at the gallery was no doubt her contact. His expression of indifference did nothing to denote his satisfaction that he would be able to complete his Mexican mission in less than ten days.

"We'll unpack after we come back," he suggested. "I have to talk to a priest about marrying us in between your shopping sprees."

Vanessa nodded. "I want to change into a pair of comfortable walking shoes before we leave." Her delicate leather sandals were pretty, but not practical for the cobblestone streets.

Joshua released her and checked his supply of Mexican pesos. If necessary, he would offer a generous "donation" to the priest for waiving the necessary waiting period. Now that Vanessa had agreed to marry him before they left Mexico, he wanted nothing and no one to thwart them.

Joshua sat at a small round table in an outdoor café near the *zócalo,* smiling at Vanessa as she slipped off her sunglasses and ran the back of her hand over her forehead. A warm breeze failed to stir the fronds of an overhead palm tree.

"I think I'm going to spend the *siesta* here," she threatened softly. Most of the pedestrian traffic in the main square had cleared out for the beginning of the two-hour period when most banks and businesses closed.

"We can always go back to the hotel and take advantage of the air-conditioning. It's your call," he continued, noting her weariness.

While they had spent the past three hours sightseeing and browsing through the colonial heart of Oaxaca, the temperature had reached ninety-one before the noon hour, and had continued to climb steadily even after the sun reached its zenith.

She stared down into a glass filled with chilled, bottled water and lemon slices. "I thought you wanted to talk to a priest." Her head came up and she returned his steady gaze.

Reaching across the table, he held her hands gently. "We will. Relax and finish your drink. I doubt whether we'll find a church open during *siesta.*"

Her fingers tightened on his. "Then we'll wait here."

Vanessa sat next to Joshua in the coolness of the rectory of the tiny church where Father José Hidalgo y Peña had said mass for more than six years. The elderly priest had granted them an audience, but they'd had to wait for more than an hour for his return after he'd been summoned to anoint a sick parishioner.

He walked to the sitting room, gesturing with a heavily veined hand as Joshua rose to his feet. "Please sit down, my son," he ordered in whispery Spanish. "My housekeeper tells me that you want me to marry you." He sat down on a worn armchair, crossing his dusty, sandaled feet at the ankles.

"Sí, Padre," Joshua confirmed, the Spanish flowing fluidly from his tongue. *"Mi novia* and I would like you to marry us without posting banns."

The minute lines in the priest's face deepened, and he frowned at them from under lowered lids. "That would be highly irregular."

"But it is not impossible," Joshua said quietly.

The priest paused, lacing his gnarled hands together. "I have church law to follow."

Joshua leaned closer. "This is Mexico, not Rome, *Padre.* I'm certain you find yourself not following the law in particular cases."

"I have my bishop to answer to," Father Peña insisted.

"Who answers to his archbishop, who answers to Rome, which is thousands of miles from here."

He nodded. "You're right about that. What you ask is irregular, but not impossible." He paused again, this time to take off his glasses and wipe a layer of dust from the lenses before replacing them on the end of his prominent nose.

He directed his attention to Vanessa. His bushy gray brows lifted slightly as if he had noticed her for the first time. "Are you with child?" he questioned in Spanish.

"We are uncertain at this time," Joshua replied, answering for her. "We've taken a vow that we will not engage in any further sexual intercourse unless we're married."

Vanessa stared at the two men, unable to understand any of what they were discussing. Judging from Father Peña's expression she knew he wasn't very pleased with Joshua's proposal.

Lacing his fingers together in his lap, Father Peña shook his head. "Temptations of the flesh are very strong, and too many babies are conceived outside of marriage." He sighed heavily. "I will marry you, but first you must receive the Sacrament of Reconciliation and give me your word that the child will be baptized in the Catholic faith."

Joshua glanced at Vanessa, then turned his attention back to Father Peña. He knew Vanessa wasn't a Catholic, but *he* was, and it had been years since he'd confessed his sins to a priest. He also knew instinctively that the Mexican priest would not perform the Sacrament of Holy Matrimony unless he agreed to his prerequisites.

"When?"

"In three days. Be here at four-thirty in the afternoon and I will perform the marriage at five."

Joshua leaned forward on his chair. "She is not a Catholic."

"But you are?"

"*Sí.* Not a good one or a practicing one, but still a Catholic."

"We'll let God judge your soul, my son. I must have your word that your children will be Catholic."

"You have my word." What he didn't say was that he would have to talk to Vanessa about the conditions under which they would be married.

Padre Peña smiled for the first time. "You can always come back for me to baptize the child."

"I'll discuss it with my wife," Joshua replied noncommittally. Rising to his feet, he handed the priest an envelope. "A modest donation."

Padre Peña accepted the envelope. "This donation does not exempt you from Reconciliation, my son."

"I didn't think it would." He extended a hand to Vanessa and pulled her smoothly to her feet. "We'll return in three days."

Vanessa waited until they left the coolness of the building before she spoke. "Will he do it?"

Joshua gathered her to his chest and placed a kiss on her mouth. "Is three days enough time for you to plan for a wedding?"

She stared up at him, her heart pounding loudly in her ears. The shock of what was going to happen hit her full force, rendering her speechless, while a warm glow flowed through her body. Nodding, she rose on tiptoe and pressed her lips to his, giving him his answer.

Cradling her face between his palms, he stared down at her delicate face. "He'll marry us, but not without a concession."

She frowned. "What?"

"I gave him my word that our children would be baptized and raised in the Catholic faith."

An eyebrow shifted. "You did?"

"I had to, Vanessa."

"Did he ask that I convert?"

"No." The single word was filled with a tone of uncertainty. He had gotten the priest to violate the regulations of his vocation, while she balked at agreeing to the conditions of their marrying.

Exhaling and nodding her head, Vanessa forced a smile. "Okay, Joshua. You have my word. But I still want them to attend an AME church with me."

He returned her smile with a bright one of his own. "Not only will they attend services with you, but I'll also come along." Holding her hand firmly within his grasp, he led her back to the car for their return trip to the hotel. Sitting in the passenger seat of the rental vehicle, she closed her eyes at the same time Joshua started up the engine. In three days she would become Mrs. Joshua Kirkland after having been in Mexico for only eight days, and she knew once she exchanged vows with the enigmatic man she had fallen in love with she would never be the same.

Chapter 13

Vanessa was quiet and reflective as she unpacked her luggage. She moved silently around the large dressing room as if she feared waking a sleeping person. She felt rather than saw Joshua staring at her, but she refused to acknowledge him while she struggled to bring her drifting thoughts into focus.

His fingers curved around her wrist, stopping her from hanging up a pair of slacks. He pulled her close, cradling her gently against his chest.

"What's bothering you?" His voice was soft, comforting.

She pressed her nose against his shoulder. "I can't believe I'm planning a wedding where I can hardly pronounce the city where I'll exchange vows, or understand the language of the man who'll marry me. I've always believed my father would walk me down the aisle of a church filled with family and friends."

Joshua rested his chin on the top of her head and stared out across the room. He knew she was uneasy—any normal woman would be if she had consented to marry a stranger within a week of their meeting. He also knew that the feelings she'd confessed to him were real—very, very real. The fact that they'd fallen in love so quickly was startling as well as frightening. However, they were not children. They were thirty-three and thirty-eight, mature and sensible, and it was as if they had been waiting for each other to come into their lives.

Leading her back to the bedroom, he sat down on a love seat, pulling her down beside him. "Your family expects you to have a large wedding?"

Vanessa smiled up at him. "My mother never asked much from me and my sister except that she wanted us to have a what she calls a 'little something if we decided to marry.' When my sister Connie married Roger that 'little something' turned out to be an extravaganza with more than three hundred invited guests."

Joshua arched an eyebrow at this disclosure. He doubted that he'd met three hundred people who knew him well enough to attend his wedding.

"We could always repeat our vows for your mother."

"I'm certain that would pacify her. But what about your family? Your father?"

Suddenly his face went grim, the familiar, impassive mask back in place. How could he tell Vanessa that it had been more than four years since he'd seen or spoken to his father? That it pained him to be in the same room as the man?

Vanessa, puzzled by the sudden shift in his mood, asked, "You do have family, don't you?"

"Yes, I do." The admission was a low, barely spoken whisper. "I've been estranged from my father for years."

She sensed his disquiet and chose her words carefully. "How many years, Joshua?"

He met her direct gaze, his pale eyes boring down into hers. He had to answer her because she had a right to know that much about him. Her family would become his, and his hers.

"All of my life." The four words held a note of finality, as if the estrangement would continue until one of them ceased to exist.

Vanessa closed her eyes, stunned by his bluntness, then opened them to find him watching her with an expression that dared her not to pity him.

She didn't pity him; she was willing to wait for him to feel comfortable enough to disclose the reason behind the alienation between him and his father.

"Do you have any brothers or sisters?"

"I have two half-brothers and sisters."

"Will they attend?"

"You're asking questions I'm not able to answer. The only thing I'm certain of is that one of my brothers will come."

She wound her arms around his waist. "It doesn't matter, Joshua. We're going to be a family—just you and I."

Just you and I, he repeated to himself, savoring the peace he'd discovered since Vanessa had come into his life.

Vanessa lay in his embrace, wrapped in a cocoon of contentment. Her earlier apprehension eased, then dissipated like a lingering wisp of rising smoke, and she looked forward to marrying Joshua with a joyful anticipation that made her want to shout out the euphoria welling within her.

"I'd like to go dancing tonight," she said against his warm, brown throat.

Joshua chuckled softly. "I thought you didn't dance." A mysterious smile played around his firm, masculine mouth, while his luminous eyes sparkled in laughter.

"That's before I met you." Pulling back, she returned his smile. "I want to dance until the sun comes up."

He ran a forefinger down the length of her nose. "That translates into we'll have to make our own music for."

"I hum very well."

"But I don't hum or sing," he admitted.

"You compensate very well with other talents."

"What talents are those, Angel?"

Vanessa took a long and admiring look at him, her eyes betraying her lust for the man who would become her husband in another three days.

"I think you know what they are."

Joshua registered the breathless quality in Vanessa's voice, the low, husky timbre cloaking and seductive. He sat motionless as he saw the smoldering invitation in her gaze. The air around them seemed electrified by their visual interchange, and he knew if he didn't move away from her he never would honor his promise not to make love to her until they were married.

"If I've forgotten, then you can show me—on our wedding night." Lowering his head, he brushed a quick, hard kiss across her mouth, not giving her the opportunity to come back at him. He stood up, pulling her up gently with him while she clucked her tongue.

"You have a one-track mind, Joshua Kirkland. I was referring to your facility with languages, and that you play a mean game of racquetball. Your lovemaking isn't a talent, my darling, but an incredible gift." Turning, she retraced her steps and walked back to the dressing room.

He stared at her departing figure, giving her an imperceptible nod. "*Gracias,* Angel," he whispered.

They didn't dance until the sun came up, but returned to their bungalow several hours past midnight, exhausted and euphoric. Joshua showered while Vanessa lingered in the bathtub, soaking her tired legs and feet.

She slipped into bed beside him, coming into his welcoming embrace. She inhaled the clean odor of soap on his bare flesh as she pressed her face to his chest.

He moaned as if in pain when her silken thigh grazed his hair-roughened one. "You're not making this easy for me," he whispered through clenched teeth in the darkened bedroom.

"What?"

"Not making love to you when you come to bed without a nightgown."

Vanessa wiggled against him, trying to find a comfortable position. "I didn't bring one with me."

"Why not?"

"I don't like them. If my coming to bed nude bothers you then you should put on pajamas."

"I don't own a pair of pajamas."

She sat up. "One of us can sleep on the convertible love seat."

Joshua pulled her down as quickly as she had sat up. "We've made a promise to share our lives, and that means we'll share a bed."

She wiggled against him for the second time, pressing her buttocks against his groin. "I've heard that a cold shower helps."

"Stop wiggling and go to sleep or I'll force you to take a cold shower with me," he threatened softly. He didn't tell her that cold showers did nothing to quell his desire for her, that he knew Vanessa was a woman he would never tire of.

Day Five—It would be another three days before he could claim the woman sleeping beside him as his wife.

The sun was high in the sky by the time Vanessa and Joshua wove their way through the charming streets of the pre-Columbian city. She lingered in one of the exquisite shops along the *Galeria de Arte de Oaxaca,* studying a tray of silver jewelry inlaid with precious and semi-precious stones. The expertly crafted replicas of pieces were designed by the Zapotec and Mixtec Indians, who had erected an important religious center in the Oaxaca Valley in 600 B.C. and the Tenth Century, respectively.

Joshua stood at the opposite end of the showcase, watching her intently. She was calm and relaxed, and as she asked questions of the English-speaking proprietor her voice was even and controlled. There was nothing about the interchange to indicate that the man was her contact.

She picked up an exceptionally beautiful necklace—a pendant with inlaid turquoise dangled from the links of silver that spilled over her delicate fingers like liquid water. "It's exquisite," she said, smiling at Pablo Mendoza, who hadn't taken his gaze off her face from the moment she walked into his boutique.

"Would you like to try it on, Señorita?"

"Yes, please, Señor Mendoza," she replied, handing him the necklace and presenting him with her back.

The proprietor leaned across the showcase and looped the necklace around her throat. His fingers lingered on the nape of her neck as he lifted several strands of hair and tucked them into the pins she had secured at the back of her head, then fastened the clasp.

She turned toward Joshua, giving him a questioning look. He nodded, smiling. Straightening from his leaning position, he closed the distance between them as her fingers traced the outline of the pendant.

"Do you want it?" he asked.

Slight frown lines formed between her eyes. "I'm trying to decide whether my sister will like it."

"You're thinking of buying this for your sister?"

"Yes." Tilting her chin, she gave Joshua a steady look. "I never know what to buy Connie for her birthday."

"Does she like silver?"

"She prefers it to yellow gold," Vanessa confirmed.

He recalled The Shadow's report that Vanessa had purchased silver jewelry for a female at *Bazar Sábado* in Mexico City, and wondered if that was also for her sister.

"Do you wear silver?"

"No. I prefer yellow gold."

Joshua was suddenly alert, all of his reactions functioning on full power. Why was she buying more silver jewelry in Oaxaca, if she'd purchased several pieces in Mexico City?

Reaching out, he cradled the pendant in the palm of his hand, measuring its weight. There was no seam along the edges, eliminating its use as a locket.

"It's a one of a kind," Pablo announced confidently, hoping for a sale.

Vanessa managed a half-smile. "I'd like to think about it. I'll be back tomorrow."

Pablo nodded. "I'll put it aside for you. If you don't come back by closing time tomorrow I'll put it back in the showcase."

Joshua removed the necklace and returned it to the shop owner. "Thank you for your time."

Holding Vanessa's hand, he led her out of the boutique, studying her expression for a sign that would indicate that her visit with Pablo Mendoza was prearranged. Her face gave nothing away, while he'd noticed that Mendoza couldn't take his gaze off Vanessa.

They wove their way through a narrow alley lined on both sides with tiny shops boasting of authentic, locally produced handicrafts. Vanessa stopped to examine several handwoven baskets before she moved on to look at a stack of colorful blankets.

"Aren't you going to buy anything for yourself?" Joshua queried.

"I am buying for myself."

"I see you looking at things for your home and family members, but nothing for you."

She stopped flipping through the blankets and gave him a long, searching look. "When I buy an article to decorate my home, it *is* for *me*," she argued softly.

"What about jewelry?"

"What about it?"

"Don't you want a necklace? Or a bracelet? The only jewelry I've seen you wear is a pair of earrings and a watch."

"I have other pieces at home."

"How would you like to take home a few more?" His voice was low, mysterious.

He cradled her face in his hands, caressing it gently. "I want to give you a wedding gift."

Her gaze raced over his handsome face as a warm glow brought a flush to her body. "You're my gift."

"I want you to have something that'll remind you of me whenever we're apart."

Suddenly she remembered what he did for a living, and she wondered how many nights she would lie awake wishing he was beside her when he had left her for a business trip.

"Okay," she conceded.

He retraced their steps and led her into a jewelry store situated on the same street as the one operated by Pablo Mendoza. An elderly man greeted them in Spanish, and Joshua told him quickly what he wanted to see.

Vanessa sat on a chair, watching as Joshua was shown more than a dozen gold bracelets. He shook his head, explaining that it was to be a wedding gift. The proprietor shifted an eyebrow, disappeared into the back of the shop, then reappeared with a length of black velvet rolled into a cylinder.

He unrolled the cloth and Vanessa caught her breath, while Joshua smiled and nodded his approval. "Perhaps these will please the Señor?"

"Very much," Joshua confirmed, taking a length of glittering diamonds set in platinum with eighteen-carat gold. He fastened the bracelet around Vanessa's delicate wrist and secured the safety clasp tightly.

"I'll take it," he stated firmly, not waiting for her approval or disapproval. "And she'll also need a ring."

Vanessa was at a disadvantage because she didn't understand what the two men were talking about, but when her ring finger was measured she knew that she wanted to be the one to select her wedding ring.

Twenty minutes later she decided on a band in eighteen-carat gold with channel-set diamonds. The band was narrow, not too ostentatious for everyday wear.

Joshua signed the credit card receipt, then tucked his purchases into the breast pocket of his jacket. "Let's go, darling. It's time for *siesta.*"

They returned to the rental car and Joshua drove back to the bungalow. Vanessa stared through the windshield behind her sunglasses, silent.

She had one more day as a single woman before she exchanged vows with the man sitting beside her.

I love him. I love him enough to give up my independence and share the rest of my life with him.

The silent declaration was enough to calm the anxiety that had surfaced when she least expected it to. She covered his right hand with her left, squeezing his fingers gently.

Joshua took his gaze from the road and stared at her before returning his attention to the traffic ahead of him. He felt the quickening of her pulse in her wrist as he reversed the position of their hands. His thumbs made soothing motions over her fingers until she relaxed and her pulse slowed.

When they arrived at the bungalow, she permitted him to carry her into the bedroom where he undressed her slowly, then himself, before they lay on the bed together.

Cradling her gently to his chest, he pressed his lips to her forehead. "I love you," he confessed reverently.

Vanessa closed her eyes and let out her breath. He loved her and she loved him, but why did fingers of fear sweep over her when she least expected it, blanketing the happiness she should feel?

"Hold me, Joshua," she pleaded. "I don't know why, but I'm so frightened."

He went still. "Of who? What?"

"I don't know." Her voice was muffled in his chest.

Easing away from her, he stared down into her eyes. "I promised to protect you, didn't I?"

"Yes." Her voice was low and breathless.

He smiled. "There's nothing to worry about."

I hope he's right, she told herself.

He buried his face in her hair, silently cursing Vanessa for allowing herself to become involved in a game where the stakes were so high that if she made a single mistake she would forfeit her life as quickly as a blink of an eye.

Day Six—Vanessa had one more day as a single woman, and one more day to make contact with the Central American agent before she exchanged vows to become Mrs. Joshua Kirkland.

Chapter 14

Vanessa stood at the window in the bedroom, her body swathed in a lace-trimmed dressing gown, watching the sun rise. The deep gorges and valleys below the Sierra Madre del Sur were bathed in shadowy shades ranging from pink to violet, turning the entire scene into a breathtaking, picturesque still life.

She'd gotten out of bed before sunrise, unable to sleep because of the troubling, swirling thoughts disturbing the peace and joy she should've felt.

She had fallen in love with Joshua Kirkland, and she felt passionately that she truly loved him. But all of it had happened so quickly that it unnerved her. She'd rationalized that her period of self-imposed celibacy had enhanced her response to his commanding physical presence, but their promise to not make love until they wed had not diminished her desire or love for him.

The heat from the sun warmed her face through the glass while another source of heat seeped into her body. Without turning, she knew Joshua stood behind her. He'd been so silent that she hadn't heard him leave the bed or detected his approach.

Curving his arms around her narrow waist, he lowered his head and kissed the nape of her neck. "Why did you get up so early?"

Vanessa leaned back against his solid chest. "I couldn't sleep."

"Don't you feel well?"

"I feel well enough." Turning in his embrace, she smiled up at him. "I suppose I've been thinking too much. I think I'm experiencing premarital jitters."

Her dark gaze lingered on his mouth, then inched up slowly over his features. In less than thirty-six hours she would become this man's wife, and it was as if she were seeing him for the very first time.

What she had acknowledged as attractiveness was passionate male beauty. His lean face with the elegant ridge of high cheekbones, straight, narrow nose, and firm, sensual lips, was hypnotic. The pale hair, close-cut and coarse, lay against his scalp without a hint of curl, and that shocking silver hair highlighted the deep, rich gold undertones in his mahogany brown face. He stared back at her as the rising sun slanted over his face, illuminating his dramatic, electric green eyes framed by long, charcoal gray lashes.

Joshua smiled down at her. "You will make a beautiful bride."

She returned his smile. "Speaking of becoming a bride—I have a ring, but no dress or shoes."

Joshua rolled his eyes upward, shaking his head. "More shopping, Angel?"

"Don't you dare complain," she scolded in a soft tone. "I came to Mexico to shop, and shop I intend to do until I board that flight to return home."

"Do you shop this much in the States?"

"No," she replied shaking her head woefully. "Unfortunately I don't have the time, with my increased workload at GEA. It's taken nearly two years for my house to look lived in."

He brushed several strands of hair away from her cheek with the back of his hand. "GEA?"

"Grenville-Edwards Aerospace. Have you heard of it?" she questioned when his eyebrows shot up in surprise.

"Who hasn't? GEA, as you call it, has become quite a giant in the field of aerospace. How long have you worked for them?"

"Almost three-and-a-half years," she replied without hesitating.

"Do you like working for GEA?"

"I like what I do," she replied honestly.

Bending slightly, Joshua swept her up in his arms. "Let's go back to bed and talk." He made his way to the bed and lowered Vanessa onto a mound of pillows; he lay down beside her, cradling her to his bare chest. "Just what is it you do?" he asked smoothly.

"I'm one of three assistants to the chief financial officer. I head the contracts division."

"Who do you contract to?"

She went completely still, her body rigid. Joshua was asking a question she couldn't answer. "I can't reveal that."

"Why not?"

Although his voice was quiet, Vanessa did not register the ominous quality in his query. "Because it's classified."

Releasing her, he rose on an elbow and stared down at her, meeting her direct stare with one of his own. Neither of their gazes wavered.

"Are we going to begin our life together with secrets?"

A slight frown marred her smooth forehead as the tension between them increased with every second that she refused to answer him. It appeared that even before they married there would be dissension between them. He wanted her to divulge classified information, while he worked for a foreign-based corporation she knew nothing about.

"There won't be any secrets between us if you're able to get a Justice Department security clearance," she stated tersely.

He wanted to tell her that he *did* have clearance from the

Justice Department—clearance, and the authority to investigate and gather evidence that could possibly indict her. She could spend the remainder of her life in a federal prison.

Leaning over, he brushed his mouth over hers in a comforting gesture. "I'm sorry, baby. I don't want you to compromise yourself—not even for me."

Vanessa exhaled audibly, smiling. "Thank you for not making me choose."

"Choose between what?"

"Whether to compromise my ethics or not marry you."

His eyes paled to a transparent green. "Are you saying that if I pressure you to tell me about your job, you won't marry me?"

She flinched at the tone of his voice, but she wouldn't back down. "Yes." The single word rang with finality.

"What about love, Vanessa?"

"What about it?"

"I'm asking the questions," he shot back.

Vanessa sat up, her temper rising quickly. "Don't you dare talk to me as if I were a child."

The silence that ensued was deafening, punctuated only by the sound of their labored breathing, and Joshua saw Vanessa in a whole new light for the first time. What he saw was a woman who was a lot stronger than she appeared, a woman who wasn't easily frightened or intimidated, who refused to disclose to a man she'd promised to marry that she was involved in the sale of classified military components to a foreign agent.

He cursed to himself because she had trapped him. He'd disobeyed orders and become involved with her; he had also exacerbated his involvement by falling in love with his target and offering marriage.

And now it was down to a race against time. They had only two more days in Mexico before they were to return to the States. Two days during which he'd report his findings to his superiors, and disclose that he had married Vanessa Blanchard.

He wanted her to trust him enough to confide in him. What

she didn't know was that *only he* could protect her from prosecution. More importantly, he knew that he couldn't afford to alienate her—not before or after they married.

"I'm sorry, Vanessa. I had no right to speak you that way. And you're right. You're not a child."

Her right hand grazed his cheek, the stubble of an emerging beard rasping under her fingertips. "What are we doing, Joshua? We aren't even married and we're fighting about our careers."

He grasped her wrist and pressed his lips to her palm. He glanced up, not releasing her hand. "You aren't the only one experiencing premarital jitters," he whispered against the silken flesh.

Vanessa wound her free arm around his neck, pulling his head down to her breasts. "I can't imagine you getting upset by anything. You always seem to be in complete control of everything that you do or say."

"I'm not in control right now," he admitted.

She felt the uncanny strength in his slender hands as they tightened on her waist, easing her back to the softness of the bed. "Why not?"

Settling his body over hers, Joshua supported his greater weight on his elbows as he studied the face of the woman he would protect with his own life. "How am I going to leave you?"

A cold knot formed in her stomach, moving up slowly and not permitting her to draw a normal breath. They weren't even married, and he was talking about leaving her.

"You're…you're going to leave me?" The question came out as a breathless whisper.

"Whenever I leave for a business trip," he explained.

The tense lines on her face relaxed with his explanation. "What do you want me to say?"

"I want to know if you're going to mind my traveling."

"How often will you be away?"

"It varies. Sometimes a week, and sometimes a month or longer."

Vanessa was keenly aware of Joshua's scrutiny and knew he was testing her and her responses. "What is it you want me to say? That I'll miss you?" He didn't move or speak. "Of course I'd miss you," she continued. "Any normal woman who loves her husband misses him if he's not with her. But don't expect me to make your decision for you. If you choose to travel to earn your living, then I'll have to accept that. But if you decide to work for a company based in Santa Fe, then you'll find out every night how pleased I'll be to have you home with me."

The harsh lines in his face softened in a smile. "That sounds like an offer that would make me the world's biggest fool if I refused to consider it."

She stared wordlessly, again caught off guard by the man who appeared to change in front of her eyes. He'd changed from an erudite world traveler to an uncompromising interrogator when he questioned the security staff at La Mérida about the break-in at her room, then to a laid-back tourist strolling through the centuries-old streets of Oaxaca with her while she shopped for hours. He had also become the consummate seducer, and she had succumbed to his spell, fallen in love with him, and given him her promise that she would become his wife and the mother of his children.

Pinpoints of happiness brightened her dark eyes as she returned his smile. There was no need for her to tell him how much she loved him, because her eyes spoke volumes for her.

Joshua buried his face between her scented shoulder and neck. He mumbled softly in Spanish before repeating the phrase in French and in Italian.

"What did you say?" she asked, her soft breath whispering over his ear.

"I just asked for strength to make it through one more day of shopping," he translated.

Her tongue grazed the ear seconds before her teeth caught the lobe gently. "Apologize," she threatened, not releasing his ear.

Joshua gasped aloud from the pressure of her sharp teeth. "No."

"Apologize." Vanessa tightened her hold on his ear seconds before she screamed in surprise, freeing him. "That's not fair," she sputtered as his hand swept up her thigh and covered the soft, furred mound concealing her femininity.

"That's because *you* don't play fair."

The heat from his hand aroused her lust for him, and she couldn't stop her body's natural response when a rush of dampness signaled her body was ready for his.

He raised his head and stared at her. Her gaze was wide and filled with uncertainty. He'd promised her that they would not make love again until after they were married, but the nectar flowing from Vanessa and bathing his fingers threatened to make him break his vow. He had also told Father Peña that he would not make love to his wife until after they'd received the sacrament of Holy Matrimony. He had many sins to confess before the elderly priest married them, and he didn't want to add a new one to the others he'd amassed over the years.

His hand moved around to cradle her hip. "I don't know about you, but I'm ready to shop."

Her gaze widened. "Shop?"

"It's either that or break a vow." He moved quickly off the bed and headed for the bathroom.

"Vow?" Vanessa whispered after he'd disappeared. She quickly forgot about his cryptic statement when she eased her body out of bed, her head filled with plans for her upcoming wedding.

She found her dress and shoes in a boutique that featured vintage clothing and accessories. The sleeveless, silk, champagne colored dress boasted an Empire waist with four-leaf-clover embroidery from neckline to the hem, which graced the toes of matching satin slippers with just a hint of a heel.

She paid for her purchases, agreeing with the saleslady when she suggested she wear her hair in a twist entwined with orange blossoms. "Orange blossoms are a traditional wedding motif, and signal a long and happy marriage," the woman whispered, glancing over at Joshua, who sat on a delicate chair flipping through a magazine.

Vanessa saw the direction of her gaze and smiled. "Do you have something I can use as a wedding gift for the groom?"

"Does your *novio* wear shirts with French cuffs? Because I happen to have a pair of cuff links that are simply exquisite."

A frown creased her brow as she tried recalling whether Joshua had worn cuff links with any of his shirts. Then she remembered—the night they'd shared dinner at Le Mérida he'd worn a shirt with French cuffs!

"*Sí Señora,* he does," she replied.

Vanessa took one look at the gold oval cuff links inlaid with minuscule rubies, diamonds, emeralds, and sapphires. The overall design resembled the many mosaics on the floors and walls of churches and museums she had seen during her stay in Mexico.

Pushing her credit card across the counter for the second time, she said, "I'll take it." Within minutes the transaction was completed, the gift gaily wrapped and placed in the shopping bags with her other purchases.

She walked over to Joshua and handed him the bags. "I'm ready to leave now."

He took the bundles, rising to his feet as a mysterious smile curved his mouth. "Where to *now?*"

"I want to go back to the jewelry store we went to yesterday and pick up the silver necklace for my sister Connie."

Joshua glanced at his watch. "We'd better hurry before they close for *siesta.*"

They made it to the tiny shop in the *Galería de Arte de Oaxaca* moments before Pablo Mendoza placed a sign in the window signaling he was closed.

The skin around his dark eyes crinkled as he smiled. "I see you've come back for the necklace."

Vanessa smiled, nodding. "I'd never forgive myself if I left Mexico without it."

Pablo clasped his hands and pressed them against his heart. "I must confess that I knew you'd return for it. I cleaned it and wrapped it up after you left yesterday. I'll make out a sales receipt and it's yours."

Joshua, moving to Vanessa's side, reached into his jacket pocket and withdrew a small leather case filled with several credit cards. "I'd like to take a look at the necklace again before we pay for it." There was no way he would permit Vanessa to accept the package without knowing its contents.

Pablo Mendoza hesitated. "*Pero, Señor,* it is wrapped so prettily."

"Then unwrap it and rewrap it so prettily," he demanded facetiously in flawless Spanish.

The shopkeeper's eyes widened in astonishment. It was apparent that the man with the very beautiful *Americana* spoke Spanish quite well. "*Sí, Señor.*"

Joshua watched as Mendoza removed the paper from the box containing the necklace, then flipped open the lid to display the magnificence of the silver and turquoise chain and pendant.

"*Muchas gracias, Señor Mendoza.*"

Pablo Mendoza's jaw tightened, but he managed a conciliatory smile for Joshua as he called to a salesclerk from the rear of the shop to rewrap the box.

Vanessa waited until they left the shop and returned to where Joshua had parked the car before saying, "What was that all about back there?"

He started the car. "What are you talking about?"

"Why did you make Mr. Mendoza unwrap and rewrap the package? I—"

"There was no way I was going to let you walk out of that place with a package that you *assumed* contained a necklace," he interrupted.

"What do you think it could contain, if not a necklace?"

"A couple of worthless coins. Or even a piece of glass. And **if the necklace wasn't there, would you come back and confront him?**"

"Of course not. It wouldn't be worth it."

"That's why I did what I did."

"Thank you for making me aware of what could happen. I suppose I'm somewhat too trusting."

Wrong, Vanessa. Spies aren't trusting at all, he thought. His right hand covered her left. "You're quite welcome, Angel."

Her eyes brightened in laughter as she studied Joshua's perfect profile. "I just realized that tonight will be my last night as a single woman."

"Have you planned anything special to celebrate the rite of passage?" he teased.

"Celebrating it with you."

He gave her a wide grin, displaying all of his straight, white teeth in his darkly tanned face. "Doing what?"

"I don't know. You'll have to help me out with the list of possibilities." He wiggled his eyebrows and gave her a lecherous grin. "Not that," she giggled.

"Not what?" He affected an expression of innocence.

"You know, Joshua."

He registered her demure smile, and it took all of his self-control not to maneuver over to the side of the road and pull her across his lap, where he could devour her lush, sweet, tempting mouth.

"No, I *don't* know," he said after a long, comfortable silence. "But I'd be willing to have you show me tomorrow night."

A warm flush swept over Vanessa's face. She turned her head and stared out the window as Joshua hummed off-key under his breath.

Day Seven—In less than twenty-four hours Vanessa Blanchard would become Vanessa Kirkland.

Chapter 15

Vanessa stared at her reflection in the full-length mirror on the door of the armoire. The stylist at the hotel's salon had shampooed and blown out her hair, then pinned up her shoulder-length tresses in a style reminiscent of a Gibson Girl's. A circle of fresh orange blossoms sat atop the raven strains like a delicate halo. The hairdo was perfect for her Regency-style dress.

Joshua walked into the dressing room, slipping a Windsor-knotted, chocolate brown silk tie into place under the spread collar of a crisp, pristine white shirt. His stride was purposeful when he closed the distance between them and stood behind her. He wore a pair of wheat-colored tailored trousers that matched the jacket she'd seen him wear on the flight to Mexico City.

She smiled at his reflection. "If you're going to wear that shirt, then I think you should wear something I bought for you." Reaching into a drawer of the armoire, she withdrew a gaily wrapped package. "My wedding gift," she stated, turning and handing him the small parcel.

Smiling broadly, he wagged a finger at her. "You didn't have to buy me anything."

"I know I didn't, but I wanted to."

"Why?"

She gave him a sensual smile, her lids lowering slowly. "Because I love you, that's why."

His hands were steady as he unwrapped the box containing his wedding gift. Flipping the top, he stared down at the flash of diamonds nestled among the spray of rubies, emeralds, and sapphires inlaid in an oval of burnished yellow gold. The decorative paper and bow floated to the floor when he reached out with one hand and pulled her to his chest.

The hard lines of his slim body and the heat from his flesh burned Vanessa through the delicate fabric of her wedding dress as Joshua wordlessly and passionately thanked her.

"I'll treasure them always," he said, his clean breath sweeping over an ear. What he didn't tell her was that it was the first time a woman had ever given him anything other than her body. But Vanessa was not just any woman—she was to become his wife in less than two hours.

Pulling back, he handed her the box containing the cuff links. "Put them in for me." Within minutes she'd removed his conservative, solid gold, monogrammed cuff links and replaced them with the elegant jeweled ones.

Rising on tiptoe, she kissed his smooth, freshly-shaven, brown cheek. "Now it's your turn to help me put my bracelet on." Joshua secured the diamond bracelet around her right wrist, lingering to kiss her scented arm.

"I don't know about you," he began quietly, "but I'm going to a wedding, and I don't want to be late."

"Why are we leaving so early? You told me Father Peña will marry us at five, and it takes less than twenty minutes to drive to the church."

Joshua withdrew his jacket from the armoire. "Father Peña wants to see me at four-thirty."

"Why?"

Turning back to Vanessa, he studied her intently. Would she understand that he was obligated to reveal to the elderly priest what he could never tell her? "In lieu of us attending Pre-Cana—the Catholic premarriage counseling—he has requested that I receive the Sacrament of Reconciliation."

"Reconciliation?"

"Confession."

Her expression revealed confusion. "It sounds so profound."

"Profound as it might sound, it's necessary. Father Peña did not allow me an option."

Vanessa watched as Joshua put on his jacket and adjusted his shirt cuffs. "And you're going through with it, because without it he won't marry us?"

His hands slipped up her bare arms, bringing her closer. "If I had to walk on water to marry you, then I'd do it."

The eyes that could freeze and heat her body with a glance bore into hers with a strange, new savage fire that pulled her in and refused to let her go. Everything that Joshua Kirkland felt at that instant she felt. They had become one—in mind and in spirit.

Again, swallowing to relieve the dryness in her throat, she whispered, "Let's go get married."

Vanessa waited for Joshua to translate the priest's words before replying in English, while Father Peña's housekeeper, doubling as their witness, smiled.

She had taken the vow to love and cherish her husband, and to forsake all others. Joshua placed the ring on her finger, then Father Peña placed his heavily veined hand over their clasped ones and prayed in a softly musical voice, while her new husband stared down at her bowed head. Father Peña withdrew his hand, smiling, then told Joshua that he could kiss his wife.

Vanessa felt the repressed passion in the kiss as Joshua's mouth covered hers possessively. She was now a married woman. Eight days after meeting Joshua Kirkland for the first time on a flight from Santa Fe, New Mexico, for Mexico City, Mexico, she had become Vanessa Kirkland.

"*Te amo,* darling," he whispered in her ear.

"And I love you, too," she whispered back, her eyes filling with tears of happiness.

Father Peña made the sign of the cross over them, saying, "Go with God to love and serve the Lord, my children. May your lives be filled with peace and love and blessed with children from this most precious sacrament of service."

Joshua shook Father Peña's hand, nodding in reverence as he thanked him for everything.

The elderly priest returned the nod, smiling. He had heard the younger man's confession, and it was no doubt that he loved the woman he'd married. He only hoped that the beautiful young bride would not be drawn into the danger her husband had elected to pursue in his career.

The housekeeper nodded to Father Peña. He inclined his head once, then turned his attention to Vanessa and Joshua. "Señor and Señora Kirkland, you would honor me if you joined me in a humble, post-wedding repast."

Joshua's brow furrowed slightly. He'd planned to take his wife to *La Morsa,* a restaurant set amid tropical gardens and fountains, for their wedding dinner, but at the priest's request he decided it could wait for the following evening. After he met with Cordero Birmingham in San Miguel he'd return to Oaxaca, where he and Vanessa would share their meal at *La Morsa* before returning to the States the next morning.

"The honor would be ours," he replied as he curved an arm around Vanessa's waist.

Leaning down, he whispered in her ear that Father Peña wanted them to share an early dinner with him, and that he had accepted the offer.

Her eyebrows arched in surprise. "How generous."

Following the priest out of the chapel, Joshua said quietly, "I told him that you agreed to raise our children as Catholics." His hold on her waist tightened. "He was quite pleased with your decision."

"And how about you, my husband? Does it please you?"

Staring down at her, their gazes met and held. "You please me, Vanessa Kirkland. Everything you do, everything you say, pleases me."

Father Peña's housekeeper was an excellent cook, and she had prepared several seafood dishes with distinct, trademark Mexican flavors: tomatoes, onions, bell peppers, and garlic were the foundation when blended with hot peppers, *achiote,* cloves, smoky cilantro and sweet *canela,* Mexican cinnamon. Lime juice, capers, and green olives stimulated the palate instead of overpowering it.

The three dined on *Huachinango a la Veracruzana, Salpicon de Huachinango,* and *Shrimp Mojo de Ajo,* with salsa, avocado, and sweet plantains. Vanessa drank two glasses of a heavy, rich red wine, while Joshua and the priest shared a bottle.

Her lids were drooping slightly when dinner ended, and she required her new husband's assistance as they rose to leave. Joshua offered Father Peña another generous "donation" for the less than prosperous parish, then escorted his wife out to the car.

She sank down in the passenger seat and closed her eyes, pressing the back of her head against the headrest. The effects of the wine and succently broiled shrimp and red snapper fish concoctions, with the accompanying salsa, lingered on her tongue. She had eaten sparingly, yet she felt unusually full.

Joshua glanced over at her composed features as he maneuvered the rental car back to their bungalow at the Victoria. "How are you feeling, Mrs. Kirkland?"

Vanessa smiled without opening her eyes. "Slightly intoxicated, Mr. Kirkland."

"On two glasses of wine?"

She nodded. "I don't know how you and Father Peña finished that bottle."

"It was easy because we're *men*," he teased with a smile.

Her eyes opened, and she glared at him. "Oh, no, you didn't go there, Joshua Kirkland. Because you're a *male* you think that makes you a better drinker?"

His smile vanished. "I was only teasing you, Vanessa. I've known a few women who could drink a lot of men under the table."

"Known how?"

Slowing the car, he gave her a penetrating look. "Jealous?"

Shrugging a bare, slender shoulder, Vanessa said, "Could be."

"I'll never give you the opportunity to feel jealous of another woman. I told you before that I'd always be faithful to you."

Her eyes crinkled with a smile. "Don't be so serious, Joshua. I was *teasing* you. Do you think I would've married you if I suspected that you wouldn't be faithful to me?"

"I know you wouldn't have," he replied confidently.

He steered the car along the path leading to the bungalow and shut off the ignition. Turning to his right, he stared at the woman he'd married. His world was perfect, balanced for the first time in his life. It had taken him thirty-eight years to find a woman he could love unconditionally, and eight days after their meeting he had claimed her as his wife.

Vanessa returned his direct stare, visually admiring the man she had married. His lips were full, firm, but did not appear feminine; his hands were slender, yet possessed uncanny strength; his eyes—pale, cold—burned with electric green sparks that hypnotized and made her his willing prisoner. And, like a transfixed rabbit unable to free itself from the spell of a larger predator, she sat waiting, waiting to experience why she had been born female.

Joshua reached out and traced the underside of her delicate jaw with his fingertips before he pressed his mouth to her parted lips. Inhaling her familiar, feminine scent, he breathed into her mouth, saying, "Let's go inside."

Even though she and Joshua had made love before, Vanessa knew this night, this time, would be different. Their roles had

KIMANI ™
ROMANCE

An Important Message from the Publisher

Dear Reader,

Because you've chosen to read one of our fine novels, I'd like to say "thank you"! And, as a special way to say thank you, I'm offering to send you two more Kimani™ Romance novels and two surprise gifts— absolutely FREE! These books will keep it real with true-to-life African American characters that turn up the heat and sizzle with passion.

Please enjoy the free books and gifts with our compliments...

Glenda Howard
For Kimani Press

Peel off Seal and

Place Inside...

FREE GIFTS
EDITOR'S SEAL THANK YOU

(K-ROM-10RS2)

We'd like to send you two free books to introduce you to Kimani™ Romance books. These novels feature strong, sexy women, and African-American heroes that are charming, loving and true. Our authors fill each page with exceptional dialogue, exciting plot twists, and enough sizzling romance to keep you riveted until the very end!

KIMANI ROMANCE...LOVE'S ULTIMATE DESTINATION

Your two books have a combined cover price of $13.98, but are yours **FREE!**

We'll even send you two wonderful surprise gifts. You can't lose!

2 FREE BONUS GIFTS!

THE EDITOR'S "THANK YOU" FREE GIFTS INCLUDE:

Two Kimani™ Romance Novels
Two exciting surprise gifts

YES! I have placed my Editor's "thank you" Free Gifts seal in the space provided at right. Please send me 2 FREE books, and my 2 FREE Mystery Gifts. I understand that I am under no obligation to purchase anything further, as explained on the back of this card.

PLACE
FREE GIFTS
SEAL
HERE

About how many NEW paperback fiction books have you purchased in the past 3 months?

❑ 0-2   ❑ 3-6   ❑ 7 or more

E7XY   E5MH   E5MT

168/368 XDL

Please Print

FIRST NAME

LAST NAME

ADDRESS

APT.#   CITY

STATE/PROV.   ZIP/POSTAL CODE

Thank You!

▼ If offer card is missing write to: The Reader Service, P.O. Box 1867, Buffalo, NY 14240-1867 or visit www.ReaderService.com ▼

BUSINESS REPLY MAIL

FIRST-CLASS MAIL   PERMIT NO. 717   BUFFALO, NY

POSTAGE WILL BE PAID BY ADDRESSEE

THE READER SERVICE

PO BOX 1867

BUFFALO NY 14240-9952

NO POSTAGE
NECESSARY
IF MAILED
IN THE
UNITED STATES

changed from lovers to husband and wife. They had taken a vow to love each other for all time.

Standing in the middle of the dressing room, she stared up at her husband as he slowly and deftly removed his jacket and shirt. He placed the jeweled cuff links and his gold watch on a small round table beside a straightback chair.

Vanessa noticed for the first time that his chest was several shades lighter than his face, indicating that Joshua probably spent an inordinate amount of time in the sun. His shoes, socks, trousers, and briefs followed, leaving him standing before her naked—and very male, as the evidence of his desire for her was blatantly displayed.

He took a step forward and removed the wreath of orange blossoms from her hair, then unpinned the expertly coiffed strands until they floated down around her long neck.

Closing her eyes, Vanessa felt the brush of his fingers and the whisper of fabric as he removed her dress and underwear until she stood before him equally naked and pulsing with desire.

She didn't have time to catch her breath before he swept her up effortlessly into his arms and walked out of the dressing room and into their bedroom.

Tightening her arms around his neck, she buried her face against his throat, savoring the texture and smell of his skin. Her prior anxiety vanished as the love she held in her heart for the man she had married surfaced, filling her with an inexplicable joy.

Joshua lowered her gently to the bed, his body following as he cradled Vanessa's face between his hands. He tasted her mouth tentatively, teasing her until her hands moved up and captured his head. His lips left hers to nibble at her earlobe, then returned, leaving her mouth burning with a simmering fire.

Her fingers tightened on his scalp, pulling him closer while she tried slowing down the desire racing headlong down her body. Her rising need was communicated when his mouth became more demanding.

"Open your mouth," he ordered softly. His tongue slipped

inside, awakening a foreign wantonness that scorched the hidden place between her thighs.

"Now, Joshua. Please," she pleaded without shame.

She opened her large eyes, and he saw the shimmering tears turning them into polished onyx. He didn't disappoint her or himself as he buried his rigid flesh deep within the softness of her moist, pulsing body.

The pleasure he found in Vanessa's body was so exquisite that Joshua feared it would be over too quickly. He had planned a long, leisurely session of lovemaking, but having been denied her body for four days had taken its toll on his self-control.

Her quickened breathing resounded in his ear, and the soft, sensual moans coming from her parted lips were his undoing. His own movements quickened as he drove into her again and again, over and over, until reality ceased to exist and he was transported to a place where light and dark merged, heaven greeted him, where his private hell vaporized, leaving in its place a gentle peace that made him want to weep with joy.

He didn't cry, but Vanessa did. Hiccuping uncontrollably, she whispered, "I love you, I love you, I…"

His mouth covered hers, stopping her litany as he drank again from her honeyed lips. "And I love you, too, my Angel," he confessed in a deep voice which carried all of the emotion he'd ever felt for a woman.

He shifted slightly, supporting his greater weight on his arms, but did not withdraw from her body. He couldn't—not now. He wanted to savor the oneness for as long as possible.

Day Eight—He'd married Vanessa, and tomorrow he would meet with Cordero Birmingham and outline the details of Operation MESA and pass along Pablo Mendoza's name for a complete background investigation.

Chapter 16

Joshua glanced at his watch as he secured the clasp. He had three hours before he met Cordero Birmingham in San Miguel. It was more than one hundred forty kilometers between the two cities, and he estimated that it would take him at least two hours if he stayed on Highway 175.

Slipping his arms into his suit jacket, he patted the inside breast pocket to make certain the small, leather-bound bible was secure. All of the maneuvers for Operation MESA were printed in the text of the bible.

Something caught his attention, and he turned to find Vanessa watching him. He'd left the bed to shave, shower, and dress without waking her. A wealth of raven hair fell over her forehead as she wrapped her slender arms around her waist over an above-the-knee, pistachio green, silk coverup.

"What time will you be back, Joshua?"

He drew in a deep breath. Her gaze was steady, but there was no mistaking the longing in her voice. Was that the way it was going to be—her waiting for him to come back from some secret mission?

He smiled, making his way across the dressing room and closing the distance between them. "I'll be back for dinner." Curving an arm around her waist, he pulled her against his chest. "This is to be our last night in Mexico, so we'll celebrate."

Her gaze raced frantically over his features, committing them to memory. Vanessa didn't know why, but she couldn't smile. She'd planned to spend ten days in Mexico—alone—but now she didn't want to be alone. She wanted Joshua by her side until she returned to a place she was familiar with, and a place she called home.

Rising on tiptoe, she kissed him. "Be careful out there."

He returned her kiss, his aftershave enveloping her with sensual memories of their wedding night. After they'd made love the first time it seemed as if they were insatiable, and Vanessa would not be surprised if she returned to the States pregnant. They had made love without the benefit of contraception, and it was the most fertile time of the month during her menstrual cycle.

"You be careful," he countered. "If you want to go into town have the front desk call a taxi. A woman traveling or shopping alone can become a prime target for a clever pickpocket."

"I'm shopped out," she said, smiling.

He gave her a look of utter disbelief. "No."

"Yes." This time she did laugh. "I'm going to relax here until you come back."

His hold on her waist tightened as his attitude became more serious. "I meant what I said about walking into town, Vanessa."

She bit back the words forming on her tongue. She wanted to tell Joshua that she had taken care of herself before she met him and she would continue to do so, but knew it was not the time. Once they were back in the States he would get to know the true Vanessa Blanchard-Kirkland.

"You'd better get going," she said instead.

Threading his fingers through her hair, he held her head

firmly and kissed her mouth. "Love you," he whispered, then released her and turned on his heel and walked out of the room, leaving Vanessa staring at the space where he'd been.

"Love you, too," she whispered to the air.

Joshua made it to San Miguel with time to spare. He drove past *La Iglesia de los Santos,* parked several streets from the ancient structure, then returned to the church on foot. He stood at the rear of the church until mass ended, then sat down on the last pew after most of the early-morning parishioners filed out.

His gaze swept over the ornate interior. Like most churches in Mexico, it was beautifully decorated.

His gaze shifted to a shirtless young man who walked into the church with a shuffling gait. What had caught his attention immediately were the angry red welts marring the man's otherwise smooth back.

Joshua moved to help the young man, whose knees threatened to give way, but was thwarted when his throat was caught in a vicious grip which threatened to crush his windpipe.

The young man he'd attempted to assist whirled quickly, and Joshua saw light pouring in from stained-glass windows glinting on the blade of a stiletto before it found its target.

He was caught between the two men as fire spread rapidly across his middle; the flickering candles burning throughout the church dimmed before his eyes in a macabre dance of death.

The two men eased him down onto a bench, propping him up until he leaned against the back of the pew. His head dropped forward as if he were deep in prayer, while his life's blood pooled at his feet.

At exactly zero nine hundred Cordero Birmingham walked into *La Iglesia de los Santos* and spied Joshua Kirkland immediately. He slipped onto the pew bench beside him, a frown forming between his topaz blue eyes when he stepped into a dark liquid. Lifting his feet gingerly, he grimaced. It was only when he glanced at Joshua's pallid face, then down at the widening red stain on the front of what had been a white shirt that he realized that his shoes were resting in a pool of blood. Joshua Kirkland's blood.

His fingers snaked around Joshua's throat, feeling for a pulse and finding one. It was weak, but it was there. Pulling Joshua up, he struggled several times, but managed to pick him up. Carrying him, he walked out of the church, yelling at anyone who glanced his way.

"Médico! Médico!"

It was another thirty-six hours before Joshua realized where he was. He was back in the States—and without Vanessa!

Turning his head slowly in the semi-dark room, he knew from the sounds and smells he was in a hospital. He stared at the clear tube taped to the back of his hand, filled with liquids that would nourish his injured body.

A slim figure moved closer to the bed. "Colonel Kirkland?" He turned toward the sound of the feminine voice. "Please don't try to talk, Sir."

The woman moved away from the bed, and the stream of light on the polished tiled floor widened with an open door. "He's awake," the woman said softly to the two uniformed men standing outside the room. One came to attention immediately and signaled to another seated on a chair at the end of the corridor.

Twenty minutes later Harry Blackwell walked into the room where Colonel Joshua Kirkland lay motionless. He barely noticed the nurse sitting at the bedside who watched the machines monitoring her patient's respiration and blood pressure.

He'd been briefed on Joshua's condition and knew it wasn't encouraging. He had been close to death when he'd arrived back in the States, and even though his prognosis was upgraded, his condition was still critical.

What Harry Blackwell wanted were answers, answers about

whether Operation MESA had been compromised. As an associate director of the FBI, Harry had given his full support to the director of the Drug Enforcement Administration, because someone within that agency had leaked classified maneuvers for drug raids throughout Mexico, and continued to.

Harry had officially recruited Colonel Joshua Kirkland from the Pentagon to devise a cryptograph filled with dates, times, and places where United States and Mexican drug enforcement personnel would strike targeted high-level traffickers.

Harry leaned over Joshua, noting the unhealthy pallor of his normally deeply tanned face. "It's Blackwell, and I'm going to make this quick. We need to know about Operation MESA. When is it going down, and where?"

Joshua swallowed several times to relieve the dryness in his throat. He recognized the voice. "The bible," he said in a croaking tone.

Joshua opened his eyes and stared up at the dark brown face belonging to the associate director of the FBI. "Did you find the bible?"

"Birmingham said he found a marked-up bible in your jacket. What does it have to do with Operation MESA?"

Joshua's chest rose and fell heavily with the exertion it took to speak. "Sit down and take notes," he ordered Blackwell. He waited until Harry pulled out a pad and pen from his jacket pocket. "Deuteronomy, chapter five, verse eight, is Durango, June fifth, at oh eight hundred." His voice was a raspy whisper. "Judges, chapter five, verse eleven, is Jalisco, June fifth, at eleven hundred. Genesis seven, eighteen, is Guadalajara. Luke six, twenty-one, is Leon. First Corinthians eight, thirteen, is Cuernavaca…"

Harry scribbled quickly, awed as Joshua enumerated every detail he'd set down for Operation MESA. He'd heard rumors regarding the man's photographic memory, and now that he'd witnessed it firsthand he was astounded by the amount of information Joshua carried in his head. He had listed eighteen cities with corresponding dates and times for raids by a concert of Mexican police and military, and U.S. Drug Enforcement personnel. The raids would stem the flow of illegal drugs from Mexico and ports south, crippling powerful cartels for years to come.

There was another matter he wanted to discuss with Joshua Kirkland. "What happened with Vanessa Blanchard?"

Joshua closed his eyes, tension tightening the lines around his mouth, while the delicate nostrils of his nose flared visibly. "What about her?"

"I'm asking the questions, Colonel Kirkland," Harry countered harshly, coming to his feet. "You reported that you'd made contact with her."

He nodded. "I did," he admitted.

"Where is she?"

Again swallowing to relieve the dryness in his throat, he said, "I left her in Oaxaca."

Harry replaced the pen and pad in his pocket. "I'll have her picked up."

Joshua struggled to sit up, but the nurse moved quickly and eased him back to the mound of pillows cradling his shoulders. "I'm sorry, Colonel, but you're not permitted to get out of bed."

"Don't touch her, Blackwell," Joshua ordered, struggling weakly against the nurse's grip.

Harry frowned, crossing his arms over his broad chest. "Why the hell not?"

"Because she's my wife."

The older man whispered a savage expletive, the single word exploding in the small room, then sank back down to the chair he'd just vacated. He would not have expected this scenario from Joshua Kirkland. "Dammit," he snarled, standing up again. "You know what this means, don't you?"

Joshua stared at Harry, freezing him where he stood. "No, I don't," he said sarcastically. "Why don't you tell me?"

"I think you know very well, Colonel. The only thing I'll ask is, is she worth it? Is she worth you being court-martialed?"

There was only the sound of breathing from the three occupants as they stared at one another. The tension in the small room at Walter Reed Medical Center swelled until Joshua broke the silence.

"Yes. She is. She's worth every day I'll have to spend in Leavenworth."

"Fool," Harry spat out. Then he turned on his heel and walked out of the room. "Guard him," he ordered the two Marines who stood at attention outside the room.

Vanessa sat in the office of the Chief of the Oaxaca Police Department, praying that someone from his staff had uncovered something about her missing husband. She had extended her vacation a week, waiting for Joshua's return.

What had begun as annoyance had turned into anger, then fear, when Joshua did not return from his business trip. Her emotions vacillated between episodes of rage and tears. She thought he'd married her and abandoned her in a foreign country, while he flew to another to seduce and marry another unsuspecting woman.

When she lay alone in her bed at night she gave in to a torrent of tears that left her spent and dazed. *He lied to me. Liar, liar, liar!*

The voices taunted her as she slept, so she sat up nights to avoid them. With the rising of the sun came the realization that she was alone, and that Joshua was never coming back.

The police chief gave her a warm, comforting smile. "Señora, I promise you that if I hear of your husband I'll contact you myself."

Vanessa rose to her feet, extending her hand. "Thank you for all of your help. You've been very kind to me."

The chief rose with her. "If you accompany one of my men to the airport, he will make certain you board your plane for your trip back to the United States."

She thanked him again and walked out of the building housing the police department with the officer who had been assigned to take her to the airport. She slipped into the car beside the young officer, with her luggage and Joshua's stored in the trunk, and stared straight ahead, willing the tears not to fall as he drove toward the Oaxaca airport.

She had lost Joshua Kirkland, and she was not carrying his child.

She was going home—alone.

PART TWO

The Stranger

Chapter 17

"That's it, Connie," Vanessa concluded, staring down at her folded hands in her lap.

Connie Childs's large eyes were fixed on her sister's composed features. "I don't believe you. There was no way it could've happened. If you'd married I would've known it."

"I wouldn't lie to you, Connie."

"But…but you didn't seem any different when you got back. All you said was that you called Warren and extended your vacation because you were having so much fun. Little did any of us know that your fun meant you'd gotten married."

"I wouldn't call having my husband of one day walk out on me fun."

"Maybe something happened to him and he couldn't contact you."

"Get real, Connie. It's been thirteen months. If he wanted to contact me, he would've done it."

"Does he know where you live?"

"He may not know my exact address, but he knows where I work. He admitted he'd heard about GEA."

"What if he's—"

"Dead?" Vanessa said, completing her sister's sentence. Connie nodded. "Well, if he isn't, he'll wish he was if I ever meet up with him again."

"What did you do with his clothes?"

"I've stored them in the closet in the small bedroom."

"This is so unbelievable," Connie continued.

Yes it is, Vanessa confirmed silently. She didn't know why she'd packed Joshua's clothes and personal belongings and brought them back with her. At first she thought she wanted something of his to hold on to, but even that had vanished when she realized that he was never coming back to her. She'd locked the closet and had never opened it again. Joshua Kirkland and everything he represented was lost to her—forever.

"You still don't believe me, do you?" Biting down on her lower lip, Connie glanced away, giving Vanessa her answer. "You think I could make something like this up?"

"I don't know what to think anymore."

Vanessa rose to her feet. "Come with me."

Connie followed her up the staircase and into the large, sunny room Vanessa had selected as her bedroom. She was always astounded by the furnishings in her younger sister's home. Each piece had been selected with the utmost consideration. Each piece of pottery, plant and wall hanging blended perfectly with the existing decor as if it had been chosen by a professional decorator.

Opening the door of a massive, bleached pine armoire, Vanessa withdrew a small box covered with a colorful green and yellow plaid fabric. She removed the top and handed it to Connie.

"He bought those for me."

Connie's mouth dropped slightly as she stared at the diamonds in the wedding band and bracelet nestled on a bed of black velvet. Handing the box back to Vanessa, she said, "I could use a cup of strong, black coffee right about now."

Vanessa returned the box in its place, closed the armoire, and accompanied her sister as they retraced their steps. It was only after she had brewed a pot of coffee and she and Connie had drunk two cups that Connie spoke again.

"Are you going to tell Mom and Daddy?"

She gave Connie a long, penetrating look. "No. It's my past, and there's no need for anyone else to know."

Connie circled the table in the dining area and hugged Vanessa, offering the sort of love and support they could always count on from each other. "Your secret is safe with me."

Vanessa maneuvered into her assigned parking space in the garage beneath the building where the administrative offices of Grenville-Edwards Aerospace were housed. Even though it wasn't quite eight o'clock, the garage was nearly filled to capacity. It was late June and she wondered, *whatever happened to people taking vacations?*

She grimaced as the word *vacation* attacked her. It had been more than a year since her last vacation, and she knew she had to get away from GEA for a while...even if it was for only a long weekend.

A satisfied smile softened her tight features. She'd solved her own dilemma. She would take her vacation as long weekends. Perhaps she would fly to Los Angeles to see her parents, or visit with her former colleagues at the small college where she had taught courses in accounting.

Stepping out of her late-model Toyota, she slipped her arms into a hip-length, peach-colored linen jacket that matched a slim, fitted sheath. Reaching for her leather tote and shoulder bag on the passenger seat, she heard a familiar voice behind her.

"Isn't it a shame about Preston breaking both of his legs?"

Whirling quickly, Vanessa stared at her assistant, Shane Sumners. Her pulse quickened. "What did you say?"

Shane's large hazel eyes widened behind the thin wire frames of his glasses. "I guess you didn't hear the news because you were out yesterday. The word is that Preston climbed up to the roof of his house to adjust his satellite dish and fell off."

"The silly, stubborn, cantankerous, eccentric fool," she sputtered. "What Preston fails to realize is that he's an accountant, not an engineer."

Shane fell in step beside her as they headed out of the parking garage to the elevators that would take them directly to the office, where Grenville-Edwards Aerospace occupied an entire floor in the modern office building.

"Is he in the hospital?"

Shane let Vanessa enter the elevator before him, then stepped in and pushed the button for the seventh floor. "He's at St. Mary's. He'll be there for a few more days before he's released. We took up a collection yesterday and sent him flowers and a fruit basket."

"What he needs is a new set of brains," she said, frowning. "Last year he almost electrocuted himself because he *thought* he knew how to rewire his house, and now this. What Preston ought to do is get a girlfriend to occupy his free time, so he can stop tinkering with things around his house."

Forty-eight-year-old Preston had spurned the advances of every woman who had seemed remotely interested in him, saying he didn't have time for a relationship. The only things he had time for were his numbers and his do-it-yourself projects, which on more than one occasion had resulted in his being hospitalized.

Shane smiled, nodding. "You're right about that. There must be something about working at GEA that prevents forming relationships."

"What do you mean, Shane?" The doors opened at the seventh floor and they both stepped out into a carpeted reception area.

"Look at you, me, Jenna, Warren, Preston. And too many others who work here and are in their thirties and forties and aren't married. Why? Because we're married to GEA. We earn fantastic salaries, but for a price. We have no life outside of GEA."

That's where you're wrong, she wanted to say to the tall, slender, thirty-seven-year-old accountant with smooth pale skin, rakishly long, dark brown hair and gentle eyes. *I am married.*

She gave him a sidelong glance. "I thought you were going to some of the clubs that hosted after-work happy hours."

"I did for a while, but I didn't like it," he admitted. "Everyone seemed so plastic."

Vanessa smiled up at him. "I wouldn't worry so much if I were you. You have a lot going for—"

"Don't say it," he interrupted, returning her smile. "I know the line."

"If that's the case, then you have nothing to worry about."

He shifted his eyebrows. "That's what I keep telling myself."

"I'll talk to you later. I have to get to my office and see what's on my desk. If I'm out one day it seems as if I need three just to catch up."

"What did I say about GEA taking over your life?" Shane teased as he headed in the direction of the employee lounge.

Vanessa made her way down the carpeted hallway leading to her office. Shane wasn't entirely wrong about GEA taking over the lives of its employees. Many worked beyond their scheduled seven-hour workday. Their workplace was very conducive to spending many hours there.

All of the offices were large, with windows and vistas that looked out at the Sangre de Cristo Mountains, while the employee lounge was furnished with all of the latest electronic equipment including a large-screen television, a library stocked with popular magazines, daily newspapers from major U.S. cities and bestselling hardcover and paperback books. All of the building's employees were offered sizeable discounts at the health spa housed on the lower level, and most ate in the building's cafeteria, which offered a cross section of cuisine, including restricted diets and those for the health-conscious extremist.

Opening the door to her office, she was met with a space

which reflected her personality. Pieces of sculpture and artifacts from African-American and Native American cultures dotted the tables and shelves. A large cactus sat in a corner where bright sunlight lingered throughout most of the day once the vertical blinds were opened. Thickly-bound reports were stacked on a worktable behind her desk, along with a set of accounting manuals and binders containing updated government regulations. Nowhere in the office was there a photograph of Vanessa or any member of her family. She had made it a practice to never combine her personal life with her career.

Closing the door behind her, she tossed her handbag and tote on a comfortable, taupe-colored leather chair before she slipped out of her jacket and hung it in a closet concealed along a wall. A small clock on a side table chimed eight o'clock as she sat down to retrieve her telephone messages.

"Vanessa, this is Warren" came a soft voice she would recognize even if he failed to identify himself. "I've scheduled a meeting of my *key* people for tomorrow morning at nine-thirty. We will meet in my office rather than in the conference room."

She listened absentmindedly to the other messages as she mulled over the word *key*. What was Warren saying? That because Preston was out on a medical leave she was to fill in for him? Shrugging her shoulders, she replayed the other messages, scribbling notes on a legal pad. Whatever Warren wanted would be revealed at the nine-thirty meeting.

Vanessa met Lisabeth Nelson as she made her way toward Warren McDonald's office. "What's going on other than Preston's broken legs?" she asked the petite personnel director in a hushed voice.

Lisabeth shook her neatly braided head. She shifted her professionally arched eyebrows seconds before her dark brown eyes sparkled, and formed an attractive smile. "Your guess is as good as mine, Girlfriend. But you know Warren. He orders, and we snap to attention."

"You've got that right," Vanessa agreed, smiling.

The gleaming brass plate on the solid mahogany door with Warren's name and title silently acknowledged the man's rank in the corporate structure before one set eyes on him, and the size and furnishings in his magnificent office mirrored Warren McDonald's passion for luxury and the exotic. Remington bronzes and Chinese ivories only captured one's gaze briefly before a nine and one-half foot long and five-foot wide desk of rosewood and marble in the center of the rosewood floor demanded full attention.

The size of the table never ceased to overwhelm Vanessa, and rumor had it that a steel frame had been anchored into the floor to lend sufficient support for the heavy piece of furniture.

"Ah—the ladies are here," Warren announced in a softly modulated voice that belied his size and strength. He crossed the large room with a light swinging gait, again throwing one off guard with his two hundred forty pounds evenly distributed over a six-foot-five frame. His unlined dark face was as smooth as an oiled, African ebony mask. His equally dark eyes swept appreciatively over the women before he closed the door.

"Please have a seat," he offered, gesturing toward two empty leather chairs. Vanessa and Lisabeth murmured thanks and sat down.

It wasn't until Vanessa glanced around the room that she felt as if the space had shrunk. The walls seemed to close in on her. There were more than ten people in the expansive office, but there might as well have been only one. Her gaze fixed on the stoic face belonging to Joshua Kirkland!

It has to be him, a silent voice screamed; she was grateful that she was seated, because she doubted whether her trembling knees would support her body. How many men claimed a pair of eyes that could burn and freeze at the same time? And how many men claimed close-cut, silver hair that shimmered against mahogany brown skin layered with burnished gold? His gaze met hers and moved slowly over her face; nothing in his expression indicated that he'd seduced her and married her. It was as if they were strangers.

He was as elegantly dressed as she remembered, his light gray trousers falling at just the right break above his highly shined black imported loafers. The matching gray jacket hung with perfect precision on his broad shoulders, and she recognized his trademark Windsor-knotted tie under a spread collar, white shirt.

Vanessa let out a breath as Warren stood behind his desk, his hands clasped tightly behind his back. "There have been a lot of rumors floating around GEA over the past few months about mergers and restructuring, and I'd like to give you an update, as department heads.

"Firstly, I'd like to inform everyone that our own resident Bob Vila slash Martha Stewart, a.k.a. Preston Richards, has been hospitalized *again*. Preston will be placed on a medical leave for the remainder of the summer. Which brings me to the next announcement. Vanessa will be filling in for Preston as Acting Chief Financial Officer until his return."

There was a spattering of applause of approval as Vanessa focused her attention on Warren for the first time. So that *was* what he'd meant by *key*. She managed a tight smile.

"I suppose some of you are wondering who this gentleman is," Warren continued. "I met with the Board of Directors several months back, and the majority recommended that before GEA entertains a merger or downsizing we hire an expert on corporate efficiency. Joshua Kirkland is that expert. He will be meeting with each of you over the next two weeks, and I've assured him of your complete and absolute cooperation.

"Mr. Kirkland has been given your résumés along with evaluations, so he is aware of your strengths and weaknesses. I assured him that the weaknesses are few, otherwise you would not claim the distinction of being GEA employees. I've also given Mr. Kirkland your vacation schedules, so he'll work around the days when you'll be away from the office. Are there any questions?"

"Is he married?" Lisabeth whispered *sotto voce* without parting her lips.

Yes, he's married, Vanessa answered Lisabeth silently. *He's married to me!*

There was silence and a wagging of heads from the assembled. Most of the department supervisors were anxious to get back to their desks, where they were engaged in neverending races to complete forms and reports before impending deadlines.

Warren shrugged wide shoulders under his tailor-made suit jacket. "Thank you for your time."

Lisabeth grabbed Vanessa's ice cold fingers as they walked out of the CEO's office. "Can you believe that, Girlfriend? We finally get a man at GEA who could get a rise out of a dead woman, and the brother's an outside consultant. Damn! Talk about bad luck!"

Vanessa did not respond, but jerked her hand away. She wanted Lisabeth to stop talking.

Lisabeth gave her a sidelong glance. "What's wrong?"

She stared at Lisabeth. "Had you known that Warren was going to bring him in as a consultant?"

The personnel director shook her head. "It never came through my office. Why?"

How could she tell her that she knew the man in Warren's office? That the man who'd looked at her as if he'd never seen her had married her, then disappeared.

"I thought that as Personnel Director you would've known, that's all."

"You have to remember that GEA is still part of the Old Boy's Club. Just because I'm the only female department head, that doesn't made me privy to all of their decisions. Now that you're Acting CFO I'll have an ally."

"The word is *Acting.* I'll have to get used to the fact that I'm going to have to do Preston's job along with my own," she lied smoothly, trying to slow down her pounding heart. She had to get away from Joshua Kirkland. It was either that, or everyone would know she'd been fool enough to trust a stranger and marry him within a week of their meeting.

"How about lunch?" Lisabeth asked.

"I can't today."

"Tomorrow?"

"You're on. Make it late."

"One-thirty?"

"One-thirty it is," she confirmed, rushing down the corridor that would take her back to her own office.

Vanessa made it to the sanctuary of her office and closed the door. Walking across the room on shaking legs, she collapsed onto the chair behind her desk.

Why had he come to her? Why now, and not months before? And why had he pretended not to know her?

The uneasiness she had felt when she first met Joshua Kirkland returned. The fears and doubts she thought she had put to rest once she had agreed to marry him chilled her, despite the warm rays of the summer sun flooding the office through the expansive wall of glass.

In the brief seconds when their gazes met in Warren's office she had detected a distrust in Joshua. He'd known that she lived in Santa Fe and worked for Grenville-Edwards, and he had followed her. Why?

She covered her face with her hands. What she wanted to do was scream, scream out her fears, frustration, anger, and relief.

At least she now knew the lying, sneaky, duplicitous, immoral snake was alive and breathing! And if their marriage was still valid she wouldn't have to search him out in order to serve him with divorce papers.

There came a soft tapping on the door, and her hands fell away from her face. Within seconds she had composed herself. She rose from the chair and took a deep breath.

"Come in."

Joshua Kirkland stepped into her office and closed the door softly. His electric green eyes measured her reaction as she floated limply down to the chair, her fingers tightening noticeably on the armrests.

"Hello, Vanessa."

She stood up again, unable to believe that he'd sauntered into her office and greeted her like it was something he did every day.

"What the hell are you doing here?" She didn't recognize her own voice because it was so low and breathless. Leaning against the door, he crossed his arms over his chest. "Get out!" she ordered before he could answer her query.

His eyes hardened like cold stones, while a muscle twitched along his lean jaw. "Your boss already explained why I'm here."

"Get out of my office." There was no mistaking the coldness in her command.

He continued to stare at her, unblinking. "I'm leaving, but I want to caution you that *no one* is to know that we're married." His warning was issued in a quiet tone that froze her where she stood.

Her ringless fingers tightened into fists. "That should be easy, because it's true. We are *not* married."

His impassive expression did not change. "We are," he insisted as if she hadn't refuted it, "and we'll remain married until the end."

She moved away from the desk, took a few steps toward him, then stopped. "Until the end of what?"

Joshua stared at the woman he had fallen in love with, the woman he still loved beyond description. He wanted to go to her, hold her close, and bare the secrets he was sworn to hide from her.

For the second time he had promised his superiors that he would give them what they wanted: the person at Grenville-Edwards Aerospace passing classified military data *and* their missing two million dollars.

"Until the end of our lives," he said instead. Without giving her the opportunity to come back at him, he opened the door and walked out of her office.

Chapter 18

Vanessa stared at the door, struggling to control her runaway pulse. The man who had haunted her dreams was no apparition, but flesh and blood. His image had plagued her dreams—for the first time on the anniversary of their meeting in Mexico—and continued over the past two months. It was as if his spirit had called out and connected with hers while she slept.

She'd left Mexico, had successfully purged the memory of Joshua Kirkland and all that she'd shared with him, and focused all of her energies on her career and decorating her home. She joined her coworkers in many of their after-work social mixers, and dated several men she met at the building's health spa.

Joshua Kirkland had come into her life for a second time, but now she was better prepared. There would be no seduction, and she would make certain that there would be no marriage.

Returning to her desk, she picked up the telephone and dialed the receptionist's desk. The receptionist answered with the familiar, "GEA." There was a slight pause before she continued. "Good morning, Vanessa."

"Good morning, Anne. I want you to call everyone in Finance and have them meet me in Preston's office at eleven."

"Consider it done."

She replaced the receiver in its cradle, then picked it up again. Pressing a button for an outside line, she secured the number of St. Mary's Memorial Hospital and was connected to Preston Richards's room. The accident-prone accountant's voice was soft and slurred from the effects of a painkiller, and she ended the call in two minutes, promising Preston that she would come to see him during afternoon visiting hours.

Vanessa sat at a conference table in an alcove in Preston Richards's office with the four men and three women who made up the finance unit.

"I want to thank all of you for your promptness," she said, greeting them with a warm smile. "Warren has asked me to fill in for Preston until his return." She paused, watching the reactions on the faces of those sitting around the table. It was only a pulse beat, but she saw a myriad of expressions from shock to smug amusement.

"How long do you expect Preston to be out?" questioned Frank Stevenson.

"He'll be out for the entire summer." She studied Frank as a frown furrowed his lined forehead. The last time Preston had gone out on a medical leave *he* had assumed the CFO's workload.

"I assume you'll be doing Preston's work?"

Vanessa registered his passive hostility immediately. "Warren has appointed me as Acting CFO," she responded diplomatically. She knew the overzealous Frank would attempt to challenge her authority, but never Warren's.

Giving him a direct stare, she continued. "To ensure a smooth transition I will continue to handle the sub-contract budgets."

"Are you going to be able to manage both?" Shane questioned.

"Not efficiently," she replied honestly. "That's why I called this meeting. Shane, you'll assist me with contracts. Frank, you'll be responsible for direct supervision of everyone in our unit except George."

George Fender, along with Frank and Vanessa, was an assistant to the Chief Financial Officer, but he preferred to work alone. He made it a practice to lock himself in his office when he arrived, and did not emerge unless it was for a meeting or to go home. His work was accurate, his reports flawless. He had refused the position as Chief Financial Officer when the position had become available.

Vanessa's gaze swept around the table. "Instead of meeting monthly, we'll meet in this office every other Monday at eight. I'll need your vacation schedules, so I'll know how much to order for breakfast. I expect everyone to be on time and prepared to give an update on their projects. Any questions?"

George shook his head. "None from me."

She stood up and everyone rose with her. "Thank you for your cooperation."

Everyone filed leisurely out of the office, talking softly to one another. Only Shane remained.

Bracing a hip against the edge of the table, he crossed his arms over his chest and stared at Vanessa. "Warren's asking a lot from you."

She gave him a questioning look. "Did you say the same thing to Frank when he filled in for Preston last year?"

A slight flush crept up the young accountant's neck and spread to his hairline. "It has nothing to do with you being a woman."

Arching a delicate eyebrow, she glanced up at him from under her lashes. "Who mentioned gender?"

He glanced down at the floor. "Touché, Vanessa," he countered softly before returning and capturing her gaze. "I'm just concerned that you'll be taking on too much."

"It's only for a couple of months, and what I can't handle will be picked up by you and George."

"You know George and I don't work well together."

"Stop whining, Shane," she admonished in a soft tone. "George knows more than all of us collectively."

"He's paranoid," he mumbled.

"And Preston couldn't have picked a worse time of the year to go out on leave, because we're down one person and we'll have to contend with vacations. We'll do what we can, and if we can't finish during our normal workday, then I'll authorize and approve compensatory time for anyone who wants it."

He managed to look apologetic. "I'm willing to put in the extra time if you need me."

Vanessa gave the bookish Shane Sumners a gentle smile. "Thanks. It's comforting to know I can depend on you." He winked at her, then turned and walked out of the office.

She let out an audible sigh, shaking her head. She did not envy Preston's position as a department head. Not only was he responsible for a multi-billion-dollar budget, but he also had to contend with the various personalities and unpredictable mood swings of his subordinates. The old adage *You pay the cost to be the boss* elicited a smile from her. One thing she didn't want to be was *the boss*. At least not at GEA.

Glancing around Preston's office, she noted the systematic clutter. Bound reports were stacked in corners, and binders filled with financial statements covered every surface of his large desk. The only unencumbered space was a workstation claiming a computer and printer. The inside joke was that gadget-oriented Preston Richards was traumatized whenever he switched on a computer. He preferred to make manual entries on analysis sheets before he gave them to Shane to input them into the computer.

She returned to her own office and began mapping out what she needed to do to put her career and her private life in perspective. Drawing a line down the middle of a legal pad, she wrote down GEA and VB at the top. Under the column with her initials she listed: *call lawyer*—DIVORCE!!

* * *

Joshua sat in the office he'd been assigned for his tenure at GEA, staring out the window. The Santa Fe sky was cloud-free and a startling, pale blue. Rugged mountain peaks shimmered in the distance, and he was awed by the natural beauty of the rugged landscape. He now realized why Vanessa had not wanted to leave Santa Fe.

What she did not know was that he'd spent the last two months following her before making his presence known earlier that morning. Seeing her emerge from a popular downtown Santa Fe restaurant for the first time in almost a year had not prepared him for the turbulent emotions sweeping over his body like the rushing waters of a typhoon. What had shocked him more than seeing her mesmerizing smile was watching Vanessa press her lithe body against that of a tall man who couldn't take his gaze from her beautiful face.

He'd sat in the leased car, numbed, watching another man embrace his wife, watching as she smiled seductively at her date, and watching them disappear into the dark confines of a late model car and drive away.

Closing his eyes, he still could see the delicate bones that made up her fragile face, the sensual shape of her full lower lip, the natural, glossy blackness of the thick hair that she now wore in a more sophisticated style than the one she had affected in Mexico. It was shorter, the heavy strands straightened and blown out until blunt ends fell in perfect precision around the nape of her long, graceful neck.

When he had stepped into her office, the familiar scent of her perfume brought back vivid memories of their passionate love-making. In that brief moment he'd relived the texture and taste of her velvety skin when his fingers sculpted the supple lines of her body and his tongue had journeyed from her lips to the soles of her feet. He had come to know every inch of her body and revel in the pleasure he derived from her uninhibited responses whenever they had shared a bed and their bodies.

Opening his eyes, he continued to stare out the window, unseeing. He had spent almost a month in the hospital after the attempt on his life, then waited another nine months under house arrest before his activities in Mexico were reviewed by the Pentagon. The overwhelming success of Operation MESA overrode his being court-martialed, and he agreed to undertake the same mission: identify the person at Grenville-Edwards selling classified military components and recover the Defense Department's two million dollars.

His guise was that of a corporate efficiency expert, evaluating Grenville-Edwards Aerospace's position for a possible merger with another aerospace company in the northwest. This time he had been given sixty days to complete his mission instead of ten.

American officials had conducted an in-depth background investigation on Pablo Mendoza and had come up with nothing that might possibly connect the Oaxaca merchant to any subversive activities in Central America; it had also become apparent that Vanessa Blanchard had not made contact with a foreign agent during her trip to Mexico.

Joshua wanted to believe that his wife was not responsible for passing the classified data or for the missing monies, but his superiors did not want his opinion; they wanted the traitor *and* their money.

Turning away from the window, he glanced down at the vacation schedule on his desk, his gaze sweeping quickly over the names and dates. Vanessa had not indicated that she was taking a vacation during the months of July and August, and a satisfied smile softened his firm mouth. She would be available to him for the next sixty days.

He caught movement out of the corner of his eye and glanced up to find a petite blond woman standing in the doorway to his office. He recognized her immediately as Warren McDonald's private secretary.

Rising to his feet, he inclined his head. "Please come in."

Jenna Grant floated into the room with a controlled, exaggerated rolling of her narrow hips. Moistening her lips with the tip of her tongue, she smiled up at Joshua. "Warren wanted me to ask you if you needed anything. Supplies," she added when Joshua arched a questioning pale eyebrow.

"I could use a few hangers. There weren't any in the closet."

Jenna glanced at the suit jacket he had draped over the back of a chair before her gaze roamed leisurely over his stark white shirt tucked into the waistband of his tailored trousers. "Hangers, and what else?"

Crossing his arms over his chest, he stared down at the woman. Jenna Grant was deceptively beautiful. Her naturally blond hair was cut in a flattering style in which a flaxen wave fell over her forehead and partially concealed one of her brilliant emerald green eyes. He knew most of her face had been surgically reconstructed after a head-on automobile accident had mangled her features three years before. He'd learned more than he wanted to know about GEA employees after reading their personnel histories.

"That's all I can come up with at this time," he replied.

"Warren said that I should handle your correspondence until he assigns someone to you for your exclusive use."

"How would you prefer that I give you my correspondence—on tape, or direct dictation?"

Jenna smiled, revealing a mouth filled with dazzling porcelain crowns. "Direct dictation."

He nodded again. "I'll check with Warren on how we'll divide your time."

"Would you want me to order lunch for you?"

"That won't be necessary. I'll pick up something from the building cafeteria."

"They deliver," Jenna informed him.

"That's all right." He wanted to get out of the office and observe as much of the day-to-day activities of GEA's administrative staff as he could. He wanted to match faces with names and job titles.

Jenna gestured to the workstation positioned to the left of his desk. "You'll need your own password if you want to log on to our computer system. Once you choose one you should give it to me for our master log."

"It's VOWS. V-O-W-S," he spelled slowly when she stared at him with a blank expression.

Jenna repeated it to herself, then asked, "As in marriage vows?"

Joshua's eyes paled. "Precisely." The single word reverberated throughout the space like the crack of a rifle. He stared at Jenna until she dropped her gaze, then turned his back.

Staring at the width of his broad shoulders and slim waist, Jenna realized that he had dismissed her without a word. Shrugging her shoulders, she turned and walked out of his office.

This was only the second time that she had come face-to-face with Joshua Kirkland, and what she had observed and admired the first time reinforced the promise she'd made to herself: she would marry before the end of the year. She had recently celebrated her thirty-fifth birthday, and while she viewed all single men as potential husbands there were but a select few that she seriously considered pursuing. Joshua Kirkland had become one of the few.

An expression of amusement softened Joshua's features as he turned back and stared at the empty doorway. The company rumor mill was filled with gossip about Jenna Grant's flirtatious behavior. If she had actually been flirting with him it was subtle. Charmingly subtle.

Chapter 19

Vanessa walked slowly down a corridor of St. Mary's Memorial Hospital's fourth floor, searching for Preston's room in the wing designated for orthopedic cases. Finding the room number, she glanced inside. Preston lay on one of the two beds, both his legs elevated by a hoist.

"Can I get a dance?" she teased, making her way into the room.

Preston Richards's bruised and swollen face split with a wide grin. "Get my shoes and I'm all yours."

Sitting down on a chair beside the bed, she grasped his hand. Preston was forty-eight, but appeared years younger. He was a small man, standing only five-foot six and weighing less than one hundred thirty pounds, but what he lacked in girth and height he compensated for with his mathematical aptitude. Vanessa had known him to do complicated equations in his head. "How are you feeling?"

Preston ran a free hand over his straight, dark brown hair,

frowning. "I'd feel a helluva lot better if I could get out of this place and get back to work."

"How long do they plan to keep you?"

"The doctor who set my legs said I should be out in a week. But there's talk about me having to go to a rehab center for physical therapy."

Vanessa's dark eyes met Preston's equally dark ones. "Did Warren talk to you?"

Preston shook his head. "Each time he called I wasn't able to talk to him. Why do you ask?"

She didn't want to be the one to tell Preston that he wasn't expected to come back to work until after Labor Day, but she wasn't allowed an option. She had to find out what he was working on.

"What's going on at GEA, Vanessa?"

Withdrawing her hand, she stared at his legs encased in plaster. "Warren has authorized you to take a two-month medical leave. He's asked me to fill in as Acting Chief Financial Officer until you return."

Her supervisor's eyelids fluttered wildly before they closed. All of the natural color drained from his face, leaving it as white as the pillowcase cradling his head. "I should've expected this. Warren wants me out."

Rising from the chair, Vanessa sat on the side of the hospital bed and leaned over to drop a light kiss on his bruised cheek. "Preston, please. Warren doesn't want you out any more than I want your title." His eyes opened and he studied her face. "I like handling our contract companies."

He smiled. "You're very good at what you do."

She returned the smile. "I know that." There was a hint of modesty in her admission.

Inhaling and letting out his breath audibly, Preston shook his head slowly. "You're going to be up to your eyeballs with closing out the fiscal year, Vanessa. All contracted budgets expire on June thirtieth, which means you're going to have to close out fifty-seven direct manufacturers and your own sub-contracts."

She winced. "How many have you begun?"

"I've completed twelve. They were the ones who spent all of their monies before their year end. In between preparing new budgets for the upcoming contract year I've been working on the corporate projection for next year. With all of the talk about a merger, I promised Warren that I'd have it to him before the middle of July."

She thought about Shane's warning that she would be taking on a lot of work. "Is the projection a priority?"

"The highest," he admitted. "The consultant will need it when he comes on board."

"He's on board."

"When did this happen?"

"This morning." She gave Preston a long, penetrating look. "Why didn't you tell me that we were bringing in an outside consultant?"

"Warren wanted it kept confidential."

"But why?"

"I don't know, Vanessa. I suppose he had his reasons."

They spent the next quarter of an hour outlining all that needed to be done before Preston was to return, he reassuring Vanessa that he would be available to her whenever she needed assistance.

It was nearly three o'clock when she finally glanced at her watch. The attorney who handled all of her legal affairs was expected to return her call at three-thirty.

Reassuring Preston that she would come to see him the following day, she kissed his cheek and rushed out of the hospital.

She made it back to GEA within fifteen minutes, and after parking her car in the underground garage she took the elevator to the seventh floor.

As she walked out of the elevator she came face-to-face with Joshua Kirkland. His cold gaze wouldn't permit her to move.

Somewhere, somehow, she found her voice. "Yes, Mr. Kirkland?"

"I need to meet with you, Miss Blanchard."

"When?"

"Now."

"I can't," she shot back.

"I'm expecting an important call."

"Let your voice-mail pick it up," he countered.

"I need to speak to this person."

"The only person you need to speak to right now is *me*."

Vanessa saw Anne watching her, and knew that the reception- ist had overheard every word of their exchange. She swallowed hard, trying valiantly not to reveal her anger. Joshua had delib- erately humiliated her in front of one of her subordinates.

Raising her chin in a gesture of defiance, she said, "Let me put my handbag away."

"Bring it with you," he ordered. He walked in the direction of his office, not glancing over his shoulder. It was obvious he expected her to follow him.

Anne shook her head and raised her hands in a gesture that signaled hopelessness. Vanessa managed a tight smile as she walked down the hall to Joshua's office.

He stood at the door and allowed her to proceed him before he followed her and closed the door. "Please have a seat, Miss Blanchard."

Vanessa rounded on him. "I'd rather stand, thank you."

He closed the distance between them until they were standing less than a foot apart. He stood close enough for her to feel the whisper of his warm breath on her face.

"Don't *ever* challenge me like that again, Vanessa. I'm here to do a job, the same way you're here to do your job."

Her temper flared. "I won't challenge you if you don't order me about. A request is not only more professional, but I also find it just as effective."

"I don't have time to court, woo, placate, or mollify. I have less than two months to conclude who should be retained at GEA and who will be let go with a generous severance award. Let me know now if you're ready for an early retirement."

Her fingers tightened into fists. "You wouldn't!" she gasped as a threat of hysteria rose in her throat.

"I would." The two words were cold and exacting.

Vanessa floundered in a maelstrom of despair. Who was he, this man, this stranger, who seemed intent on disrupting her life? How had she thought she loved him? How had she lain with him, then married him?

"You're a sick monster, Joshua Kirkland."

He recoiled as if she'd slapped him. *I'm a soldier, not a monster,* he screamed silently at her. He was only following orders. But he wanted to disobey those orders and take her in his arms and love her until time stood still for both of them.

Successfully concealing his anguish, he smiled down at her angry expression. "There was a time when you said that you'd love me forever."

Vanessa was stunned by the shift in his mood. First he'd threatened to have her fired, then he caught her off balance by acknowledging the unspoken bond between them.

A brittle smile parted her lips. "I lied, Joshua," she whispered. "There's a time for love, and a time for letting go. And the time for my letting go came the day you walked out on me."

The fingers of his left hand locked around her upper arm. "Sit down." Steering her over to the chair beside his desk, he eased her down on it.

Joshua removed his jacket and hung it up in the closet before returning to sit down behind the desk; his gaze captured hers and held. She looked thinner, fragile, while still appearing ardently fragrant and utterly sensual. She was the woman he'd fallen in love with and continued to love; she was his wife, his partner, and he was forced to interact with her as if they were strangers; she was the woman who had haunted his dreams and his days for more than a year, and she was the woman he would willingly forfeit his own life to keep safe.

"I need an overview of your people, including their job titles and functions."

She noticed a file on his desk with Shane's name typed on the tab. "Do you want to begin with Shane Sumners?"

The charcoal gray lashes bordering his luminous eyes concealed them from view when he glanced down at the file atop a stack of others from the Finance Unit.

His head snapped up. "No. I'd like to begin with you. I want to know *everything* you've done since your first day at GEA."

Everything in her manner was detached as she related the information he had asked for. Not once did he pick up a pen to make a notation on a blank pad next to the folders, and she suspected that perhaps he was secretly recording their session.

Joshua interrupted her once when he excused himself and called Jenna to have an order of iced tea delivered to his office. She was grateful for the delay. She stood up and paced the length of the office while tugging at the earring in her right lobe as he waited for the tea.

He watched her pace, silently admiring her well-formed legs and remembering the first time he'd noticed their incredible length—when she strode across the lobby of La Mérida in Mexico City. He had sought to set a trap for her, and instead of becoming the hunter he'd become the prey.

"Are you all right, Vanessa?"

The deep, rich resonant sound of his voice stopped her, and she glanced over at him. "I'm fine."

"Why are you pacing?"

"I pace when I'm thinking."

"I never noticed you doing that before."

"That's because I didn't do much thinking. All I did was react."

She watched him as he rose to his feet and moved toward her. The motion was so fluid, effortless, that one moment he was sitting and then he was standing close to her. The heat and the scent of his body washed over her, and she was lost, lost in the memory of the man who had seduced her with a passion that robbed her of her common sense.

"Don't," she breathed out even though he hadn't touched her.

Leaning in to her, he whispered, "Why don't you ask me, Angel?"

Closing her eyes, she let out her breath in a long shudder. "Ask you what?"

"Why I left you." Her eyes opened and she stared at him. "Ask me," he taunted in a hoarse whisper.

"Why—" The question was left unspoken when there was a soft knock on the door.

Joshua made his way to the door at the same time Vanessa sat down on a leather love seat. He opened it and Jenna strode in carrying a small, white plastic shopping bag.

"I had them put the sugar and lemon on the side," she reported cheerfully.

He took the bag from her, glancing at the receipt stapled to its side. Withdrawing several bills from his trouser pocket, he handed them to her. "Thank you."

Flashing a winning smile, she wiggled across the room. Just as she neared the door, she noticed Vanessa. Her smile vanished quickly and a hard line settled around her pouting mouth, marring her perfect features. Jenna closed the door, but not before Joshua registered her sudden shift in attitude.

He turned his attention to Vanessa as she stood up. "Would you like some tea?"

"No, thank you."

"I have enough for two."

"I don't like iced tea."

"Why didn't you tell me that when I had Jenna order it?"

"Forget it, Joshua. I'd like us to finish up here so I can get back to my office."

He noticed the strained tone in her voice and decided to relent. He had taken up more than an hour of her time with the pretense that he wanted to know what she did at GEA. That information he had gleaned from her evaluations.

"We'll continue this tomorrow."

"At what time?"

"At a time that is convenient for *you,* Vanessa."

She gave him a slow smile and Joshua sucked in his breath. He had waited months to see her smile at him, and now that she had he feared losing control.

"I'll call you as soon as I set up my schedule for tomorrow."

"Call Jenna. She'll be scheduling my meetings for me."

They stood staring at each other, their chests rising and falling in unison until Vanessa broke the spell. "Good afternoon, Joshua."

He inclined his head, escorted her to the door and watched her until she walked down the hall and disappeared from his line of vision.

An hour with her hadn't been enough. What he wanted was a lifetime.

Vanessa stared at the neatly handwritten figures on Preston's spreadsheets. She had spent the last two hours entering them into her computer. She'd had to correct several entries because she couldn't rid her head of the sound of Joshua's resonant voice taunting her when he urged her to ask him why he'd left her.

Whatever his reason, it no longer mattered, because she had returned her attorney's call and had set up an appointment to meet with him at the end of the week to begin divorce proceedings.

The tiny numbers on the monitor began blurring before her eyes and she knew it was time to quit. She stored what she entered on a disk and reached for her handbag for the key to a file cabinet.

The drawer where she usually stored her handbag was empty. Anxiety spurted through her as she looked around the office. Where could she have left it?

Don't panic, she told herself. She mentally retraced her steps.

She had it when she left the hospital, because she could not have driven her car without her keys.

She had left it in Joshua's office. "Dammit!" she ground out between clenched teeth. It was after six, and she prayed he hadn't left and locked her bag in his office.

She left her office quickly, rushing toward his. Only recessed lights glowed in the reception area and the doors to many of the offices were closed, indicating that most of the GEA staff had left for the day.

Light spilled out onto the champagne-colored carpeting outside Joshua's office, and she breathed a sigh of relief. He was still working.

He glanced up as she walked into the room. He appeared totally relaxed. His tie hung loosely around his unbuttoned collar. He had removed the cuff links from his shirt and rolled back the cuffs.

Leaning to his right behind the desk, he straightened and held up her black, patent leather shoulder bag. "Are you perhaps looking for this?"

Vanessa pressed her hands over her pounding heart. "Yes, thank you."

He rose to his feet, her bag dangling from his forefinger. "Now what do I get for taking such good care of this for you?"

Her mind refused to register the significance of his words as she reached for her handbag, only to have him pull it out of her reach.

"I thanked you," she spat out.

He grinned at her, shaking his head. "I don't want your thanks."

A wave of heat flooded her face. "What do you want?"

Wrapping the strap tightly around his fist, he moved over to the door and closed it, then let the bag slide down to the carpet. Pressing his back to the door to prevent her escaping him, he extended his arms.

"I'll take a hug for starters."

Crossing her arms over her chest, she shot him a cold look. "No."

Joshua crossed his arms over his chest in a similar gesture. "Are you telling me that you'd rather spend the night here with me instead of going home?"

Her eyes narrowed. "Get away from that door."

"Or what? You'll scream?" He gave her a sly smile. "Don't bother, Angel, because everyone's gone home."

Her arms fell to her sides. "I could dial nine one one."

"And tell the police that your husband asked that you hug him?"

"How many times do I have to tell you that you are not my husband?"

All evidence of Joshua's teasing evaporated. "Have you divorced me, Vanessa?"

"Not yet," she threatened.

His eyes paled until they seemed devoid of color, and a shiver wracked her until she couldn't stop her legs from shaking. He stepped away from the door at the same time she reached for her handbag. Moving with the speed of a bird in flight, he caught her arms and pulled her up close to his body.

"Let me remind you that until the divorce *is* final you're still *my* wife."

He didn't give her the chance to refute him as his head came down and he claimed her mouth with the power of a volcano ripping the earth asunder. The cruel ravishment of his mouth mirrored his frustration, but it lessened as she moaned under the sensual assault.

Vanessa clung to Joshua like a drowning swimmer. The pain and distrust she'd carried for a year was propelled to the back of her mind while her heart sang with the renewal of passion racing out of control throughout her body.

His searching tongue challenged her mouth, thrusting forcibly until her lips parted. Her knees buckled and he tightened his grip, supporting her sagging body. Nothing had changed. His kisses still had the power to make her weak in her knees.

"No," she pleaded, trying to escape his marauding mouth.

Pulling back, Joshua stared down at her eyes, which were filling with tears. "I didn't want to leave you," he confessed. "I would never leave you."

Vanessa blinked back the tears threatening to overflow and stain her face. "But why did you?"

"Someone mugged me."

His grip on her loosened and she stepped out of his embrace. "Where? How?"

"In San Miguel. I was stabbed and left for dead."

He'd said it so matter-of-factly that she couldn't believe him. Her eyes widened as she watched him pull the hem of his shirt from his trousers and unbutton it so that his chest and torso were exposed. A thin pale line, running from belly to breastbone, marred the smooth, golden brown flesh.

Bile rose in her throat and she clapped her free hand over her mouth and swallowed painfully. Breathing heavily, she whispered, "Why didn't you tell me? Why didn't you come to me?"

"I couldn't come to you until now," he answered honestly. He had been ordered not to contact her until his cover had been established. He was forced to wait thirteen months to come to her, and after kissing her he knew the wait had been worth it.

"What happened to the man who attacked you?"

"The authorities caught him."

What he couldn't tell her was that the two men who had attacked him were apprehended by Mexican police during Operation MESA. The hired killers were contracted by a rogue senior U.S. DEA agent who knew Joshua Kirkland had planned the dates, sites and times of the drug sweep. Jorgé Martín resisted capture and died from his injuries before he was to return to the States for prosecution.

Her face clouded with uneasiness. "What's going to happen now?"

"To us?"

She nodded. "Yes."

"If you want a divorce I won't contest it."

Vanessa tried to force her flustered emotions into some semblance of order, like her column of numbers. But the events in her life hadn't added up as easily as her financial statements. "And if I decide not to go through with it. What then?"

"You have two months to decide," he replied cryptically.

"Why two months?"

"I'll be finished with my assignment. After that we'll be able to live openly as husband and wife."

Her brow furrowed. "Why not now?"

"I uncovered an arcane clause in GEA's personnel policy. Members of the same family cannot be employed simultaneously."

"You're saying that our marriage would constitute a violation of this clause?"

"Yes."

She lifted her chin and met his direct stare. "What do you want to do, Joshua?"

"What I *don't* want is a divorce."

What he was offering her was a chance to heal, to trust, and to become whole again. They had been given a sixty-day reprieve.

But should she accept it? Could she afford to believe him and wait? She'd waited a week for him to return to Oaxaca. The week became a month, the month two, then thirteen. She had waited thirty-three years to become a wife, and now, at thirty-four, she had to wait a second time. She had succumbed to Joshua's seduction before—it would not happen again.

"I'll meet with my attorney and have him draw up the papers. I'll also instruct him *not* to file them until I authorize him to do so," she offered as a compromise. "If our marriage is worth saving, then there won't be a divorce."

"And if it isn't, Vanessa?"

"Then I won't wait the two months."

Joshua felt as if he'd won a small victory. He had gotten her to delay filing for a divorce. He'd almost lost her once, and he'd make certain it would never happen again.

Leaning down, he pressed a kiss to her silken cheek. "This will be the last time I'll ever touch you at Grenville-Edwards Aerospace."

She nodded, praying silently for the two months to pass quickly.

Chapter 20

Vanessa opened the door of her house to the ringing of the telephone. She was tempted to let voice mail pick up the message, but changed her mind.

Reaching for the receiver, she picked it up before it switched over. "Hello."

"How was your day, Beautiful?"

Berating herself for answering the telephone, Vanessa recognized the silken male voice coming through the receiver. She'd gone out with Stanton Reid a half dozen times in three months and they continued to see each other, though both knew their liaison would never progress beyond friendship.

She didn't want to talk to Stanton—not now. Not when her head was filled with conflicting issues regarding *her husband*. Regardless of how much she denied it or protested, Joshua Kirkland was legally still her husband.

"Long."

There came a sensual chuckle. "I take that to mean that it wasn't good."

"It was tiring, Stanton."

"If that's the case, then I'll keep this brief. Are you available for Saturday evening? My brother is throwing a little something for his wife's fortieth birthday, and he wanted me to bring someone."

Dropping her handbag and leather tote onto the small round table, she cradled the telephone receiver between her shoulder and chin. "I don't know," she replied honestly. She'd planned to go into GEA to get a head start on Preston's corporate budget projection.

"When will you know?"

"To be frank with you, I don't know. I have to go into the office on Saturday, and I have no idea how long I'll be there."

"All work and no play make for a dull Vanessa," Stanton teased.

"The last time we went out you told me I was very exciting."

"And you're that, and more. What if I play it by ear and call you around six? If you're up to it, then we'll go. If not—no problem."

"Okay," she conceded.

"I'll talk to you Saturday."

"Bye, Stanton."

She hung up the phone, kicked off her low-heeled, black, patent leather shoes and headed for the staircase leading up to her bedroom. What she needed was time to think and time to relax, and she could do both quite well in a tub filled with soothing bath crystals.

Within minutes she'd stripped off her clothes, filled the over-sized sunken bathtub with warm water and a profusion of redolent lavender crystals, and stepped into the tub amid an extravagance of silken bubbles.

Resting her head on a large sponge bath pillow, she closed her eyes, still seeing Joshua's image looming behind her lids. What was it about him that made her doubt her own sanity?

There was no doubt that she'd been attracted to him at first sight, and that the intensity of attraction had escalated with each day she spent with him. But a week was hardly enough time to know him or develop the enduring trust that is one of the hallmarks of love. What she had done was mistake love for attachment, or for the hope of fulfilling a fantasy.

She had prepared herself to marry Kenneth, but when that hadn't manifested she had substituted Joshua for Kenneth. She smiled. There was no real mistaking the two men, because they were complete opposites—in and out of bed.

Why, she continued to ask herself, had Joshua confessed his love for her within days of their meeting, and why had he proposed marriage? A marriage he still did not want to end in divorce. Was it possible that he actually loved her?

Opening her eyes, she stared at the brass fixtures along the outer ledge of the bathtub. She'd lost Joshua in Oaxaca, and he'd come to her in Santa Fe. But why hadn't he come to her before he presented himself in Warren's office?

She hadn't known whether it was shock or rage that had rendered her speechless when she saw him for the first time in more than a year. Whatever it was she had remained in control, enough control to give her the opportunity to assume a role where everyone would believe that she and Joshua were strangers.

Vanessa had to be honest with herself—did she still love Joshua? Could she love him enough to give their marriage a second chance?

Vanessa headed toward the cafeteria to order breakfast before going up to her office. She'd slept fitfully throughout the night, her dreams filled with images of the days and nights she had spent in Mexico. The dreams were not reminiscent of the ones she experienced before Joshua walked back into her life, but were fraught with erotic visions of their passionate lovemaking. The recollections were vivid enough to wake her, and she lay waiting until her traitorous body quieted with the ebbing passion. She waited until the sky brightened with the beginning of a new day and left her bed, deciding to go in to work early.

As she walked into the cafeteria she spied him immediately. He sat facing the entrance, but he wasn't alone. His head was tilted at an angle as he listened intently to what Jenna Grant was saying. His rapt expression indicated that he was enthralled by whatever she was telling him as her fingers rested on the sleeve of his suit jacket.

Vanessa stared, experiencing a range of confusing emotions. Was she to stand by and watch another woman openly flirt with her husband and not react? She remembered Lisabeth's rejoinder when Warren had introduced Joshua. *Is he married?*

Her husband. For the first time in more than a year she thought of him that way. At that moment she realized she still wanted him—as her husband.

Making her way to the counter where trays of breakfast foods were lined up, she picked up a plastic container and filled it with sliced seasonal fruits. Moving along the counter, she filled cups with orange juice and coffee. The cashier greeted her with a bright smile, rang up her purchases, bagged them, and chatted incessantly about the beautiful weather they were experiencing.

Vanessa had to agree with her, although she hadn't taken full advantage of it. She had to find a way to take her vacation in days, despite her increased work schedule. Even if it meant working longer hours during the week, she needed to take some time off and get away from GEA, where she wouldn't be constantly reminded of the man who had seduced her and continued to seduce her, with just his presence.

She made it to her office without encountering anyone and closed the door firmly behind her. Switching on the computer, she entered her password and waited for it to boot up between bites of fruit and sips of coffee and juice. Then she began the onerous task of entering Preston's figures from his spreadsheets.

The buzzing sound of the intercom startled her, and she jumped. Glancing at the clock on a side table, Vanessa realized she had been working steadily for more than ninety minutes.

Swiveling on her chair, she pushed a button on the telephone console. "Yes?"

"Warren wanted me to remind you that you're late for this morning's meeting."

Vertical lines formed between her eyes as her gaze swept over the large calendar on her desk. "I don't have anything down for this morning, Jenna."

"Aren't you filling in for Preston?"

Mumbling an oath under her breath, Vanessa realized that she hadn't checked with Preston for his listing of regularly scheduled meetings.

"Tell Warren I'm on my way."

It was only her second day as Acting CFO and she was going to be late for a meeting. And how, she thought as she saved the numbers she had put into the computer, was she going to make her deadlines if she spent all her time at meetings? Gathering a pad, pen, and the keys for her office, she headed for Warren's.

Jenna flashed Vanessa a facetious smile as she neared her. "I just want to let you know that Warren is on the warpath."

She shot the flirtatious woman a derisive half-grin. "Thanks for the warning."

What she wanted to tell the secretary was that she'd seen Warren in the full throes of his celebrated temper, and not once had she ever felt threatened. What unnerved her more was the silent rage she'd occasionally glimpsed in Joshua Kirkland. The paling of his eyes and the stillness in his body never failed to cause a shiver of caution within her. Something unknown, unspoken, communicated that he was more than he'd presented to her.

She walked into the opulent office, noting that the thunderous expression on Warren McDonald's dark brown face vanished as his gaze swept over her.

Warren stood up and came around his desk to greet her. "In case you're not aware of it, Preston and I usually meet at nine-thirty every Wednesday morning."

Vanessa smiled. "Are there any other meetings I should know about?"

He cupped her elbow and led her over to a love seat in an alcove facing a wall of windows. "Check with Jenna and she'll fill you in." He seated Vanessa, then dropped down beside her.

She looked at Warren beneath lowered lashes, wondering why she had not succumbed to the man's overall captivating manner. He was in his mid-fifties, and appeared more virile and appealing than men half his age. His large, powerful-looking body was magnificent, his dusky skin smooth, and his short, cropped hair was liberally sprinkled with gray. His dark eyes were clear and sharp, always assessing everything and everyone quickly.

He stared at her profile, his gaze caressing her hair and body before returning to her face. "How are you holding up with the additional workload?"

Turning her head, Vanessa stared at him staring back at her. "I don't know yet. I'm coming in early and staying late. Preston told me that you need next year's budget projections before the middle of next month, so that has become a priority for me."

"Let me see if I can't get an extension for you." Leaning over to a side table, he pushed a button on an intercom. "Jenna, please tell Kirkland that I'd like to see him in my office."

Vanessa bit down on her lower lip in frustration. She didn't want to see Joshua again—not after seeing him with Jenna in the cafeteria earlier that morning.

Her mental objections were ignored when he entered Warren's office and stared at her seated beside Warren. His gaze shifted to the other man's arm stretched out over the back of the love seat.

"Have a seat, Kirkland," Warren ordered, pointing to a side chair several feet from where he sat with Vanessa.

Joshua complied, draping one leg elegantly over a knee. Dark brown socks with minute tan checks complemented his tan slacks and brown, Spanish cordovan slip-ons. His gaze shifted leisurely from Warren McDonald to his wife. Jenna had been more than willing to suggest that Warren was in love with Vanessa. Judging by the older man's body language Joshua concluded that the chatty Jenna was right.

Warren squared his wide shoulders under the finely woven fabric of his custom-made shirt and smiled at Joshua. "What is the *very* latest possible date you'll have to have the budget projections?"

The arching of one pale eyebrow was the only change in Joshua's impassive expression. "I thought you had committed to July tenth."

"I know," Warren conceded, "but Vanessa may need more time."

Joshua stared at Vanessa. "How much more?"

Vanessa calculated quickly. It would take her at least a week to transfer Preston's figures to the computer, and another week to put together three, six, nine, and twelve-month projections.

"An additional week."

Joshua crossed his arms over his chest. "You're asking the impossible. I can give you three days, but not a week. "I must have it by July thirteenth, or—"

"I'll submit it to you by the *thirteenth*," Vanessa interrupted. She swallowed and tried successfully not to reveal her annoyance. Turning back to Warren, she gave him a warm, inviting smile. "I need your approval for my vacation schedule. I'd like to take Mondays and Fridays off during the months of July and August."

Warren stared down at her, his gaze softening. "Take whatever time you need."

"Thank you," she countered softly.

"Miss Blanchard?"

Vanessa's head swung around and she stared at Joshua. There was no mistaking the sudden chill in his voice when he'd said her name. Her gaze narrowed as she tilted her chin in a defiant gesture. "Yes, Mr. Kirkland."

"I'd like to know why you're taking time off, while asking in the same breath for an extension for the budget projections."

She took his chiding tone as a personal affront. It was the second time he'd humiliated her in front of a co-worker, this time in the presence of her boss.

"*Mr. Kirkland,* do you really think I would not have factored in my days' off when I projected submitting the budget projections?" The air in the office was suffocating as she glared at Joshua.

Warren missed the undercurrent of stinging tolerance between the two other occupants. "Jenna's typing a memo that will go out to everyone in our administrative office before the end of the day. There's been a lot of uneasiness about the impending merger, and I want to put everyone at ease by inviting them to my home next Saturday evening for what could be termed as an extended staff meeting." He smiled at Joshua. "It will also give you an up close and personal look at everyone in a more relaxed setting."

"Is this a mandatory staff meeting?" Vanessa questioned as a slight frown marred her smooth forehead.

Warren nodded, amusement inching the corners of his mouth upward. "I'd say so. The only other requirement is that everyone bring their spouse or significant other."

Feeling the heat from Joshua's gaze on her face, she refused to look at him at the mention of spouse. She would attend Warren's dinner party, but not with her husband. She would ask Stanton to escort her.

"Will you need me for anything else?" Joshua asked Warren. He wanted to get out of the office and away from Warren McDonald. It disturbed him to see Vanessa doing to Warren what she'd done to him the night he met her at La Mérida. She was silently seducing the CEO.

"No. And thank you for your time."

Joshua stood up and walked out of the room without saying another word, leaving Vanessa staring at his retreating back. Was their marriage worth saving, when they were at each other's throats each time they met? It was obvious they could never work together, and she wondered if they would ever be able to live together.

Chapter 21

"I don't like what's going on around GEA," Lisabeth Nelson complained softly as she leaned over the table at the restaurant where she and Vanessa usually shared lunch. "People are coming into my office asking if they're going to be laid off. And now we get a memo from Warren mandating that we come to a party at his house next week. I see it as a gesture to fatten the calf before it's slaughtered for the feast."

Vanessa pushed the contents of her plate around with a fork. She had eaten two forkfuls of her salad before feeling full. Glancing up at her dining partner, she shook her head. "None of us know what our future is going to be. If this merger doesn't go through this time, there's always a possibility of another in the future."

Lisabeth stared at Vanessa, her eyes narrowing slightly. "Do you know something I don't?"

She shook her head. "I know what you know."

"Joshua Kirkland has everyone spooked."

The mention of his name garnered Vanessa's complete attention. "What about him?"

"He intends to personally interrogate every employee. If there is one thing I do know, it's that every employee of GEA is loyal and competent."

"What is he trying to ascertain using this method?"

"Assess everyone's efficiency," Lisabeth replied.

"I don't know about manufacturing, but we in administration are unquestionably overworked and understaffed."

"There's no waste in manufacturing, either."

"Then what does he want?" Vanessa felt it strange that she could discuss her husband so objectively.

"I asked him the same thing, and he said that when he offers GEA to this other company he wants to make certain there's no excess fat. And if he has to, he will streamline GEA to the point where it can almost run itself without employees." Lisabeth paused and took a sip of sparkling water. "The scary part was that he was smiling when he said that. There was this half-smile on his lips, but his eyes were cold as ice. I didn't wait to hear any more. I ran the hell out of his office as fast as I could. Warren will have to fire me for insubordination if Joshua Kirkland ever calls me back to his office."

Vanessa knew what Lisabeth was talking about. She'd seen the cold stare from Joshua often enough to know how intimidating it could be. "There are always losers with mergers, and it seems as if it's the little guys who lose. Top-heavy CEOs never have to give up anything."

Lisabeth's dark brown gaze was fixed on her dining partner's face. "I don't think you'll have anything to worry about. Human resource specialists are a lot easier to replace than an accountant with your experience."

"Don't sell yourself short, Lisabeth. You wouldn't be where you are at GEA if you weren't good. You of all people should know about the Old Boy's Club."

She smiled. "Well, it's not as if I don't have other options. I could always move back to Atlanta and marry Tyrone."

"You wouldn't!"

"Why not," Lisabeth said glibly. "How many sisters have a brother calling them across the country and proposing marriage at least once a month?"

Vanessa laughed, shaking her head. "You've got a point."

Lisabeth sobered. "What about you, Vanessa? What are you going to do if you're laid off? We're in different financial positions. I don't have a mortgage to pay each month."

How could she tell her friend that the threat of being laid off did not trouble her? That she would sell her house before she lost it? That she had family in Santa Fe who would take her in? That she was married to a man who owned a home on the island of Jamaica and another residence in Palm Beach? That she was certain Joshua would take care of all of her financial needs?

"I don't know," she replied as honestly as she could.

"Enough about GEA," Lisabeth said cheerfully. "Who are you bringing to Warren's soirée?"

"I'll ask Stanton. How about yourself?"

"I'll probably come with Otis Nichols."

Vanessa shifted her eyebrows. "I thought you had stopped seeing him."

Lisabeth made an attractive *moue*. "I felt sorry for the poor fool when he came down with chicken pox at thirty-six, and I played Florence Nightingale. There was a serious epidemic at his school this past spring, and he caught it from the kids."

Both of them laughed, relieving the solemn mood, and concentrated on enjoying their lunch.

Vanessa returned to her office and retrieved her voice mail. There was a message from her sister, reminding her that she was to attend her six-year-old nephew's birthday party on Sunday afternoon at four.

Checking her appointment book, she noted the entry. Connie

would never forgive her if she missed her own godson's birthday. She made a notation to pick up the video game Eric had not so subtly hinted that he wanted.

She spent the remainder of the afternoon behind her door entering numbers. Taking time out to call Preston, she promised she would come to see him the following day, reassuring him that his unit was operating smoothly in his absence, and that she would keep him updated on everything.

It wasn't until she pulled out of the underground garage hours later that she thought about what she would tell Connie when she saw her on Sunday. She had to let her sister know that Joshua was in Santa Fe, and that they were working together. Connie would think she was crazy. There were several times over the past year that she had doubted her own sanity.

She maneuvered through downtown Santa Fe traffic, leaving the business district behind, and drove for several miles before she realized she was being followed. The car was so far behind her that she couldn't identify the driver. Whoever was driving knew how much distance to keep between the two automobiles.

It was nearly eight o'clock and dusk was descending, making it difficult to see the driver's face clearly. She recognized the black car as a Saab with a matching convertible top. Slowing, she tried making out the license plate number, but failed.

Vanessa continued along a local two-lane highway before turning off to the one lane road leading to her house. Glancing into the rearview mirror, she breathed a sigh of relief. The black car was nowhere in sight.

It wasn't until she'd parked her own car in the attached garage and locked the door behind her that she felt completely safe.

The next two days passed quickly for Vanessa. She did not get a glimpse of Joshua, but heard the quiet grumblings from other employees after they'd been sequestered in his office.

It had become the norm for her to arrive at GEA before eight and leave twelve hours later, and she visited Preston on alternate days and updated him on her progress.

There were nights when she was too exhausted to notice anyone following her home, but realized she'd been grinding her teeth after she locked the door behind her.

She called Stanton, saying she couldn't attend his sister-in-law's birthday celebration and inviting him to accompany her to Warren's house the following Saturday. Stanton accepted and she rang off. Even though it was a Friday night, she wanted to go to bed early because she'd planned to work the next day.

Joshua sat in the darkened living room at the Santa Fe hotel where he was to reside for the next two months. He had watched the lengthening shadows as the sun sank down behind the nearby mountains until the last sliver of day was swallowed up by a clear blackness.

He sat motionless, frustration mirrored on his lean face. His first week at GEA had yielded nothing. He'd learned more about the private lives of the corporation's employees than he would ever care to know.

Jenna had become his confidante, offering tidbits of gossip each time he called her into his office. What surprised him was that she never divulged what was deemed "classified" by Warren McDonald. There was no doubt that she could be trusted to not breach her boss's confidentiality.

Reaching out, he flicked on a table lamp. The soft glow of light filtered over the typical hotel furnishings. His gaze swept over the objects filling the room, and his frustration intensified. He had come to detest his existence—living in hotels and sleeping in strange beds. He wanted to come home every night to his own home and share his own bed with Vanessa. The visions of preparing meals and vacationing with her filled his days and escalated at night. His superiors had given him sixty days, and if he could he would complete the assignment in six. He wanted it over, because this time when he retired he would *never* come back.

He was utilizing his managerial expertise to streamline GEA, while he had transferred total control of his own company to someone else. A cynical smile touched his mouth. He had spent all of his adult life serving others—his superior officers and his country. But now, for the first time in thirty-nine years, Joshua Kirkland—his desires and his needs—had become a priority. He would take care of himself *and* all that belonged to him.

Rising in one fluid motion, he strode to the bathroom with long, determined strides.

Vanessa awoke immediately, sitting up on her bed. The sound reverberated again throughout the downstairs. There was no mistaking the chiming of her doorbell. She turned and glanced at the lighted numbers on the clock on a bedside table. It was ten-fifty.

She swung her legs over the side of the bed at the next chime, reaching for a celery-green silk robe. Belting it tightly around her waist, she headed toward the staircase, wondering who would come to her home at this hour. She pressed a switch on the wall at the top of the stairs, flooding the downstairs with golden light.

The bell chimed again. "Hold on," she mumbled under her breath as she moved quickly down the staircase.

Peering through the security eye in the door she recognized the magnified face of Joshua staring back at her. Her pulse quickened. Why had he come to her home?

She unlocked the door and opened it, letting in the cool night-time mountain air and the familiar scent of his aftershave. He leaned against the entrance, his hands thrust into the pockets of a pair of well-worn jeans. Her gaze swept over the navy blue T-shirt stretched over his chest and down to his running shoes, then back to his face. Their gazes met and she felt a ripple of awareness run through her body.

"What do you want?" she asked, unaware of how sensuous her voice sounded to him.

Joshua smiled, crossing his arms over his chest. "I can't believe you'd ask me that. Isn't it obvious what I want?"

Vanessa couldn't believe his arrogance. "Not here, and not tonight," she retorted, moving quickly to close the door. She was fast, but he was faster as he braced an arm against the solid wood surface, thwarting her attempt to shut him out.

"I need to talk to you," he said quickly.

"Call me tomorrow." He didn't move or blink, and Vanessa felt a thread of panic settle in her chest and prayed that he wouldn't attempt to force his way into her home. She wasn't ready for a volatile confrontation with Joshua—not tonight.

"Look, Joshua, I'm exhausted," she said wearily. "I need to get some sleep, because I'm planning to work tomorrow."

His gaze softened when he noticed the evidence of strain in her face for the first time. Her large eyes were sunken, and her cheeks gaunt.

His arm came down slowly to his side. "What do you say that I pick you up after you're finished and we go somewhere and relax?"

Vanessa shook her head. "No, Joshua. It's not going to work. You can't rip my heart out at the office, then try to put it back when we're away from GEA."

Joshua successfully concealed his disappointment. "I need to be with you."

"You talk about what you need, but what about me? What I don't need is for us to sneak around with each other at night, then pretend we're strangers during the day. Unlike you, I can't turn my feelings off and on like a faucet. I want to be given the option of openly acknowledging you as my husband before God and the world. But until that can become a reality—stay the hell away from me!" She slammed the door and locked it as tears filled her eyes and overflowed, staining her cheeks and the silk robe.

Turning, she braced her back against the door and sobbed softly. She loved him! As much as she didn't want to admit it to herself, she still loved him.

She loved a man who could be as cold and cruel as he was seductive and passionate. Pushing away from the door, she made
her way slowly up the staircase, to her bedroom, and her empty
bed.

Joshua's claim that he needed to be with her echoed her own
silent yearnings. He was honest enough to verbalize it, while she
had taken the coward's way out.

Joshua leaned forward, resting his forehead against the cool
wood. What he wanted to do was pound his head against the door
for being a fool. He'd come to her vulnerable and with all of his
emotions bared because he loved her enough to humble himself,
to beg. Her rejection cut deep, deeper and more painful than the
knife wound which had almost cost him his life. He was bleeding
for a second time, his life's blood flowing invisibly and weak-
ening his resolve, until he found it difficult to draw a normal
breath.

His fingers curled into tight fists as he whispered a solemn
promise. He would never give her the opportunity to reject him
again.

Chapter 22

Vanessa watched a profusion of helium-filled balloons tied to the backs of folding chairs sway gently in the night breeze. The balloons, colorful streamers and several plastic bags filled with discarded wrapping paper, plastic cups, utensils and paper plates were the only visible remnants of what had been a raucous birthday celebration.

Constance Blanchard-Childs flopped down on the wrought-iron, cushioned love seat beside her sister, groaning. "Whoever thought of birthday parties should be drawn and quartered."

Closing her eyes, Vanessa smiled. "I think it was quite successful in spite of all of the noise. Why must children scream so much?"

"I don't think anyone has an answer to that question."

Connie glanced over at her sister, seeing the fatigue in her composed features, and wondering if she was still being plagued by recurring dreams of her missing husband.

"Is everything all right, Vanessa?"

"What do you mean by everything?"

"Are you still having nightmares?"

Opening her eyes, Vanessa gave Connie a long, penetrating look. She had intended to tell her sister about Joshua, but decided to wait until after her nephew's birthday party. Now the waiting was over.

"There's no need for me to dream about Joshua anymore," she began cryptically, "because he's here."

There was a stunned, pregnant silence before Connie found her voice. "What!"

Vanessa slowly and methodically related everything, including his late night visit to her home.

Connie's gaping mouth closed as she shook her head. "I can't believe you didn't let him in."

"Why? So he could climb into my bed!"

"Did you think that maybe it wasn't about sex?"

Vanessa felt her temper flare. "Sex brought us together, and it was because of sex that we married. And the sex was good, Connie. It was hot, raw, unbridled and delightfully satisfying. But it's not enough to base a marriage on or build a future. I need more than the love he professes." Her lower lip trembled when she sought to stem the tears welling up in her eyes. "I need to trust him.

"How do you explain it, Connie?" she continued vehemently. "I can accept his being assaulted, but I can't accept the amount of time it took for him to let me know that he was still alive. Why couldn't he have called me instead of showing up mysteriously at a meeting he knew I would attend? He knew where I worked, and it would've been easy enough for him to get my office extension and call me with some advance warning. He had no way of knowing whether I would blurt out his name before he was introduced."

"Maybe he counted on you being too shocked to say anything," Connie rationalized.

"And he was right."

Running her fingers through her blunt cut hair, Vanessa closed her eyes and tried slowing down her runaway pulse. "Why does he have to work for GEA?"

"From what you've told me, Vanessa, he doesn't work for GEA. Didn't you say that he's a consultant? And to my knowledge, consultants aren't employees."

Her eyes opened quickly and she stared at Connie. "You're right! And that means that we don't have to keep our marriage a secret. It would also stop Jenna Grant from throwing herself at him. When I saw her practically sitting in his lap the other day I wanted to slap her blind and snatch her baldheaded."

Throwing back her head, Connie squealed with laughter. "You sound just a little bit jealous, sister. Could it be that you're in love with the man you claim as your husband?"

Vanessa felt heat flood her face. She'd given herself away. "I never said that I didn't love him."

Connie cocked her head at an angle. "So, you *didn't* marry him just for the sex?"

Staring up at the star-littered summer sky, she shook her head slowly. "No. I consented to become his wife because I loved him. And as crazy as it may sound, I still do."

Connie draped an arm around her younger sister's shoulders. "It's not crazy at all. How many people meet and know within days that they want to spend the rest of their lives with each other?"

"I don't know about spending the rest of our lives with each other."

Connie's delicately arched eyebrows drew together. "Why not?"

"Joshua's the only man I've known who can bring out the worst in me. One wrong word from him can set me off, and I'm ready to explode."

Connie's frown disappeared. Resting her head against her sister's, she said softly, "It's called passion."

"I think I prefer the other form of passion."

"Who wouldn't?"

The two women sat under the stars for another hour, talking quietly. Vanessa listened intently to her sister who was trained in social work, as Connie objectively analyzed all that she had revealed to her. Their conversation took a different turn when Roger Childs emerged from the large house and joined them.

Roger ran a hand over his face and let out his breath slowly. "No more, Connie. This is the last time we're going to have a kids' party at the house."

"You said the same thing last year, darling," Connie reminded her husband. "The kids come here because of the pool."

"I'm going to fill it in."

Connie and Vanessa looked at each other and shared a secret smile. Roger Childs's size and gruff demeanor were deceptive. He was compassionate, a Santa Fe cardiologist who had earned a reputation as one of the best surgeons in the Southwest.

"You're spoiling Eric," Roger continued, wagging a finger at his sister-in-law. "He asks for one video game and you buy him three."

"That's because I don't know an Xbox from a PlayStation. Besides, as his aunt and godmother I have a right to spoil him."

"Once you're married and have your own children we'll see if you're going to be so indulgent," he countered.

The two women shared a knowing look. What Roger did not know was that Vanessa *was* married, and that her first wedding anniversary had come and gone.

When Vanessa walked into her office early Monday morning she spied a beautifully curved, crystal vase filled with a profusion of pale pink flowers. As she made her way slowly to the desk, her gaze widened when she recognized the same variety of flowers that had made up the bouquet Joshua had sent her at La Mérida. Unlike the other bouquet, this one had been delivered without a card. A sensual smile softened her mouth and her expression as she leaned over and inhaled the heady fragrance of a delicate orchid.

Reaching over, she picked up the telephone and dialed

Joshua's extension. His voice-mail switched over after four rings. She waited for his recorded message to end. "Mr. Kirkland, please call Miss Blanchard," she said softly into the receiver.

She hung up at the same time Shane walked through the door. Her smile was dazzling. "Good morning. You're in early this morning."

Shane gestured toward the vase. "I suppose it is a good morning for you. Very nice." He winked at her. "Are you celebrating something we should know about?"

"Of course not." There was a hint of laughter in her voice. "I hope you didn't come to work this early to engage in office gossip."

He stared at her with rounded eyes behind the lenses of his glasses. "No way. I need the backup on the Kroff account."

She gave her assistant a puzzled look. "I gave it to you last week."

Shane ran a hand through his long, tousled hair. "You did?"

Vanessa sat down and dropped her handbag into the lower drawer of the desk. "Yes, I did. See if you can locate it before I have to print out another hard copy."

"I've looked everywhere, Vanessa, and I can't find it. Why don't you give me the disk, and I'll print out another copy. It'll save valuable time for both of us."

She hesitated, then nodded, saying, "Okay." Unlocking the file cabinet under the workstation, she ran her fingertips over the indexed computer disks and withdrew the one containing all of the financial data on the Kroff subcontract account.

Handing it to him, she ordered, "Make a copy for yourself, then return it to me."

"Thanks, Vanessa. You're a lifesaver."

"Don't forget to return the original to me."

"You're beginning to sound like Preston," Shane teased.

"As long as we don't begin to look alike, you'll be okay."

Shane laughed and walked out of her office, waving the disk above his head. Vanessa was amazed that everyone in her unit was able to maintain a normal, easygoing manner in spite of their additional work assignments. She would complete entering all of the data from Preston's spreadsheets within hours. Then she could begin work on the budget projections for Joshua.

She did not think of Joshua again as she became totally engrossed in her work, stopping only to order her lunch from the building cafeteria.

A shiver of delight raced up her spine when she did hear his sonorous voice as he said, "Are you planning to work all night?"

Swiveling on her chair, she turned and stared at him. He stood in the doorway with a mysterious smile on his lips. She glanced at the clock and groaned. It was seven-forty.

Threading her fingers through her hair, she rose to her feet. "I suppose I lost track of time."

His luminous gaze lingered briefly on the vase of flowers on a side table before sweeping back to admire the woman who managed to look enchantingly fresh despite the late hour.

He made his way into the office and stood less than a foot from her. "I picked up a message from my voice-mail that you wanted me to call you."

"And you came instead of calling," she said matter-of-factly.

"I don't like communicating by telephone," he confessed. "It's too impersonal."

Vanessa stared at him, mesmerized. He was standing close to her, too close, and his closeness was like a powerful narcotic, drawing her, lulling her into a state of gluttonous euphoria where she never wanted to surface.

It was as if she were seeing Joshua Kirkland for the very first time. He was as stunningly virile as he was when she first saw him. A rush of heat swept over her body, settling in her breasts and inching lower like a slow-moving stream of molten lava.

He watched her like a falcon, unmoving, only his eyes betraying his lust. They darkened to a deep, rich green, examining her every reaction as her breasts swelled, the nipples tightening against the lace of her bra and silk of her blouse.

Every pleasure point in her body tingled as if he'd touched her, and Vanessa realized that Joshua knew what he was doing to her. Without touching, without speaking, he was seducing her, and she did not protest or resist.

She'd stopped asking herself what it was that drew her to him and made her love him the way she had never loved another man, refusing to acknowledge that their attraction was only physical, because she knew now that it wasn't.

There was something profound, unspoken, that communicated itself and told her that she would always be protected with Joshua Kirkland. A silent voice shouted, *He will always take care of you!*

He had protected her when her hotel room was ransacked in Mexico City, but she hadn't been able to protect him when someone assaulted him and left him to die—alone in a foreign country. She had judged him unfairly. She had no right to judge anyone, especially not the man with whom she had exchanged vows.

He hadn't deserted her. He still loved her, she still loved him, and she didn't want their marriage to end.

"I wanted to thank you for the flowers." Her voice was a throaty whisper, the underlying sensuality caressing Joshua like a gentle brush of silk on bare skin.

"You're quite welcome," he said just as quietly.

The sound of his voice broke the spell, and Vanessa turned back to the columns of numbers on her computer screen. Pressing a key, she saved her work.

"How's it going?" Joshua asked behind her.

"I've completed the long-term capital expenditure budget, allowing for segment expenditures by years."

Moving around the desk, he picked up a page of printed numbers. "Why did you decide to do it that way?"

She gathered all of the pages from the printer and stacked

them neatly. "This segmentation is required for coordination with the annual, or short-term, capital expenditure budget. Inclusion of a project in the annual capital project does not necessarily provide automatic authorization to spend funds or incur financial obligations with respect to that budget."

A slight smile touched his firm mouth as he crossed his arms over his crisp white shirt. "What about controls?"

"Controls are generally exercised at three stages," she continued as she cleaned up her workstation. "Usually inclusion in the budget, approval of appropriation of funds, and finally, the authorization of the expenditures."

"Why?"

Her head came up quickly and she stared at him. "I've done it that way to allow and maintain flexibility in changing the annual capital budget if unforeseen circumstances arise." She tapped the page in his hand. "The starred projects are classified as priority groups."

"You're almost finished, aren't you?"

She took the single sheet of paper from his loose grip. "I should have everything done by Thursday."

She wouldn't need the extension. The budget projections would be submitted two weeks before the original deadline of July tenth.

His left eyebrow rose a fraction. "You're very good, Vanessa." There was no mistaking the pride and *surprise* in his voice.

"And you doubted I could do it." There was a hint of laughter in her accusation.

"I didn't doubt *you, Miss Blanchard.* I just had my doubts whether you would submit your projections on time. I know—" Whatever he intended to say died on his lips when he noticed the direction of Vanessa's gaze. Turning around slowly, he found Shane Sumners standing in the doorway watching them.

"I—I didn't mean to interrupt, Vanessa," Shane stammered. "I just came back to give you your disk."

Vanessa beckoned to him. "You're not interrupting. Please come in."

Shane's normally pale face was flushed with high color as he entered the room and nodded to Joshua. "Mr. Kirkland."

Joshua inclined his head. "Sumners."

Shane handed her the disk. "I've closed out Kroff, so that's one less you'll have to do."

She gave him an appreciative smile. "Thanks, partner. I don't know what I'd do without you."

"Anytime, partner." Returning her smile, he backpedaled out of the office. "Good night, folks."

"Good night," Vanessa and Joshua replied in unison.

Joshua turned his attention back to Vanessa. He watched as she put away the disk and the pages of the budget in the file cabinet and locked it.

"Do you always lock up your work?"

She glanced at him before she dropped the key in her handbag. "Always. I left a disk on my desk once and it disappeared. I made myself a promise that it would never happen again." She gave him a half-smile. "I don't know about you, Mr. Kirkland, but I'm calling it a day." Reaching over, she picked up her handbag, secured the strap over her shoulder, and walked to the closet for the matching jacket to her slim, lime green, linen skirt.

"Have you eaten dinner?"

Her hand stilled on the doorjamb. "No, I haven't."

"Are you hungry?"

She arched an eyebrow, not turning around. "A little."

"How much is a little, Miss Blanchard? A steak little, or a salad little?"

"Neither—tonight."

He crossed the room and stood behind her. "When?"

"Tomorrow."

He leaned close enough for her to feel his breath on the nape of her neck. "What time should I come by your place and pick you up for our *business* meeting?"

"Seven."

His expression softened with a satisfied smile. "Thank you, *Miss Blanchard.*"

"You're welcome, Mr. Kirkland. Good night."

"Good night, Angel."

Vanessa waited until he walked out of her office before she let out her breath, astonished at the sense of fulfillment flowing through her. Before she made the decision to end her marriage, she had to give it a chance; she had to give *them* a chance.

Chapter 23

Vanessa knew the day was going to be unique when she woke to the fury of a violent thunderstorm. A flash of lightning lit up the bedroom as a roll of thunder shook the earth with an angry rumble.

Rolling over, she peered at the clock and groaned. It was only four-seventeen, and she had spent a restless night dreaming of Joshua. When would she ever stop dreaming about him? When would she ever purge him from her mind?

Never, a silent voice whispered. Never, because she knew Joshua would never give her up, and more importantly she did not want him to. He was her husband, they had consummated their marriage, and she wanted to spend the rest of her life with him, a stranger who seemed to know her and her body better than she knew herself.

She had mulled over the possibility that the arcane marriage clause would not apply because Joshua wasn't a GEA employee, and they could live openly as husband and wife. But after hearing the grumblings from her coworkers about Joshua interrogating them—he referred to it as "interviewing"—she decided not to broach the subject with him. He would be at GEA for two months, and that would give them both enough time to resolve their matrimonial status.

Rolling over onto her stomach, she folded her arms over her head and did what she hadn't done in weeks—she went back to sleep and waited for the clock alarm to go off.

Vanessa raised eyebrows when she strode through the reception area fifteen minutes before nine. She had made it a practice to always come in before eight-thirty, and with Preston out on medical leave her day now usually began at seven-thirty. She smiled at two secretaries standing around the receptionist's desk, whispering and giggling to each other.

"Good morning, ladies."

The two women returned her smile. Anne looked up from the compact mirror in which she was dutifully outlining her lips with a lip liner before applying a layer of her celebrated, dragon red color. "Good morning, Vanessa," the three chorused.

Before she had taken three steps she heard Joshua's name whispered. Shaking her head, Vanessa knew why the administrative offices of GEA had been dubbed *Peyton Place* by the workers at their manufacturing plant in a suburb ten miles northeast of the city. Gossip was rampant, and everyone had stopped counting the number of ill-fated office romances. Even without lingering in the employee lounge, she knew Joshua's name was being slowly and finely ground through the rumor mill.

She walked into her office and opened the vertical blinds. The rain had stopped, but the sun had yet to put in an appearance. Moving behind her desk, she sat down to check her voice-mail. Finding none, she retrieved the key from her handbag and opened the file cabinet beneath her workstation.

Frowning, she stared at the lower shelf. The pages of the budget she'd printed out the night before were scattered about.

She remembered stacking everything neatly; she knew she hadn't thrown the papers in haphazardly. She never did!

She tried slowing down the runaway beating of her heart, telling herself that she was imagining things. Maybe she hadn't stacked them, or they had been unsettled by the motion when she closed the drawer. The same eerie feeling she had experienced when her hotel room in Mexico City had been ransacked came back. No one had touched her, yet she felt personally violated.

Get a grip, Vanessa.

Swallowing painfully, she closed her eyes and inhaled deeply, utilizing the breathing exercises she had learned in the Tai Chi classes she had taken at the health spa. Within sixty seconds she was calm enough to review her actions of the night before.

Joshua had come to her office and his presence and nearness had unsettled her. A knowing smile touched her mouth. He had kept his promise not to physically touch her at GEA, yet he had.

In his own way he managed to emit an invisible sensual stroking that she was powerless to resist. He was maddeningly arrogant and self-assured at the same time; and he knew if he persisted he could break through any wall of defense she set up to thwart him.

In his role as consultant she had found him to be willful, relentless, tenacious, inflexible and recalcitrant. But as her lover and husband he was tender, protective, passionate, and generous.

She knew little or nothing about the very private Joshua Kirkland. She knew him to be thirty-nine, and that he spoke fluent Spanish. He'd revealed that his mother was dead, he was estranged from his father, and that he had half-brothers and sisters. She knew nothing of his education or childhood. The realization that had plagued her for months was more evident now than when she first married him. He truly *was* a stranger, a stranger she would love forever.

The chiming of the telephone broke into her musings and she reached over and picked it up. "Good morning. Vanessa Blanchard."

"You sound quite chipper this morning. That must mean you're handling everything that's being thrown at you."

"How are you, Preston?"

"Wonderful," came his reply. "I'm being discharged this morning. The good news is that I won't have to go to the rehab center."

She leaned forward on her chair. "Does this mean you're going home?"

"Yes. I'll have an aide come in and help me for a few hours a day until the casts come off."

"That's wonderful, Preston. I'm going to give you a few days to settle in. Then I'll be out to see you."

There was a lengthy pause before Preston's voice came through the wire. "I want to thank you for everything—for carrying on beyond the call of duty."

"Get well, and get your butt back here as soon as you can," she teased good-naturedly.

"Labor Day will be here before you know it, and then you can take a nice long vacation like you did last year."

She winced at the mention of *vacation*. "I'm going to take long weekends in July and August, and when you come back I'm going to put in for several weeks, go somewhere exotic and romantic, and never come back."

"Bite your tongue, Vanessa. You keep talking like that, and I won't approve a vacation for you."

"Now, you know Warren has final say on vacation approvals."

"What I *do* know is that everyone at GEA says that Warren McDonald is your magic genie. You rub him the right way and he grants your every wish."

She was momentarily speechless, in shock. Preston had just verbalized the rumors circulated by the people they worked with. "Do you believe that, Preston?" she questioned breathlessly.

"No, I don't. But I do know that he likes you. He likes you *a lot*."

She ended her conversation with Preston, sat back on her chair, stared out across the room, and thought about the two men in her life: Warren McDonald, who pursued her indirectly, and Joshua Kirkland, who wanted to keep their marriage a secret.

Mentally switching gears, she threw herself into her work, completing all of the three-month and half of the six-month projections. She ordered lunch in, eating lightly because she was to share dinner with Joshua.

It was five-thirty when she cleaned up her desk, this time making certain that her reports were neatly stacked on the lower shelf of the file cabinet and that the computer disks were filed correctly. All of the disks were labeled and color-coded, so she knew at a glance how to identify each sub-contract budget.

She walked past George Fender's office on her way out and saw him engaged in a heated discussion with Shane. The tension and hostility between the two men was unmistakable.

A large vein throbbed in George's forehead as he waved a sheaf of papers. "I told you before that I won't accept this format. All of next year's budgets will use deficit funding."

"I bust my hump for two days, and now you tell me that we're using deficit funding?" Shane shouted.

"Is there a problem, gentlemen?" Both men turned at the sound of her voice.

George's angry glare swept from Vanessa and back to Shane. "There won't be, if he does what he's told to do."

Shane's fingers curled into fists, the muscles in his forearms tightening, while his face was flushed a bright red. Never had she seen Shane this enraged.

"Shane, go home. Now!" she ordered in a stern tone. "You and I will talk tomorrow."

"I can't go home," he mumbled through clenched teeth. "I have something I have to finish tonight."

"Whatever it is can wait until tomorrow."

"I don't want to wait."

Vanessa went still, her mood varying from annoyance to anger, and she reacted quickly to Shane's defiant behavior. "You will *not* work on anything tonight. And from here on out you *will* check with me personally on a daily basis for approval of overtime."

The blood drained from the younger man's face as his normally gentle hazel eyes hardened with contempt. "I hear you, boss."

He stalked out of the office, his shoulder brushing Vanessa's, and she fell against a wall to keep her balance. She looked up and saw Joshua standing less than five feet away at the end of the corridor. There was no doubt he had seen Shane deliberately shove against her.

"Sumners!"

Shane stopped in his tracks when he heard the crisp sound of his name, spoken quietly yet carrying like the crack of a whip. Turning slowly, he saw Joshua Kirkland leaning against the textured wallpaper, arms crossed over his chest. He gave Joshua a long, penetrating glare before retreating to the office he shared with another accountant.

George walked over to Vanessa, offering her a rare smile. "Are you all right?"

"I'm okay. Thanks for asking."

She smiled at the taciturn man with the snow-white crew cut he had affected since the late nineteen fifties. For the first time, she saw George Fender in an entirely different light. She looked past his remote, blue gaze. He was thought of as a dinosaur compared to other GEA employees. They claimed he was a throwback to another era, eschewing everything unless it was work-related. His wife of thirty-six years had passed away the year before, and he withdrew even further. What she saw was a man who did not trust. George glanced at Joshua, nodded, then returned to his office and closed the door.

Joshua came toward her, his face a mask of scalding fury. "Did Shane hurt you?"

"Of course not."

"I'll take care of him tomorrow."

Vanessa shook her head. "No, you won't. I supervise him. Therefore, I'll take care of him."

"Don't argue with me, Vanessa."

"And don't *you* undermine my authority. I have to supervise Shane long after your work here is done. And I'm not going to have him in my face because he thinks I can't stand up for myself."

Joshua studied her for a long moment, seeing pride and frustration on her delicate face, and knowing she was right. "I'll let you handle it, Vanessa," he conceded quietly. "But if Sumners ever touches you again I swear I'll kill him."

Her breath caught in her throat as if a hand had choked it off. He'd uttered the warning as calmly as he would ask for a glass of water. She'd glimpsed elements of danger in his personality during their stay in Mexico, and now they had surface again.

"Would you actually kill him?" she whispered.

He didn't move or blink. "Yes, I would."

She gasped as her knees buckled slightly. Her eyes widened until she reminded Joshua of a deer, startled and hypnotized by a beam of bright light.

"Who are you?" she mumbled.

Leaning closer, not touching her, he said softly, "I am your husband."

She did not want to acknowledge that she'd married a man who openly admitted that he was capable of murdering another human being.

"Go on home," he urged gently. "I'll come by at seven."

"No, Joshua. Please don't come."

"Don't let what I said upset you."

"Why shouldn't I be upset? You just admitted that you could kill someone."

"I was just talking like a jealous husband. If I had to kill someone to protect you I would. Other than that, I would never take a life. It's too precious. Once it's gone you can never retrieve it."

She forced a nervous smile. She had given him her word that

she would share dinner with him. "Would you mind eating in tonight?"

"No, Angel. Not at all."

Vanessa moved away from him, frightened, and down the corridor like someone in a trance. *Who is he?* she asked herself for the hundredth time, and the resounding answer, as always, was *I don't know!*

She opened the door to Joshua's ring, her gaze taking in everything about him in one swift glance. He was casually dressed in a pair of lightweight black slacks, matching jacket, and a white silk T-shirt.

He clutched a large bouquet of wildflowers in one hand, while the other held a decorative silver shopping bag. His smile widened to a full grin when he saw the full bibbed apron tied around her neck and waist over an airy, sleeveless, ankle-length dress dotted with sprigs of lavender blossoms.

Handing her the flowers, he said, "You look beautiful and very domesticated, Mrs. Kirkland."

"I won't feel like Mrs. Kirkland until whatever it is you've been hired to do at GEA is over," she admitted.

Stepping into the entry, he closed the door behind him before pulling her against his chest with his free arm. The familiar scent of her perfumed body brought back vivid memories of their passionate lovemaking.

His eyes lingered on her hair, which was parted off-center and falling to conceal her ears. His gaze inched slowly over her face, noting that the soft, yellow-orange undertones in her brown face had not yet darkened with the intensity of the summer sun. It was apparent that she spent too many hours indoors. What he wanted to do was take her away with him for a week to where they could frolic in the ocean and offer up their bodies to the tropical sun.

Closing her eyes, Vanessa savored the scent of lime on her husband's smooth-shaven jaw. It was as if they had never parted.

She shivered with vivid recollections of the days and nights she'd spent in his arms.

"I take it you've learned to cook?" he teased, his breath feathering over her ear.

"Somewhat."

"What's for dinner?"

She extracted herself from his embrace. "Broiled lobster tails, vegetable kabobs, a green field salad with a balsamic vinegar dressing and homemade blackberry ice cream."

"It sounds wonderful."

He set the bag down on the brick-tiled floor and removed his jacket. Vanessa took the jacket and hung it on the wrought-iron coat tree in the spacious entry.

"We'll eat on the patio instead of in the dining room. I find it a bit more relaxing."

Joshua retrieved the bag and followed her across the living room, staring in awe at the contents of her home. The brick tiles in the entry gave way to terra-cotta floors covered with colorful woven rugs in Native American designs and African mud cloth prints. He admired the sand-beige leather furniture in the living room, and the look of the heavy, dark, Spanish-style dining room furniture. A black, wrought-iron wine rack along a wall in the dining room stood six feet in height and was filled to capacity.

"I don't suppose you need wine, do you?"

She smiled at him over her shoulder. "I suppose you have wine in that bag?"

"Champagne," he confirmed.

She remembered her first date with him when they shared a bottle of champagne. Her intent had been to seduce him, only to have him turn the tables on her and seduce *her*. She watched Joshua watching her, and a smile of pure satisfaction tipped the corners of her mouth. Mistrust, frustration and loneliness vanished, a deep moving peace taking their place.

Taking his hand, she led him into the kitchen. "Put the champagne on the countertop and make yourself at home."

"Do you need any help?"

"No. I have everything under control. I've prepared the salad and skewered the vegetables. We'll wait for the champagne to chill before grilling the lobster."

"Do you mind if I have a look around?"

"Of course not, Joshua. *Mi casa es su casa.*"

He placed the bag with the two bottles of champagne on a marble counter in the stainless steel and black kitchen. The color was repeated in the black and white vinyl flooring and the steel tubing of a table and four chairs positioned in a corner under a skylight.

Retracing his steps, he returned to the living room and examined the seemingly free-floating staircase leading to the upper level. He pushed his hand into a trouser pocket and withdrew a small disc measuring less than a quarter of an inch in diameter.

Quickly and methodically, he placed discs under a lamp, a table, and in the mouthpiece of a telephone. He mounted the staircase, his footfall silent as he moved along the carpeted hallway.

He walked into the first bedroom and froze, knowing instinctively that it was where his wife slept. An enormous room opened out to a more intimate sitting area. Slanting rays of the setting sun filtered over an imposing antique brass bed, firing the metal like pyrite. The bed dressings were also antique: white embroidered pillowcases, shams, crocheted coverlets, dust ruffles, and quilts. The only other conspicuous piece of furniture, which dominated the space, was a massive, bleached pine armoire.

The room beckoned, and he entered it as if he were walking onto a sacred site. This is where she'd lain while he'd spent a month at a military hospital; if he hadn't been marked for death, this was the bed they would've shared as husband and wife. His expression was one of complete detachment as he placed the minute bugs around the bedroom.

He moved over to the sitting room, his gaze cataloging everything: the floral chaise lounge, a small round table cradling a pile of books, a television, audio system, stacks of DVDs, CDs and a corner filled with lush green plants. Bugs went under clay pots, and on the ledge under a window seat cushion.

He searched the other two bedrooms. They were also charmingly decorated, claiming wrought-iron beds, antique quilts, Native American rugs used as wall hangings, and hanging plants in large clay pots.

The large bathroom enchanted him. The scent of Vanessa was everywhere. Glass shelves held bottles and jars of creams, lotions, perfumes, and soaps. Running his fingers along a black silk robe hanging from a wall hook, he held the garment to his nose. Everything that was Vanessa Kirkland seeped into his being, and for an instant he considered removing all of the electronic listening devices.

A part of him wanted to take her away to Jamaica and never return to the States, while another part—the soldier following orders—said he had to gather evidence for the Pentagon. The last part said that she was innocent.

With the scent of his wife lingering in his nostrils, Joshua made his way down the hallway to the staircase and back to the kitchen.

Chapter 24

Joshua found Vanessa in the enclosed patio. Her back was to him as he watched her position a vase with the wildflowers on a bistro table.

He smiled. The patio was large, yet intimate. She had elected to decorate it with four bistro tables, with two chairs at each, giving it the look of an outdoor Parisian café. Small, lighted votive candles were on all of the tables, their flickering lights resembling twinkling stars in the encroaching darkness.

"Everything looks beautiful."

Turning quickly, Vanessa smiled at Joshua. He stood in the shadows, making it impossible for her to see his expression clearly.

"The champagne is chilled, so we can begin with the salad."

He didn't know whether it was the setting or the mood, but it was the first time he'd noticed the rich timbre of her voice. The register was lower than he'd remembered. There were so many things he knew about his wife, yet he did not truly know her.

He stepped away from the shadows. "I'll help you."

"No. Please sit down. You're a guest."

Moving toward her, he reached out and held her shoulders in a firm grip. "How can I be a guest in my own wife's home?"

Vanessa stared up at his angry features, shaking her head. "That's not what I meant, and you know it."

"I don't know anything of the sort. We're married, Vanessa," he whispered harshly.

"Yet we're not," she countered. "I can't live openly with you as your wife, so right now I don't feel very married."

His grip on her shoulders eased. "What is it you want me to do? Kiss you? Taste your body? Do you want me inside you? Say the word, Vanessa. Just say it," he taunted, "and I'll have you for dinner right here, on this—this table!"

She was so turned on by his erotic suggestions that she couldn't form the words to come back at him for several seconds. "I want that, *and* more," she said in a breathless whisper. "I want to be able to come home every night and have you sleep beside me. I don't want to have to eat alone. I want someone to laugh with me, and someone to comfort me when I hurt. I want to share all of the things a man and his wife plan for. I want a child, Joshua. Your child. Is that too much to ask? Is it too much to want from you as your *wife?*"

Lowering his head, he buried his face in her hair. His hands moved down her back to her waist and hips, fusing her body to his. "No, it's not too much to ask or want, Angel. I can give you all of it, and more. I just can't do it now."

Vanessa drew in a deep breath. She would not become a willing victim to his seduction. Not again. "If that's the case, then consider yourself a guest in my home until you can openly give me what I *want* and *need.*"

His hands fell away, and she turned and made her way back into the kitchen. Curses—raw and violent—exploded in his head, warring with the frustration he'd carried for more than a year.

Rage paled his eyes until they lacked all traces of color. If Vanessa wasn't responsible for selling the components or stealing the two millions dollars, then he rued the one who was, who had unknowingly come between him and his wife.

He stared at the night sky. Clouds raced swiftly across a full moon; the eerie light from the moon reflected off the nearby Sangre de Cristo Mountains, altering their shapes so that they resembled spires rising above a medieval Gothic cathedral.

Vanessa returned to the patio, carrying an ice bucket with a bottle of champagne and cradling a large salad bowl against her chest.

Joshua moved quickly and took the ice bucket from her, placing it on the table. "May I have the honor of popping the cork?"

She glanced up at him, seeing a half-smile softening his mouth. "Yes, you may. You'll find a towel in the narrow cabinet next to the dishwasher." Placing the salad bowl on the table, she spooned portions onto two salad plates, then positioned the bowl on a low, wrought-iron table in a corner before returning to the kitchen.

"Did you find the towel?" she questioned softly. Joshua stood at the cooking island in the center of the kitchen, peering under a foil-covered tray.

He turned his head slightly, giving her a sidelong glance. The overhead light illuminated his silver hair and sun-browned face. The white silk T-shirt was a startling contrast to his firm brown arms, and she drew in a breath as her gaze moved down the length of his tall, lean frame. His tailored slacks hung with perfect precision from his slim waist to his hips, and down his long legs.

His luminous eyes twinkled. "I was just checking out dinner," he explained, wiggling his pale eyebrows.

Removing her apron and laying it on a tall stool, Vanessa moved closer to where he stood. "Do I get a passing grade?"

"If it tastes as good as it looks, then you can expect an excellent grade."

She turned on the range-top grill, adjusted the temperature, then flicked on the exhaust fan. "I'll turn on the grill while we eat our salad. It'll only take minutes for the lobster and kabobs to cook."

"What would you say to preparing a meal together?"

Vanessa gave him a questioning look. "Is that what you want?"

He nodded. "I've dreamed of doing that ever since I met you."

Pulling her lower lip between her teeth, she nodded. "Okay. When?"

"Sunday," he replied without hesitating.

A frown furrowed her smooth forehead. She had promised Connie she would come to her house for Sunday dinner. The frown vanished as quickly as it had formed.

"It can't be this Sunday, because I'm invited to my sister's house for dinner. Why don't you come with me?"

His gaze narrowed. "Does your sister know about us?"

Vanessa nodded slowly. "I had to tell her."

"Who else knows?"

"Connie's the only one. I swore her to secrecy. Not even her husband knows."

He cocked his head at an angle. "It sounds as if it's going to be an interesting gathering."

"You'll come with me?"

Nodding, he gave her a reassuring smile. "Of course."

"Good. Then we'll cook together the following Sunday."

Flashing a boyish grin, he said, "I think I'd better get that towel."

They returned to the patio, and Joshua seated Vanessa before he quickly and expertly removed the cork from the bottle of champagne. He filled two flutes with the pale, sparkling liquid. Still standing, he stared down at her and raised his glass in a toast.

"Vanessa, I love you more than you'll ever know. And may this night signal a beginning of a new life for us in which we'll learn to trust each other as much as we love each other."

Rising to her feet, she raised her own flute, her gaze locked with his. "Joshua Kirkland. I love you," she stated simply.

A delicate ring chimed in the stillness as they touched glasses before putting them to their lips. Joshua put down the flute, came around the table, and pulled Vanessa into his arms. He eased the stem of the wineglass from her fingers and placed it on the table beside his.

Champagne-scented breaths mingled and met when his mouth covered hers. With one hand cradling her face, Joshua took her mouth gently, successfully concealing the turbulent passions racing throughout his body.

She curved her arms around his neck, rising on tiptoe and fastening her mouth to his, her tongue meeting his demanding one. Her body cried out for his, and he answered the call. His mouth was everywhere—on her jaw, throat, ears, and then moved even lower, to her shoulders.

Passions she had locked away with his clothes and her wedding ring surfaced, exploding and shaking her from head to toe. She wanted and needed him. She didn't want to need him, but she did.

"Tell me to stop, baby. Just tell me and I will," Joshua pleaded.

Her breath came in soft, hiccuping gasps. "I can't. You know I can't," she chanted over and over.

He was seducing her again. She'd promised herself that she would not succumb, but the moment he touched her she knew she'd lied, and had been lying to herself for more than a year. He couldn't stay away from her, and she couldn't resist him.

Swinging her up in his arms, Joshua cradled her to his chest and carried her through the kitchen and up the staircase to her bedroom. Neither of them gave it a thought that this scene was a repeat of the one at his hotel in Mexico City. Their food lay uneaten on a table while they looked to partake of another feast.

He walked into the bedroom and lowered her to her feet beside the bed. The sensors along the baseboards filled the large space with soft, warm light, and set the mood for their joining.

Standing over Vanessa, his gaze never straying from her face, he undid all of the minute buttons on her dress and pushed it away from her chest, exposing the soft swell of her breasts rising above the lacy demi-cups of a pale, blue bra. He deftly un-snapped the clasp and cradled her small, firm breasts as the scrap of satin and lace fell from her shoulders. In one motion the wispy fabric of her dress pooled around her sandaled feet.

Only then did his gaze drop to her flat belly and the flare of her hips, encased in pale blue lace. Kneeling, he eased her bikini panties from her hips and down her legs, then removed her sandals.

Vanessa closed her eyes as a trembling wracked her body when she felt his mouth follow the path of his fingers, fingers that feathered up her inner thigh and lingered near her sex.

Her chin fell forward on her chest at the same time her fingers gripped his head, tightening on his scalp. Bracing both hands on her inner thighs, he spread her legs apart and drank the drink of a man dying of thirst. His tongue was relentless, not stopping until she collapsed over his head as shudders of ecstasy echoed her calling out his name in an unending, breathless litany.

Joshua eased her gently to the floor, then pulled back the bed covers. He shed his clothes quickly before placing Vanessa on the center of the bed. She moaned softly when he moved over her languid body, then gasped sharply as he entered her with a driving thrust that rekindled her waning passion all over again.

Every thrust, every stroke, symbolized the nights he had been apart from her, and when his soaring lust exploded the ebbing passion was similar to the weakness he'd felt when his life's blood pooled on the marble floor of the church in San Miguel. He had glimpsed death a second time. The difference was that this *muerte* was in the arms of his wife.

He reversed their positions, cradling Vanessa atop his chest. She struggled to free herself, but he tightened his hold on her waist. "Stop wiggling."

"I don't want to hurt you."

"You don't weigh enough to hurt me."

She raised her head and stared down at him. "Don't your chest and belly hurt?"

"No," he laughed. "I've healed completely."

Picking at the coarse strands of hair on his head, she frowned. "How serious were you?"

"I received three units of blood."

"Joshua—"

"Don't, Angel," he interrupted. "I can't talk about it."

What he did not want to do was lie to her. There was no way he could tell her about the attempt on his life without disclosing what he actually did for a living. He knew he would have to tell one day—but not now.

She pressed her forehead to his. "I invite you to eat and we wind up in bed. I'm not a very good hostess, am I?"

Brushing his lips over hers, he said, "You are a wonderful hostess, and I did eat. You were the appetizer." She pressed her face to his shoulder and he felt the heat in her cheeks. "Did I embarrass you, darling?"

"You're a wicked man, Joshua Kirkland."

"That's because you're a wicked, sexy woman."

"Let's get up and take a shower. Then we'll see if we can't behave long enough to sit down and eat."

Joshua rolled her over on the bed, smiling. "Someone should've told you about me before you consented to become my wife."

She flashed a saucy smile. "Told me what?"

"That I'll never be able to behave. I'm what people call a *bad boy.*"

"I suppose I can't help myself. I seem to have a penchant for bad boys."

His expression stilled and grew serious. "Who else are you involved with?"

"I'm not involved with anyone."

"Have you been seeing anyone since we married?" It was a question he knew the answer to, but he needed to hear her reply.

Combing her fingers through her mussed hair, Vanessa pushed it off her forehead. "I'm seeing someone as a friend. His name is Stanton Reid, and I've invited him to come with me to

Warren's party." She noticed that Joshua's eyes paled. "Is that what you want to know?"

Rolling off her body, he sat up. "It's enough."

Vanessa sat up, staring at his solemn face. "Are you sure that's enough?"

Arching a pale eyebrow, he smiled again. "What I do know is that you couldn't be sleeping with him. The moment I entered you I knew that."

She rose on her knees and settled down on his lap. His arms curved around her body as she leaned into his strength. They sat silently, holding each other until they rose as if on cue and headed for the bathroom.

The glow of being loved throughout the night was still visible the next morning when Vanessa walked into her office. She had just sat down behind her desk when Shane appeared.

"I came to apologize," he said quickly. "I was out of line, and I have no excuse for acting the way I did."

"Come in and close the door, Shane."

He complied, then walked over and sat down on the chair beside her desk. She stared at him for several seconds, trying to understand what could've triggered his display of hostility the night before.

"Are you having personal problems?" she questioned softly.

He stiffened. "What kind of personal problems are you talking about?"

"Love? Money?"

He shook his head vehemently. "No, Vanessa. I told you before that I can't work with George. The man's paranoid."

"You were insubordinate," she countered.

"I wasn't insubordinate. George didn't give me correct direction. I swear to you, Vanessa, that he never told me we were setting up the budgets using deficit funding."

She stared at her assistant. His outburst of the night before was not only foreign but totally unexpected, because Shane had always been cooperative. He, along with many of the others in the Finance Unit, were unable to work directly with George Fender, and because of this Preston had permitted George to work alone.

"Would you prefer to work with Frank?"

"Sure. Anybody but George."

"I'm going to do you a favor, but first you have to do something for me." His head bobbed up and down in a nervous gesture. "I'm going to warn you just this one time. If you ever attempt what you pulled last night, you're out! And because GEA doesn't have a union, there's no one to advocate on your behalf."

His gaze dropped, his head following. "I promise you that it won't happen again."

"Don't promise, Shane. Just don't do it. You don't have to worry as much about me as you do about Joshua Kirkland."

Shane's head snapped up. "What about him?"

"He saw everything. And he has the power to recommend that you stay or be released." What she didn't say was that Joshua would intervene if he ever attacked her again.

"Did he say anything to you?"

Not wanting to lie, she said, "Yes, he did."

"What did he say?"

"I'm not at liberty to reveal that to you. As of now I'm reassigning you to Frank. I'll let Frank know that he's to expect you."

Shane ran a trembling hand through his wavy, dark hair, smiling a nervous smile. "Thanks, Vanessa."

She stared at him until he rose to his feet and walked out of her office. Exhaling audibly, she shook her head. She'd felt like an ogre, admonishing another adult. One she liked a lot.

It appeared Joshua did not have a problem admonishing or intimidating anyone. All he had to do was turn his frigid gaze on someone and they trembled.

Closing her eyes, she recalled the passions they had shared the night before. They showered, ate, cleaned up, then returned to the bedroom, where they made love for hours. She fell asleep at midnight and awoke at four to find Joshua gone; an iris from the bouquet he'd given her lay on the pillow where he'd slept, its fragrance blending with the lingering scent from his body. The smell of him was everywhere—on her bed and on her skin. She loathed washing it away when she got up to prepare for the day.

Picking up her telephone, she called Frank and informed him that he would be responsible for Shane's supervision. Frank was pleased with her decision. He had unofficially become the Chief Financial Officer, supervising everyone but Vanessa and George.

A satisfied smile softened her mouth as she unlocked her file cabinet to begin the onerous task of completing the budget projections.

Chapter 25

Joshua parked his car in the space behind Jenna's. He'd berated himself over and over for asking her to accompany him to Warren's house. Maybe it had something to do with Vanessa and another man—a man he knew she wasn't sleeping with, but that did not stop pangs of jealousy from disturbing his sleep.

Walking the few steps to the front door of her duplex garden apartment, he rang the doorbell.

The door opened, and Jenna stood before him completely nude except for a pair of black satin mules. She tossed back a wave of flaxen hair with a flip of her head, smiling. "Please, come in."

He didn't know whether to laugh or walk away. He decided on the latter. "I'm going back to my car to wait exactly fifteen minutes for you to get dressed. Take one minute longer, and I'm leaving."

Jenna laughed, blowing him a kiss. "I only need a couple of minutes to slip into something."

The door closed and, much to his surprise, he did laugh. There wasn't an ounce of modesty in the tiny woman. He wondered how many men had taken her up on her unorthodox greeting.

Jenna strutted out of her apartment after ten minutes. An emerald green midriff top and a matching short, tight skirt were an exact match for her eyes. Her provocative attire exhibited her body's best features: a tiny waist, flat middle, and strong legs. Joshua opened the passenger-side door and she leaned over, providing him with a more than ample view of her breasts.

He slammed the passenger-side door violently and circled the car. Slipping in behind the steering wheel, he glared at her. "Show out with me, and I'll bring you back home so fast that it'll make your head swim."

She placed a hand on his shirt sleeve. "Oh, Joshua, don't be so serious. I was only playing with you."

He jerked his arm away. "I didn't play when I was a boy, Jenna. And I certainly don't have time for it now."

Her jaw snapped loudly, and she turned away from him and glared out a side window. Most men would've followed her up to her bedroom and taken what she was offering, but it was apparent that Joshua Kirkland wasn't most men.

Vanessa half-listened to what Stanton Reid was telling her as her gaze was directed toward the area set aside for parking. Joshua'd said he was going to attend Warren's *staff meeting,* but he hadn't put in an appearance even though it was after six o'clock.

A rising wind lifted the long, silk chiffon skirt of her irides-cent, fuchsia camisole dress above the grassy lawn, revealing a matching color on her toes. Layers of the sheer fabric of her dress floated over her body like breaths of wind. Her well-groomed feet were cradled in a pair of high-heeled, silk sandals in darker hues of varying shades of pink and purple.

"I asked if you would like me to get you something to drink."

She looked at her date as if he had two heads. "Yes, please," she replied after registering what he'd said. "A glass of white wine."

Stanton walked away at the same time Joshua strode around the rear of the sprawling, one-story, hacienda-style structure. Her suppressed smile froze on her face once she saw the woman clinging to his arm.

How could he? How could he have brought Jenna? And there was no mistaking that the woman was more than pleased to have accompanied him, as evidenced by her wide grin.

Their gazes met across the expanse of lawn and, not wanting him to see her annoyance, she smiled. He nodded imperceptibly, placing a hand in the middle of Jenna's back and leading her over to where an outdoor bar had been set up.

"I wonder if he's already slept with her," said a familiar feminine voice close to Vanessa's ear.

Turning, she glared at Lisabeth. "Why don't you ask Jenna?"

Lisabeth tucked in a stray braid that had escaped her elegantly coiffed braided hair. "She looks quite satisfied. The way she's grinning you can see all thirty-two of her bought and paid for porcelains."

"Pull in your claws, Lisabeth. Jenna's not worth it."

"She gives women a bad name."

"Jenna gives Jenna a bad name."

"I don't want to be here, Vanessa. I have better things to do on my Saturday nights than hang out at Warren McDonald's house."

"Do you think this is fun for me?" she hissed between her teeth.

She couldn't tell Lisabeth that she and Joshua had spent the past four nights together. After the first night they couldn't stay away from each other. The pull was too strong for them to resist. He came to her house after the sun set and left before sunrise.

Stanton returned with her white wine and she smiled up at him. Stanton Reid was heart-stopping, breathtakingly handsome. The former professional football player, now a sportscaster for a major television network, broke hearts whenever he displayed his lopsided, dimpled smile.

Twice-married, Stanton dated several women at the same time, refusing to commit to any of them. This suited Vanessa just fine, because she couldn't marry Stanton even if she wanted to. She was still legally married.

Curving an arm around her waist, he covered more than half of her back with his large hand. His large, clear brown eyes twinkled with his trademark smile. "You're gorgeous, Vanessa."

"So are you, Stanton."

Throwing back his head, he laughed loudly, garnering everyone's attention. Vanessa took a sip of her wine, peering over the rim at her husband. There was no mistaking his displeasure when he saw Stanton's hand on her waist.

Excusing himself and leaving a pouting Jenna staring at his back, Joshua made his way toward Vanessa and Stanton. There was no doubt that Stanton Reid and Vanessa were an extremely attractive couple, but she was *his* wife.

Extending his hand, he said quietly, "Joshua Kirkland. I was a big fan of yours when you played for the Cowboys."

Stanton took the proffered hand, his patent smile in place. "You from Texas?"

"Originally from Florida. I've decided to settle out here in Santa Fe."

"Beautiful landscape," Stanton stated soberly.

"Beautiful landscape, beautiful weather, *and* beautiful women."

Stanton looked at Vanessa, then back to Joshua. "I suppose you two know each other?"

"Of course," they replied in unison.

"Mr. Kirkland is an independent consultant for GEA," she explained for Stanton.

Joshua's knowing gaze moved slowly over the now softly curled hair framing her face. She was aware of his preference for curly hair. Pinpoints of brilliant green grazed her bared shoulders and the soft swell of breasts rising above the revealing garment's décolletage.

Politely excusing himself, Joshua returned to Jenna, noticing that she was frowning at something Shane was saying to her. He slowed his approach, watching the exchange as the fingers of Shane's right hand curled around Jenna's upper arm before she jerked it from his grasp. She glanced down at her arm, fearful that his savage grip had left it marred.

Joshua walked up behind Shane, catching him off guard. "You seem to have an inclination for physically abusing women, Sumners. I'm going to recommend that you go for counseling."

Shane spun around, startled, then turned and strolled casually across the lawn as Jenna continued to massage her arm.

Cupping her elbow, Joshua examined her arm. "I don't think you're going to bruise." He stared down at her. "What was that all about?"

She shrugged. "Nothing."

"Nothing? He wanted to hurt you."

Jenna turned away before he saw the tears well up in her eyes. Not tears of pain, but tears of frustration. "I'd rather not talk about it."

A slight frown marred his smooth forehead as he stared at her back. "Do you want me to take you home?"

"Please."

Placing a comforting hand on her shoulder, he pulled her head to his chest. "Wait near my car for me." She nodded and made her way to the area set aside for parking.

Joshua searched the crowd for Vanessa. Meeting her gaze, he raised his left hand and beckoned with his forefinger. Within seconds she was at his side.

"I'm going to take Jenna home."

"Are you coming back?"

"No. Warren briefed me on what he was going to say. I'm going back to the hotel. Call me at the Meridian when you get back home, and I'll come and get you."

"Get me?"

He winked at her. "You're going to spend the night with me."

Joshua drove Jenna back to her apartment in complete

silence. He took surreptitious glances at her profile as she stared straight head, her deceptively composed features revealing nothing.

When he maneuvered into the driveway behind her late-model Saab convertible coupe, she said, "You don't have to see me in."

Pushing open the door, she stepped out and walked to the entrance of her apartment. She unlocked the door, walked in, and closed it behind her.

He sat in the car for several minutes before putting it in reverse. Instinctively he sensed that something was going on between Jenna and Shane. What it was, he intended to uncover.

Twenty minutes later he pulled into the parking lot of the Meridian Hotel. Like most of the employees at the administrative offices of GEA, he hadn't wanted to attend Warren McDonald's so-called staff meeting dinner party, yet had felt obligated to go.

Warren looked at the occasion as a morale booster, because he was willing to underwrite the cost of food and live entertainment. Rumors of mergers and takeovers usually meant givebacks and layoffs to employees, not promotions or raises.

Taking Jenna home had provided him with an excuse not to stay and listen to Warren's gung ho speech to people he referred to as his troops, nor to watch Stanton Reid covet his wife.

Joshua entered the small hotel and headed for the concierge's desk. He had chosen the Meridian over the better-known major chains because of its charm and elegance. One hundred years ago it had been a popular mission along the Santa Fe Trail.

He picked up his key and several telephone messages, flipping through the messages as he walked slowly toward the staircase. Vertical lines formed between his eyes when he saw the name on one of the slips of paper. His gaze swept quickly over the neatly printed message: *CALL HOME. VERY IMPORTANT! Martin Cole.*

Taking the stairs two at a time, he raced down the hallway to his room. It took him less than sixty seconds to unlock the door and dial the number of his half-brother's residence. The telephone rang twice on the other end before the connection was broken.

"Cole residence" came a drawling female voice.

"Martin Cole, please," he snapped with barely controlled patience.

"Hold on, sir."

He didn't realize he'd been drumming his fingers until he heard the familiar voice. "Martin Cole."

"What's up, Martin?"

There was a conspicuous pause before Martin's voice came through the line again. "It's Sammy."

Joshua's pulse quickened. "What about him?"

"He's—"

"Is he dead, Martin?"

"No, Josh. He's not dead, but he's close to it. He's suffered a stroke."

Closing his eyes, Joshua pressed his head against the cushion on the sofa. "How bad is he?"

"There's some paralysis on his right side, and some speech impairment."

"Why are you calling me?"

"Because he's asking for you, Buddy."

"How the hell can he ask for me when he can't even talk, Martin!"

"He can't speak in complete sentences, but he can say your name." There was another pause. "Let it go, Josh. Let go of the bitterness just this one time. Come and see your father before he dies."

"Damn him," he whispered harshly. "Damn his soul to Hell."

"He may be damned, and he may be going to Hell, but he's still your father."

Joshua clutched the telephone receiver in a death grip as he struggled to control his breathing. The man he could never acknowledge as father, could never call "father," was lying in a hospital in Florida and asking for him. For what? To ask for forgiveness? To make peace? To try and make up for more than thirty-nine years of denial?

"Where is he, Martin?" His expression was a mask of stone as he listened to his brother's voice, nodding slowly. "I'll be there tomorrow."

The telephone receiver fell from his limp fingers back to its cradle. Resting his elbows on his knees, he buried his face in his hands. Vanessa—his angel. Just when he'd found her again he had to leave her.

Dreading the inevitable, Joshua picked up the telephone and dialed Vanessa's number. His voice was a monotone when he left his message on her voice mail. Depressing the hook, he dialed the operator and asked for an airline carrier, to secure a reservation for his flight from Santa Fe to West Palm Beach, Florida.

Chapter 26

Vanessa sat with Stanton, Lisabeth, and her date at one of the ten round tables set out on the expanse of lawn at the rear of Warren McDonald's house.

He tested a portable microphone given to him by one of the musicians he had hired for the evening's festivities.

"Good evening." His pleasantly modulated voice carried well in the open space. "I know most of you don't want to be here." There was an undercurrent of laughter and gesturing protests from the assembled. "But I'm going to make it worth your while having to give up whatever it is most of you do on Saturday nights. Thanks to our budget projections for the upcoming fiscal year, no one, and I repeat, *no one,* will be let go with the impending merger."

Vanessa smiled at Lisabeth, who clapped wildly at the news. Everyone rose to their feet, applauding, while several of the men placed fingers in their mouths and whistled loudly.

"I want that in writing!" a man from the legal department shouted.

A wide grin split Warren's handsome, brown face. "You have my word, John. Shouldn't that be enough?" Everyone nodded in approval. "Now that I've gotten everyone's attention—let's have a damn good time tonight!"

His short speech set the tone for the celebrating with an inexhaustible quantity of food, liquid beverages and live music that continued well into the night.

Vanessa pleaded fatigue around eleven-thirty and asked Stanton to take her home. Now that she had submitted the budgets she would cut back on her hours, but she needed to catch up on her sleep.

She was also looking forward to spending the night with Joshua and being able to sleep late for the first time in two weeks. It also would be their first night together when he wouldn't have to leave her bed before dawn.

She hadn't told Connie that she was bringing Joshua to dinner with her, and she wondered what her sister's reaction would be when she finally met the man who was responsible for her younger sister's disturbing dreams.

Stanton turned off the local road and onto the private one where Vanessa's house sat in a cul-de-sac with twelve other Spanish style townhouses.

He pulled into her driveway and put his two-seater Porsche in park. "It turned out to be a very good party."

Vanessa smiled at him. "It had all of the makings of a wake until Warren's announcement." Unbuckling her seat belt, she leaned over and pressed a kiss on Stanton's cheek. "Thanks again for coming with me."

Resting an arm along the back of her seat, he trailed his fingers over her jaw. "Thanks for inviting me." He smiled. "We get along so well that there're times when I think about asking you to marry me."

"That's when we'd stop getting along."

Stanton nodded. "You're probably right. I've always been a better boyfriend than a husband."

Pulling his hand gently away from her cheek, Vanessa examined his pleasant features. "Even if I wanted to marry you, I couldn't." Not when she was already another man's wife. She kissed Stanton again, then pushed the car door open, stepped out into the cool summer night, and walked the half dozen steps to her front door. She unlocked the door, waved to him, then closed it behind her, shutting out the night and Stanton.

Bending over, she eased her feet out of her high-heeled sandals. The colorful straps dangling on a forefinger, she walked barefoot across the living room and up the staircase to her bedroom.

The blinking red light on the bedside telephone glowed eerily in the room.

Making her way to the table, she punched in the code and listened intently as Joshua's voice came through the speaker. The moment he'd said her name she knew something was wrong. He wanted her to call him as soon as she got in.

Waiting until the message ended, she dialed the number of his hotel. He picked up the phone after the first ring.

"Kirkland."

"It's me."

"I'm coming over."

His terse message sent a shiver of uneasiness through her. What had happened between the time he left to take Jenna home and returned to his hotel? Vanessa refused to imagine.

She heard the sound of a car's engine and opened the door to find Joshua striding up the path. An idling taxi waited in her driveway.

Her frantic gaze swept over his drawn features. He had exchanged his suit for a pair of slacks and a lightweight summer jacket. He stepped into the entry and partially closed the door.

"Where are you going?"

Joshua registered the tremor of fear in his wife's voice, but refused to acknowledge it. He had to remain indifferent. If not, then he wouldn't be able to leave her.

"My father has suffered a stroke."

Vanessa's eyes widened at his disclosure. "How is he?"

"I'm told that he's been stabilized."

Her arms went around his neck as she buried her face in his warm throat. "How long will you be away?"

Reaching up, he removed her arms from his neck. "I don't know." Tightening his hold on her hands, he brought them to his lips and kissed her fingers as his gaze bore into hers. "I wanted to spend the night with you."

"Go to your father, Joshua. He needs you more than I do right now."

He wanted to tell Vanessa that he needed her more than his father did him. He, who had never needed anyone, needed her. "I'll call you from Florida."

She managed a smile. "I'll say a prayer for him."

He nodded. "Thanks." Leaning over, he kissed her mouth lightly. "I have to go or I'll miss my flight."

Turning, he opened the door, then closed it. Vanessa stood staring at the door for a full minute before she turned the lock. This time she'd had Joshua for two weeks instead of one. She wondered how long she would have to wait to see him again.

The slight puffiness under Joshua's eyes mirrored his exhaustion as he walked into Samuel Cole's hospital room. He had taken the red eye from Santa Fe to El Paso, Texas, before catching a connecting flight to West Palm Beach. He'd stopped at his apartment in Palm Beach long enough to shower, change clothes, then returned to West Palm Beach.

Martin Cole sat on a chair near the bed, asleep. His once raven black, curly hair was liberally streaked with gray, adding character to his forty-five-year-old face instead of age.

Joshua placed a hand on his half-brother's shoulder and shook him gently. Martin woke up, staring up at him with a pair of eyes that were as black as pitch.

Rising slowly to his feet, he gave Joshua a quick, rough embrace. "Thanks for coming, Buddy."

Joshua turned his gaze on the prone figure on the bed for the first time. Various machines monitored Samuel Cole's respiration, blood pressure and other vital signs, the beeping sounds reverberating loudly in the silent room.

"Why don't you go home and get some rest?" Joshua urged softly.

"I'll do that after I check on M.J."

"How is she holding up?"

"You know my mother. She's not one to go to pieces in front of anyone. The doctor sedated her, so she's holding up as well as can be expected."

"I'll stay here until you get back," he offered.

Martin Cole stared at the man whose height was the only physical characteristic they had in common—other than the blood of their father.

Joshua stood at the foot of Samuel Cole's bed a long time after Martin left. He'd tried to rid himself of the bitterness that had taken root at another time and another place, but failed.

His cold gaze lingered on Samuel's face, seeing a man whose political influence and money were now as worthless as a single drop of water in the desert. Moving closer, he noticed that the debilitating stroke had taken the rich color from the golden brown face and withered the solid bulk Samuel had carried well into middle age. Even the thick, white hair he wore with pride was sparse and brittle. For the first time Samuel Claridge Cole looked every year of his seventy-three years of living.

Moving slowly to the head of the bed, Joshua sat down on a chair, reaching out and running his fingers along the back of his father's inert hand. For a man of his height and bulk, Samuel Cole had incredibly slender hands, hands Joshua had inherited from him, along with his coloring.

"You wanted to see me, Old Man," he whispered harshly to the sleeping patient, "and I'm here. Just what the hell did you want to see me about? Did you want to tell me how sorry you are that you ruined the life of a young woman you just had to have? That even though you had a wife of your own you just couldn't stay away from her?

"You claim that you hate me—well, the feeling is mutual, Old Man. I hate you, too. I hate you for the self-indulgent bastard that you are. You're a taker and a user, Samuel Cole, and I hope you rot in hell for all of the dirty dealing you've perpetrated over the years."

Leaning closer, he peered down at the composed features of the man he despised more than any other human being he'd ever known. "You gave Teresa Maldonado a job in your company. Then you set out to seduce her. She was only eighteen, a first-year college student and a virgin, and you, nearly twice her age, used intimidation and bribery to rob her of her innocence.

"And when she came to you with the news that she was expecting your child you gave her hush money, bribing one of your trusty corporate flunkies to marry her so that she wouldn't disgrace her devoutly Catholic, immigrant Cuban family.

"She despised Everett Kirkland as much as she loved you. She didn't think I knew that she cried every time he exercised what he considered his conjugal rights. And because you were paying him, the greedy bastard hung around for sixteen years. He realized the money wasn't enough when I told him that I would kill him if he ever touched my mother again.

"I had only one argument with my mother, and that was when she mentioned that you were able to help me get into West Point. For seventeen years she never asked you for anything for herself. But she swallowed her pride, hid her feelings, and came to you for *me*. And no matter what she said, I know I would've gotten into West Point without your intervention.

"And what I could not fathom was that she loved you, Sammy. Why, I don't know. She never stopped loving you, not even on her deathbed.

"I hope you can hear me, Old Man, because I want you to lie on your back for a long time and repent, repent for all of the lives you've manipulated and ruined."

Emotionally drained, he stood up and walked out of the room, his chest rising and falling heavily; he was unaware that Samuel Cole's eyes opened briefly, the lids fluttering weakly, as a single tear trickled down his drooping right cheek.

Joshua Kirkland stood in the silent, empty hallway, head bowed. He had waited all of his life to unburden himself to Samuel Cole, but having done so he felt no measure of satisfaction. He'd spewed his pain, his venom, leaving a void that needed filling. He had let go of the bitterness, but needed something else to take its place.

His troubled thoughts turned to Vanessa, wanting and needing her more than he wanted or needed anyone else in his life. He glanced down at his watch and sighed heavily. It was three o'clock Mountain Time. He couldn't call her—not yet.

Turning, he reentered the room, sat down on the chair Martin had vacated, and waited.

The ringing of the telephone jerked Vanessa from her much-needed sleep Sunday morning. Groping for the telephone, she picked up the receiver after several attempts.

"Hel-lo."

"Vanessa?"

She sat up, her pulse accelerating. "Joshua? How was your flight? How's your father?"

"One question at a time, Angel. My flight was okay, and my father is holding his own."

Bracing her back against a mound of pillows, she pulled her knees to her chest. It had taken a catastrophe for Joshua to reconcile with his father. "What do you mean he's holding his own?"

"He's not on life support."

Vanessa wanted to ask him how *he* was holding up. If he had made his peace with his father. But more importantly, she wanted to know when he was coming back to Santa Fe. She didn't have to wait long for the answer.

"I'm not certain when I'm coming back, Angel. Once there's a change in his condition—either way—I'll be back."

As casually as she could manage, she said, "Keep in touch."

There was a punctuated pause from Joshua. "I will."

Those were the last words they exchanged before they hung up simultaneously.

Chapter 27

The next three weeks had come and gone quickly for Vanessa. Joshua called her every morning and at night, reporting that his father's condition had not changed. His calls always ended with a declaration of love, and that he missed her. Hearing his voice buoyed her spirits, allaying the foreboding that his absence would signal a repeat of what had happened in Mexico.

She found it hard to believe that it was five weeks since he had come back into her life, because the time had passed so quickly. Within another three they would be able to live openly as husband and wife.

Rescheduling her own time to accommodate her approaching shorter work week, she met with her staff and Warren. Shane worked well with Frank, which helped to speed the process of closing out the fiscal year.

She also met with Preston on alternating evenings for what had become enjoyable dinner meetings. Preston, who developed a passion for Chinese food after a trip to China and Hong

Kong, always greeted her arrival with a variety of dishes from an excellent take-out restaurant.

The phone on her desk buzzed twice, indicating an inside call. She picked up the receiver. "This is Vanessa."

"Girlfriend, want to do lunch?"

Glancing at her appointment calendar, she smiled. Her afternoon was free. She could always count on Lisabeth to get her out of the office. "You're on. Where do you want to go?"

"There's a place in the Plaza that serves wonderful fajitas."

The Plaza was so close, so they didn't have to take their cars. "What if I meet you downstairs in ten minutes?"

"Make it fifteen, Vanessa. I have to fix my face."

As she readied herself to go to lunch with Lisabeth, Warren rapped lightly on the open door, his solid bulk filling out the doorway. He flashed a winning smile.

"Do you have a few minutes?"

She stood up. "Yes—a few."

Closing the door, he walked into the office. His dark gaze lingered briefly on her face, then shifted to a point over her head.

"Sometimes I don't say it often enough, but I wanted to let you know that I appreciate how you've filled in for Preston. The work you did on the projections was truly exceptional."

She smiled. "Thank you, Warren, but I just do what I'm paid to do."

"You do much more. I've watched you become a very capable administrator. I…"

Her gaze narrowed. "What are you trying to say?"

He gave her a direct stare. "I'm considering reassigning Preston and giving you his position."

Vanessa chose her words carefully. "Does Preston know?" Warren shook his head. "You've made this decision without conferring with him?"

This time he nodded. "I see no need to discuss it with him."

She stared back at her boss, unable to believe what she'd just heard. "Then I can't accept it. I will not take the man's position while he's practically flat on his back."

"You may not have a choice, Vanessa."

Heat flared in her face. "I will not be a party to what I think of as an act of deception."

Warren's expression softened as he closed the distance between them. "I'm doing this for *you*, Vanessa. I shouldn't have to wear a sign around my neck to let you know how I feel about you."

She was uncomfortable with the fact that he'd finally confessed his feelings for her. Always before she had perceived his interest through innuendoes.

"You've complimented me with your persistence and patience in pursuing me. I acknowledge your feelings, but my answer is no. I will not accept Preston's title, nor will I do anything to encourage your advances."

Pulling back his broad shoulders, he smiled. "I suppose you can't get any plainer than that, can you?"

"No, I can't."

He inclined his head. "Thank you for your honesty."

She flashed a gentle smile. "You're very welcome."

Warren returned her smile, turned on his heel, and walked out of her office. Vanessa fell limply back down on her chair, grateful that he had taken her rejection without a confrontation. Warren was well aware of the laws regarding sexual harassment in the workplace, and he had been very, very careful not to test it.

If, she thought, she could reveal that she was married, then she wouldn't be dating Stanton or sidestepping Warren's advances.

Most women complained that there weren't enough men to date; she had a husband and two other men who were interested in her, and all she wanted was to be a wife to the man who had captured her heart and refused to give it back.

Gathering her handbag, she rose to her feet and left the office to meet Lisabeth.

* * *

"How about a drink?" Lisabeth said conspiratorially as she studied her menu.

Vanessa shifted her eyebrows. "For lunch?"

Lisabeth nodded her braided head. "Why not? I had a rough morning." She chewed her lower lip. "I think I'm going for a frozen margarita."

"I'll pass on the alcohol. But a virgin piña colada looks very tempting right now."

Lisabeth stared across the table at her co-worker. "Are you still working late?"

"Not too late. Six."

"Yeah, Girlfriend, you're learning."

A waitress approached their table and they gave her their orders. Within twenty minutes they were sipping icy cold drinks and inhaling the spicy ingredients of chicken and beef fajitas.

Vanessa hadn't taken more than two bites of her chicken dish when she felt the beginnings of her stomach rejecting her food. Clamping her napkin over her mouth, she pushed back her chair and walked quickly in the direction of the rest rooms.

She returned to the table, her face drawn from a violent bout of retching. The rising nausea had emptied the contents of her stomach.

Lisabeth peered closely at her when she retook her seat. "Are you all right, Girlfriend?"

Taking a sip of water, she shook her head. "I don't know. I must have eaten something that didn't agree with me."

"Either that, or you're pregnant," Lisabeth said glibly.

Lines appeared between Vanessa's eyes as she frowned, and she became more uncomfortable by the minute as her apprehension increased. Calculating mentally, she realized she was late!

No, she pleaded silently. She couldn't be pregnant. She didn't want to be pregnant—not now! Her hand trembled noticeably as she took another sip of water.

Lisabeth watched her intently. "Are you, Girlfriend?"

She lowered the glass. "Am I what?"

"Pregnant?"

"Of course not."

"But you are seeing Stanton Reid, aren't you?"

"Seeing, but not sleeping with him." What she couldn't tell Lisabeth was that she had slept with a man—a man who was her husband. Leaning back on her chair, she said, "I think I'm going to skip lunch."

She ordered a cup of lukewarm tea with lemon, hoping it would help settle her stomach. However, the tea was not the antidote for her nausea, and she spent the remainder of her lunch break watching Lisabeth eat and drink.

She returned to her office, stopping short when she saw Frank Stevenson going through a stack of papers on her desk. His back was to her, so he hadn't seen her come in.

"What do you think you're doing?"

Frank spun around, his face flushed. It was apparent he had not expected her quick return. "I—I was looking for something."

"I can see that!" Vanessa tried bringing her rising temper under control. "Couldn't whatever you need wait until I came back?"

"Warren asked for the latest balance sheets on the direct contractors. I couldn't find my copy."

Folding her hands on her hips, she walked slowly into the room. "Warren could've waited."

"He said he needed it right away."

"I don't care what he said. If you misplaced your copy, then that's on you. I don't want to find you going through anything in my office ever again."

Glaring at her, Frank crossed his arms over his chest. "There's no need to get your nose out of joint, Missy."

"Get out of my office and stay out!" Frank dropped his arms, complete surprise mirrored on his face. "Now!"

It was a full thirty seconds before he registered the seriousness in her voice and knew enough not to challenge her further. He strode past her and walked out, slamming the door behind him.

Making her way over to the chair behind her desk, Vanessa flopped down on it. Why, she thought, did men find it so difficult to take direction from a female superior?

After the incident when she'd found her papers disturbed in her locked file cabinet, she did not want to set up the opportunity for it to happen again. She didn't want her reports missing like Frank's.

Picking up the telephone, she dialed Warren's extension. Jenna answered, and she told the secretary that she would bring the balance sheets for her to photocopy. She also told Jenna to tell Warren that she was taking the afternoon off.

She then straightened the papers on her desk, locked them away, and called Frank and told him to fill in for her. He seemed pleased with her decision, because that meant she would begin her four-day weekend earlier than planned.

Making certain everything was locked, including the door to her office, she left.

Vanessa sat on a stool in her bathroom, numbed. She'd sucked in her breath, trying to hold raw emotions in check. However, the tightness in her chest forced her to expel it, her gaze fixed on the wand in the glass filled with a yellow liquid. The strip had changed color.

She could still see Lisabeth Nelson's distinctive, copper brown, rounded face with sparkling dark eyes, pert nose, and full mouth as she said, "Either that, or you're pregnant."

Lisabeth was right. She *was* pregnant! And she knew exactly when it had happened—the first night Joshua had come to her house; the first time they had made love after a thirteen-month separation.

She sat on the stool for what seemed hours until the ringing of the telephone forced her to move.

* * *

A moan floated across the room and Joshua sat up quickly, moving to Samuel's bedside. He'd berated himself for remaining in Florida each time he spoke to Vanessa, but knew he had to experience closure. His father was expected to recover, with limited use of his right arm and leg. The neurologist predicted some speech impairment, but with intensive therapy Samuel Cole would be able to communicate with some facility.

Leaning over Samuel, he stared down at the intelligent dark eyes struggling vainly to focus.

"Jos—"

"It's me, Old Man."

Samuel closed his eyes, his chest shuddering with every effort it took to form the words he tried forcing through his lips. "I—I sor—ry."

"So am I, Old Man. I'm sorry you can't talk, because I'd love to go a few rounds with you right now. I want to hear all of your lies before I curse your soul to hell and back."

Samuel's head rolled back and forth in frustration. His eyes opened again and he stared at the son who was more like him than the two who claimed his name.

Tears pooled in his eyes as he swallowed, trying to bring his emotions under control. "I…love…you," he said slowly, stringing the words out and breathing heavily from the exertion.

A shadow of anger tightened Joshua's features. "You don't know how to love."

Nodding slowly, Samuel mumbled breathlessly, "I do." His suddenly alert gaze was fixed on his son's face. "You need to marry. It—it will be good for…" His words trailed off.

The hardness and pain fled his cold, green gaze as Joshua studied the face of the man he'd claimed he hated, but couldn't. "I am married," he confessed. "And unlike you, I'll always be faithful to her."

Groping over the sheet with his left hand, Samuel reached out and caught Joshua's wrist in a firm grip. Despite the debilitating stroke, he still possessed a great deal of strength. He ran his tongue over his lower lip in slow motion. "Call…call…"

Joshua's gaze swung to the machines monitoring Samuel's vital signs. Nothing had changed. "Who do you want me to call?"

Samuel's increasing frustration was evident by the lines creasing his forehead. "Call me…please."

"Call you what?"

"Father." The single word was strong and unwavering.

Pulling his wrist free, Joshua shouted, "No!" He stalked over to the window and stared out, not seeing the fronds of towering palm trees bowing gracefully from a hot breeze, not seeing the traffic moving fluidly along a multi-lane highway, and not seeing the stretch of beach meeting the gray waters of the Atlantic Ocean, because of the tears filling his own eyes. For the first time in his adult life he'd shed tears for someone who didn't deserve them.

Turning away from the window, he stared at the broken-spirited man whose name and money had controlled and changed lives with a wave of his right hand. Now, that hand lay lifeless at his side.

He retraced his steps and stood over the sobbing Samuel. Picking up the useless right hand, he caressed it gently as a smile lifted the corners of his mouth.

"It's all right," he crooned softly. "Everything's going to be all right, *Father.*"

Samuel's tears streamed down his face, into his hairline, and onto the pillow cradling his head. He tried smiling, but the muscles in the right side of his face wouldn't move, and the smile resembled a pained grimace.

Joshua leaned over and pressed his lips to his father's shriveled cheek. "I have to leave now. I have to see about my wife. I've left her for too long."

Samuel nodded, closed his eyes and surrendered to exhaustion. It had taken a great deal for him to ask his son for his forgiveness. Joshua pulled a sheet over his chest.

Martin Cole walked into the room, stopping and recognizing the gentleness in Joshua's touch as he comforted their father. "How is he?"

"He's asleep." Turning, he smiled at his brother. "He's going to be okay."

"Where are you going?" Martin asked when he saw Joshua reaching for his jacket on the back of a chair.

"I'll be in Ocho Rios if you need me. I'll call you and let you know where I'll be when I return to the States."

Martin embraced his brother, then watched as he made his way down the hospital corridor until he disappeared from view.

Vanessa answered the telephone after the third ring. "Hello."

"Hello yourself, Angel." The greeting was a fluid, husky whisper.

"Where are you, Joshua? The connection sounds weak."

"That's because I'm in Ocho Rios."

"Ocho Rios?"

"I want you to get yourself to the airport. I've made reservations for you for a nine-twenty flight to Miami. You'll only have forty-five minutes to make a connecting flight to Kingston on Air Jamaica. I'll be at the airport waiting for you."

"Joshua, I have something to tell you."

"Tell me when you see me, Angel."

She looked at the receiver when she heard the steady drone of the dial tone. He had hung up.

An hour later, Vanessa fastened her seat belt and prepared herself for the flight to Jamaica, wondering what had happened that sent Joshua to Jamaica. She remembered him saying, *"It's a refuge if you're hurting, and need a place to heal."*

Had he gone there to heal? Shrugging a shoulder, she closed her eyes. She would find out soon enough.

Chapter 28

As promised, Joshua was waiting for her when she left the customs area. He rose from the chair where he'd sat waiting for her flight to arrive and walked toward her.

Vanessa noticed that he had a long, fluid stride, and that his right foot turned in slightly. She also noticed that he'd lost weight; his face was leaner and his cheekbones were more pronounced. A gentle smile lit up her eyes as he extended his arms. Dropping her single piece of luggage, she threw herself against his chest.

"Thank you for coming, Mrs. Kirkland," he whispered.

"You're…" His demanding kiss stopped her words and robbed her of her breath.

"Let me get you out of here," he crooned against her moist lips. Picking up her bag, he curved his free arm around her waist and led her out of the airport to the parking area.

Vanessa watched Joshua store her bag in the trunk of a Mercedes Benz sedan that had to be more than thirty years old. "You didn't give me time to pack much."

"You won't need much where we're going."

"How far is Ocho Rios?"

"We'll arrive there in time to see the sun come up." He helped her into the car, then came around and sat beside her. His right hand caressed her knee over her cotton slacks. "Did you sleep on the way down?"

She shook her head. She couldn't sleep. Not when she'd just found out that she was carrying a child, his child.

Closing her eyes, she settled down in the seat. "I won't be able to see much of the landscape in the dark, so please wake me up when the sun comes up."

Joshua did not wake her as they traveled west through Spanish Town en route to Ocho Rios. The sun shone brightly in the sky when he arrived at the house and carried her into the bedroom they would share. She didn't stir when he undressed her and covered her with a sheet. Removing his own clothes, he lay down beside his wife and adjusted the mosquito netting around the antique four-poster bed. Cradling her close to his chest, he joined her in a deep, dreamless sleep.

Vanessa woke up, startled. At first she didn't know where she was, then her arm brushed a solid shoulder. Turning over, she stared at Joshua staring back at her. A sensual smile crinkled her face as he returned it with one of his own.

"Good morning."

She wrinkled her nose. "Good morning to you, too."

Holding the back of her head in one hand, he brushed his lips over hers. "Welcome to Jamaica."

She snuggled close to his chest, her nose pressed against his throat. "I have something to tell you." Her voice was low and mysterious.

Joshua combed his fingers through her hair. "What?"

"We're going to have a baby."

He stiffened, then sprang up, pulling her up with him. His gaze burned her face with its intensity.

The nostrils of his thin nose flared noticeably when he finally let out his breath. "What did you say?"

Vanessa blinked back tears. It was apparent he didn't want the child. "You heard damn well what I said, Joshua Kirkland."

"Are you sure? Did you see a doctor?"

She bit down hard on her lower lip, shaking her head. "I took a home pregnancy test yesterday, and it came out positive. I didn't have time to make an appointment with my doctor."

Her apprehension vanished as he rested a hand on her chest, his fingers gently outlining the shape of her breasts. Then she was in his arms. He held her so tightly she had trouble drawing a normal breath.

"Joshua! You're crushing me."

"I'm sorry," he apologized, loosening his grip. "How did it happen? When?"

"I don't think I need to tell you how. When? The first night you came to my house for dinner."

He let out a triumphant laugh. "That was the night I had you for the appetizer!"

Vanessa pounded his hard shoulder with her fist. "This is serious, Joshua."

Turning her on her back, he moved over her body and supported his greater weight on his elbows. Tenderness lit up his eyes. "You've just given me the best news I've ever had." He pressed a soft kiss on her forehead. "How can I thank you, Angel?"

"Thank me by being a supportive husband and a loving father."

"That shouldn't be too hard to do with you."

"You're not sorry?"

He stared down at her. "How can I be sorry, Vanessa? I've waited a long time for someone like you to come into my life. Loving you has helped me to let go some of the bitterness I've carried for a long time."

Her large eyes searched his features. "Have you made peace with your father?"

He nodded slowly. "I had to. I couldn't carry the hate any longer. It was eating me up inside, and I knew it would eventually destroy me."

Curving her arms around his neck, she pulled his head to her breasts. "Have you forgiven him?"

"It's myself I had to forgive. I'll tell you everything later."

Joshua, caught up in the joy that he was to father a child, refused to think of the possibility that Vanessa could be indicted by the very people he worked for. He would worry about that later—much later.

Vanessa waded into the clear, blue-green waters of the Caribbean, nimbly dodging the waves rolling gently against the beach bordering Joshua's house.

After a light breakfast, which she was able to keep down, Joshua gave her a tour of the two-story, white stucco structure with a red tile Spanish roof. Everything about the house was wholly West Indian in character—from its design to the furnishings—and she was totally enthralled with the beds, armoires, tables, chairs, desks, china, linen and serving pieces from a bygone era.

She had opened all of the Creole jalousie shutters on the second floor, letting in the cooling breezes from the sea. When she'd stood looking out at the lushness of the property, the distinctive smell of salt water and tree-ripened fruit had filled the large rooms which overlooked a veranda enclosed by elaborately designed wrought-iron.

She'd felt a special thrill when Joshua told her that the house now belonged to her, and she could decorate it any way she wanted it.

She sat down in the water, feeling more like a child than an adult. She'd missed the ocean. When she first moved to New Mexico she had been awed by the unending landscape and the mountains, and hadn't realized how much she missed seeing the ocean until she returned to California to visit her parents.

Joshua said he was willing to relocate to Santa Fe, and she wondered if he, too, would miss living near the water. He had the Atlantic Ocean in Palm Beach and the Caribbean in Ocho Rios.

Her thin cotton dress was soaked through by the time she stood up and walked back to the beach where Joshua lay face down on his folded arms, naked.

At first she had been startled when he walked down to the beach, shed his clothes, and swam nude. He'd explained that he owned more than five miles of the surrounding beach. Even knowing that the beach was private, she hadn't felt comfortable enough to swim nude. Not yet.

The tropical sun had bleached his hair white and tanned his skin until he was almost as dark as she was. And the contrast between his face and eyes was shockingly hypnotic.

Sitting down beside him, she wrung the water out of her dress. Without warning, he sprang up and eased her back to the sand. His penetrating gaze rested on the shape of her bare breasts clearly outlined through the damp fabric.

She held his gaze with her own. "Who did you get your eye color from?"

He shifted a pale eyebrow, seemingly surprised by her question. "My hair and eyes are my mother's. My height and coloring are my father's."

"What about the rest of your face?"

He smiled at this question. "It's my maternal grandfather's."

He continued to stare at her, and Vanessa felt an increasing uneasiness under his penetrating examination.

"I'm married to you, yet I know very little about you. Why is that, Joshua?"

"Because you haven't asked, that's why."

"I'm asking now. I want to know everything you're willing to tell me."

He released her, and she sat up. Undoing the buttons on the front of her dress, she slipped out of it and spread it out on the sand to dry. She then removed her panties and lay them on the sand beside the dress.

Joshua stared at her perfectly formed, ripening feminine body. "How do you expect me to concentrate when you're tempting me?"

Combing her fingers through her wet hair, she turned her face up to the sun and closed her eyes against the blinding rays. "There's nothing to concentrate on. Just open your mouth and tell the truth."

His hands went to her shoulders, holding them gently. "The truth is that I love you and that I've missed you."

A seductive smile curved her sensual mouth. "Missed me how?"

"Like this," he said softly as he touched his lips to hers. "And this." His mouth moved lower to the base of her throat. "And especially this." He fastened his lips to her belly, his tongue tasting the salty particles clinging to her velvety flesh.

"Hello, little baby," he crooned against her flat belly. "This is your daddy. I want you to be good to your mommy while you grow strong inside of her. And when you're ready to be born I'll be right here to love and protect you."

Vanessa cradled Joshua's head as her eyes flooded with tears of joy. Lowering her cheek to his hair, she whispered, "Make love to me, darling. Now!"

His head came up, his eyes wide and questioning. First she'd balked at swimming nude, and now she wanted him to make love to her under the heavens.

Pulling her dress closer to where they lay, he eased her down on it, then moved into her outstretched arms. The heated blood rushed to his groin, leaving him lightheaded with the rising passion.

Settling himself between her thighs, he kissed her mouth with the lightness of a butterfly's wing. Her slender arms tightened around his neck, increasing the pressure of his mouth on hers.

His hand had barely touched her breast when the nipple

hardened against his palm. There was no doubt that she was as aroused as he was.

Adjusting his body, he angled for position and eased his swollen flesh into her, both of them sighing with the intense pleasure of flesh meeting flesh.

She had asked him to love her, and he did. He took her, alternating between long, deep thrusts and shorter, quicker ones that prolonged the ecstasy neither of them wanted to experience—not yet.

The sun burned brighter, hotter, but it could not match the torrid lust fusing the two people on the beach into one.

What Vanessa and Joshua could not do was put off the inevitable; they could not prolong or temper the blinding, scorching passion screaming for escape.

Lifting her hips, and cradling them in the palms of his hands, Joshua surrendered his passion, breathing out the remnants of his explosive release into her open mouth at the same time Vanessa abandoned herself to the explosive ecstasy shattering her into tiny bits of brilliant light.

They lay on the beach, spent, their passions sleeping until the next time.

Joshua rolled over, bringing Vanessa with him. He smiled up at her and was rewarded with the sensual smile that never failed to melt his heart.

"Let's go inside before we burn," he suggested. "I'll wash your back if you'll wash mine, and I'll tell you whatever it is you want to know about me."

Vanessa sat beside Joshua in the vintage automobile as he drove expertly along a narrow road in what he'd called *the back country*. He had promised to take her to a restaurant where she would sample some of the best Jamaican food served on the island.

Maneuvering into a large clearing, he turned off the engine. She sat up straighter and stared out at more than a dozen bungalows painted in tropical pinks, yellows, and blues. Each had a matching red tile roof.

Her eyes brightened. "Oh, Joshua, they're charming."

He smiled at the excitement lighting up her face. "The restaurant is another two hundred yards. Do you mind walking?"

"Of course not." She unlocked her door and waited for him to circle the car and help her out.

His arm went around her slim waist as he led her through what looked like a small village. The scent of her perfumed body wafted in the night air, reminding him of the passion they'd shared earlier.

He'd told her of his mother's affair with Samuel Cole and detailed his being estranged from his half-brothers and sisters until his older brother, Martin, sought him out a month before he entered college. What he did not tell her was that the college was the Military Academy at West Point.

He also revealed that his relationship with his siblings improved slowly over the years until they had developed an accepting respect for one another.

His fingers grazed the smooth flesh over her bared back. When he told Vanessa they were eating dinner out, she had put on one of the few dresses she'd brought with her—a slim, white halter dress with a generous slit up the front that ended several inches above her knees which flattered her slender body and rich, dark coloring. Her high-heeled sandals clicked rhythmically over the narrow cobblestone path laid out along the perimeter of the pastel-colored bungalows to a larger, lime green stucco structure.

The distinctive sound of steel pans playing an upbeat tune drifted from the ocean windows, along with the sounds of laughter and voices raised in song.

Vanessa glanced up at Joshua, smiling. "It sounds like a fun place."

"It is," he confirmed with a mysterious smile.

A white-jacketed waiter stepped aside as they entered the restaurant. Inclining his head slightly, he flashed a warm, inviting smile, displaying a set of beautiful white teeth.

"Good evening, Mr. Kirkland. We've been expecting you."

"Thank you, Duncan." Pulling Vanessa closer to his side, he glanced down at her. "I'd like to present my wife. Vanessa, this is Mr. Duncan Alton."

Duncan bowed again. "Mrs. Kirkland."

She flashed her winning smile. "Mr. Alton."

"Come right this way. Your table is ready."

Vanessa looked around her as they were shown to their table. The restaurant was larger than it appeared from the outside. There were dozens of tables, all of them crowded, a bar, an area set aside for a dance floor and an elevated stage where a quartet played a rocking rendition of a popular calypso.

The rattan furniture, potted palms, banana trees, the orchids hanging from poles rising high above the wooden floor, were all in keeping with the tropical locale, while the mouth-watering aroma of food wafting from the kitchen reminded her of the need to put some food into her stomach. She had eaten sparingly, not wishing to undergo another bout of nausea similar to the one she'd experienced when she'd shared lunch with Lisabeth.

When they reached their table Duncan stepped back politely and permitted Joshua to seat his own wife. He waited for Joshua to take his seat, then said, "Lindsay will serve you tonight."

Vanessa smiled across the small table at her husband. He'd elected to wear white: a banded collar linen shirt, a pair of loose-fitting linen slacks and an unconstructed matching linen jacket. His overall appearance was breathtaking with his sun-bleached white hair; it was an attractive contrast to his shimmering, sun-browned face.

A young man approached their table, a shy smile softening his already youthful face. Vanessa guessed he was no more than seventeen or eighteen.

"Good evening, Mr. Kirkland." He gave Vanessa a surreptitious glance. "Mrs. Kirkland. It will be my pleasure to serve you this evening."

He's so charming, she thought, giving him a warm smile. He was a younger, darker version of Duncan Alton. Even his voice was the same: soft, refined, with a hint of a British accent.

"How is your sister, Maryeles?" Joshua questioned.

"She is well, Mr. Kirkland. She boasts a great deal, saying she does a fine job taking care of your house while you're away."

"And she does, Lindsay. A very fine job indeed."

Lindsay stood up straighter, flicking a nonexistent piece of dirt from the sleeve of his pristine white jacket. "Are you and your lady ready to order?"

"Can you give us a few minutes to study the menu?"

"But you wrote the menu, Mr—" Lindsay clapped a hand over his mouth when he realized he had made a serious faux pas.

Joshua did not glance up, but continued to study the selections printed on the menu. "But Mrs. Kirkland is not aware of what is on the menu."

"I—I will be back whenever you are ready," Lindsay said quickly, then scampered away.

Moving the small votive glass with a burning candle to a corner of the table, Vanessa leaned forward and stared at Joshua's bowed head. "Now, what was that all about?"

He pretended interest in the menu. "Nothing."

She placed a hand over his. "Do you own this place?"

His head came up slowly. "Yes. And my brother Martin and I are partners in three other ventures just like this one."

Her eyebrows shifted. "All in Jamaica?"

He nodded. "Ocho Rios, Montego Bay and Port Antonio."

"What else are you hiding from me?" she questioned softly as her gaze narrowed.

"Nothing else."

"You're not lying to me are you, Joshua Kirkland?"

"No." And he wasn't. If he didn't deny something she'd questioned, then he wasn't lying.

Removing her hand, Vanessa turned to study her menu. "I want something to drink. What do you recommend?"

"Try the soursop. It's like a milkshake."

"What about the food? If it's spicy it's not going to stay down."

"Mama's got to eat, and baby's got to eat," he mumbled to himself. "What do we order?"

Vanessa managed to eat a small portion of baked swordfish, plain white rice and several slices of sweet plantains. They settled easily in her stomach, along with the deliciously chilled soursop. Joshua watched her carefully with each forkful she put into her mouth.

"Do you feel like dancing?" he asked after she finished.

"No, Joshua."

Pressing his fist to his mouth, he shook his head. "I remember you enjoying a dance with me on more than one occasion." Rising to his feet, he circled the table and gripped her elbow. "Up on your feet, Mrs. Kirkland."

"I can't," she whispered, protesting with every step she took as he led her out to the dance floor.

Pulling her flush against his body, he held her firmly. "Follow me, Angel."

And she did, dipping and swaying to the rocking calypso beat. Everyone in the restaurant was up on their feet, gyrating and grinding, and when Joshua swung her out Vanessa found herself in the arms of another man who swung her around wildly, then handed her back to her husband.

A trio of singers joined the band and they played an extended version of "Dollar Wine." After twenty minutes on her feet Vanessa told Joshua she had to catch her breath. He led her outside, both of them laughing and breathing heavily.

Without warning, he bent slightly and swept her up into his arms. "Let's go home and have our own private party," he whispered seductively in her ear.

"That sounds like a wonderful idea."

He carried her to the car, where they hummed and gyrated on their seats until they arrived at the house where they would reaffirm their love—over and over throughout the night.

* * *

Vanessa felt a rush of disappointment the moment the plane touched down at the Santa Fe airport late Monday afternoon. It was back to reality and back to living a lie. The man she had spent three full days with had given her a glimpse of what her life would be like if they could live openly as husband and wife, and she had wanted that to last—forever.

They were silent as they sat in the back of the taxi. The driver would drop her off first, then take Joshua to his hotel. Making certain she was safely in her house, he kissed her passionately. Then, without saying a word, he turned and walked back to the waiting taxi.

Vanessa stood in the entry, listening until the sound of the departing car's engine faded completely. Then, she made her way slowly up the staircase to her bedroom. Falling across the bed, she closed her eyes and slept until the alarm woke her early the following morning.

Chapter 29

Vanessa strolled into the reception area of GEA tanned and relaxed.

"Nice tan," Anne commented when she exited the elevator.

She smiled. "Thanks."

"Looking good, partner," Shane complimented as he passed her. Turning around, he backpedaled, winking.

"Thanks, partner," she returned, waving.

Walking into her office, she dropped her leather case on a chair, opened the vertical blinds, and flopped down on the chair behind her desk.

Before she had the opportunity to pick up the messages on her voice-mail the phone rang. Inhaling deeply, she picked up the receiver. "This is Vanessa."

"I heard you were back, Girlfriend. Now, tell me, where did you go to get your tan?"

"Lisabeth," she whispered softly. "I'm not back three minutes, and the gossip mill is grinding."

"When you work for GEA you don't have a private life."

"Tell me about it."

"No. Tell me where you were over the weekend."

"Give me a few minutes to make a phone call, then come on around to see me."

Vanessa rang off, then flipped through her Rolodex for the number of her gynecologist. She spoke to the nurse at the doctor's office, explaining her findings, and the nurse gave her an appointment for later that afternoon.

The moment she replaced the receiver in its cradle Lisabeth stood in the doorway, hands folded on her rounded hips. Her sharp gaze took in Vanessa's radiant face.

"Hey, Girlfriend, you look wonderful."

Vanessa waved her closer. "I feel wonderful."

Lisabeth wagged her head. "No more nausea?"

"Nope."

Walking into the room and sitting down on a chair beside the desk, Lisabeth leaned over and glanced up at Vanessa from under her eyelids. "Tell me something. Where did you go?"

Vanessa opened her mouth, then closed it. Joshua stood in the doorway, trapping her within his mesmerizing gaze. Lisabeth, seeing the direction of her gaze, turned slowly on her chair. Standing up quickly, she gave him a tight smile. "Mr. Kirkland."

He waited until she was abreast of him, then stepped aside. "Miss Nelson." Closing the door behind the departing personnel director, he leaned against it. His tender gaze reached across the space separating him from Vanessa, enveloping her in a cocoon of warmth.

She frowned at him. "Why do you do that to her?"

He arched a pale eyebrow. "Do what?"

"Intimidate her."

"I didn't come here to discuss Lisabeth Nelson."

"Why are you here?"

"To see what everyone is gossiping about. They're whispering about how beautiful you look."

Waves of heat flooded her face. "And I have you to thank for that. The weekend was wonderful."

"It was more than wonderful, Angel. It was perfect."

Nodding, she stood up and walked over to him. "I have a doctor's appointment for three o'clock this afternoon."

"Do you want me to come with you?"

"No."

"Are you sure you want to do this by yourself?"

"I'm sure, Joshua. Stop worrying," she admonished softly. "I'll be all right. I'll let you know everything when I get back."

"I'm going to be out of the office later this afternoon. Call me at the hotel and leave a message for me if I haven't returned."

Resisting the urge to kiss him, she smiled instead. "I'll talk to you later."

"I love you," he whispered softly.

"Same here," she whispered in return.

His declaration of love lingered with her throughout the morning as she resumed the task of closing out the last of her sub-contract budgets.

Picking up a yellow-coded disk, she inserted it into her computer. Three more budgets and she would be finished. Three more before she would start the process all over again for the coming fiscal year.

She stopped long enough to eat several carrot sticks and a cup of yogurt. After saving her figures on the disk, she filed it back in the cabinet. Staring intently at the disks, she noticed something was different. What, she couldn't identify.

Running her fingers over the disks, she counted them carefully. Exhaling, she shook her head. They were all there. But why, she thought, did she feel something was wrong?

Picking up the one for the Kroff account, she looked at the

front, then the back. Tapping the label with a fingernail, she
shrugged her shoulders. It would come to her later.

The question nagged her on the drive to the doctor's office
later that afternoon, but once she lay on the examining table she
pushed it to the recesses of her mind.

The doctor confirmed her own findings—she was pregnant,
and he estimated that she was approximately a month into her
first trimester. He examined her thoroughly, and patiently explained what she could expect with each trimester.

He wrote a prescription for the supplements he wanted her
to take and gave her an appointment to see him in another month.
As she filled the prescription at the pharmacy located on the
lower level of the medical office building, pangs of hunger
gripped her, and she decided to stop at a downtown diner before
returning to the office.

Joshua walked into the field office of the Santa Fe FBI and
was shown to the office of the man who headed the site.

Extending his hand and not pausing for preliminaries, he
asked, "What have you come up with?"

Special Agent Patrick Lewis shook the proffered hand and
waited until Colonel Kirkland sat down before taking his own
seat. "Not much. We've tapped all of the phones of everyone at
the administrative office and have come up with *nada.*"

"What about Vanessa Blanchard's?"

"Again, nothing. My men were in two weeks ago and in-
stalled cameras in all of the offices, and again we're drawing a
blank."

Joshua stared at Patrick Lewis. The man was as nondescript
as a male could be. He was of medium height with straight,
close-cut, brown hair and brown eyes. He claimed no distin-
guishing features. He could easily pass for a Little League
baseball coach, or the manager of a local fast food restaurant.

"What have you come up with on Shane Sumners and Jenna
Grant?"

Patrick smiled, shaking his head. "Now that's a strange combination."

Joshua leaned forward. "Why would you say that?"

"There's nothing to suggest that they're involved with one another, except that he drives her car on occasion."

"I want you to bug her car. Better yet, bug both of their cars."

"We'll do it tomorrow."

"Are any of the people in Finance meeting regularly with anyone in Manufacturing?" Joshua questioned.

"It appears as if everyone at GEA gets together after hours. Most of them meet in a place near the Plaza for happy hour on Fridays."

"I'm not talking about Fridays," Joshua insisted.

"I'd like to accommodate you, Colonel, but I don't have enough men to spread around."

"Call your boss in Washington and ask him for more men. Do I have to remind you that my boss and your boss want their two million dollars, *and* a traitor? It's been almost three years, and the big boys on Capitol Hill have exhausted all of their patience."

"I'll try," he conceded. His brow furrowed. "We did come up with some interesting footage last week."

Joshua leaned closer. "What?"

"It appears as if Vanessa Blanchard has an open-door office policy."

"No one at GEA locks the door to their offices. If they want privacy they simply close it."

"I'm not talking about that. Come. I'll let you see for yourself."

The rush hour was over when Vanessa finally maneuvered into her parking space in the underground garage. She thought about not returning to the office, but something about the disks continued to nag at her.

She rode the elevator to the seventh floor, but when the doors refused to open she knew everyone had gone home.

Searching her handbag, she found her key and inserted it in the panel which would allow the doors to open and permit her access to the floor.

Only a table lamp in the reception area remained on, giving the space an eerie glow. Flicking a wall switch, she lit up the corridor where her office was located. Her footsteps were silent as she made her way down the carpeted corridor.

As she pushed open the door she wasn't given the opportunity to scream. A tall figure loomed in front of her. A large, gloved fist smashed into her face. The hand covered her mouth, and she was forced backward and down to the floor. Struggling against the nausea rising from her throat from lack of oxygen, she felt a wave of blackness descend on her.

Don't hurt me. Please don't hurt my baby, she pleaded silently as she clawed at the hand over her face. Her struggling grew weaker, then stopped altogether. Darkness covered her like a comforting blanket, shutting out the light from the lamp on a table, the waning sunlight coming through the partially closed blinds, and her fear.

Joshua paced the length of his hotel room, clenching and un- clenching his hands. It was after nine, and he hadn't heard from Vanessa. He had left three messages on her cell and voice mail at home, and she hadn't returned any of them.

He knew she hadn't returned to the office, because *he* had— after meeting with the special agent in charge of the Santa Fe field office. He'd wanted to question her about the video footage on Frank Stevenson.

He was relieved that their electronic wiretaps hadn't picked up anything on her. They had recorded his calls to her, her calls to her sister, and several calls to her parents and co-workers. There was nothing on the tapes to indicate that she was even remotely involved in a conspiracy to commit espionage.

He had her sister's number, but didn't want to call the woman and alarm her. It would've been different if they'd met, but they hadn't.

"Dammit, Vanessa," he cursed under his breath. "Where the hell are you?"

As if in answer to his question, the telephone rang. He took two steps and picked it up. "Kirkland."

"Josh—"

His heart pounded wildly in his chest. "Vanessa! Vanessa, where are you?" He didn't realize he was shouting into the receiver.

"He hurt me. Come get me. Please, come get me," she pleaded weakly.

A wave of moisture swept over his body. "Where are you?"

"In my office."

He could hear her sobbing. "What the hell are you doing in your office at this hour?"

"Just come get me." A distinctive sound followed.

"Vanessa!" She had hung up the phone.

It took him less than two minutes to retrieve the automatic handgun he'd concealed in the false bottom of a piece of luggage. He slapped in a fully loaded clip, pulled on a holster, and concealed the gun under a lightweight jacket.

His tactical training in navigating vehicular obstacle courses prevented him from wrecking the rental car as he maneuvered out of the hotel's parking lot on two wheels.

He pulled into the underground parking garage at the same time Vanessa stumbled off the elevator, dragging her handbag along the ground. Her legs buckled as she groped her way to her car.

Swinging her up in his arms, Joshua placed her on the rear seat of his car, slammed the door shut, then slipped behind the wheel and headed for the nearest hospital.

He didn't wait for a stretcher as he carried Vanessa through the emergency room entrance, shouting at the first white coat he saw.

"Can I get a doctor here? Someone attacked my wife!"

A nurse approached him. "Was she raped?"

He glared at her, and she took a step backward. "I don't know. But she is pregnant."

The nurse turned quickly and shouted for an orderly to bring a stretcher. It appeared miraculously. A young doctor joined the nurse, checking the swelling along the left side of Vanessa's face. Her left eye was closing quickly.

"What's her name?" he asked Joshua.

"Vanessa Kirkland."

The resident doctor looked at Joshua, frowning slightly. He leaned over Vanessa and studied her face. "This is Childs's sister-in-law. I met her once at his house." Turning to the nurse, he ordered, "Page Dr. Roger Childs, STAT. Tell him we have a family member in the E.R."

Joshua wasn't permitted in the examining room as Roger Childs took over seeing to his sister-in-law. He paced the floor outside the room, praying. Vanessa was conscious, but she was quiet. Too quiet.

Forty minutes later, Dr. Roger Childs stepped out of the room and motioned for Joshua to follow him. He led him to a small space that appeared no larger than a utility closet, and closed the door.

"What are you to my sister-in-law?"

Joshua glared back at the tall man, who matched his height but outweighed him by at least forty pounds. "She's my wife."

Roger slipped his large hands into the pockets of his lab coat and flashed a feral grin. "I'm going to ask you the same question again, and I expect to hear the truth."

"Save your breath," Joshua countered. "She's my wife. Vanessa and I were married last year in Oaxaca, Mexico. She has a marriage license to prove it. If you don't believe me, then ask your wife. She knows all about it."

Roger looked stunned. "Connie? Connie knows?"

"Does she also know that her sister is pregnant?"

Roger removed his hands from his pockets and ran them over his head, shaking it from side to side. "What the hell is going on here? You bring Vanessa in looking like she went a couple of rounds with a boxer, then you tell me that you're married."

"Is she going to be all right?"

Dr. Roger Childs managed a smile. "She's just a little beat up."

"And the baby?"

He smiled for the first time. "The baby is just fine. There's no sign of bleeding."

Covering his face with his hands, Joshua let out his breath slowly. He dropped his hands and stared at the man who was his brother-in-law. Roger Childs looked more like a linebacker than a doctor. His nut brown face was round, his chest broad and deep, and his shoulders were thick and wide.

"Do you know who did this to her?" Roger questioned.

"No. But whoever did better be long gone."

Roger shivered as if a breath of cold air had swept over the back of his neck when he saw death in the eyes of the man standing in front of him.

Joshua extended his hand for the first time. "Joshua Kirkland."

Studying the slender hand, Roger finally enveloped it in his larger one. "Roger Childs. This is a helluva way to meet, Brother."

"You've got that right, Brother."

Roger released his hand. "Now, tell me why you and Vanessa have kept your marriage a secret."

"I've been contracted as a consultant at GEA for a couple of months. There's a company policy that states members of the same family cannot be employed at the same time, so we decided to keep it a secret until my contract ends."

"That makes sense. But didn't you say that you and Vanessa married last year?"

"That's a long story, and I'd rather not go into it now. Is it possible for me to see her?"

Nodding, Roger placed a heavy hand on his shoulder. "Sure. Come with me."

He found her in a small room, lying on her back on a narrow bed, holding an icepack to the left side of her face. Sitting down beside her, Joshua smoothed back several strands of hair from her forehead.

"How are you, Angel?"

"Okay." She breathed out.

Leaning over, he kissed her forehead. "Did you get a look at who did this to you?"

She shook her head. "I know it was a man."

"Why a man?"

"By his height and his strength. He was too strong to be a woman."

"Was he as tall as I?"

"I don't think so. He may have been somewhere around five-ten or eleven."

"What was he wearing?"

Closing her eyes, she tried remembering everything up to the time she passed out. "I can't remember. The only thing I can recall is that he was wearing perfume."

Joshua stared at her, frowning. "Don't you mean aftershave?"

Her eyelids fluttered. "No. It was definitely perfume. I just can't recall the fragrance."

"Why would anyone want to attack you, Vanessa?"

"I don't know."

His features hardened. "Are you certain you don't know?" She sat up, but he pushed her back down.

"Why are you interrogating me, Joshua?"

"I'm not."

Her temper flared and she flung the ice pack across the room. "You *are* interrogating me, as if I'd done something wrong. All I did was go back to the office to check on my disks and—"

His eyes paled. "What about your disks?"

"I noticed something was wrong with my disks, but I couldn't figure out what it was until I got back to the office.

"I color-code all of my disks by contracts. Hudson is leaf green, Aronson, sepia, Robertson, melon pink, Wallace—"

"What's your point?" he interrupted.

"The one for the Kroff account wasn't the right color. When I set up the account on the disk I used a sunflower yellow, but the one in the drawer was a lemon yellow."

"What the hell is the difference?"

There was enough exasperation in his tone to annoy Vanessa. "I *know* the difference, Joshua. As a child I knew every color in the Crayola crayon box, could tell the colors without looking at the labels."

"Who worked on the Kroff account beside you?"

"All of us at different times."

"Exclusively, Vanessa."

Her fingers grazed her injured cheek. "Myself. Shane and Frank."

"Was there anything on the disk that would be of interest to anyone?"

"You keep asking me questions I can't answer. For the last time, I don't know." Gritting her teeth against a spasm of pain, she closed her eyes. "Please take me home."

"I'm going to ask you one more question before I take you home. Who would have a key to your file cabinet?"

"I'm the only one. Warren has a copy of the keys to every lock at GEA. If we lose one it becomes a big production number, because the locks have to be changed. All of our keys are stamped with *Do Not Duplicate.*"

He kissed her again, this time on the lips. "Let me check and see if you can be released."

She sat up. "I don't want to stay here."

"You won't have to stay if your brother-in-law says you can go home."

"You met Roger?"

"Yes, I did."

"His bark is bigger than his bite."

Joshua nodded, smiling. "I've discovered that."

Dr. Roger Childs signed the release, arguing softly that the police should be notified. Joshua reassured him that he would make certain to report the incident to the police and to the office building's security department.

Vanessa made Roger promise not to tell Connie about the attack or the baby. "I'll tell her when I see her."

"She's going to go off on you when she finds out," he warned.

"I'll deal with it when it happens," Vanessa countered, leaning against Joshua for support. "I can walk," she protested after he'd swung her up in his arms.

"Carry her out to the car," Roger ordered Joshua. "You've got your work cut out for you if she's anything like her sister. Bossy, opinionated and a shopaholic."

"Tell me about it, Brother," Joshua confirmed with a wide grin.

"I'm telling Connie," Vanessa threatened.

"Tell her," Roger called out. "She'll just agree with me. Will I see you around, Joshua?"

"Most definitely."

"Take good care of Vanessa. She's very precious to me."

Joshua nodded. "Not as precious as she is to me."

He carried her to the car, and the return trip took twice as long as the one to bring her to the hospital. Because of her condition Vanessa could not take anything for the pain, and he drove carefully to avoid any uneven road surfaces.

"I need you to do something for me, Joshua."

Stopping at a red light, he stared at her. "What?"

"I want you to go back to the office. I need to see what's on the Kroff disk."

"Someone just went upside your head, and you want to go back for some more?"

"Please don't argue with me. I know whoever attacked me wanted something in my office. And instinct tells me that it has something to do with the Kroff account."

"If they wanted the disk it's probably gone by now."

"And if it isn't?"

"Then it can wait until tomorrow," he insisted.

"Take me back to pick up my car."

"You're not driving anywhere tonight."

Vanessa gritted her teeth as a wave of pain radiated up her jaw to her temple. The pain hit her at the same time her stomach tightened with a contraction.

"Let me out here," she mumbled. "I'm going to be sick."

Joshua stopped the car with a squealing of rubber hitting the roadway. Vanessa was out of the car the moment he put it into Park. Supporting her back against the bumper, she leaned forward until her stomach stopped the violent churning.

Joshua's hand made soothing motions along her back as she gulped in a lungful of air. "Breathe deep, darling. That's it."

She recovered without retching. Turning to him, she curved her arms around his waist. "That was close." Pulling back, she looked up at him. Light from a nearby streetlamp gave his face a sinister look. "I don't want to leave my car overnight in the parking garage."

He shifted an eyebrow. "Are you trying to get over on me, Vanessa?"

"No. I can drive. You can follow me in your car until I get home."

He stared down at the battered face he loved beyond description. "Okay. We'll go back and get your car." Rising on tiptoe, she kissed his cheek. "Roger's right," he grumbled under his breath. He found that he couldn't deny her anything.

They returned to the underground parking garage, discovering that Vanessa's car wasn't the only one parked on the first level. The health spa did not close until eleven, and many of the members worked out until closing time.

Joshua pulled alongside her car, got out, and examined the interior before he'd let her get into it.

Opening her handbag, she searched along the bottom for her keys. Her fingers closed around a hard, square object. She pulled out the Kroff disk, holding it out to Joshua.

"I had the disk all along."

"You know you're not permitted to take anything off the premises."

"I didn't take it deliberately," she argued. "I was so caught up with going to the doctor that I must have dropped it in my bag by mistake." She grabbed his hand. "Let's go upstairs and see what's on it."

He gave her a skeptical look. "If you're lying to me about not knowing you had the disk—"

"Don't you dare call me a liar," she interrupted. "I never lie!" Her voice echoed loudly in the near-empty garage.

"Okay, Angel. Calm down."

Holding her arm firmly between his fingers, he led her toward the elevator, all of his senses on full alert. Vanessa had been attacked once, and he didn't intend to let anyone attempt it twice in the same night.

Chapter 30

Vanessa moved closer to Joshua after he inserted her key in the elevator panel. Her prior bravado fled quickly when she recalled the smothering darkness sucking the air from her lungs.

"It's all right, Angel," he reassured her as he held her hand firmly.

There was a deafening silence awaiting them as they moved silently down the corridor to her office. Joshua stood outside the door, listening for movement, then walked in, Vanessa following.

The office was as if she had just left it. The table lamp burned softly, and there was no evidence of the struggle earlier that evening.

She made a move to turn on the overhead light, but Joshua stopped her. "Don't. In case someone is watching from the outside," he warned quietly.

Nodding, she took the keys from his loose grip and walked over and unlocked her file cabinet. Nothing appeared to have been disturbed.

Turning on her computer, she told Joshua about the time she found her reports scattered around her file cabinet after she was certain she had stacked them neatly before locking the drawer.

The light from the computer monitor glowed eerily in the dimly-lit space. She punched in her password, then slipped in the disk.

Joshua pulled over a chair and sat down beside her. "Do you recognize these numbers?"

Blinking, she tried focusing on the screen. Her left eye was almost closed shut. "Can you please get me some ice from the lounge? Having the use of only one eye is going to make this a little difficult."

"Give me your keys."

"Why?"

"Because I'm going to lock the door behind me."

Her uninjured eye widened. "You're going to lock me in?"

"You're safer locked in here than out in the corridor. Whoever attacked you may still be lurking around."

Nodding slowly, she said, "Okay." Picking up her keys, she handed him the one to the office door.

Dropping a kiss on the top of her head, he moved silently out of the room and locked the door behind him.

Vanessa had lost track of time even though it was only a few minutes when she heard the click of the lock sliding open. "That was fast," she said, not bothering to turn around.

"And you're very stupid," said a familiar male voice behind her.

Turning, she stared at Jenna Grant and Shane Sumners. Both of them were clothed entirely in black. "What are you doing here?"

Shane stalked into the room, his normally pleasant features twisted in an angry scowl. "I told Jenna you'd be back. She didn't believe me. Now get the disk, Jenna."

"I want no part of this, Shane," she sobbed. "When I gave you the keys I never thought it would come to this."

"Get the damned disk!" Shane shouted at the trembling Jenna.

Vanessa stood up, watching the secretary as she inched closer. Her gaze swung to Shane. "You were the one who hit me."

He shook his head. "I didn't want to hurt you, but you left me no choice."

"Why? Why are you doing this?"

"Why don't you ask *yourself* why, Vanessa? I gave GEA my life, and when you walked in here and batted your lashes at Warren I knew it was over for me. I was supposed to be Preston's first assistant and eventually take over after he retired. You took everything I wanted, so I decided to fix you."

"Fix me how?"

He laughed, sounding deranged. "Oh, wouldn't you like to know?" He turned his attention to Jenna. "Didn't I tell you to get that disk?"

Jenna's eyes were unnaturally large in her pale face as she shook her head. "No, Shane. I—"

Whatever she was going to say was left unsaid as Shane lunged across the room and pushed Jenna to the floor. He reached out for the disk at the same time Vanessa swung her right hand in a curving arc and connected with his left eye. Pain radiated along her arm, and she shook her fingers while Shane howled liked a wounded animal.

He recovered quickly, and for the second time that night Vanessa found her throat caught in a savage grip as Shane pulled her up until her feet dangled above the carpet.

"Get the disk, Jenna, or I'll break her neck."

"Let her go."

Shane swung Vanessa around when he registered the quiet voice. He eased his grip slightly, but then, without warning, she felt the press of cold steel along the side of her neck.

"You move, and she dies," he threatened. "I swear I'll cut her throat."

Joshua's eyes glowed like a trapped animal's when he raised his left hand. The muted light glinted off the powerful handgun he pointed at Shane's head.

Vanessa could smell the acrid scent of fear rising from Shane's body. She couldn't believe what was happening. Shane Sumners—a man she'd worked closely with ever since she had come to work for GEA—wanted to kill her. Because he thought she had taken his position and title.

Joshua's gaze never wavered as he stared at Shane, measuring how much space he had if he was to pull the trigger. He had to be careful, because Sumners was using Vanessa as a shield.

"I'm going to say it just one more time before I drop you like a sack of manure. Let my wife go."

"Wife?" Jenna questioned, rising slowly from the floor.

Shane raised his arm at the same time Joshua pulled the trigger. The explosion sounded like a bomb in the confined space, and everyone went still.

Joshua shoved Jenna out of the way and she fell back to the carpet, weeping hysterically. He walked over to Shane, who stood staring numbly at his shattered arm. Drawing back his right hand, he slapped Shane across the face. The accountant's glasses were dislodged from his face from the savage force of the blow.

"That's for hitting my wife." Shane swayed, and Joshua caught him by the throat, righting him and keeping him from falling. His fingers tightened around the injured man's windpipe, cutting off much needed oxygen. "Hit me, you bastard," he growled against the younger man's flushed face. "Hit me! What's the matter, you twisted punk? You like hitting women?"

Vanessa hadn't realized she was screaming as she tried pulling Joshua's hand away from Shane's throat. "Let him go, Joshua! Please, don't kill him," she pleaded.

He heard her screams and eased his grip, shoving Shane away as if he feared contamination. His gaze swung to Jenna as she crawled toward the door.

"Where do you want your bullet, Miss Grant?"

She stopped and collapsed, sobbing uncontrollably about how Shane had forced her to help him.

Vanessa made her way to a corner and sat down, while Joshua

picked up the telephone on her desk and dialed a number. Her gaze was fixed on the automatic handgun he'd placed beside the phone.

She shivered when she heard him say, "Special Agent Lewis. Tell him Colonel Kirkland needs to speak to him." There was a pregnant silence before he continued. "Have some of your men come over to the office of GEA. You should also bring medical personnel. Yes, there is an injury."

Vanessa lay on the love seat in Warren McDonald's office, eyes closed, while an ice pack lay over the left side of her face.

She listened to the different voices of the men in the office, trying to understand what was being discussed.

"I resent not being told what was going on in my own company," Warren stated angrily.

"I was not at liberty to inform you," Joshua countered.

"I wanted to say something to you, Warren," George Fender said in a quiet tone, "but I couldn't."

"You're a government plant," Warren said to Joshua accusingly.

"A plant who saved your butt."

Warren shook his head. "I can understand Shane's hostility because he felt he was passed over for a promotion, but why Jenna? She's always been loyal to me."

"And she is, Colonel," Joshua confirmed, using Warren's military rank for the first time. "She had no idea that Shane intended to use her. When she gave him the key to Vanessa's file cabinet she never knew what she was going to be drawn into. It was the same when she lent him her car. She had no way of knowing that Shane was meeting someone from manufacturing, who in turn was selling the specs for the laser-guided bombs."

"What about the two million dollars?" Warren asked Joshua.

"Shane was brilliant enough to hide it among Vanessa's subcontracts. Most of the money was concealed in the Kroff account. He made up a dummy disk, but he panicked when

Vanessa took over from Preston. He was certain she would discover that the account had more money than was allocated once she compared her figures with Preston's master sheet. What he needed to do was to get the actual disk back and undo all of his transactions."

Warren shook his head. "What did he hope to prove by hiding the money?"

George looked at Joshua, who nodded his approval. "He knew that eventually the auditors would discover the missing monies, and what he wanted was for her to take the blame. With her out of the way he would move into her position."

Warren covered his face with his hands and shook his head. "How much did he get for passing along the specs?"

"Not a cent," Joshua confirmed. "He just acted as the go-between."

"But why?" Warren continued. "Why spy, if not for financial gain?"

"You'll have to ask Sumners personally. Perhaps he thought computer hacking was enough without adding espionage to the list of charges." Joshua didn't say that murder could have been another charge, if he hadn't shot Sumners.

Warren glanced at Vanessa, then swung his gaze back to Joshua. "Damn man, I was making moves on your wife."

"If she hadn't stopped you, I would have. But you don't have to worry about chasing her ever again, because today was her last day at GEA."

Vanessa sat up quickly, her mouth gaping. The sudden motion made her lightheaded, and she floated back down to the love seat, cursing him under her breath. Joshua had no right to tender her resignation.

Joshua rose and extended his hand to Warren. "I have a few business investments in the Caribbean that will take up most of her time."

Warren grasped the proffered hand. "I'm going to miss her, Colonel Kirkland."

"You'll probably get to see us around. We plan to stay in Santa Fe until the baby comes. After that, we'll do some traveling."

"A baby, too?" Warren mouthed softly. "You just met her."

"Wrong. We met and married over a year ago."

Warren and George exchanged puzzled looks as Joshua walked over to where Vanessa lay sprawled on the love seat. Going to his knees, he caressed her bruised face. "Are you ready to go home?"

She glared at him. "I don't think you want to go home with me, *Colonel* Kirkland," she hissed through clenched teeth. "You really don't want to hear what I have to tell you about your double life. I don't like liars, Joshua."

"I didn't lie to you, Angel. I just never told you the complete truth."

"You handed in my resignation, and I'm going to make a demand of my own. You have exactly twenty-four hours to retire, Colonel. I'm not going to wait around and have you disappear on me every few months. I will not raise this baby alone."

He smiled at her angry expression. "I beat you to it. My resignation was official the moment I picked up the phone and called the FBI."

She let him assist her until she stood up. "Tonight has been one big nightmare." She managed a sensual smile. "But I'm glad it's over. I was beginning to wonder whether I actually am Mrs. Joshua Kirkland."

"Oh, but you are. As soon as you're better I'll give you a special in-house demonstration."

Smiling, she rested her head against his chest. "Let's go home."

She took several steps, glanced over her shoulder, and smiled at Warren and George. Warren nodded, while George flashed a rare smile and waved.

Arm-in-arm, she and Joshua walked away from GEA to begin to live out their marriage vows.

Epilogue

Six-month-old Emily Teresa Kirkland sensed it was a special occasion. She opened her eyes and smiled at her father at the exact moment the taxi stopped in front of the large house in West Palm Beach. Designed in Spanish and Italian revival styles with barrel-tiled red roofs, it had a stucco facade, balconies shrouded in lush bougainvillea, and sweeping French doors that opened onto broad expanses of terraces with spectacular, panoramic, water views.

Joshua stepped out of the taxi and held his daughter in one arm while extending the other to his wife. Turning, he saw the large group of people standing by the entrance waiting for his daughter's arrival.

Martin Cole walked forward and held out his arms. "Let me see the princess." Joshua handed him his niece. Throwing back his head, he laughed. "Her last name may be Kirkland, but this little girl is all Cole." Turning, he walked back to the house, everyone following him.

Joshua pulled Vanessa gently to his side. "Don't worry, Angel. They'll take good care of her. Come, let me introduce you to my family."

Vanessa walked into an entryway with an African slate floor, then followed Joshua to a living room filled with priceless antiques and exquisite reproductions. She looked around for her daughter, and found the man she assumed was Martin cooing softly to Emily.

She stared at an elderly man leaning heavily on a cane with his left hand. She smiled and he returned it, nodding. "I am Sammy, Joshua's father," he said slowly.

Moving closer, she kissed his cheek. "Hello, Sammy."

His eyes misted. "You are very, very pretty. All Cole men love pretty women."

Joshua steered her over to a tall, white-haired woman who had retained her incredible beauty even though she was in her late sixties. "This is Marguerite Josefina Diaz Cole. She's the matriarch of this somewhat unruly brood."

"Everyone calls me M.J." She extended a hand. "Welcome to the family."

Vanessa accepted M.J.'s handshake before she was directed to the man holding her daughter. "Martin is my older brother," Joshua began, "and the beautiful woman standing beside him is his wife, Parris."

Parris leaned forward and pressed a kiss to Vanessa's cheek. Her clear, green-flecked brown eyes were friendly. "Welcome. We'll get together and talk later," she whispered softly near her ear.

Joshua bent down and picked up a petite, dark-haired, dark-eyed toddler who was a carbon copy of Martin Cole. "This little flower is Arianna. She just turned two, and is the undisputed boss in her house. And this serious little guy is her brother, Tyler."

"He's three going on thirty," Parris volunteered, running her fingers through her son's curly hair.

Joshua looked around the room. "Where's Regina?"

On cue, a tall and strikingly beautiful teenager with a curtain of curling black hair falling to her tiny waist floated into the room.

"Uncle Josh," she squealed. She sprinted across the room and threw her arms around his neck seconds after he'd handed Arianna to her mother.

Lifting Regina off her feet, he swung her around, kissing her cheek. "How's my favorite girl?" he asked as he set her down.

Regina Cole stepped back and folded her hands on her incredibly slim hips as twin dimples winked attractively in her brown cheeks. "Your third favorite girl, now. Daddy told me that your wife is first and Emily is second." Her head spun around. "Where are they?"

Vanessa extended her hand to Martin's eldest daughter. "Hello, Regina. I'm Vanessa."

Regina ignored the hand, hugging Vanessa instead. "Gosh, you're pretty. Uncle Josh is very lucky to have you. Where is my cousin?" she queried, not pausing to take a breath.

Vanessa gestured to Martin. He stood in the middle of the living room with what appeared to be a crowd of people. There were two women whose resemblance to M.J. was startling, and she knew these were Joshua's half-sisters. More than a dozen young people ranging in age from mid-teens to early twenties stood together, talking excitedly.

"Your father has her," she told Regina.

"Daddy's a mush for little girls." She walked over to her father and whispered in his ear. Martin placed the baby gently in her outstretched arms.

Regina looked down at the infant girl who claimed a head filled with dark, curly hair. Emily yawned and opened her eyes, staring back at her older cousin, while Regina shifted her delicately arching eyebrows.

"Excuse me. Miss Thang has Uncle Josh's green eyes. Watch out world—she's here!"

Vanessa couldn't keep track of all of the names and faces as she was introduced to Joshua's half-sisters, their husbands, and children. One of his sisters had become a first-time grandmother, giving Sammy and M.J. great-grandparent status.

It took more than a quarter of an hour to seat everyone in the formal dining room. Joshua sat beside his wife, but periodically found himself glancing over his shoulder at his daughter sleeping in a cradle that had once belonged to M.J.

His life was good; he had let go of the bitterness, replacing it with peace, peace and love from his family.

There was a moment of silence as everyone at the oversize table bowed their heads to say grace before the meal was served.

"Am I too late to meet the new princess?" asked a tall man with a melodious voice, breaking the silence.

"Must you always come late, David?" M.J. admonished softly.

Joshua leaned closer to Vanessa. "That's my youngest brother." She arched her eyebrows at the sensually attractive man with a wolfish, dimpled grin. "He's quite a character."

Vanessa met David's gaze, smiling when he sat down opposite her. Her smile widened when he winked at her.

Joshua had told her many tales about the Coles, but after seeing them for herself she realized they were quite extraordinary. Quite extraordinary indeed.

* * * * *

REQUEST YOUR FREE BOOKS!

2 FREE NOVELS
PLUS 2 FREE GIFTS!

KIMANI™
ROMANCE

Love's ultimate destination!

KROM10R

THE *MATCH MADE* SERIES

**Melanie Harte's exclusive matchmaking service—
The Platinum Society—can help any soul find their
ideal mate. Because when love is perfect,
it is a match made in heaven...**

Book #1
by *Essence* Bestselling Author
ADRIANNE BYRD
Heart's ♡ Secret
June 2010

Book #2
by National Bestselling Author
CELESTE O. NORFLEET
Heart's ♡ Choice
July 2010

Book #3
by *Essence* Bestselling Author
DONNA HILL
Heart's ♡ Reward
August 2010

www.kimanipress.com
www.myspace.com/kimanipress

KPMMSP